VIPERS

AND

VIRTUOSOS

SAV R. MILLER

FIRST EDITION

Cover Design: Cat (TRC Designs)
Editing: Ellie McLove (My Brother's Editor)
Proofreading: Rosa Sharon (My Brother's Editor)
EBOOK ISBN: 978-1-7376681-3-8
PAPERBACK ISBN: 978-1-7376681-4-5
HARDCOVER ISBN: 978-1-7376681-5-2

 Created with Vellum

AUTHOR'S NOTE

Vipers and Virtuosos is a dark, contemporary romance inspired by the myth of Orpheus and Eurydice.

It is NOT fantasy or a retelling.

This book contains <u>stalker</u> and <u>bully</u> themes and includes many triggers, such as graphic violence, explicit sexual scenes, and other mature situations. For a detailed list of triggers, visit savrmiller.com

Aiden may not be a mafia guy, but he is an *antihero*. He will do things you won't like, and he may not be sorry about them. If you're not comfortable with that, don't read this book.

For the people still learning to love themselves.

"What madness destroyed me and you, Orpheus?"

— VIRGIL

PLAYLIST

"Getting Older" — Billie Eilish
"Ghost" — Justin Bieber
"Billie Bossa Nova" — Billie Eilish
"DEAD TO ME" — blackbear
"What a Time" — Julia Michaels, Niall Horan
"The Other Side" — Conan Gray
"An Unhealthy Obsession" — The Blake Robinson Synthetic
Orchestra
"Let's Fall in Love for the Night" — FINNEAS
"that way" — Tate McRae, Jeremy Zucker
"Pretty Venom" — All Time Low

Part One

PROLOGUE

There's blood everywhere.

It soaks my clammy palms.

Burns my eyes where it drips down my forehead.

The smell of death singes my nostrils, permeating the air like noxious fumes, and all I can think about is how angry my mother will be when she gets home.

My vision blurs as I try to move—from the blood, or the sudden sharp pain that licks down my spine, I can't be sure. Whatever the cause, it immobilizes me, and I choke out a puff of air.

What if he comes back?

Oxygen rattles from my lungs, catching on the thick sludge blocking my throat.

A throbbing sensation prods at the base of my skull, then seems to echo all over; in my ribs, across my collarbone, and zinging down my legs.

I manage to wriggle a hand up, sliding it over my stomach. My index finger snags on a slit in the fabric, but that can't be right.

I'm wearing a dress.

It was finally warm enough outside after a cold start to spring, so I put on a dress.

Why is there a slit in the middle?

Wetness gushes around the pad of my finger as I press down. It stings, but I keep pressing, keep investigating. Maybe if I figure out what's happened, I can fix it.

Agony ripples through my abdomen, but for some reason, I don't register it completely. It's a tsunami breaking before it hits the shore, whipping against me with the dull aftershocks.

I'm leaking, bleeding out on my mother's white carpet.

God, she's going to be so pissed.

With every bit of strength I can muster, I will my body into motion. I have to get out of here before it gets worse, although it's hard to imagine how it can at this point.

Shards of glass dig into my back as I shift, attempting to find some sort of purchase on the floor.

Footsteps, deliberately heavy, thud beneath my head. Fear sprays down my spine like a broken faucet, my body recognizing the danger before my brain has even caught up.

Goose bumps prick along the back of my neck, and I fall as still as humanly possible, hoping it's enough. That maybe if he thinks I'm dead, he'll leave me be.

I should know better, though.

The men my mother dates aren't satisfied until they've tasted the slaughter.

A shadowy figure breaks through my hazy gaze as he looms over me, clutching a piece of broken glass in one palm.

Manic, yellow eyes glare down at me and a sinister smile stretches across his face.

His belt is unbuckled, pants undone, and crimson in the shape of desperate fingerprints paint his neck, his face, his white shirt.

My brain revolts against the image, disgust rising like a high tide in my chest, but my body doesn't respond.

All I can do is stare.

Watch as he bends, sliding the sharp edge of the glass across my face. I feel it glide up from the corner of my lip to just below my eye, and for the briefest moment, I pray.

Pray he gouges them out, so the last thing I see before I go is darkness and not his face.

I pray he finishes me off quickly.

Worst of all, I pray my mother's not too angry when she gets home, because there's only one thought playing in my mind when my vision blurs again, then goes totally black.

And that thought is that there's blood.

Everywhere.

1

MY MOTHER USED to say beautiful things were wrought from the most unimaginable pain.

Then she'd put her cigarette out on my stomach, in case I needed a reminder that whatever beauty I possessed was still a work in progress.

When she died, I know people expected me to mourn her.

That's what kids are *supposed* to do when they lose a parent.

Then again, most parents don't try to sell their kids to

their crime lord boyfriend, who deals almost exclusively with sex trafficking.

The only thing I mourned was that I didn't light the match.

My brother Boyd insists that's a good thing; he says murder changes you. Rewires your soul into something bleak and broken.

But so does trauma, and I'd much rather be haunted by the sounds of my mother's last screams than the echoes of my own. Maybe the pain would be a bit more bearable if I'd gotten to witness her suffering, too.

When I swallow, familiar discomfort wrapping around my windpipe, the scars on my cheek and at the corner of my mouth throb. The only remaining evidence of memories I can feel, but not picture.

Besides, I certainly don't see my brother losing any sleep over it.

In fact, watching him adjust the cuff links of his neatly pressed, dark-gray suit in the hotel bathroom, Boyd looks more rested than ever.

"Riley," he grunts, his hazel eyes focused on their task. "Stop looking at me like that."

I swing my legs off the king-size mattress tucked in the corner. "Like what?"

Boyd's jaw tics, irritating the pulse in his throat—not that you can really see it beneath the tattoos. Ink spans the entirety of his body from the neck down, a plethora of images etched permanently into his skin. Standing there with his dark-blond hair slicked back and frown lines framing his lips, he looks more like a member of the Mafia than his friends who are *actually* made men.

Not that I'm supposed to know any of that. Boyd likes to pretend the security firm he's an engineer at is totally legitimate, but I've done my homework. And I know that no one in little King's Trace, Maine, lives outside the scope of organized crime.

He doesn't answer my question. "I can stay another night, you know. I'll push back my meeting, tell the company to wait until Monday for me to return."

My eyes flicker to the massive window across from us, sweeping over bustling Fifth Avenue twenty stories below. The sun's beginning to set just beyond the Empire State Building, a blanket of pastel orange and pink covering the sky as the city makes way for darkness.

A shiver skates across my skin, goose bumps sprouting along the surface as I think about navigating New York on my own.

Well, *kind of* on my own. Technically, this is a class trip, so I'm rooming with two girls—Aurora Jackson and Mellie Simmons. Boyd wasn't supposed to be here at all, but no one says no to your requests when you have enough money to silence them.

"You can't keep putting off work to stay here," I say finally, dragging my gaze away from the glass. "We both know that place doesn't function well when you're gone."

"I haven't taken a vacation in a decade. They owe me."

"Right, and we agreed you'd stay here three days, and then go home tonight."

"No, I said I'd stay as long as I felt you needed me to." His hazel eyes jump to mine in the mirror. "I've spent the last three days watching you fold into yourself, so forgive me for not exactly being confident that you're able to handle this."

His words sting. A little pinprick reminder that I'm not as good an actress as I think.

My fingers curl into fists, my nails digging into the flesh of my palms and burrowing until the physical pain replaces the ache in my bones. I suck in a deep breath and pull my feet up on the bed, the black polish on my toenails contrasting with the white comforter beneath.

"How will we ever know I'm ready if you don't let me try?"

Boyd grips the edge of the counter, watching as I yank on a pair of socks. "What if I let you, and something happens?"

"Like what, someone attacks me? Been there, done that, have the ECG report with a lapse in activity to prove it." The joke tumbles from my lips before I have a chance to swallow it down.

My gut thrashes, matching the intensity in my brother's eyes.

He doesn't say anything.

He never does.

I exhale, my tongue thick as it sticks to the roof of my mouth. "I'm just saying, I could get hurt anywhere. You can't guarantee my safety in New York City any more than you can King's Trace, so what's the point of you staying?"

Turning, he leans against the sink, cocking an eyebrow. "You don't think you're any safer with me than you are alone?"

"But I'm not even going to be alone. I have *roomies*, remember?"

Scoffing, Boyd looks out the door to the empty hallway of our suite. "Right. Because they've been great companions so far."

He's not wrong; even though school guidelines require roommates to stick together during group outings, Aurora and Mellie have been content to leave me every chance they've gotten. Although, I suspect it has something to do with the fact that I refuse to engage in polite conversation with the two overly enthusiastic girls.

Or maybe it's because I'm still the awkward new girl from the "wrong side of town" where my classmates are concerned. You can take the girl out of the trailer and stuff a bunch of money into her bank account, but that doesn't mean your peers will stop seeing you as trash.

I shouldn't care what they think, I know. But my freedom hinges on their willingness to attend things with me. Boyd would never leave me here otherwise.

"It's one night," I say, leaning back and spreading my fingers out on the mattress. "If something goes wrong while you're gone, then you never have to let me out of your sight again."

He stares at me in silence for a long time, roving over my face as if trying to commit it to memory. I fidget, the fear that he'll say no palpable as it notches down my spine, making me sit up straight.

I attempt a smile, kicking out my legs and crossing one over the other. Prim and proper, the picture of ease in my oversized Grateful Dead hoodie and fuzzy purple socks.

Maybe if I at least try to pretend I'm not nervous, he'll believe it.

Perception is reality, or whatever bullshit his girlfriend Fiona is always spewing.

Finally, when it feels like I might die under his perusal, my brother heaves a leaden breath, pushing off the counter as he comes back into the room. He lifts his arm, the sleeve falling back slightly, and checks the massive Rolex strapped to his wrist.

"Phone calls every hour, on the hour until you're in bed

for the night." He drops his hand, pointing a long finger at me. "If I don't hear from you, I'm on the first flight back here. I'm sure I don't need to remind you that no matter where you're at, I'll find you."

Excitement bubbles up in my chest, and I leap off the bed, skipping over to wrap him in a hug. My forehead barely touches his collarbone, his muscles tensing as my arms encircle his waist.

One of his hands comes down, resting between my shoulder blades; a whisper of a touch, the way you handle something fragile that's been broken before. As though the fractures haven't fully healed, and you're afraid that any pressure might split them wide open again.

I pull away before he can feel the phantom sutures unraveling, and paste a wide, fake smile on my face. There's no telling if he believes it or not, but at least he doesn't comment further.

Later, after I've ushered Boyd into the back of a cab before he could change his mind, I rush back up to the hotel suite and am just coming out of the bathroom when Aurora and Mellie return. Both girls have a myriad of shopping bags draped over their forearms, and they drop them off en route to the bedroom they've been sharing, disappearing the second I step into view.

Resentment burns in my throat, but I stuff it down, turning left and heading to my room. I flop onto the mattress, already regretting sending my brother away.

I mess around on my laptop for a bit, working on a website mock-up for my professional portfolio—the one I'm collecting in case I decide I want to apply to any design programs after high school.

It was a suggestion of an old therapist that I find a hobby

after my assault and my mother's death left me emotionally stagnant, and so for the last two years, I've been dabbling in web design.

I'm no expert, but I'd be lying if I said it didn't boost my serotonin levels significantly.

A knock on the door pulls me from my screen, and I sit up, pushing the laptop onto the mattress as Mellie pokes her head in.

Her platinum-blonde hair is streaked with royal blue, and she tucks a piece of it behind her ear as she quickly glances around the room.

"Mr. Kelly's gone?" she asks, and I bite the inside of my cheek to keep from rolling my eyes at the formality. Like I don't know every girl I go to school with masturbates to the thought of my brother.

I could *hear* Aurora getting off to him in her imagination last night while she showered, the sounds of her pleasure obvious in the shared living space. He heard it too, and promptly called his girlfriend and went to the lobby to talk to her.

"Left a little while before you guys got back," I say, voice flat, picking up my phone from the bedside table. I unlock it, scrolling aimlessly through social media apps, trying to pretend as though her presence doesn't unnerve me.

"*Awesome.*" Pushing the door open all the way, Mellie bursts into the room, dragging a long dry-cleaning bag behind her. Unzipping it, she pulls out a scrap of dark-green silk fabric and tosses it my way. "Quick, put this on."

I catch the garment, furrowing my brows as I clutch the soft material. "What is it?"

"It's a dress, you troll." Aurora strolls inside, her deeply bronzed skin glowing against the sparkly, hot pink number she's wearing. The sequined hem hits her mid-thigh, showing off her toned calf muscles, and she's in the middle of pinning her black, curly hair up.

"Ror," Mellie scolds, offering me an apologetic smile.

Aurora rolls her brown eyes, shrugging as she turns to look in the mirror. "Oh, come on. Riley knows I'm joking. But what kind of question is that?"

Heat sears my cheeks, and the scar on one pulses to life. I finger the green fabric, noting the plunging neckline as I spread it over my lap.

"This is really fancy," I say slowly, confusion worming through my brain. "We went to the opera last night, and Le Bernardin the night before... what do we need to get dressed up for tonight?"

"It's a charity event." Aurora arches a brow. "You're familiar with *charity*, right?"

My eye twitches.

"Because your brother's girlfriend's family hosts a lot of fundraisers," she continues, a little grin tugging at the side of her mouth. I want to smack it off her.

It's true, at least—the Ivers family is a staple of generosity back home, and Boyd's girlfriend, Fiona, is the figurehead for fundraising ever since her mom passed.

But still, I don't believe that's what Aurora meant.

"Yeah, I guess you could say I'm used to dealing with the less fortunate." I hold her gaze when I speak, a little flare of fire sparking through me. Determination to not let her bitchy ass ruin my night.

"Great." Her tone is overly sweet and flaky, like spun cotton candy. "We have tickets to *the* gala of the year, and we need to look our best."

My stomach rolls as I grip the dress tighter. "Why?"

Mellie beams at me, coming over with a tiny leather pouch. She drops it on the bed beside me, then starts pulling out various tubes of makeup, holding them up to my face as she decides which to keep out.

"Word is Aiden James is gonna be there," she gushes, uncapping a bottle of liquid foundation. "And he's looking to place a bid at the live auction."

I lean back, my insides knotting together at the thought of being in the same building as the rock *god* I spent my formative years drooling over. At one time, I would've already known he was in the city.

I'd probably have planned to arrive at the gala myself.

But a lot's changed over the last two years. My obsession lessened—or at least, I thought it had.

The sweat beading along my hairline suggests otherwise.

"So, what? You guys are gonna try to talk to him?"

"Why not?" Mellie says, shrugging. "Might as well try to get him to see what we have to offer."

"We aren't a charity, though. We don't have anything for him to bid on."

Mellie and Aurora exchange a snicker, and then Aurora's walking over and bending in front of me, cupping my knee. She squeezes slightly, the gesture condescending as she offers false pity.

Or maybe she really does pity me—I can't tell what's worse.

"Oh, sweetie," she says, her lips stretching back over pearly white teeth. "A live auction means they bid on *you*."

2

"YOU'RE LATE."

My fingernails drum on the polished surface of the dining table. The dull, rhythmic thud follows the patter of my heart as it beats woodenly, a hum I try to ground myself in as I stare down my father.

With the New York City skyline looming through the ceiling-to-floor windows behind him, Sonny James almost looks like the king he fancies himself.

Tall, though not as tall as me. A lean, athletic build that resembles mine, although it bears the evidence of his age.

Dark-brown hair that he keeps combed back over his

head to hide the dime-sized bald spot at the crown, and a face chiseled by the gods themselves, crossed with wrinkles and heavy with the unmistakable weight of failure.

For a moment, I see what the rest of the world once did as he steps out of the shadows. A flash of charisma and ease, chin held high as if he doesn't have a single care in the world.

"My flight got delayed." He pulls out the velvet-backed chair at the opposite end of the table, sinking down with a sigh. "Your mother was supposed to tell you."

Pausing the tapping of my nails, I press the edges of each tip into the wood, my jaw clenching of its own accord. The silver rings adorning my inked fingers glint in the dim lighting, cast by the muted crystal chandelier above.

Twisting the thick bloodstone on my thumb, I stare at the red oval until bright splotches form at the edges of my vision. I curl the digit inward, hiding the face of the jewel, and reach forward with my left hand for the glass tumbler of Jack and Coke in front of me.

Music industry royalty, *Forbes* once called the James family—*technically*, the James-Santiago family, given that my parents never married and the latter is my official last name. With a washed-up Colombian pop star sensation as a mother, and a composer turned label owner as a father, the world supposes I have more talent in my pinkie finger than most people can fathom.

More problems, too.

My stomach pinches as I think about the state of the walk-in closet off my bedroom. Hidden behind a pocket door, the mess inside is something the gossip rags would *love* to get their grubby hands on.

Piles and piles of clothing, some mine and some from my

parents, my ex, and my best friend. Some that don't fit, and some that never belonged to anyone in the family—just items I've picked up from various events and hotel rooms over the years.

Things I simply can't part with.

Just in case.

Bringing the glass to my lips, I toss a drink back, reveling in the way the burn soothes my worries, quelling the obsessive thoughts before they can cement in place.

"*Callie* doesn't tell me anything until the moment before it's supposed to happen." I pause, daring my father to disagree about my mother's reliability.

He won't, of course. Her poor time management skills are only one of the reasons he strayed from their relationship.

The promise of fresh, young pussy was the other.

"Remind me why you made her your manager over me," my father says, swiping the other glass from the middle of the table. He mimics me, taking a sip without breaking eye contact, the sleeve of his navy Brioni suit riding up as he lifts his hand.

I run my tongue over the front of my teeth. "Well, for starters, I don't have to worry about her fucking my girlfriend."

He blinks, and the large vein in his forehead throbs, the way it always does when he's annoyed.

Well, join the club. Finding you with your dick inside the only girl I've ever been with wasn't exactly a walk in the park for me.

"I see we're still holding grudges."

Lifting one shoulder, I point my tumbler at him. "Are you still fucking her?"

"Aiden."

One of my eyebrows cocks.

Reaching up, he rubs at his temple with his thumb. "Don't ask questions you don't want the answer to."

I can't deny that the betrayal stings, but it's been long enough at this point that Sylvie Michaels is practically a fever dream to me now.

A painful one that left scars, but distant nonetheless.

"Then I'll say the same thing about why Mom is my manager." Crossing my arms, I shrug. "Besides, she knows what she's doing."

If nothing else, the woman is dedicated to her job.

Being a mom, not so much.

Grunting, he sets his glass down and leans back in his seat. "And I don't? Son, I think you're forgetting who taught her what she knows."

My grip on the tumbler tightens, rage scratching at my throat with his use of the word son, as if that's not a privilege he lost.

Placing my glass on the table, I straighten my spine and check the bulky Chanel watch on my wrist.

Part of me wants to drag this out. Make him squirm. But I know Callie will be pissed if I'm late for the gala, since I'm supposed to be the headliner of the event, and I don't feel like dealing with her right now.

"I want to talk about my contract."

He freezes, the oxygen around us evaporating with his stillness. "Why?"

My expression flattens, and he shifts in his chair, pulling at the knot in his tie.

Buying time.

Finally, my father sighs. "Aiden, I'm not sure that's a good idea."

Slipping my thumb beneath the band of my watch, I

smooth the calloused pad over the corrugated flesh there, grounding myself in the sting of new ink. The latest reminder.

"Why not?" I prod, poking my nail into the linework; a simple pair of wings, something random I got before last night's show in Detroit.

"Because..." He drags a hand over his mouth. "There's a *lot* of money on the line."

My index finger taps on the tabletop, the ring at the base clinking with each downward pump. "I'm aware of that fact. It's *my* contract, after all."

The switch to his label, Symposium Records, was not one made lightly; however, after being dropped from the previous one due to some hits my reputation took, I didn't have much of a choice.

And while a typical contract spans a single year, with the potential to renew for future releases, the contract I'd been asked to sign roped me in for three years and as many albums, minimum.

Not necessarily unheard of for a firm as large as Symposium, but still. It's the principle; being stuck living under my father's thumb, the way I have my entire life, becomes less appealing every day.

His mouth twists. "I get it. You're tired, we *just* finished the Argonautica tour, and you're feeling flighty. Every performer gets that way. Once you see the eight-figure projections, you'll feel differently."

I grit my teeth. "It's not the money. I'm not jonesing for cash. I'm just not sure I want to work with your label."

The penthouse apartment gets extremely quiet, the only sound that of the busy East Fifty-Seventh Street below.

Gripping the armrests of his seat, my father swallows

audibly. The unspoken words hang in the air between us, the implication heavy: I don't want to work with *him*.

But because this is the music industry, and I'm legally bound in more ways than just one, I don't get a fucking say. Before he speaks, I can feel his words in the pit of my stomach, like a large stone disrupting a shallow pond.

"Guess you'll just have to learn to live with it."

CALLIE'S VOICE is barely discernible through the din of the gala, even though she's got her mouth pressed against my ear.

I can feel her pink lipstick staining my skin as she informs me of my role tonight for the millionth time; the show's over now, a stagehand having already taken my acoustic guitar up to the penthouse, leaving my hands feeling very empty.

Autographs have been signed, and I'm supposed to sit on stage and look pretty for the rest of the night.

Until the auction, that is. Then, I'm supposed to be attentive and friendly to entice the crowd—as if any woman here wouldn't crawl on her fucking knees for a chance to breathe the same air as Aiden fucking James.

That's not even ego talking; it's just how it is. Rabid fans flashing their tits in the hopes that I'll see and want to take them home with me. It's the main reason I stopped doing VIP events after concerts.

"Think you can handle sitting here and not causing a commotion?" Callie asks, pushing some of her dark coppery hair off her shoulder.

"Do I think I can handle something you can teach a dog to do?" I hook one ankle over the opposite knee, resting my hands on my lap. "Yes, you've trained me well."

She rolls her eyes, reaching to adjust the collar of her red blazer. "*Ay*, such a smart-ass. I can tell your father is around."

Her accent peeks through her irritation, so I don't bother correcting her; he left right after telling me to nut up and get over my reservations with the label, presumably to rejoin my ex-girlfriend in whatever luxury hotel they're at for the weekend.

Since I had this event scheduled, there was no time to press him on it.

"See any *causes* you might wanna bid on?" Liam, my best friend and publicist, asks as Callie walks away to bother some of the catering staff. He pulls a hand through his dirty-blond hair, tossing a quick look around the room, as if we haven't been through the prospects twice since arriving.

I shake my head, glancing around quickly for the millionth time; black satin cloths mask each round table lining the ballroom, and candles sit at their centers, drowning the partygoers in darkness.

They all look the fucking same at these events; the men in their expensive three-piece suits, eyes roaming no matter their attachments. There's always someone willing to put themselves up for sale, if only for the night.

Far be it from any of these men to deny themselves temporary carnal pleasure.

The women are all dressed in similar black gowns, unable to deviate from the status quo for even a second.

It's positively fucking boring.

A flash of green catches my eye, and I squint into the shadows, trying to make out more than just a silhouette.

I spotted her the second we walked in, my eyes drawn to her like moths to a flame. She'd been flocked by two giggling girls and dragged around the room countless times, so I hadn't had a chance to fully soak her in; the girls have since gone, and now that I'm looking, I don't ever want to stop.

She sits at the corner of the bar staring into an empty champagne flute, right leg cocked on the bottom rung of her stool, revealing pale flesh through the high slit in her dress.

And fuck me, the dress.

Deep, emerald-green silk molds to every curve of her lithe body, and the way she folds her arms over her chest has her tits spilling from the ridiculous neckline.

Light emanates from the chandelier just above her head, casting a warm glow over her honey-colored hair, and even though her face is hidden, she looks like a fucking angel.

An uneasy fish out of water... but an angel, no less.

My gut tightens, twisting with each passing second spent not in her presence.

For some inexplicable reason, I want to taste the discomfort radiating off her skin. Want to be the sole cause of it.

But that's *insane*, and I'm trying to prove to the world that I'm not. So, instead of marching over and thrusting myself into her existence, I swallow down my arousal and ignore it.

Gripping my armrests, I blow out a breath and groan loudly, ignoring the immediate swarm of attention the sound brings. I tower over everyone on stage, sticking out like a sore thumb, and while I'm used to those stares, right now, I'm not in the mood.

Besides, *she* doesn't look my way, and I don't like the hollow feeling that sprouts in my chest at that notion.

"You have to donate *something*." Liam raises his brows. "We're trying to improve your image here. Do you know how bad it'll look if you attend a charity function and don't actually do anything?"

"I don't really give a shit how it looks. This was *your* idea."

He frowns, pointing an index finger at my chest. "You hired me to fix your reputation."

My stomach burns, reality clawing at my skin and trying to slip inside. God, you trash a few hotel rooms in a fit of grief, and suddenly you're the poster child for mental instability.

Biting down on the inside of my cheek, I snatch the laminated pamphlet we were given when we walked in from his hands.

I scan the itemized list, looking for something that catches my eye. Airbnbs, wellness consultations, dates with celebrities—all things I can get any day of the week without dropping half a million dollars beforehand.

"What is this even benefiting?" I ask, tossing the pamphlet back. "Women putting themselves up for celebrities to bid on, like this is some sort of cattle show?"

Liam catches it in his lap, shrugging. "It's benefiting homelessness." He pauses, glaring at the paper, and turns it over. "Or... maybe AIDS research? I can't remember now."

Folding the pamphlet, he reaches up and tucks it inside his suit jacket, lifting his hand in greeting to someone over my shoulder. His smile lights up his face, fading the second his gaze drops back to mine.

"It doesn't have to be anything huge. Bid on a random, see how shit turns out." He nods his chin in the direction of the blonde at the bar. "Want me to find out her deal?"

"No." The word's too quick. Too sharp. Liam catches on immediately, a grin slowly stretching across his freckled face.

"You've been staring at her all night, you know. Why don't you just go over? There's no rule saying you can't fraternize with guests. Sample the goods before you purchase." He leans back in his seat, crossing one leg over the other.

I hook my thumb over my shoulder to where Callie stands, likely berating a member of the event staff, if the distraught look on her face is any indication. "Are you saying I should risk *her* wrath?"

He shrugs. "No, I'm saying that if *you* aren't going to buy the girl's evening, someone else is."

His comment has me sitting forward, clamping my palms down over my knees as my eyes find the girl again. White-hot jealousy rips a fiery path up my spine, making my stomach clench around itself as a tall man with silver hair approaches her, his hand reaching up to grip her bare shoulder.

Every fiber of my being wants to rip it clean off his arm. Maybe grind it down into mush and feed it to him.

Would serve him right for breathing the same air as someone as exquisite as she is.

A sharp pang tears through my chest, possessiveness unlike I've ever known rearing its head inside me. It slithers like slime along my tendons, coating them in thick darkness and damn near pushing me across the room.

My fingers tighten around the armrests of my chair, and I feel a couple of the calluses marring my palm split open from the pressure. The man says something that makes the girl laugh, and I grit my teeth against the urge to do something stupid.

I'm practically vibrating with anger, my insides clenching

so hard it feels like I might pass out. My hands shake where they're clutching the seat, nausea rolling up through my stomach like a cloud of smoke, desperate to be set free.

Even an act as natural as breathing becomes labored the longer I watch the two interact.

I pull my eyes from the bar and push onto wobbly feet. A dense fog collects in my mind as I try to ignore the emotions battling inside me, and I suck in a deep breath, steadying myself.

"I'm gonna go for a smoke."

Liam sighs, rubbing at his clean-shaven jaw. "Your mother's going to ask where you went."

"So, lie." I reach down, patting his cheek once, twice, adding a bit of extra oomph with the second one. *"That's what I hired you for."*

"Fine," he grumbles, shoving my hand away. "But I'm putting a bid on something for you. You're not gonna make me look bad, too."

I pause, my throat thick as I stare out into the crowd again. My heart thumps like a wild animal against my ribs, *painful* in its revolt, and my gaze flickers to the girl again.

This time, she is looking; no, that's not quite the right word.

She's *watching*. Pointedly turning away from the man at her side to stare me down across the room.

I can't see the exact shade of her eyes, but I feel the weight of their acknowledgment.

It stabs at something in my chest, poking at the crazed organ inside, and I reach up to absently rub the spot, unable to tear myself from her sight.

"Her," I say, tipping my chin. "Bid on her."

3

I'M STARTING to remember why I don't go out much.

The man at my side—supposedly a senior investor at some Wall Street firm he refuses to name—leans into me for the third time since sitting down, running his pudgy index finger along the rim of my empty champagne glass.

"It just isn't right for a little lady as stunning as yourself to sit here alone all night," he says in a low voice that I feel against my hair.

He's been scooting toward me in tiny increments as if I can't tell he's just trying to get a better angle of my cleavage in this dress.

My discomfort grows tenfold, and I'm cursing myself for not putting up more of a fight when Aurora and Mellie gave me this dress. But I didn't feel like arguing, and I'd already made them late having to apply my own makeup.

Mellie wanted to, but there was no way she'd be able to cover the scar on my cheek as well as I've learned to.

I offer the man a thin smile, well versed in the art of warding off creeps. That was my mother's favorite brand, after all.

"Like I've said, I'm not *alone*. My friends are in the bathroom."

His lips purse, and I lean back on my stool to do a quick sweep of the ballroom, wondering where the hell my "friends" have disappeared to. The second we arrived and got our tickets, Mellie and Aurora made themselves scarce.

Presumably, to mingle and look at auction items they might be able to afford, but part of me can't help feeling purposefully abandoned.

I wouldn't be surprised if they've left the building entirely. Probably slipped out the same time Aiden James did, hoping to get close to him.

Warmth floods my cheeks at the memory of our gazes colliding just moments ago; I'm still not even sure if it was me he appraised from the stage across the room, but it felt nice to temporarily entertain that idea.

The distance between us made it easier to pretend. From his vantage point, there's no way he'd have been able to see my scars, or the anxiety threading through my nerves.

That was the most exciting thing to happen all night.

At my side, the man inches even closer, his breath coasting over my jawline as he blatantly gapes at my chest.

My opposite hand creeps up my sternum, fingers

grasping at my neckline, pulling the skintight material as far over my cleavage as it will go. *This, Riley. This is what Boyd warned you about.*

The man reeks, like stale booze and popcorn, and apprehension coils tight in my stomach, though I can't pinpoint the exact cause.

It's always this way when I'm around strangers, though— a numbing sensation of unease holding my insides with an iron-clad grip, refusing to let go or tell me *why* I feel this way.

Deep down, I know it has to do with the assault from two years ago. The fact that I can't remember anything about it, though, is what tortures me the most.

But it wasn't *always* like this.

Once upon a time, I was blissfully ignorant of how the world can break a person.

Now, awareness sits like a brick in the core of my being, alerting my body to danger. But the memories are hazy, frayed at the ends, and I can never latch on to them long enough for my brain to process fully.

I don't know what I'm afraid of. Just that I am.

"They've been in the bathroom an awfully long time," the man drawls, his fingers slipping from the flute to the bar top, spreading out so they're millimeters from mine. "Maybe they went home with someone."

My face scrunches up despite my best effort to remain apathetic. "They wouldn't leave without telling me."

He smirks, his thumb hooking over the metal edge of the counter, disturbingly close to where my hand is covering my chest. As he leans in, I feel his other arm snake around the back of my stool, and he plants his palm beside my ass.

"They might if their ticket's been picked up. Buyers don't

always give their prizes time to say goodbyes, especially if they're particularly... keyed up."

I turn my head slightly, frowning. "What do you mean?"

His low chuckle vibrates against me as he presses his lips to the crown of my hair; I hear him inhale, and my entire body locks up, so rigid it makes my bones ache. The hand on the counter slips off, his knuckles dragging over mine where I'm still clutching my dress, and then he reaches forward for the little buzzer an usher gave me when I entered the building tonight.

"Don't play coy." His voice is breathy, and I swallow over the bile rising in my throat. "You know exactly what you signed up for."

"I didn't *sign up* for anything."

The man's lips twitch. "Every person that steps into one of these events signs up. You're automatically added to the ballot once your attendance has been confirmed. Technically, you can decline, but it has to be before you enter the event. Did no one explain that to you at the door?"

A live auction means they bid on you. Jesus, I hadn't thought Aurora was serious.

How is that even legal?

I shake my head. "Well, I need to speak to someone, then, because clearly I wasn't expecting this—"

"Dressed like that? You're practically begging for it, sweetheart." He presses the buzzer against my thigh just as it roars to life, rippling against my skin. "Oh, look at that. Someone must've purchased your company for the night."

The hand on my stool slides up, cupping my hip, and I jerk in the opposite direction, trying to wrench away from his grip. His fingers tighten on my thigh, pain sparking where his nails dig into the bare skin, and terror spreads through my limbs like a fast-acting poison, destroying my nerve endings.

Swallowing, I lean harder to the left, my eyes frantic as they scan behind the bar again, wondering why no one is paying attention. A girl is being accosted in public, and yet there isn't a single person who seems to mind.

Then again, if this is the kind of place you can buy someone's time, I guess maybe they don't see it as a big deal.

"Want to know what I'm gonna do with you?" the man asks, parting my hair with his nose and scraping his lips over the shell of my ear.

I shiver, a ball of anxiety unraveling in my gut, and he takes it as a sign to continue. "We'll get you out of that dress, for starters. Maybe before we even make it out of the building."

A memory flashes across my vision as he speaks, horror spiking in my chest and pulsing outward. The smell of burned flesh and blood floods my nostrils, and I fold into myself and squeeze my eyes shut, willing it to be over.

Something slaps against the bar top, the sound ringing through my ears over the din and chatter floating around the ballroom. I jump, fear launching headfirst into my throat, and exhale when the man's hands immediately stiffen against my body.

Peeling my eyes open, I find the source of the intrusion; my gaze trails slowly, beginning at long, tapered fingers as they curl around the edge of the counter. Silver rings, some thick and bejeweled while others are thin and plain, adorn each digit, and ink winds up from his knuckles over large veiny hands, disappearing beneath the sleeve of a light denim jacket.

I suck in a heavy breath as the new man leans against the

bar. His cologne is the only part of him that reaches me—
something spicy and masculine, like pine and cardamom.
Somehow, it feels as though I've been engulfed in flames.
I don't dare look any higher.

The pervert at my side huffs, sitting back in his seat, but
he doesn't remove his hands. The buzzing on my leg doesn't
cease, making the skin beneath go numb.

"Can we help you, son?" he snaps, not bothering to stifle
his irritation.

"She's not for sale."

The stranger's voice is deep with a slight rasp, like melted
chocolate topped with bits of coconut. I want it to dissolve
on my tongue.

It's also... familiar.

"I beg your pardon?"

Releasing the counter, the tattooed hand whips out,
snatching the buzzer from the other man's grip. I watch,
mesmerized, as the stranger turns it over with deft fingers
and hits a button that lights up the little screen.

"I didn't stutter," he says, and I can't stop staring at his
hand—the way his veins bulge against the Medusa design
covering the back of it. Her serpentine hair stretches out
over each of his fingers, her eyes practically glowing even
though the design is just line work and shading.

Heat flares between my legs, and I shift, clenching them
together against the foreign sensation.

Tension hangs heavy in the air, and I'm not sure if I'm
even breathing anymore. The pervert clamps down on my
thigh, and I can already feel the bruises sprouting there.

"I'm not going to fight with you over her—"

"You're right, you're not. We aren't *fighting* at all. You were
just leaving."

The stranger's hand moves, and then he brings the buzzer down on the bar, sending shards of plastic and metal pieces flying.

My eyes slip, temptation winning out; I see black jeans with holes in the knees. A Sex Pistols hoodie beneath the denim jacket and a single silver chain peeking out from the neckline, bright and shiny against more tattooed skin.

Continuing up, my stomach somersaults, and it feels like I've just jumped from an airborne plane with no parachute.

I *know* this man.

Well, as much as you can know someone from behind a screen or magazine spread. Or a shared look across a room.

Aiden fucking James. My former idol, when celebrity worship was my favorite pastime.

The lump that forms in my throat, hard and sticky, says that maybe I haven't moved on as much as I thought.

Or maybe it's just because when I lift my gaze, stormy gray eyes sear directly into my soul, stealing the breath right from where it rests on my tongue.

He's mesmerizing in person.

Sharp. Raw.

Intense.

Angry.

Even though it's not directed at me, I find myself recoiling slightly, taken aback by the murderous glint shining in his irises.

Still, my pulse kicks up, both in my chest and lower.

"Get your fucking hands off her, before I remove them myself," Aiden clips, a darkness bleeding into his tone that indicates he isn't messing around.

"Whatever. I could tell she wasn't gonna be any fun, anyway." The pervert practically spits at him, jostling me as he yanks back and hops from his stool. "Good luck with your dead fish, *dick.*"

Embarrassment scorches my cheeks, and I absently touch a finger to the scar at my mouth, trying to keep his comment at bay.

Pushing back the broken bits of the buzzer as the man slinks off, Aiden lets out a breath, reaching up to drag a hand through his hair. The dark-brown locks curl slightly over his forehead, and he flips them up, rolling his shoulders.

"You're..." I start, unsure of where the sentence is going the second I open my mouth. I should just thank him and leave, but the weight of relief coursing through me compels me to stay.

Even as my mind screams to run. Not to let my broken soul taint his genius.

"Parched," he cuts in, raising a hand and finally catching the attention of the bartender. The middle-aged blonde comes over for his drink order, a bored expression on her wrinkled face. "Scotch neat, please." He steals a glance at me, then nods to her. "And a vodka soda."

My eyes widen, and I reach out, spreading my palms on the metal counter. "Oh, no, that's okay. I'm not—"

But the bartender scurries off to fill the order, ignoring my protests. I cover the stamp on the back of my right hand, unease tightening around my sternum.

"This seat taken?" Aiden asks, slipping onto the stool on the opposite side of where the pervert was.

We sit in silence a few moments, and finally the bartender returns. She slides our drinks across, scoops up the remnants of the buzzer, and then slinks down to the other end to assess more customers.

"I was here for an hour without anyone even asking me

39

what I wanted to drink," I say finally, reaching for my glass. Wrapping my fingers around it, I let the surface cool my heated palms, and take a tentative sip.

"You mean that asshole felt you up, but didn't offer a beverage first?"

"Well, you know what they say." I shrug, turning my head to look at him. It's a little alarming how easy I find it to talk to him, all things considered. "Chivalry is dead, and all."

He grunts, bringing his tumbler to his lips with a smirk. "That it is."

After a beat, he drops his arm, returning his glass to the counter.

"What's your name, angel?"

I sputter, choking on the alcohol as it works down my esophagus. Both at his question, and the fuzzy feeling I get in my center when he calls me angel.

Fuck, how I could ruin this man.

If he were anyone else, I might even try—but the sixteen-year-old buried deep inside me is begging me not to.

She still clings to the hope that one day, we'll be whole again. That the stains on our soul might disappear if enough time passes.

But I know better; the darkness in us is a quicksand, seeking out others to devour.

So, I decide not to tell him my name, rock star or not.

I spin on my stool and down my drink, buying time. Try to play quirky and aloof, even though everything inside me is spinning out of control for a million different reasons.

"I can't tell you all my secrets. Where's the fun in that?"

His smirk grows as he takes another drink, and so does the fire in my belly. Goddamn, I should say thank you and go find my friends. Leave what is sure to be a disaster here at the bar.

Dragging the rim of his glass along his bottom lip, his eyes darken on me. They grow heavy. Hungry. I shift, uncrossing and crossing my legs, trying to alleviate the pressure between them.

"The *fun*," Aiden says, letting his gaze drop to my mouth, then lower and back up, "is that I know what to call you when I collect my dues."

My eyebrows scrunch together, and his jump.

"You weren't for sale to him, angel, because I already paid for you."

4

THE LAUGH that tumbles past the girl's lips makes my cock twitch attentively. In part because it's an inherently melodic sound, soft and lilted, but more so because she seems surprised by it.

Like laughter isn't something she's used to.

Her crystalline blue eyes widen a fraction, and she covers her mouth with a dainty hand.

"Sorry," she says around her fingers. "I just wasn't expecting you to say that."

"Would you rather I ease you into the idea?" I lift a shoulder, holding the tumbler to my mouth.

I don't know why I ordered a drink—it's been months since I tasted a drop of alcohol, and yet I've had hard liquor twice tonight.

My mother's disappointment is almost palpable, but when I glance around the room, she's nowhere to be seen, so I ignore the discomfort and take another drink instead.

Besides, drinking was never a *problem* for me. Not like pills were for her.

It was always just something I did in an attempt to make the emptiness inside me a little less glaring.

The girl beside me clears her throat, gripping the edge of the bar in one hand. Her fingers strain against the metal top, as if that connection is the only thing keeping her upright.

"I'm not, uh..." she trails off, licking her lips once. Twice. Three times. I feel each swipe of her tongue in my balls, and goddamn if I don't want to ravage her right here.

Lay claim to her where everyone would see, and inevitably inform the rest of the world that this stranger is off-limits.

With how much you can get for an Aiden James story, and how fast celebrity gossip travels, everyone would know before she even left the building tonight.

I blink, clearing the fog of desire from my brain. *Jesus. Get a fucking grip.*

Sucking in a deep breath, I set my glass down and push it away, trying to calm the erratic beating of my heart. I shouldn't indulge. Shouldn't let arousal take root in my gut, or let my cock do the thinking.

But there's just *something* about this girl.

She smells like warm peppermint, and those wide blue eyes say more than her pretty pink lips ever could.

This isn't like me, and it's *definitely* not like her—I can tell

43

she's not enjoying the gala by the way she's curled into herself, face pinched as if just waiting for it all to be over.

"I'm not a hooker," she rushes out finally, the words escaping like a gust of wind. She spins slightly on the stool, making eye contact with my chin. "I know my dress maybe doesn't scream *innocent patron*, but to be fair, I didn't pick it out."

My eyebrows rise. "Not your style?"

"No." Her throat ripples as she swallows, and I find myself fascinated by the movement.

I'm still gazing at the creamy expanse of skin when I ask, "What would you have rather worn?"

Please say nothing.

She shrugs, shifting so her hair veils the slope of her neck. "I wouldn't have come at all."

Leaning back in my chair, I scrub at the light stubble lining my jaw. All around us, gala patrons flit about, engaging in conversation, purchasing drinks and auction items. Going about their evenings, unperturbed by the way ours has stalled.

I have a schedule to keep. A full five hours of sleep to catch before hitting the gym with Liam, then vocal exercises and a briefing of tonight's show before we hit the road. People depend on the schedule, need me to keep it so they can continue on with their own lives.

Normally, I'm fine with the rigidity of it. Keeps my mind from wandering and puts a degree of order to what is otherwise chaos.

Right now, though, I have no desire to return to the land of the living. I'm frozen in my seat, in time, entranced by this complete stranger for no reason.

And that is all the more reason to stay.

Not to mention the ungodly amount of money I dropped on her ticket.

"What would you rather be doing?" I ask after the silence has stretched too far between us. "If not attending a charity ball with New York's elite."

Her shoulders relax the slightest bit. "I don't know. I've never been here before."

"You're a tourist?"

She nods.

"Ah, a Big Apple *virgin*." I chuckle at the blush that creeps up her neck, enhanced by the low fluorescent bar lighting. "So, what brings you to the city?"

"Class trip."

I lean against the counter, waiting for her to elaborate. A lone worry niggles the back of my mind, and I squint at her, trying to gauge her age. "*Class*? Where do you go to school?"

As if sensing the reason for my unease, a small smile plays at her mouth. "Don't worry, rock star. I'm legal." She pauses, seeming to consider her words. "Not that it matters."

I've heard that before, though I suppose if she'd come here with that angle tonight, she'd have been walking around talking to guests rather than hiding in the corner. Most girls who come to events like this, when they aren't allowed, overcompensate in that way.

Still, I make a mental note to have Liam double-check. "It matters," I mutter, letting my eyes drift over her body, my cock jerking slightly.

"My birthday is in October, just past the cut off, so I'm a year behind other eighteen-year-olds in school," she explains, and I find I quite enjoy the sound of her voice. It's got a soft grit to it, as if rusty from lack of use.

Okay. I can work with a four-year difference.

45

"I see. Are you off to college in the fall, then?"

She twirls a strand of hair around one finger. "I haven't decided yet."

Again, I wait for her to elaborate, but it never comes.

Slipping from my stool, I slap the soles of my black steel-toe boots to the floor and stand upright. I stare at her for a beat, though she doesn't look back at me.

That shift is oddly refreshing; usually, I'm the one being watched and doing the hiding. The chasee, not the chaser.

Pursuance is... alluring.

Turning my hand up, I hold it out in her direction. She glances at my fingers from the corner of her eye and slowly lifts her gaze.

"Well?"

She blinks. "Well, what? I already told you I'm not a hooker. I don't know what you want from me—"

"You think I need to pay for sex, angel?" I press my lips together, stepping closer. Not so close that she feels preyed upon, but enough so she's aware that her personal bubble is no longer her own. At least, not for tonight. "If I did, I could get it a lot cheaper elsewhere."

Those blue eyes glisten, oceanic depths I want to dive to the bottom of. Discover the secrets hidden beneath.

"How much did you pay?" She reaches forward, pulling a leather clutch to the lip of the bar. Popping it open, she rifles through the contents, yanking out a wad of cash and holding it up. "Maybe I can pay you back?"

"Sure." I stand up straighter, shoving my hands into my jacket pockets as she starts sifting through bills. "You carry five million around in your purse, or should we stop at an ATM?"

Her body stills, thumb on the tip of her tongue. She

looks up, eyes narrowing. "You paid five *million* dollars for a night with a stranger?"

"I paid for an adventure." I lift a shoulder like it's no big deal.

Though I think we both know it is.

My father will likely shit a brick when he finds out what I donated, and to who—but frankly, I don't give a shit.

Dropping her hands, she taps her knee, eyes glazing over as she contemplates. The inside of her clutch illuminates, a phone screen flashing with an incoming call, but she ignores it.

Taps some more.

My threshold for patience is wearing thin, and I take another step toward her, noting that we're beginning to draw something of a crowd. Onlookers slink closer, predators circling in, desperate to get a look at what's captivating the always-mobile Aiden James.

"My friends forced me to come tonight. I didn't know what I was signing up for."

"Friends?" She nods, and I reach out, possessed by some inhuman force that needs to touch her. My fingers tuck a strand of soft hair behind her tiny ear, slipping under her jaw and tilting her chin up. "They made you come, and left you by yourself?"

"I don't think they like me very much."

Scoffing, I shake my head. "How is that possible?"

Her head tilts. "You can say that because you just met me."

"Well, I *haven't* met your friends, and I think they sound dreadful. That they could *force* someone else into doing something and then ditch them when they get what they want says enough."

The girl quiets, eyes dark as she studies me. I don't know what she's thinking, and the ignorance is unnerving. I want to climb inside her mind and see what she thinks of me.

See what she's afraid of, what makes her tick.

For a long moment, neither of us says a word. Anxiety slicks down my spine, the hairs on the back of my neck prickling as more eyes fall to us.

I start to worry she's still going to refuse. A plea digs into my tastebuds, bitter as it bleeds into me. I don't fucking beg, and yet I find myself on the verge for this stranger.

It's all-consuming, this sudden need for her to come with me.

Completely unhinged.

Obsessive.

But I'm not ready to let her go.

My hand falls to my side, and she glances at it, tracing the lines of the Gorgon inked there.

"An adventure." She licks her lips, then pushes to her feet. I have to dip my chin downward to meet her gaze, and the position makes my chest swell with arousal. "Okay, then. Let's go."

5

I'M NOT sure where I'm expecting him to take me.

Before we leave, Aiden pulls a Yankees ball cap and a pair of red hipster-style glasses from his hoodie and slips them on. Not the greatest of disguises, but with his hair covered and the collar of his jacket pulled up, I almost don't recognize him.

We slip out a back exit, my pulse thrumming like a turbulent storm, and part of me anticipates being shoved into a back alley and taken advantage of.

Even though I try to convince myself a *celebrity* wouldn't hurt me, not in such a public space, I can't fully shake the fear. It cinches tight in my chest as Aiden pulls me under a strip of scaffolding behind the building, my throat constricting from the nerves.

The other, slightly more optimistic part of me is prepared to duck into the back of an SUV, secret service–style, so we can navigate Manhattan unnoticed. But as we weave through the crowded sidewalks, he makes no move to get inside any vehicles.

Pain splices up the arches of my feet as I sprint to keep pace with him, cursing my short legs and unfamiliarity with heels.

This is by far the craziest thing I've ever done, and if my brother could see me now, he'd definitely have me committed. Frankly, I'm feeling a little out of sorts myself, but my options for the night weren't great.

I owe it to the old me to indulge in this, even if it still seems like some kind of fever dream.

Sixteen-year-old Riley, who was obsessed with this man and his music is sated, at least.

The tall, tattooed rock star comes to a standstill at a busy intersection, spinning in a circle to pin me with a bright smile. "Do you smell that?"

Pausing midstep, I cock my head and inhale.

A myriad of scents assault me; expensive perfumes from passersby, damp concrete, and the unmistakable smell of garbage. It's hard to pinpoint any one thing, really, because they all sort of mesh together like a rainbow of paints mixing to make the color brown.

"Uh... you'll have to be more specific." Chilly air whips across my bare skin, but I hardly feel it with the adrenaline coursing through me.

Aiden jogs over, shaking the sleeves of his jacket so more

of his ink is revealed; on one arm, I see an animated compass, its face shattered, and the shards morphing into a flock of birds taking flight. On the other, I see the bottom half of a Rubik's cube, one of the first tattoos he ever got.

My nose scrunches up. It's weird to have such intimate information on someone, without having been told it by them.

"Don't make that face," Aiden says, walking behind me. "You can't judge before you've experienced it."

"I don't know what I'm—"

His hands come down over my eyes, and on instinct, I pinch them closed, my entire body going stiff as a board. The rings on his fingers are cool against my skull, but the compromising position keeps me from being able to enjoy it.

Reflexively, my hands reach up, grabbing his wrists.

It's a mistake; they're thick, and the pulse in his corded veins has mine flaring to life, as if I've just been resuscitated.

And I would know—I've been brought back to life once before.

A shiver works through me, goose bumps sprouting along my skin at his touch, mingling with the cold air.

"Relax," he coos, words coasting across my hair. No other part of him touches me, just his hands and damp breaths. "We're on a crowded street in New York City. Every other person that passes by can't help but look at you, so I'm sure there'd be no hesitation to step in if someone thought you were in danger."

I scoff, my shoulders still tight. "They're probably looking at you."

"If they noticed *me*, we'd be swarmed by a sea of paps right now. Trust me, angel, all eyes are on you."

Ignoring the way my insides deflate a little, I slowly

release his wrists, my hands dropping to my sides. "Why do you keep calling me that?"

He doesn't answer me, forcing my legs into motion, and a fresh wave of panic floods me. "Tell me what you smell."

You! That spicy cologne of his invades my senses, overpowering literally everything else. Makes it difficult to breathe or concentrate on anything but the fire zipping along my spine.

On the one hand, *Aiden James is touching me!* And Jesus, he smells better than any magazine ever described him.

On the other, a complete stranger has stolen my vision, and every lesson from my brother—even my absentee father—comes hurtling back, filling me with a severe sense of dread.

Leaning forward, I try to lessen the weight of his hands on me. It doesn't work; he continues moving with me, as if this is a game.

"Don't you have security?" I ask. "Aren't they gonna wonder where you went?"

"I'm not a prisoner," he says, though there's a sudden edge to his voice that makes me wonder if he really believes that. "*What do you smell?*"

"Oh, my *god*, you're annoying!" Huffing, I stomp my foot on the ground and jerk against him, redoubling my efforts as I suck in a lungful of air. It burns, like ice filling my chest, but I get a hint of something else.

Something warm and fresh, like my favorite bakery back home.

"What is *that?*" My eyebrows draw together, and he slowly slides his hands away, fingers grazing my cheekbones.

When I open my eyes, I'm staring into the storefront of a dilapidated dry cleaner. The red awnings are tattered, the glass windows in dire need of a wash, and there's a broken padlock hanging off the front door.

I glance up at Aiden as he grins, rocking back on his heels. Confusion threads through my paranoia, and I frown. "Your idea of adventure is... taking me to the dry cleaners? You know, these exist outside the city."

"I'm aware, yes." Walking over to the door, he wrenches it open, pushing it back against the wall. With a sweep of his arm, he gestures for me to go inside. "Adventure comes in many forms, though, and I thought ours would go smoother if we got you into a change of clothes."

My cheeks heat and I cross my arms, digging my fingernails into my biceps. "You don't like the dress?"

Shame coats my skin like a thin layer of sweat, and I berate myself internally for thinking he might. For thinking it was attraction that made him bid on me, rather than something like pity for the lonely little girl at the bar.

"Didn't say that." His smoky eyes rake over me, agonizingly slow in passage, and I see his throat bob as he swallows. "I just thought you'd be more comfortable."

Our gazes stay locked for several beats, and I swear I could pass out from having his undivided attention.

Lifting a shoulder, I acquiesce, ignoring the pounding of my heart. "Why a dry cleaners, though? We must've passed a dozen different boutiques."

Grinning, Aiden nods. "True, but none of those shops have the world's best, most authentic New York bagel."

My eyes narrow. "A bagel."

"You scoff, but trust me. It's life-changing bread."

Trust me. It's the second time he's said that phrase to me tonight, and even though I shouldn't... I want to.

For once, I want to believe that someone I don't know,

who isn't invested in my well-being, isn't out to get me. And if not this man, then... who? And why *not* him?

I already know more about him than he does me, so it's not like he has an intellectual advantage here. When he looks at me, I don't see the apprehension or sadness that people who know me usually have, and I like the way his gaze doesn't leave me hollow.

So, instead of running the way my brain wants me to, I let my heart push me forward, hoping this doesn't become a night I regret.

6

Aiden shoves a pair of NYU sweatpants into my arms, while the shop owner moves to the back to grab our bagels.

I glance at the gray sweats, then up at him, disbelief narrowing my gaze.

Removing his cap, he swipes a hand through his messy brown hair and the smile from before slips off his face.

"Problem?"

"How did you..." I trail off, realizing that the end of the sentence is stupid.

It's not possible for him to know I used to dream about

going to school there, or that I feel most at home in baggy clothes.

Questioning coincidence only leads to trouble.

Shaking the thoughts away, I blow out a breath and look around the tiny store. Checkered linoleum tile covers the floor, and there are racks of bagged clothes hanging against each wall. A conveyor carousel sits behind the checkout counter, occasionally moving forward when the brunette manning the register hits the button.

She's flipping through an old issue of Vogue, one I recognize from the stash I kept in my nightstand when my mother was still alive.

Aiden graces the cover, along with headlines about his favorite vacation spots and the best sex positions. My mouth grows dry as I slide my gaze from the print version to the human in front of me, trying my best to reconcile the two.

"This is weird," I say when his hand finds my elbow, and he guides me to a back corner near the family restroom.

"*You're* weird."

The brunette jumps to her feet, shoving the magazine in our direction. "You're Aiden James! Oh, my god, can you sign this magazine for me?"

He winces, stepping up to the counter. "Sure thing, sweetheart. Think you can keep my being here a secret?"

She nods wildly, practically drooling as he takes the pen she holds out. With a flourish, he signs, and then she scurries off to the back of the store without a single glance at me.

"Sorry about that," he says, once again pushing us to the back.

I make a face, jerking my arm out of his grasp. He brings his fingers together, popping each knuckle individually, and studies a spot above my head.

"Do you realize how many girls would kill to be in your position right now?"

Shifting my weight from side to side, I purse my lips. "Why don't you go hang out with one of them?"

"No refunds or exchanges when you leave the premises." Reaching into his jacket pocket, he pulls out a red cardboard ticket, holding it up in the light. "So sayeth the fine print. That's where they get you."

And of course, not reading the fine print of the guest book I signed is why I'm in this mess in the first place.

I stare at the ticket, then him. Waiting.

One of my eyebrows cocks, and his left one mirrors the movement.

He moves forward an inch. A small smirk tugs at the corner of his lips. "You feel that?"

"What?"

"Fate." He gestures between us. "It's working right here, right now."

Oh, good. My childhood crush is a crazy person.

"All I feel is annoyed." My arm lashes out, shoving him back a step. "Would you mind... not watching me undress?"

Once again, he drags his gaze over my form slowly, the heat emanating from those gravestone-colored eyes warming me all over. "I'll go check on the bagels."

Pulling my phone from my purse, I clear the texts from Boyd and triple check for any from Mellie or Aurora. My heart sinks at their lack of communication, even though I know better.

Doesn't make it hurt less.

As soon as Aiden's disappeared through the curtain separating the kitchen from the storefront, I duck behind a rack of clothes and change quickly, praying to whatever omniscient being lives in the sky that no one else comes in.

Pushing the uncomfortable dress off my shoulders, I let the silky material pool at my feet, then step out of it and pull the pants up to my waist. Heaving a sigh of relief, I secure the drawstrings and fumble around for the top, my forearm tight against my breasts as I search.

And search some more.

My throat burns as the realization sets in that I don't have a top to put on. Pushing into a standing position, I start sifting through the rack in front of me, trying to find something that isn't a suit jacket.

"Jesus, what—"

I don't hear the footsteps until they're right at my side, and the sudden warmth seeping into my exposed skin startles me; I jump back, my foot hooking on a mop bucket, and then I'm falling.

Squeezing my eyes shut, I brace for impact against the floor, my hands flailing as I try to catch myself.

Instead of tasting tile, I'm jerked backward, my spine connecting with a bulky, stonelike surface.

One of Aiden's arms wraps around my waist, pinning my hips so my ass is in line with his pelvis. The other brackets my ribs, almost crushing them as he hauls me up.

Panic tears through my chest, shredding my resolve like it's nothing more than cheap ribbon. My breasts rest on top of his forearm, and it takes me a second longer than it should to realize.

A calloused hand grazes the sliver of puckered flesh that mars my abdomen; a fat, jagged mass stretching from the outside of my left hip to my belly button. Unmistakable evidence of the one night of my life I can't remember, but when he touches it, I'm flooded with sensations.

Burning. Not of flesh, this time, or even gasoline. It's an internal fire, singeing my organs as if clearing the path for new life.

His stubble grazes my temple, and I can feel him straining. Trying to see what he feels.

"What—"

My body tenses, my jaw locking as I wrangle myself from Aiden's grasp, diving into the clothing rack like he's held a flame to my skin.

His dark brows furrow, arms falling a full minute after I've left them, as though they'd already become accustomed to my presence.

"Where the hell is your shirt?" he hisses, moving toward me. Pausing, he seems to think better of it, and shrugs out of his jacket.

"You didn't give me one!"

"Jesus *Christ*." Letting his jacket fall to the floor, he tosses his cap and glasses down. Hooking his fingers in the hem of his hoodie, he whips it over his head to reveal a plain black T-shirt beneath.

I gape as he extends his arm, holding the hoodie out for me.

"Seriously? You want to argue about this too? You're topless, angel."

My chin lifts, defiance ebbing through me like a tsunami. I'm annoyed with myself for the way the evening's panned out. Annoyed with the fact that he's seen me in such a vulnerable state—*felt* the most vulnerable piece of me, even if he didn't get a good look at it.

I'm tempted to search his gaze and find out just how

much he saw. See if it changed the way he looks at me, but I don't.

That way lies madness.

"Just put it on, please. The bagels will be done in a minute, and I really don't feel like busting Ronan's ass for looking at your tits."

Jaw clenched, I snatch the hoodie from him and yank it on, untucking my hair from where it gets caught in the hood. I look ridiculous in the oversized clothes, but I'm more comfortable in them than I have been all night.

Aiden runs his knuckles over his bottom lip as I step out of the rack, his eyes darkening like melted silver. I throw my hands out and twirl with a wide, fake smile.

"Better, *sir*?"

His hand tightens into a fist, knuckles bleaching. "*Much.* Now let's go."

He puts his disguise back on and grabs a pair of slip-on shoes too big for me in the lost and found bin. Paying for them and a clean pair of socks, he hands the items over.

I push my feet into them, letting out the softest moan when I'm no longer constricted by my heels.

Draping my discarded dress over one shoulder, I wait at the counter while Ronan—a heavyset man with a white mustache—rings up the total. He shoves a paper bag in our direction, and Aiden swipes it from the counter at the same time he hands over a wad of cash.

"Keep it," he says, holding a palm up when Ronan tries to return his change. His hand whips out, tangling with mine, and then he's yanking me from the building and back up the street.

My fingers tingle where we connect, but I stuff the sensation down and blame it on excitement.

Definitely not fate.

I still struggle to keep up, my feet flopping around in the new-to-me shoes, and he's practically sprinting up the side-walk. We bump into people, and I whisper apologies as he drags me along, aware that they likely can't hear my words.

He moves fast, with his head tucked into his chest, alter-nating between glancing back at me and at the crowd. If someone's holding a cell phone to take pictures, or a camera points in our direction, he veers as far away as he can get, blending into the darkness.

We pass by the complex where the gala is being hosted, and I still do a double take to see if maybe Mellie and Aurora are scouring the outside for me. I don't see them, and soon I don't see anyone as Aiden snags a corner and crosses the street.

I feel the water before I see it; the air gets a little cooler, a lot cleaner, and soaks into my skin with a soft breeze. He releases my hand as we reach a dead end, and I wonder if this marks the finish line of our adventure.

A coerced night with a rock star, a change of clothes, and a bagel I haven't even gotten to taste yet. I suppose there are worse ways to close out a trip to New York City.

But Aiden doesn't stay still for long; his figure moves in the shadows cast by the streetlights, and he starts up the path in front of us, pushing the chain-link gate back enough for us to slip in. I follow like a cat fiending for tuna, shuffling behind him.

Once past the wrought iron fence surrounding the area, we stop to catch our breath.

The park is compact, mostly made up of brick and concrete, dotted with gardens I suspect are probably flush with exotic flora in the spring. Right now, they're barren, the wild boar statue to my left the only real appealing thing inside.

Across from us is the East River, and I step closer, captivated by the way the city skyline reflects off the surface. A massive bridge stretches horizontally over the body of water, connecting Manhattan to Queens—which I only know because I studied the boroughs excessively before this trip.

My shins meet the concrete barrier between myself and the river, and I let out a wistful sigh.

"It's beautiful," I say softly. Reverently, as if my compliment might upset the water.

Aiden steps up beside me, resting his free hand on the rail next to where mine is curled around it. I feel his eyes on me, hot where they try to penetrate deeper, but I refuse to turn my head and get sucked in.

"Yeah," he says, the one word laced with such tenderness to it that I ache between my thighs in a way I never have before.

I clear my throat, tension coiling in my stomach. "Do you do this kind of thing often? Bid on girls and take them on crazy dates?"

"Never. I don't really..." He sighs, slipping his hand into his back jean pocket. "My life is very carefully coordinated, and for good reason. I don't usually deviate, because I'm a creature of habit. Most artists are, because it helps keep the creativity flowing when you don't have to put a lot of work into changing everyday shit up. I truly don't remember the last time I ventured off on my own like this."

"So, what? You saw me throwing a pity party and decided we should celebrate elsewhere?"

He cocks his head to the side, a tiny smirk tugging at the corner of his lips.

"You were the only one there tonight who didn't look like they wanted to be there. Everyone in my life, in the entertainment industry... we're all snakes. Everyone wants something. Your honesty is refreshing."

Trying not to focus on the fact that he said *we*, I grip the railing tighter.

I don't know what strange force has led me here tonight, or why it feels as though my world is spinning off its axis and I'm being hurtled toward the sun.

But for right now, I want to stay here.

At least for a little while.

7

"OH, MY GOD."

Swallowing hard, I steal a look at the blonde beside me. She's got one arm hooked over the armrest, staring out at the river as she bites into a strawberry bagel.

Satisfaction softens her features, and I'm once again struggling to keep my dick down as she moans into the bread.

"I'm gonna need to know your name if you're gonna keep making sounds like that."

Her eyes widen, her head whipping in my direction. "What sounds?"

My mouth falls open a little, the urge to ask if she's a virgin in the literal sense flaring on the tip of my tongue. I don't think it'd surprise me either way, but the idea of her being untouched sends a renewed spike of pleasure down my spine.

"Nothing," I mutter instead, leaning back on the metal bench.

She kicks her legs out, taking another bite as she quickly redirects her attention. I can't help noticing how different she seems, now that she's in normal clothes.

Can't help noticing how good she looks in *mine*.

My mind flickers back to when I caught her at the dry cleaners, the way her body stiffened, yet somehow still perfectly molded into me.

If she were any other girl in the world, my guess is that I'd have already bent her over and had my way in whatever dark alcove we deemed appropriate. I don't ever do that kind of thing with fans, too worried about the potential repercussions my father's always warned me about, but something tethers me here with her.

This girl's skittish. Constantly looking over her shoulder, as if anticipating an attack. It hits close to home, and I find that her fear intrigues me.

It feels like a game, and I'm racing toward victory as I try to uncover what she's afraid of.

Deep down, a sick feeling bubbles up, soaking in her terror.

I want it to be me.

Shaking my head to dispel the insanity, I throw my arm over the back of the bench, twisting my fingers in the ends of her honey-colored locks. "Well?" I press, cocking an eyebrow. "Is that not the best bagel you've ever had?"

She hums, picking a piece off with two fingers. "It's *pretty* good, I'll give you that. Not sure my life has changed because of it, though." Moaning again as the dough hits her tongue, she shakes her head. "Okay, but how? How is it so good?"

"Boiled, instead of fried. Makes them crunchy and chewy in all the right places."

Making a little sound in the back of her throat, she looks back out at the bridge, and I look at her.

Her phone buzzes, interrupting the conversation, and she reaches into her purse to pull it out. Wiping her hands on her pants, she sets the half-eaten bagel on top of the paper bag, then slides off the bench.

"I need to take this."

Shrugging, I watch as she scurries away, knowing that even if she tried to run right now, it'd take minimal effort for me to catch up. She's small and has no idea how to navigate the city.

Besides, I don't think she has much interest in ditching me at this point.

Maybe that shouldn't please me so much, but I can't deny the way my blood heats in her presence. Technically, I *could* let her go—auction rules are pretty strict, but when what you've purchased is defective or not delivering, they tend to be more forgiving about refunds in order to avoid lawsuits.

I'm just not interested in buying anyone else's time.

Awareness scratches at my insides, fascination sprouting with that familiar sense of dread the longer I watch the girl. Intrigue is a dangerous thing, and I'm plummeting like a falling star, unable to lessen the impact.

The need to know *more* about her digs into my stomach, weeds twisting around my insides until I'm practically suffocating in my ignorance.

Unhealthy coping mechanisms, my mother would say. Obsessions with things that don't matter in order to keep the darker thoughts at bay.

My gaze drops to the rings on my fingers, jaw clenching. If anyone knows about unhealthy ways to cope, it's her.

"...yes, I'm *fine*. Please do not come back here."

I glance up, finding the girl's back as she leans over a metal trash can, phone pressed to her ear. One hand grips the rim of the can, while the other reaches up to scratch at her scalp repeatedly.

"It was two minutes, Boyd. There's really no reason to be this upset."

The man's name rolls off her tongue flippantly, and it feels like a concrete block drops right onto my chest. My lungs burn with the stress, and I realize just how close to unraveling I am.

I shift, hooking my ankle over my knee, and take my phone out to distract from the conversation. Willing myself to put some distance between the intensity of the inappropriate jealousy swimming in my veins, I unlock the screen and turn away from the blonde.

Several missed calls litter my notifications—three from Callie, one from my father, and a dozen from my producer Simon, who I'm supposed to meet when we fly to LA next week.

I don't bother listening to any of the voice mails, knowing they all probably say the same things. Demands of my whereabouts, as if they aren't tracking my every move.

Like I haven't noticed my bodyguard, Jason, lurking at every corner, watching from a distance, only ever giving me the illusion of freedom.

My fingers slip beneath the band of my watch, and I

press down as I open my texts. There are three from Liam, detailing the paperwork of my donation and the subsequent rage of my father, who'd been contacted as soon as the funds transferred.

Liam: You have maybe an hour. Hour and a half, tops. Finish getting your dick wet so we can go back to the apartment before your dad murders me.

I don't bother correcting him as I send a thumbs-up emoji and put my phone back in my jacket. Let him think what he wants—maybe if my father believes I gave the money away for pussy, he'll back off.

That's his MO, after all.

Liam: The Internet knows you left the gala. Just FYI. Be on the lookout.

"*No*. If you come back right now, I swear I won't forgive you. I'm *fine*." The girl turns slightly, meeting my gaze. She exhales, her breath wisping like smoke above her head. "Yes, I promise. Jesus. Okay, I'll talk to you when we're back at the hotel."

Something heavy pulls at my chest, scraping like thorns at the tendons there. The thought of the night ending already makes my entire body sag, buckling beneath the weight of a missed opportunity.

Instead of dragging her up the street, I should've been grilling her all this time. Finding out what makes her *her*.

Why the blue hues in her eyes seem to dim when she's lost in her thoughts but brighten when they're engaged with mine.

I clear my throat, and she finally walks back over, shoving her phone into her purse. Forcing nonchalance, I watch as she settles back onto the bench, stuffing a large bite of the bagel into her mouth.

"Boyfriend?" I ask, apprehension notching along my throat.

She snorts. Shakes her head. "Brother."

"Ah." I nod, relief splashing over me like a bucket of ice water. My heart stutters as I continue. "Do you *have* a boyfriend?"

Chewing, she steals a glance at me from the corner of her eye. "I'm not sure I'm really the dating type."

"No?"

She shrugs. "I know that probably seems crazy, what with how much you know about me."

"Well, I know you're not a hooker, and that your taste in bagels is subpar, at best." I inch toward her, the heat from her body reaching out with invisible fingertips. "You just don't really strike me as the love them and leave them type, is all."

"Maybe I'm full of surprises."

"Yeah?"

Driven by some powerful, transparent force, my hand reaches out slowly, once again tangling in her hair. A light shiver skates along her spine, and I trace it with the tip of one finger, arousal collecting in my gut and spurring me on.

She doesn't ask me to stop or lean away.

"Maybe you're more attracted to danger than you've let on? You did, after all, come out tonight with a complete stranger."

"Under duress."

My fingers travel higher, twisting in the strands at the base of her neck. The urge to tug back is strong, but I resist as her pink lips part slightly, not wanting to scare her off.

"Besides..." she breathes, dropping the rest of the bagel

into her lap, eyes tilting toward the night sky. "Who says *I'm* not dangerous?"

Leaning forward, I run my nose along her hairline, inhaling that sweet peppermint perfume. "I have no doubt that you are."

A beat passes, neither of us moving.

No breaths escape as time seems to slow down, and then halt altogether.

My dick twitches, intoxicated by this girl, but then she's springing to her feet and whirling on me, throwing her bagel into the trash over her shoulder.

When she grabs my arm and hauls me up, I let her, unsure of what's happening, except that a manic smile stretches across her face in an almost blinding manner.

It's brighter than the city lights and the stars, and for some reason, I find myself not wanting to let it disappear just yet.

It's the warmest expression she's had all night.

So when she drags me back down the ramp, exiting the park the way we came, I follow.

8

GROWING UP, I admired my brother.

Kind of worshiped him, as pathetic as that sounds.

Because while life had not been kind to him, he never seemed to let adversity keep him down. It didn't matter that our mother used him, letting her friends abuse him as payment for the drugs her body craved, or that she treated him as an emotional scapegoat even after sending him to live permanently with our aunt Dottie.

On the outside, Boyd kept his cool. Waited things out and went on to become rich and powerful.

For a long time, I thought that made him strong. He was

invincible to me, and I looked forward to the sparse moments when he'd stop by mine and our mom's little trailer to give me money.

He'd barge into the shoebox I called a bedroom and make small talk, before cutting a check or stuffing cash in my backpack, where our mother wouldn't find it.

God forbid she even pretend to be interested in my schooling.

I'd spend most of that time studying the colorful artwork spanning Boyd's skin, though with the suits he wears, I was never able to get a very good look at them. A skull on one hand, dice on the other.

A canvas of experience, he'd once called them. Said every single piece had some modicum of meaning to it, and that was the only reason he didn't regret getting them.

His body told a story.

One he'd created from scratch to erase any evidence of the life he'd been written into.

That sentiment struck a chord, though he's always been strictly anti-tattoo when it comes to me. If he even knew I was standing in a shitty parlor beside an inked rock star, waiting for them to gather paperwork, Boyd would certainly have a coronary on his way to the airport.

The thought of his rage is almost enough to quell my spontaneity.

Instead, I steal a look at the man beside me, watching as he smooths his thumb over the bulky watch on his wrist. He's discarded his hat and glasses, and his eyebrows are drawn in.

Anxiety flares up between my ribs at the thought that I'm keeping him from something.

Or someone.

"We don't have to do this."

Aiden's eyes slide to mine, and my trepidation melts like butter when our gazes lock. Mine twitches, itching to focus elsewhere, but I'm trapped.

"Having second thoughts? It doesn't hurt nearly as bad as your brain makes you think."

"It's not that," I say, although now it is a little. A loud buzz splits the air, coming from one of the little cubicles behind the receptionist's desk, and it makes my teeth chatter.

"Okay." He crosses his arms, turning to look at me head-on. "Then what's the problem?"

Chewing on my bottom lip, I shrug. "Maybe there are better things we could be doing with our time? I doubt this is what you had in mind when you bid on me earlier."

His eyes narrow, and he takes a step toward me. My heartbeat picks up, pounding like a snare drum inside my chest, resisting his magnetism even as it tries to yank me into him.

"You don't know *what* I had in mind when I saw you at the gala." Those gray irises grow heavy. Dark with something unspoken that I feel in my core. "Is there something else you'd rather be doing?"

My head shakes.

His jaw tics. "You want a tattoo, right?"

I nod, my throat tightening.

"Then you're getting a goddamn tattoo. Stop making excuses, angel, and do whatever the fuck you want tonight."

What I want and what I can actually have are very different things, I almost say. Desire unlike I've ever felt before surges up in my chest as he turns away, carding a veiny hand through his hair.

I wonder what his hands would feel like on my skin.

Gliding, touching, pleasing.

An image flashes of his lips on mine, traveling lower, slicking down my navel. I rub my thighs together, trying to relieve the ache between them.

My stomach twists, knowing these are fantasies I can't act on, regardless of what he tells me. Aiden and I are from totally different worlds. He deserves better than what mine would do to him.

The pixie-haired receptionist comes out from the back with two clipboards in hand, lips smacking as she chews on a piece of gum. She shoves one at me and tosses a black pen on top, then turns to Aiden.

"You've been here before," she says, tilting her head as if just recognizing him.

"Every time I come to the city. No one I trust more than Gio to slice me open."

My face flushes and the receptionist runs her tongue over the stud in her upper lip, giving me a bland expression. "That's not how tattoos work."

Turning on her heels, she takes the other clipboard with her to the back, and I sit down on a bench in front of the window, filling out the questionnaire.

Aiden doesn't come over, eyeing the glass behind me carefully, as if he's afraid of someone peeking in and noticing him. I tap the pen on the edge of the board after writing my name.

"I used to own all your albums," I say, breaking the uncomfortable silence that starts settling in around us. "*Herculean Effort* was my favorite, for a long time."

One of his brows arches. "Oh yeah? The way you've acted tonight, I assumed you weren't a fan."

"I'm not."

"Ouch."

My head snaps up, eyes wide. He's got his hand pressed to his chest, and he's smirking. God, that fucking smirk. I drop my gaze to the silver chain around his neck, heat flooding my face.

"I didn't mean it like that, it's just... I don't know, I guess I outgrew you."

He snorts. "You're bad for a man's ego."

Pushing my tongue against my cheek, I roll my words around in my head, trying to filter out what to say next.

I want to ask about his inspiration for his songs, if there's a reason they have mythological undertones, as if he takes the public's references to him being a modern-day Orpheus to heart.

Want to ask if it's hard being talented and under constant scrutiny. I can't imagine there's much room for creativity under a microscope.

I mull over each potential question, trying to figure out what the old me—the wannabe groupie—would want to know most.

The receptionist returns before I can continue, taking the clipboard from me and holding out a manicured hand.

"License?" she asks after I've spent more than a few seconds gaping at the length of her glittery black nails.

How she gets anything done with those claws is beyond me.

Slipping the card from my purse, I place it in the center of her palm and hook a thumb in Aiden's direction. "Can you make sure he doesn't see that?"

Her dark eyes narrow, sliding from me to him. "Why?"

"I don't want him to know my name."

Aiden laughs, the sound loud as it echoes off the cement

walls. The receptionist frowns, curling her fingers around my license, and looks back at me. "This feels illegal."

Gio, a tall, burly man with a braided red beard and a silver bar through the bridge of his nose, returns to the front of the shop with stencils and a clear spray bottle. He steps into one of the cubicles and starts rustling around, though I can't see what exactly he's doing.

"It's not illegal, Jenna." Aiden rolls his shoulders, and I hate the way he says her name. "Just a little game we're playing."

Twin storms rake down over my form, traveling so slow on their ascent that it feels like a caress. My breath catches in my throat as he pauses at my lips, reaching up to scrub his jaw with the side of one hand.

Never in my life have I wanted so badly to touch another person. To be touched by them.

The longer we stand here, stuck in some sort of impasse, the heavier that want gets. It presses down on my stomach, flattening my insides until want morphs into need, and I'm tempted to launch myself across the room and into his arms.

I have no clue if he'd catch me, but it doesn't matter, because before I have a chance, Gio calls his name and gestures for him to enter the cubicle. A few moments later, that buzzing sound from before picks up, and I clench my jaw.

The receptionist watches me while she photocopies my license, and I shift in my seat, her stare unnerving. She walks back over, handing me the card, and tilts her head.

"Whatever this is," she says in a low voice, just for me. "It's not going to end well."

Slipping my license back into my purse, a wave of unease

washes over me, flushing out any good feelings I've had about tonight.

There's truth in her words, but I don't want to acknowledge them.

So, instead, I sit back down on the bench, slump down against the window, and wait. Pulling my phone from my pocket, I try not to feel too disappointed when I see there are still no messages or calls from my "friends."

Then again, I'm not sure what I expected. Outside of school, we don't really interact, and the only reason I roomed with them for the trip was because I had to.

Still, a *little* concern would be nice. Especially since they'd have to report to the chaperones in the morning, not to mention the police, if I was really missing.

Snapping a picture of the artwork hanging on the wall behind the mahogany desk, I send it to my brother's girlfriend, unsure if she's even awake right now.

I wince when the little bubbles pop up, indicating her reply. Awake, and probably getting reacquainted with Boyd after days apart.

Fiona: He's gonna kill you.

Grinning, I swipe out of the app and switch over to social media, scrolling through the boring posts of the people back home. For a town living under the thumb of organized crime, the people there sure don't have a lot going on.

Glancing up, I see Aiden's dark head of hair over the cubicle wall. The buzzing continues on, echoing ominously in my ears as I pull up the hashtag with his name, filtering through thousands of tagged photos for the first time in years.

Jealousy stabs at my chest as I soak in the pictures of him and Sylvie Michaels, with her dark hair, tan skin, and almond-shaped eyes. She looks almost regal standing next to him on red carpet after red carpet, and my self-esteem rattles inside its empty cage.

Once again, I have no idea why he's spent the night with me, but I suppose that doesn't much matter now.

The night's almost over, anyway.

Farther down, there are tons of concert photos; him posing with a black electric guitar on stage, sometimes crowd-surfing or holding the mic to the audience. Bright lights and laser shows obscure the pictures, making him little more than a silhouette performing for people.

I'm so engrossed in my findings that I don't hear anyone approach me. A shadow falls over my form, and my muscles seize as I jolt upright, nearly dropping my phone in the process.

"*Jesus.*" I exhale a shaky breath, my shoes slapping onto the floor as I lock my screen. "You can't sneak up on people like that."

Aiden grins. "You're very cagey, you know that?" I don't respond, and he extends his hand. "It's your turn."

My eyes scan the visible stretch of skin beneath his sleeve. "What did you get?"

Turning his left hand up, he shows me where black plastic is taped to the underside of his thumb. "Tit for tat. I'll show you mine after you show me yours."

I'm not sure how badly I care about new ink on him, when he's almost completely covered in it, but I nod anyway, letting him lead me to the tattooing station.

Stepping into the crowded space, I wait for instruction as Gio sits on a stool with his back to me, fiddling around with the utensils on a plastic cart. Black ink sits in a little paint dish, and the electric gun is beside that; my eyes glue to them as I take a seat on the padded table, swinging my legs beneath me.

"You've eaten recently?" Gio asks, rolling around to face me.

"Uh, yeah. Like half an hour ago."

He jerks his chin in acknowledgment and picks up the stencil on the cart. "Where are we putting this?"

Gripping my knees, I let out a sigh, trying to expel the fear from my lungs. "My hip, I think."

Aiden makes a sound in the back of his throat, and I turn to glare at him.

"You can't watch."

His eyebrows shoot up. "Why the hell not?"

"That's... too much. Too intimate, for strangers."

Pressing his lips together, his nostrils flare, and he leans over the partition. A muscle in his jaw thumps, and I can tell he wants to protest, but after a prolonged stare down, he growls in defeat.

"*Fine*, but I'm not leaving you alone back here."

"Whatever." I wave my hand pointedly. "But don't you dare look."

9

WITH MY THROAT suddenly thick and dry, I try to force a swallow, but my gut rages on.

My body's revolting at the idea of intentionally causing myself harm, bits of memory trying to worm their way in.

Tattoos are basically colored scars, Boyd told me once, when I asked if I could get one for my seventeenth birthday. *Aren't you sick of being identifiable?*

Hypocritical, yes. But maybe my brother had a point.

It's on the tip of my tongue to decline when Gio snaps on a pair of blue latex gloves and holds up the stencil, cocking an eyebrow. I blink, and then spring into action when I realize he's waiting for me.

Hopping up, I awkwardly shimmy the sweatpants down to my knees, avoiding eye contact with the artist as he leans forward. The lacy nude thong Mellie made me wear does nothing to shield me from the cold table, and I grit my teeth as I sit my bare ass back on it.

Aiden's hoodie, at least, is long enough to cover the scar on my abdomen. I hold the hem in place for good measure, though.

Swiping an alcohol wipe over the spot, he lets it dry for a moment before placing the stencil on. I hiss as the paper makes contact with my skin, but then he's pulling back and using his hand to fan the purple ink.

He holds up a little circular mirror. "Like it?"

My brain is a bit hazy as I nod, my eyes trailing over the design; it's higher and farther in than I'd imagined, in that soft crease where thigh meets hip, but it looks *good*.

I'm buzzing, something that feels a lot like excitement pumping through me when Gio tells me to lie back and relax.

I do quickly, turning my head to stare at the back of Aiden's. His dark hair sticks up in an array of angles, perfectly tousled, and I want to tangle my fingers in it. Tug on it the way he's done all night, see if I can cure my fears with him.

God, what is wrong with me? I didn't want the slimy businessman's hands anywhere near me, but the thought of Aiden James even thinking about touching me has my temperature rising.

Gio dips the tattoo gun in his ink, and I feel his eyes on me. "Ready?"

The muscles in my chest pull tight, and I force a shaky nod. He switches the gun on, and instinctively, I stiffen, my breaths growing shallow. Rickety.

They rattle from somewhere deep in my chest and sweat percolates across my forehead as shame and panic swirl around my insides.

My heart bangs into my ribs so hard I'm worried it might bruise. Worried the black and blue skin will bleed through and reveal my insecurities.

"Relax," Gio grunts as he leans over me, and I'm trying, really I am.

Fuck, I'm trying.

My eyes shoot to the ceiling, tracing squares in the popcorn material. The buzzing sound fills my ears and invades my senses; it vibrates through my body, and I clench my teeth shut to try and ward it off, but it just travels along my spine instead.

Thick bile teases the back of my throat, cutting off my air supply, throwing me further down the stairs of terror.

"It'll be over in a minute." Gio's voice is low, meant to be soothing, but for some reason all I can hear is the gravelly baritone of my mother's ex-boyfriend as he pins me down.

The image is unclear, but his words come through as if he's whispering them in my ear all over again. It's mostly muffled Italian, but that exact phrase, *"it'll be over in a minute,"* replays over and over, the only English he cared to utter.

Pinching my eyes shut, I try to force the memory away, but it doesn't budge. My hands grip the edges of the table. If Gio notices my apprehension, he doesn't say anything.

Maybe because he thinks it's all pre-tattoo jitters, and that I'll get over it when we get started.

A lead weight settles in the center of my chest, and the buzzing gets louder. Blots out everything else as it slinks up and down my skin like a familiar knife.

And then, the needle is on me, slicing or punching or whatever it is that tattoo guns do. Pain sizzles where the tool touches, radiating outward until I'm suffocating in it, my lungs giving in to the burn.

"Jesus Christ," Gio curses as an ear-piercing mewl rips out of my throat. He snaps back, switching the gun off, and I can practically hear Aiden trip over himself to turn around and assess the situation.

I don't open my eyes, struggling to regulate my breathing; fear has me in a choke hold, its claws digging into my throat and refusing to let go.

"What happened?" Aiden demands, his tone sharper than it's been all night.

"Nothing. I did *one* line and she's having a fucking panic attack. I thought you said she was good."

No one says anything for several beats, and my skin warms even more knowing they're watching me.

Waiting.

Forcing a swallow, I peel my eyelids back and blink up at the fluorescent lights, sucking in three lungfuls of air as I push into an upright position.

"I'm fine," I insist, even as my arms tremble. Crossing them over my chest, I glance down at the tattoo; black streaks across my skin, a single line mixed with a droplet of blood, and I look away before the urge to vomit resurfaces. "Seriously, I am. Let's... can we try it again?"

I don't know why I ask, since it's painfully obvious that I'm *not* okay, but I don't want to seem like a baby in front of a freaking celebrity. Especially one *covered* in tattoos.

Embarrassment scalds my cheeks, and I stare down at the ground, wishing it'd crack open and swallow me whole.

"Clearly you're not, and I'm not tattooing you if you're going to fucking pass out. I could have my license revoked for that shit."

"You can't leave her with an incomplete design," Aiden says.

"I can if it means not risking her safety. She's in no shape to continue."

"G, come on—"

Tears sting my eyes, and a solution rushes past my lips before I have a chance to consider the consequences. "What if Aiden finishes it?"

Lifting my head, both men are watching me with wide eyes, like they're surprised I suggested such a thing. I'm not even sure if that's something he's allowed to do, although I remember reading a few years ago about how he'd occasionally step into some tattoo shops around the country while on tour and fill in as a guest.

Though not an artist, he can at least trace over a simple stencil, and fans used to line up down the street for the chance to have Aiden James scar them with ink.

They're staring, clearly waiting for me to elaborate. "I think... I think I can do it, but not with a strange man looming over me, you know?"

Sliding his gaze from me, Aiden looks at Gio and lifts a shoulder. Gio frowns so hard a dimple forms in his right cheek, and then he throws his hands in the air, shaking his head.

"That doesn't make any fucking sense, but whatever." Removing his gloves, Gio tosses them in the trash bin next to the table and stalks out of the cubicle. "Make sure you sign that liability release. And I want VIP tickets to your next show in Philly."

"Done."

"She gets even a little paler, or starts gagging, you quit. Got it?"

We nod, and Gio disappears through the back with the receptionist while Aiden takes his spot on the stool. He doesn't look at me while he preps, methodically sliding his rings off and pulling on a new pair of gloves.

My ears ring in the silence that follows, and I feel extremely stupid. *This is such a bad idea.*

"Wanna talk about it?" he asks, turning toward me.

I shake my head, pressing my legs together as the reality that I'm half naked sets in. My fingers pull on the hem of the hoodie, reflexively ensuring the scar is still covered.

"Ready to tell me your name yet?" He rolls forward so his chest is level with my knees.

Again, I shake my head, and he just sighs.

"Lean back for me." My throat constricts until I can't breathe *again*, but his soft tone stirs something else in me.

Determination takes hold, and I force my body to move through the sludge of panic, pushing my weight back onto the heels of my palms.

He scoots closer, keeping his eyes on mine. With one hand, he pushes the sweatpants down a little more, then draws a damp cloth roughly over the start of the tattoo, cleaning my skin of debris. The pain is sharp, sudden, and over before I can even finish inhaling.

"You have to relax," he murmurs, reaching for the gun. I watch, rapt, as he dips the needle in ink and brings it over to the table. "In the name of adventure, remember?"

Blowing out a breath, I give a quick jerk of my chin, and

he plants his elbow between my thighs as he angles the gun appropriately.

My breathing stalls out completely, and my pulse plucks along just centimeters from his arm.

Head tilting, he purses his lips, and for a moment I worry that he's rusty and doesn't know what he's doing. That he's just using this as an excuse to get close to me and get what he paid for.

He switches the gun on, and that buzz races up my spine. I squeeze my legs against him, and the motion drags me closer, the point of his elbow digging into my lace-covered pussy.

Curling my fingers into the leather cushioning, I try to move back, but my ass is sticking to the table. Keeping me trapped against him.

That second pulse between my thighs picks up speed, racing wantonly as it craves more friction. He's *barely* touching me, and I'm seconds from unraveling.

"You've done this before, right?" I choke out, hoping like hell that he can't feel my blood rushing south.

A curt nod and a flare of his nostrils is all the acknowledgment I get before he presses the needle into my skin.

"Breathe, angel," he croons, shifting.

His elbow grinds into me even more as he moves, watching the gun work with narrowed eyes. They don't move from the site, even when I start to squirm, and he pauses. His eyebrows raise, but that's it.

"You're doing so well, pretty girl."

Tingles shoot up and down my arms like wildfires, and I get more tangled up in my confusion.

I swallow, my body warring with pain and pleasure and the fact that he's causing them both.

Still, the memories from before aren't flashing across my vision, so I consider that a win of some sort. Grabbing on to that shred of relief, I rest my head on the partition encircling us, closing my eyes and imagining that I'm a different person.

Someone strong and brave, who doesn't get panic attacks they can only partially ascertain the cause of.

"I do this after every show, you know." His breath is warm and damp as it glides over my skin, contrasting sharply with the way my flesh breaks for him. "Get a new tattoo. It's like a little good luck ritual, prepping me for the next one."

"What'd you get tonight?"

"A halo."

I'm too focused on not freaking out to fully process his admission, but I feel my brain file it away for later.

When I don't reply, he continues, the gun still scraping. "So, when you said this wasn't what I had in mind for tonight, you were wrong. I can't imagine doing anything else."

The buzzing suddenly stops, and my eyes pop open as silence falls around us. Aiden leans back, returning the gun to its place on the side table, and squirts purple liquid onto a towel. I sit up straighter, and he drags the cloth over the tattoo, wringing a tiny moan from my mouth at the instant relief it provides.

His elbow is still between my legs, his head dangerously close to my hip as he cleans me up. Emotion, tight and sticky, lodges in my throat, and I bite down on the inside of my cheek until it bleeds.

"Well?" he asks, tipping his chin up to look at me. "What do you think?"

But I'm not looking at the tattoo. Not even a little bit interested in it.

Inching forward, I tilt my hips down, my clit throbbing as I apply more pressure against his elbow. Heat flares in his gray eyes, like lightning splashing across a stormy sky, and his Adam's apple bobs violently.

"I think," I croak, my voice sounding like it's been shredded by a cheese grater. "That I'm not ready for this adventure to be over, just yet."

His mouth opens—to say what, I'll never know, because in the next second I'm shoving my fingers into his hair and yanking his lips to mine.

10

FUCK, her lips are soft.

That's the first and only coherent thought occurring in my mind as our mouths connect, crashing together in a flurry of passion. The tension we've been holding on to all night dissolves into the singular action, evaporating into the air as we get tangled up in each other.

Her fingers clutch tight to my roots, holding my face in place like she's afraid I'll move away if she lets go. Matching her movements, I rip off the latex gloves and place my palms on either side of her head, angling her mouth so I can delve deeper.

One swipe of her tongue against mine, tentative as it explores, and my knees are fucking buckling. I drop one hand, bracing myself against the table, and press harder against her, mapping out the inside of her mouth like an explorer who's just discovered a new island.

My dick throbs behind the zipper of my jeans, stiffening as she tries to bring her sweet little cunt closer.

It was all I could do to keep my composure while I finished her tattoo. Concentration was nearly lost the second I bent down, inhaling the soft scent of her arousal.

Part of me wondered if any of it came from her obvious fear.

Still, I wasn't going to act on anything—didn't need the extra set of complications.

I'd gotten started almost immediately, falling back into the motions even though it'd been a long time since I sat behind the gun. Then she'd pushed her hips forward and clamped her thighs around my arm, inadvertently rubbing her soaked crotch against my elbow, and I'd almost blown my load right then.

Given her apparent shy, reserved nature, I really wasn't anticipating the night to take this turn.

I'd hoped, of course. I've been wanting to taste her since the second I laid eyes on her.

And now that we're here, I don't intend on wasting the opportunity.

"*Fuck.*" Breaking away, I slide my hand around to her jaw, holding her head back to stare into those clear blue eyes. They're glassy, round with lust, and laced with vulnerability.

"Oh, my god," she breathes, her breath cool as it brushes my lips. Her fingers touch the corner of her mouth, and she drops her gaze to the chain around my neck. "I'm so sorry, Aiden, I don't know what I was thinking."

My eyebrows jump, nearly grazing my hairline. "Well, that's a first."

"What?"

"Never had someone apologize for kissing me. I can't decide if that's worse than you saying you've outgrown me, or not."

Her cheeks take on a rosy hue, and she lets her hand fall to her lap.

Her mostly naked lap.

Arousal rushes down my spine like a waterfall, and I slowly inch the hand resting on the table toward her leg. My fingernail scrapes over her knee, and my palm smooths over it, stopping mid-thigh and giving a tight squeeze.

She jolts forward, bringing her cunt to the edge of the table. The lace material of her underwear strains against her, caught between the two of us. It'd take almost no effort for me to slip a finger beneath the band and rip, baring her to my eyes.

My fingers. My tongue.

"I-I don't..." She licks her lips, her hand encircling my wrist. Barring entry.

"Don't what?" I bend down, dragging my nose across the crown of her head, trying to find where her peppermint perfume begins. "Don't want me to kiss you?"

"I don't know why you'd want to."

The admission feels like a brass-knuckled punch to the gut, knocking the wind out of me. My free hand moves up, cupping the back of her neck so she's forced to look up at me. Glacial eyes blink back, rife with unspoken emotion and secrets.

They're captivating, like a whirlpool that sucks you into its current, and I feel like a man who never learned how to swim.

"Fishing for compliments?" I ask, arching an eyebrow.

Her mouth flattens, the blush from before darkening. "No, just making an observation."

My fingers flex around her, my thumb finding her pulse point. It stutters beneath me, as if struggling to keep a steady beat.

"Do you think I'd be here if I didn't want to be?" Pressing my hips against her, I move so she's bowing back over the table and slide my hand into her hair, threading lightly in her roots. The tips of our noses brush as I ghost my mouth over hers, teasing but not kissing.

Desire builds in my chest, like water held back by a dam.

"That whole ballroom was stuffed full of beautiful, elegant women tonight. Women who I probably wouldn't have had to pay for."

My other hand pushes back against her, moving higher up her thigh, until I'm close to the spot I've just tattooed. She opens to me and our breaths mingle, passing interchangeably between parted lips.

"But all I saw was you."

A soft gasp escapes when my fingers drift around the tattoo, soothing the heated flesh, and I swallow it, sealing our mouths together.

Her answering moan damn near unravels me, and I'm practically climbing on top of her in my search for *more*.

More friction.

More sweetness.

More of *her*.

Wiggling her hips, she kicks out of the NYU sweatpants and wraps her legs tentatively around my waist. I feel her hands slip up my back, roving over the raised lines of each of my tattoos. My hands fall to her hoodie, hooking beneath the hem.

I draw her bottom lip into my mouth, sucking sharply as I begin lifting the hoodie up.

She jumps, yanking back for a moment, holding my hands in place. Anxiety colors her features, and I frown.

"I need to see *all* of you," I say, but she just shakes her head.

"Shirt stays on. Please."

My jaw clenches, irritation slinking through my nerves. "You realize I saw you topless earlier?"

"An innocent accident," she says, shrugging one shoulder.

It's like she thinks that remaining clothed will protect her from me.

"Fine."

Releasing the hoodie, my fingers dip lower, traveling lightly over her pubic bone. Her face seems to tighten and soften at the same time, as if she likes what I'm doing, but it pains her to admit.

"Then I want more."

Teeth sinking into her bottom lip, she hesitates. "I guess we can keep kissing—"

Snorting, I pull back and smooth a palm down the front of my jeans, cutting her off mid-sentence; her eyes widen as they track the movement, taking in the sight of my erection straining against the fabric.

"I don't have a condom," I say, cursing myself internally

for not thinking to grab one from the penthouse. Though, to be fair, I really *hadn't* planned on needing one. "But I would always regret it if I left tonight without getting to taste you."

She blinks several times, her blush darkening and crawling down her neck.

I can't help but wonder if it stretches farther.

Short breaths puff from her chest, and she glances back at the door Gio and Jenna went through. "What if someone comes back?"

"They won't. I'll be done before they do."

"They won't come back, or you'll finish before they do?" she rasps. "Those are two different things."

"*You'll* finish before they do."

"This seems like a bad idea."

"The worst," I agree. "We'll probably regret it in the future."

She frowns. "You think?"

"Undoubtedly."

I don't mention that my regrets will come in the form of an obsession, one that's been brewing on the outskirts of my mind all night. Once I've tasted her, I know I'll never have enough.

"But who the fuck cares about tomorrow? Just enjoy the right now with me, and deal with everything else later. Okay?"

I pause, watching her for signs of discomfort. It's there, veiled beneath layers she's erected in an attempt to hide it away. But I see it.

Finally, she gives a slight nod, and the pressure releases in my chest like water draining from a bathtub.

"Okay."

Dropping to my knees, I run my hands up her thighs, fitting my shoulders between them. "You smell so good. Like peppermint."

"It's a lotion," she breathes, the sound barely registering.

"Scoot closer, pretty girl. If you won't show me everything, I at least want to see this perfect cunt."

"You're extremely demanding." But she obeys anyway, shimmying forward so her ass is hanging half off the edge of the table.

"Please accept my tongue as an apology." Her thighs flex, pressing against me as if she's trying to close them. Trying to hide from me.

I curl two fingers into the lace crotch of her thong, tug it to the side, and lean back on my heels to admire the shape of her glistening sex. Like the dewy petals of a pink rose blossom, she opens up, perfection in the form of the sweetest sin.

"*Jesus*. How long have you been wet for me?" I taunt, leaning in to lap from top to bottom, spreading her arousal along her lips.

"I-I don't—"

"Were you going to keep it a secret?" Pressing the flat of my tongue against her swollen clit, I soak in the soft vibrations, flicking the tip gently. "Pretend I didn't have an effect on you, and then what, angel? Were you going to touch yourself to the thought of me tonight?"

My licks turn languid, broad swipes along her seam as I grow more starved for her.

"No," she gasps out, hips bucking up.

"You're a filthy little liar."

One of my fingers moves, teasing her slick entrance at the same time I pull her clit between my lips and suck. Her head falls back, and I moan as I watch her break apart, alternating between massaging her flesh with my tongue and swirling in circular motions.

I pull back just enough to speak around her. "But goddamn, do you taste good. So fucking *perfect.*"

Diving back in before she can reply, I take note of what has her panting and squirming and redouble my efforts. Sparks of pleasure rain down my back like hellfire, and I feel that familiar heaviness in my balls as my cock hardens to the point of pain, threatening to release from the sound of her enjoyment alone.

I'm not thinking about anything else as I work her over, pushing my index finger into her gently. She's *tight*, impossibly so, and I imagine her inner muscles suffocating my dick, milking me dry as I curl and knead, searching for that sweet spot.

Her orgasm crawls through her slowly, starting with her shaky thighs; I can feel it cresting as she pinches her eyes shut and tightens around me, practically cutting off my circulation.

"*Yes,* just like that, angel. You're fucking magnificent, coming for me like this. Such a good girl for your stranger."

Lips parting on a silent scream, her body goes rigid, tremor after tremor racing through her as she finally surrenders.

I groan, trading my mouth for my finger, and vice versa. "That's it, pretty girl. Soak my fucking tongue."

Immediately, she's trembling, fingers grabbing at my hair as I spear into her tight channel. A gush of wetness trickles along my tastebuds, and I can feel myself leaking in my jeans, my cock desperate to be inside of her.

Only when she collapses against the table, limbs going limp, do I pull away. And even that proves to be the most difficult thing I've ever fucking done.

Face flushed and drenched in sweat, she keeps her eyes closed, throwing a forearm over them.

I wipe my mouth on the back of my hand, wishing there was a way to imprint the taste of her cum on me forever.

"Well." I grin, reaching for her arm. "That was—"

Jolting up, she flinches away from my touch, shoving her way off the table. My eyebrows draw in as she scrambles to her feet, yanking her sweats back on.

"A mistake."

Arms dropping to my sides, I frown. "The only mistake was not *starting* our evening with that."

She shakes her head, running a hand through her disheveled hair. "No, no. I *told* you, I'm not a hooker. This was wrong. So wrong."

Stepping toward her, my hands slide around her waist, trying to pull her close. To calm whatever switch has just flipped. "It's not like *you* get the money I donated. What's the big deal? Did that not feel good?"

Watery blue eyes turn up at me, and her bottom lip wobbles. "I'm sorry, I need to go."

"Go?"

I should just let her, especially since I'm sure my own freedom is coming to an end. It probably won't be long before one of the bodyguards following us tonight makes himself known and escorts me back to the penthouse. Back to reality.

But for some reason, I don't want to go back yet.

I cup her cheeks, trying to lean in for a kiss, but then

she's tearing out of my grasp and darting from the tattoo station. She barely has time to remember to grab her purse on the way out, and she's bolting past the front desk and out the door before I can say anything else.

11

THE TRIP back to my hotel is a blur, and my phone rings incessantly the entire way.

My teeth chatter as I stand on the corner of East Fifty-Ninth and Second Avenue, struggling to catch my breath. I sprinted out of the tattoo parlor and didn't stop until I was swallowed up by the crowd, safe from Aiden's intensity.

By the time I manage to hail a cab, I turn my cell off completely and pull my hood up, trying to block out the sounds of the city.

It doesn't do anything, though; pressing my hands to my ears just amplifies everything, and I buckle forward, shoving my head between my knees the way my therapist used to tell me to.

God, I can smell him on me.

What he did to me.

What I let him do.

Bile burns the back of my throat, and it feels like I've swallowed a razor blade. My palms slide around to my face, fingers trembling violently against heated skin as I try to focus on getting air to my lungs.

In through the nose, out through the mouth.

"Hey, you can't puke in here, girly." The driver's voice barely penetrates, his harsh tone not loud enough to cover the way my brain screams at me.

Stupid. I'm so fucking stupid.

Every wall I've built over the last few years is nothing but rubble now, and I'm left standing, wondering how I'm supposed to pick up the pieces.

Disgust crawls over me like thousands of little bugs, and I scratch desperately at my skin, trying to eliminate the itch. The longer I sit, the worse it gets, until it feels like I've been buried alive and left as worm food.

I can feel layers of my flesh breaking away as my scratching becomes ferocious, and I'm sure the driver thinks I'm tweaking right now. He curses under his breath, something about junkies in the city, but I don't really hear it when my mother's voice echoes in the recesses of my mind.

Easy. Slut. Whore.

Insults she used to hurl at me, even though there was no merit behind them.

I've never even been on a *date*, much less let anyone have their way with me.

Until now, that is.

Now I've gone and proved her right. Eviscerated every principle, every amount of work I've done over the last few years. I can feel my progress unraveling, disintegrating as her accusations become my reality.

All because a gray-eyed man made me feel special.

Bursting from the cab as soon as we're within a hundred feet of the hotel, I toss a wad of cash up front and bolt to the front doors. My chest is tight, and my throat feels like it might be on the verge of closing permanently, but I jog past the concierge and into the elevator anyway.

Once the metal doors slide shut, I collapse against the wall, forcing a strangled gasp from my lungs. It tears up my esophagus, wheezing as it squeaks out, but at least I'm breathing.

That's what I try to focus on as the elevator comes to a stop, and I make my way across the hall to our hotel suite. I'm already looking forward to wrapping myself in the plush white bedding in my room, hiding out until we leave for the airport in the morning.

I stop dead in my tracks when I swipe my key card, push open the door, and find Mellie and Aurora lounging on the couch, watching a scary movie. They're wearing matching white silk robes, and an open bottle of red wine resting on the sofa between them.

It looks as if they've been here for a while.

Swallowing, I let the door swing shut behind me, blinking rapidly as though that might change the scene before me.

Mellie glances up first, and she grins, giving a little wave. Her platinum hair is pushed back by a rainbow headband, her almond-shaped eyes wide as they take me in.

"Well, that's definitely not what we sent you out in," she says, wiggling her dark brows. "*Someone* had a good night."

Aurora turns her head, tapping the mouth of the wine bottle. "Jeez, Riley. And here we were thinking you wouldn't be into the whole live auction scene."

She pauses, and a practiced cruelty tugs at her sharp features. "Given your familial history, though, I guess it wasn't so foreign to you, huh?"

My lips part, a retort materializing on the back of my tongue. There's no telling which part of my history, exactly, she's talking about—my mother's aptitude for whoring herself, or my brother's affiliation with the Mafia and *their* connections to the slave trade.

Though, I suppose the specifics don't really matter. They don't change the fact that she clearly equates my worth as a person with my unfortunate heritage, and I doubt there's any way I could convince her otherwise.

Once you accept something as garbage, it's very difficult to polish it afterward.

So, instead, I bite the inside of my cheek and swallow the reply. Walking over to the sink, I wash my hands, trying to scrub the feel of Aiden James out from under my fingertips.

I dry them quickly, then grab a hotel-branded water bottle from the fridge and walk over to where they sit, contemplating if I want to join them or not. Perching on the arm of the sofa, I wait for an invitation. Something to prove they don't hate me, despite *everything*.

Because I'm an idiot who seems to accept the scraps tossed her way.

Better than going hungry, I suppose.

"Where did you guys go tonight?" I ask, avoiding the gore on the television.

"Oh, you know. We walked around the event area. Tested out a few of the physical products they had up to bid on, mingled with a lot of B-listers. Boring stuff, really."

I watch Mellie's lips move as she speaks, but for some reason, I don't buy a word of it. "I looked but couldn't find you."

"We were around," Aurora says, shrugging. "Must not have looked hard enough."

"That silver fox at the bar probably stole her attention," Mellie giggles. Her thumb prods at my knee, nudging as if we're in on the same little joke.

"He looked very *Wolf of Wall Street*." Aurora raises a brow. "Hope you made him wrap it."

"*Jesus*, Ror."

My face heats, the anxiety from before flushing my skin. As it trickles down my chest like an IV drip, I push to my feet, not wanting them to know there's even a little truth to their words.

Sure, it wasn't the "silver fox" I left with, but that doesn't exactly make it better.

Excusing myself from the room, I lock myself in the bathroom and get ready for bed. Washing the day's events from my body, I push them as far from the forefront of my mind as possible, ignoring the ache between my thighs.

I don't want to think too hard about *why* I'm suddenly so sore there, so instead I sit with the detachable showerhead against my pussy for several minutes. I don't come, don't imagine Aiden's talented fingers or mouth working me over. I just let the water soothe.

Fiona calls as I'm climbing beneath the goose down comforter, and I pick up as I flip off the bedside light.

"So?" she says, in lieu of hello. My brother's girlfriend isn't one for greetings or goodbyes. "Did you do it?"

I yawn. "Do what?"

"Get a tattoo! God, it's been like an hour and a half since you texted me that picture. Is your memory that bad?"

Only when I want it to be. Clearing my throat, I stuff my hand beneath the comforter and run a finger over the fresh ink, wishing I'd thought to grab a tube of ointment before I made my escape earlier. I make a mental note to steal some from Boyd when I get home tomorrow.

"Yeah."

I pause, chewing on my bottom lip as I consider telling her more. If there's anyone I can trust to keep a secret, it's Fiona Ivers—lord knows she kept my brother as one for months, back before they officially became a couple.

"That's not... *all* I did tonight, though," I say finally, and even just the hint of a confession makes my shoulders sag with relief. "I kind of went on a date with Aiden James."

Silence fills the line, twisting my gut into impenetrable knots. I stare out the window at the dark sky, wondering how far out you have to go from the city before you can see the stars again.

Some shuffling comes through the phone, and then it sounds like a door closes, and she's back. "Okay, sorry. Definitely not something I want your brother to hear. I'm in our closet now. What do you mean you went out with *Aiden James*? The musician? *The* Aiden James you're totally in love with?"

I snort, slinking down farther beneath the covers. "I'm not in love with him, but yes. *That* Aiden James. He kind of bought my time at some weird charity gala we went to, and things kind of just spiraled from there."

"Holy shit." She laughs, the sound breathless.

I can imagine her curled up in the corner of the closet she shares with my brother, tucked between Louboutin heels with her dark-red hair pulled into the messy bun she likes to sleep in.

"That's insane. What did you do? Do you think he liked you? Did you exchange numbers so you could see him again?"

Excited chatter is one of Fiona's many features, and I can already tell she's ramping up to some questions I don't know how to answer.

"I didn't exactly tell him my name," I say, cutting her off.

"*What*? Why the hell not?"

"I don't know," I admit, and I don't. Truthfully, it was the night my dreams used to be made of and giving him my name at the end of it would've at least given him the opportunity to find me one day down the road.

Maybe that's why I kept it a secret.

I don't *want* him to find me.

"It's complicated. We... did *stuff*, and I don't know. Have you ever been... intimate with someone, and felt gross about it afterward?"

She hums. "Did he force you to do something?"

"No!" I pinch my eyes closed, not even sure what I'm trying to say anymore. "I don't know. I guess it was just a long night, and I didn't think about giving him my name. Besides, I kind of like the idea of this being a one-night thing. Two strangers passing by, looking for a way to pass the time. That kind of deal."

"God, please don't ever tell Boyd that." She laughs again, and it almost warms the icy brick of unease sitting on the floor of my stomach.

When we hang up minutes later, I feel much lighter than I did when I left the tattoo parlor, and it's that feeling I grasp on to as I drift off, pushing everything else away and letting exhaustion consume me.

I'm certainly not prepared for what I wake up to.

12

I SLEEP through my gym session with Liam.

Normally the night after a show, I go to bed early and wake up energized, ready to tackle the day. The lag in my sleep schedule from my late night is already affecting my productivity, and it's been less than twelve hours since I left the tattoo parlor.

At least, that's what I'm choosing to blame the laziness on, and not a relapse of a depressive episode.

My gaze flickers to the red velvet sofa at the foot of the bed; the green dress that little angel left behind is draped over the arm, taunting me.

I'm not sure why I took it, and I definitely had no business bringing it back here with me.

Any man worth his salt doesn't provide evidence of the nights he's trying to forget.

The golden halo etched into the skin beneath my thumb begs to differ.

The bedroom door swings open while I'm still in the bed, and Callie walks in, her dark hair pinned back with an emerald clip. Wearing a beige pantsuit and carrying a clear binder in her arms, she looks more like my manager today than my mother, and for some reason, it irritates me more than usual.

"Do you like costing me money, Aiden?" She doesn't come over, just stands in the corner, glaring down at me.

I groan, pulling one of the massive pillows over my face. "How am I costing *you* anything? Last I checked, you work for me."

She clicks her tongue in disapproval. "*Ay*, every time you sneak off when you're supposed to be networking, or promoting an album, or in general not being a hoodlum and running away from your guards, I lose a quarter-million dollars in brand investments. Paid partnerships. Label deals. Everything your father and I have worked so hard to secure for you just gets flushed down with the train."

Blinking, I refrain from correcting her; when she's upset, her accent thickens, and English phrases get lost in translation. It was worse when I was young, and sometimes downright embarrassing depending on the context, but my own Spanish translations are tepid at best, so I don't say anything.

"'*Your father and I*?' Since when are you two a unit?"

Her jaw clenches, blanching her tan skin. "When it comes to you, *hijo*, we're a unit."

"You mean when it comes to *dinero*." Sitting up straighter, I work through the stiffness in my muscles, ignoring the groggy desire that shoots through me, telling me to lie back down. "Dad tell you I asked about the contract?"

Brown eyes sharpen as they narrow, and her mouth flattens. *"Por qué?"*

"I want out, Mother."

Lips turning down, she shakes her head. "That isn't possible. Who would you sign with, or are you forgetting your father had to beg for the producers at Symposium to even take you on?"

Embarrassment flares in my cheeks; how could I ever forget? A few very public meltdowns, and suddenly you're the poster child for mental instability.

Apparently, for most labels, that's not a great brand to associate with.

"I could always go solo. Produce and upload my own shit."

"What, and be like those little SoundSky rappers? You know that's not sustainable."

SoundCloud, I want to say, but I just drag my hands down my face and stay silent.

Her face softens slightly as she stares off into space, as if the cogs inside her head are turning slowly. After a few moments, she shakes her head and cracks open her binder.

"*Ay*, never mind that. We don't have time for it. You have a postshow briefing to catch up on this morning, plus you need to make an appearance at a boutique opening down the street."

I groan, twisting the bloodstone ring on my thumb. "That sounds like a press event."

"We'll make it quick. We have to be on the road to Pittsburgh no later than ten, anyway."

With a grunt, I fall back onto the mattress and sigh. Seconds later, the dull clicking of her heels drifts farther away, and then the bedroom door closes, leaving me alone in the massive space.

I should be used to it by now. If I'm not working, there's no reason for anyone else to hang around.

Even though my body absolutely doesn't want to, I drag myself out of the bed and over to the closet, sliding the door open slowly. I don't turn on the light, refusing to acknowledge the mess inside in the hopes that maybe one day it'll go away.

Logically, I know that's not how these things work, but I'm not in the mood to deal.

Stepping over a pile of clothes, I grab on to one of the wooden shelves and feel around for the clean clothes I stacked inside yesterday. Then I slip quickly from the little room, stuffing myself into black jeans and a dark-orange hoodie.

After washing my face and finger-combing through my hair with wet fingers, I step out of the bathroom and stare at the foot of the bed. My eyes are glued to the green dress, irritation swimming in my veins that she wouldn't even give me her fucking name last night.

I can still *taste* her on my tongue, can still feel the way her cunt tried to swallow my fingers whole, and yet I'm left with nothing.

Nothing but the reminder of why I don't engage with the opposite sex.

Snatching the dress up, I lift it to my nose, inhaling that

goddamn peppermint scent until it feels like my lungs might explode.

I should burn it. Throw it away, at the very least. But when I try to toss it in the bin for housekeeping, something stops me, like an invisible hand reaching out and keeping me still.

It's stupid, I know, but I can't shake the feeling that maybe she'll come looking for it.

Commotion downstairs draws my attention, and I toss the dress into the closet along with the black heels the girl had on and shut the door.

Definitely don't want to get caught with those.

Walking over to the opposite side of the room, I fish out a new carton of cigarettes from the bottom drawer of my cherrywood dresser and leave with one between my lips.

Determined to put the thought of her as far from my mind as possible.

"Cancel it. Cancel fucking *all* of it."

My father's voice grates across my skin, shredding the little pieces of contentment swimming through my veins, forged by nicotine. His face is beet red when he steps out onto the balcony where Callie, Liam, my bodyguard Jason and I are sitting, going over the logistics of last night's show.

Callie lets out a sigh, placing her pen in the spine of her binder. "*El Diablo.* What the hell are you doing here?"

He doesn't even spare her a glance, zeroing in on me with blazing eyes. "Do you know what you've done?"

"Uh..." My eyebrows draw in, and I rack my brain for

something, coming up short. "Gonna have to give some context, if you want me confessing to shit."

"Are you shitting me? Not one of you has checked the news, or any social media outlets this morning?" His eyes bounce from each of us, and his face darkens with each passing second.

They pause on Liam, who's been plopping red grapes into his mouth; when he notices that he's got my father's full attention, though, he pauses, setting the vine back on the patio table in front of him.

"Well, great, let me be the first to welcome you all to our living hell."

Unbuttoning his black Armani suit jacket, he yanks out his phone, turning it around. A grainy photograph fills the screen, and I lean in, squinting hard to make out the picture.

When I do, my chest floods with anxiety, like a ship taking on too much water. There's nothing to plug the leak with, no way to keep from capsizing.

All I can do is hang on.

"Look familiar?" my father demands, shaking the phone in my face.

I rear back, shoving him away. As if I haven't burned the image of the girl from last night looking out over the East River permanently into my brain.

Except, it's not *just* her in the photo; I'm there, too, sitting on a bench at the park, watching her like she's the most fascinating thing I've ever seen. Her beauty surpasses all of Manhattan and Queens beyond, lighting up the nighttime in a way the buildings and stars envy.

That must be why her rejection stung so deeply.

It's not often you get to witness a true masterpiece, and I'm not used to being denied beautiful things.

"Is this why you left the gala last night?" Callie frowns, folding her hands in her lap. "For some girl?"

Her tone scrapes against the invisible sores on my chest. "It was just a bit of harmless fun. She happened to be on the ticket last night, so I bid on her, and we left."

"Harmless fun," my father repeats, voice completely devoid of emotion.

"Sir, I signed off on the paperwork with the charity myself," Liam cuts in, smoothing a hand over his blond hair. "In fact, I've got the receipts and everything, if you need to see them for tax purposes..."

Trailing off, Liam sits back in his seat, throat working over a swallow. My father just stares, not blinking for the longest time, before he looks at his phone and swipes out of the photo.

"I don't give a single flying *fuck* about taxes right now."

Callie sighs, clearly growing impatient. She waves for Jason to give us some space, and I watch as the burly bald man heads back inside, leaving just the four of us.

"Sonny, why are you being so dramatic—"

"*Dramatic*? Are you fucking *seeing* this, Calliope?" His use of her full name makes my stomach cramp, and we all lean forward at the same time to inspect the screen.

Now, the boat isn't simply flooding; it's been completely submerged by a tsunami-like wave, and there's no chance of recovery. It sinks to the bottom of the ocean, settling on the floor where it'll rot away like the Titanic, full of broken dreams and lost futures.

#AidenJamesIsOverParty

"Whatever girl you slinked off with last night is claiming you sexually assaulted her," my father says, snatching the phone back. "It's trending all over the fucking Internet right now. I've been dodging phone calls from a dozen different studio execs for the better part of the half hour, who are already wanting to drop your affiliation and void contracts."

The silence that follows his words falls over me like a vacuum, playing the first sentence over and over on a distant loop. I'm suspended in time, floating out in space where the words *"claiming you sexually assaulted her"* don't have the same gravity.

And then, I laugh.

It's an incredulous sound, desperate as it rips out of me, but a laugh nonetheless. Callie's hand comes up to her mouth, eyes watering as she swings her gaze from me, and Liam drags a hand down over his face.

My father is the only one who doesn't move. I'm not sure if he's even breathing.

Frankly, I'm not sure *I* am either.

"Please, tell me what's funny about this." My father crosses his arms, cocking an eyebrow while jutting a hip out.

It's a power move I've seen him use to put the fear of God into clients but now all it does is make me angrier.

"*Obviously*, I didn't do it." When I swallow, it's like a handful of hot coals sliding down my throat. "She's lying."

Why, I have no fucking idea, but the notion incinerates any good feelings I had about our time together, or our connection, replacing them with fiery resentment.

Maybe she wasn't as honest as you thought.

Nausea curdles in my gut like spoiled milk, and I hunch over, resisting the urge to vomit.

"Well, the truth hardly matters in cases like this, as we all know. Our next steps are going to be about damage control and finding out a way to spin the claims as the bumbling narratives of a deranged fan until the investigation finishes.

Luckily, this is the only photographic evidence anyone has come forth with yet, placing you two together."

Shaking my head, I try to clear the fog clouding around my brain. "Why don't we just find her and make her confess? You've done it before."

Jaw set, my father exhales, reaching up to pinch the bridge of his nose. "Because, son, she forged her charity papers. The name she used, the address—all of it's fake, and no one can seem to track her down."

"What are you saying?" Callie asks, fingers trembling.

She doesn't look at me, and the lack of acknowledgment stings. Like she's already writing me off in her mind, convinced I'm capable of something so disgusting.

"I'm saying, this girl may as well be a ghost."

13

EVERYONE'S STARING when our plane touches down in King's Trace, and even though I've grown accustomed to a certain level of scrutiny within this seedy small town, there's something extra about the way it unfolds today.

Heads turn, deliberate in their attempts to get a glimpse of me. Eyes narrow, tracking me as I grab my suitcase from baggage claim, and the whispers follow down the corridor to where my brother stands, looking more grumpy than usual.

Arms crossed over his chest, Boyd looks as though he's been sent to collect a debt with his crisp navy suit and the hard set of his jaw. There's a ferocity in his gaze that I haven't seen since before I moved in with him, and that, coupled with the spectators around us, has my hair standing up on end.

The cartoonish redhead beside my brother, however, alleviates some of that stress. A bright smile stretches across Fiona's face, and she bounces on her heels as I near them, clasping her hands together.

Immediately, she pulls me in for a hug, wrapping her arms around my neck. She smells like bubblegum and flowers, and I soak in it for a moment, letting her warmth partially erase the memory of the last twenty-four hours.

Mellie and Aurora were packed and checked out by the time I woke up this morning, and I couldn't find them in the crowd among our other classmates or chaperones. I'd ended up catching the shuttle back with one of the school administrators, having to listen to her drone on about how amazing the free night had been for her and a few other staff members.

I'm not sure what it says about me that I'm envious of middle-aged poker at a luxury burlesque show, especially considering who I'd spent most of *my* night with.

But I've been trying not to think about that.

"You're back!" Pulling away, Fiona grips my biceps and gives me a little shake.

"Uh, yeah." I laugh. "Surprisingly, I managed not to get beheaded in a dirty subway." My eyes find Boyd's. "Looks like someone owes me an apology."

Fiona makes a face, scanning me from head to toe. "I'm just glad to see you're mostly okay."

"Mostly?" My eyebrows draw in. "What does that—"

"We need to leave." Boyd's voice interrupts, completely devoid of emotion.

I glance at him, rolling my eyes. "You make it sound like there are people after us."

He doesn't respond. Just stares, not blinking for a full sixty seconds. Shifting, I steal a look at Fiona, who's twisting a piece of pink bubblegum around one of her manicured fingers.

"What's going on?"

"Haven't you seen—"

"Fiona." Boyd's using his dad voice, and I'm not even sure if he's aware of it. "Not here."

She worries her bottom lip, big brown eyes shining up at him. It looks like she wants to protest, push him on his insistence, but she seems to decide against it.

Looping her arm through mine, she tugs me along ahead of him, leaving my suitcase for Boyd to roll.

As we walk, I avoid looking at any other patrons, focusing instead on the tile directly in front of my path. "Did Boyd get broodier since yesterday, somehow?"

"He just worries about you," she says, shrugging one shoulder. The black sweater she has on drapes off, revealing more of her pale, freckled skin, and she resituates the cashmere as we walk outside.

Boyd's red Audi sits at the curb, and he pops the trunk, rounding it with my luggage. He traded in his motorcycle for the sedan, citing safety concerns, but I secretly think it's because he's trying to ease into settling down.

They say a man's toys are the first to go.

People mill about the sidewalk, some slowing as they enter the airport, openly gawking at us. For a moment, I don't think anything of it—it's hard not to feel temporarily stunned by Fiona's effortless beauty, and people often try to get a look at her before Boyd notices.

But these stares feel different, more pointed somehow, and with a sickening feeling sluicing through my blood, I realize they're still looking at *me*.

Muscles tight, I bow my head slightly, leaning in to speak to Fiona in a low voice.

"Okay, seriously, what's going on? Why is everyone looking at me?"

"Are they?"

Her eyes dart in a circle, pausing briefly on the two teenage boys sitting on a bench closer to the parking lot. She flips them off, tossing her hair back, and they quickly avert their gazes.

"Don't even pay attention to them. People just don't know how to mind their business in this town."

"Yeah, but... what business are they minding of mine?"

"What do you mean? Obviously, people are—"

"Fiona Ivers, I swear to God." Boyd slams the trunk shut, voice sharp.

She huffs, crossing her arms. "What? I'm not doing anything."

"Not here. Get your pretty little ass in the car so we can go home." His eyes cut to mine, though it feels like they look right through me. "You too. Now."

I stand there for a few extra beats, trying to understand what exactly is going on. Clearly, something has the two of them on edge, and immediately I'm flooded with apprehension, as irrational thoughts and fears resurface in my mind.

With a shaky hand, I pull open the back car door and climb inside, hunkering down low while Boyd shifts gears and takes off.

We speed through King's Trace at a speed that feels illegal, though no one would ever dare give my brother a ticket.

Even if he didn't have more money than most of the residents here, the police are bankrolled by the Italian Mafia, the boss of which is a client at Ivers International, Boyd's security firm.

Well, technically, the firm belongs to Fiona's family, but still. Boyd's pretty much the lifeblood of that place.

All of which I know only because I interned for him over the summer, familiarizing myself with the ins and outs of cybersecurity—and the personnel files, when he wasn't looking.

Pine trees whiz by the windows as we weave through traffic, passing downtown as quickly as we enter it. King's Trace really isn't much—a dirty little conglomerate of poverty, with a couple of groceries and a host of different small businesses, all centered around the unnavigable Lake Koselomal.

It'd be quaint, if it wasn't plagued by secrets, crime, and death.

When we pull up to the white bungalow we call home, my nerves stretch thin. Somehow, in the time I've been gone, I've been able to put off the bad memories associated with this place.

But my mother's ghost hangs around like a woman scorned, looking for souls to blacken with her talons. She's behind me as I slip from the back seat, fitting an invisible noose around my neck, cinching until I can scarcely breathe.

And then I'm reminded about last night. What it felt like to indulge in a man's attention, let him want me for a few minutes while I pretended not to hate myself.

But I do. Always have, and if my mother's presence is any indication, I probably always will.

Boyd opens the front door, and we head inside to the

place where time seems to stand still; the walls are the same bland shade of beige, the brown afghan draped over the arm of the sofa *just so*—arranged by Fiona, whose obsessive-compulsive disorder keeps things particular.

Not clean, as the dirty dishes in the sink suggest, but in order.

I head for the stairs, gripping the rail in one hand, when Boyd stops me.

"Riley. We need to talk."

My chest hollows out, air suddenly impossible to retrieve. Spinning around slowly, I see him and Fiona sitting at the oak dining room table. His hands sit in front of him, fingers interlocked, while she has a hand on his wrist, rubbing her thumb in small circles.

The gesture is inherently soothing, and it sends a spike of sourness through me. Biting down on the inside of my cheek, I abandon my suitcase and meander over to them, gripping the back of a chair.

"What's up?"

"You tell me," Boyd grinds out. "Want to explain what the hell you did last night?"

My eyes widen, flickering to Fiona. Resentment burns in my throat as she shifts, her eyes moving down to study the table.

Swallowing, my tongue darts out, tapping the edge of the scar on my mouth. Grounding myself in the present, rather than allowing the sudden pulsing coming from the ink on my thigh to distract me.

"That's it, pretty girl."

Delight hums through my veins at the memory, Aiden James's praise forever seared on parts of my soul I hadn't known existed.

But that doesn't change the fact that it never should've happened in the first place.

Blowing out a breath, I squeeze the chair and lean into it. "Look, if this is about the tattoo, I—"

"The tattoo?" Boyd scowls, his mouth forming a harsh frown. "No, Riley, for fuck's sake. This is about the fact that I woke up this morning to my sister's face plastered all over the goddamn Internet, attached to claims of sexual assault by some celebrity I didn't even know she knew. Fuck a tattoo."

He pauses, tilting his head. "Actually, no, we'll come back to that."

"*What*?" My jaw drops, disbelief and confusion knotting inside my stomach. Reaching for my phone in the back pocket of my jeans, I quickly unlock it, opening up the first social media app my fingers find.

It's the number one trending story.

Throat tight, I pull up the most popular article beneath the #AidenJamesIsOverParty hashtag, scanning the page.

A picture of my profile, as I stand at the East River while Aiden looks on, greets me at the top, and my insides wring together until I feel like I might explode.

"Early this morning, news outlets first reported the allegations of sexual assault and misconduct initiated by musician Aiden James, who is currently on tour promoting his most recent album, Rhapsodic Dreams, *which hit number one on the best sellers chart in the US at its debut."*

Vomit teases the back of my throat, and my hands shake violently as I read the next paragraph.

"Though no charges have been made, authorities are looking into these allegations, which stemmed from an anonymous source stating that Mr. James disappeared from a charity banquet last

night in order to engage in nefarious activities with a fan. Reportedly, the fan was not receptive to Mr. James's advances, though we've not heard directly from the victim, who has yet to be named. More on this story as it develops."

My heart pounds between my ears, and the phone falls from my hands to the floor. The clatter of glass hitting wood and shattering on impact almost drowns out the chaos forming in my head.

Like angry waves of deceit, reality crashes over me, and I sit stunned for several minutes, unsure of how to even proceed. My mind feels like a broken record, skipping on the portion of the article stating that I had a hand in this.

I didn't tell anyone other than Fiona that I'd even been with him last night, and as far as we knew, no one but the girl at the dry cleaners spotted him while we were out.

Though, I can't imagine she'd do something like this.

With tears stinging my eyes, I look up at Boyd. "I didn't do it."

He frowns. "What?"

Gesturing toward my cracked phone, I raise my brows, exasperation racing through me. "I didn't... I didn't contact anyone. The press, social media. I didn't tell anyone *this*. That he hurt me."

But it's exactly what you get, little girl.

My mother's voice rings louder than my anxiety, fueling the fire burning inside of me.

"So, it's not true?"

"That he assau—" The word sticks in my throat like old syrup, and I choke over it. "*No*, god. Don't you think I would've called you if he had?"

Relief seems to surge through him, and his shoulders slump as he releases a breath.

Fiona squeezes his arm. "I told you."

"Needed to hear it directly from the source." He scrubs a hand over his jaw, looking off into space as he thinks. "Well, regardless, this is very, very bad. They don't have a name yet, but the reception you got at the airport is proof that people recognize you. I doubt we have very long before your identity is revealed."

"I don't understand why anyone would lie about this." I feel faint, my heart stuttering. "What are we going to do? Release a statement?"

His fingers tap at the table, and he looks at Fiona. "Princess, do you mind giving me a moment?"

Nodding, Fiona pushes to her feet and heads up the stairs, giving me an apologetic smile. I don't respond, my grip tightening on the chair until my nails start to splinter.

"Two years ago, when you were attacked... do you remember anything about that night?"

Blood. Agony ripping up my spine, sinking its claws in my soul and refusing to let go.

A male's voice, assuring me. Wet lips on my ear, cheap cologne in my nostrils.

I shrug. "Bits and pieces."

"The men our mother associated with were heavily involved in certain... illegal trades. Worse than the normal drug running that everyone knows goes on around here."

True. The Mafia has a monopoly on drugs in King's Trace—the kids at school get their designer fixes through them, even.

"And while the man who attacked you is dead..." Boyd trails off, his face hardening, fist curling on the table. "I live in constant fear of his associates realizing you're alive, and the reason he's not. The things they would do if they found you..."

Again, his sentence goes unfinished, hanging in the air like a deadweight between us.

I can't even bring myself to imagine it.

"If we draw attention to this scandal... to you... it could be very bad, Riley."

My stomach sinks, a rock breaching the surface of a pond, and I don't want to ask what this means for me. What he's saying, even though I'm pretty sure I already know.

"You're not gonna let me make a statement, are you?" I ask, eyes brimming with tears.

His are red-rimmed, and his nostrils flare like he's as at war with the reality as I am. When he shakes his head, confirming the lack of response, a sharp, stabbing pain flares in my chest.

A knife that penetrates with little effort, twisting as it comes out the other side. Rending as much misery as possible.

"We're going to ruin his life," I whisper, a tear slipping over. Reaching up, I swipe at the liquid, the scar on my cheek rough beneath the pad of my thumb.

"I'm sorry, Riley. Really. I won't stop trying to find another way, but for now... this has to be it. I have to keep you safe."

His voice is strained. Desperate. I can see in his eyes that he feels solely responsible for my well-being, and after a lifetime of him letting me down, I'm not sure if I can stomach disappointing him right now.

I'm being ripped in half, my soul split in two, and I have no idea how to reconcile either decision.

Maybe this will blow over if they don't have anything to connect the allegations with.

Resigned to my fate, I sit with Boyd and recount the entirety of the last twenty-four hours, creating a timeline and allowing my brother to offer me the only thing he's ever been consistent with: security.

Because as much as I want to prove a strange man innocent... I can't take that chance. Not when there are other people who might want to finish what my mother and her boyfriend started.

The fear inside won't *let* me, even if I could get Boyd on board.

When I go to bed that night, even after he's scrubbed the Internet of my picture and done his best to keep my name out of things, I go to bed knowing I'm the most hated girl in America.

If not by the whole country, then at least by one volatile gray-eyed man.

14

I USED to think that outside hatred couldn't touch you when your self-deprecation screamed louder.

Thought I was protected because I'd spent an entire lifetime despising myself.

Thought the opinions of others didn't matter, because no one would ever be harder on me than *me*.

Then, I became an overnight Internet sensation—in the worst possible way—and learned that when you don't have a buffer for yourself, negativity from other people acts like kerosene, fanning the flames you've spent all your time cultivating.

Eventually, you get to a point where all you want is to be doused in the fire.

Relieved of your sentence on earth.

In the days after the catastrophe that followed my class trip to New York City, I did my best to stay off-line. I swear I did, but the temptation to look and see if there were people on my hypothetical side always seemed to win out.

Every night before bed, I'd prop myself up against the headboard and scroll through social media on my laptop, scouring news articles who updated frequently, even though there was never anything new to report. Aiden went on an indefinite hiatus, suspending the rest of his tour and refunding concert tickets, until the investigation brought some sort of closure.

Because of who my brother is, not to mention his connections, there would never be any.

Sure, people speculate about the identity of the girl—even go so far as to pinpoint her as a tourist from Maine—but nobody is saying my name. And as far as us Kellys are concerned, that's as good as a situation like this can get.

Still, guilt eats away at me, gnawing the frayed edges of my soul like parasites.

Maybe that's why I check to see what people are saying; it's as much of an honest form of punishment as my brother will allow, although if he *knew* I was searching the case online, he'd definitely revoke my Internet.

It's been days, and still no word from the girl he supposedly raped? Yeah, okay. Red flag.

Just another groupie who got what she wanted and decided to exploit a celebrity. Shame, too—I love Aiden's music. To Night And Fire are some of my all-time favorite songs!

I met Aiden James at Lollapalooza a couple years back. Nice guy. Don't believe he'd do this.

Hope that lying bitch gets what she deserves.

A flurry of concern and empathy for the accused, and yet the support for the supposed victim doesn't even compare.

Scrolling to the bottom of the page, I let their animosity soak to the bone, becoming one with my marrow until I can look at the next comment, no problem.

The shock of their magnitude of disgust never ceases to cut straight through me, no matter how many forums and articles I peruse. To these people, I'm not a girl caught in an impossible place, only trying to do what her brother says will keep her safe.

I'm not a starstruck teenager who had their dream night with their dream man completely ruined by a single rumor.

I'm subhuman.

Garbage.

Once again, proving my mother right.

When I shut down the laptop at night and shove my head beneath the pillows, it's her whispering the comments in my ear.

Never letting me forget.

NOT LONG AFTER THE INCIDENT—AS those of us on my side are calling it—I ask Boyd to let me finish high school from home.

Most of my classmates at King's Trace Prep seem entirely too suspicious of my identity, and while no one will come out and say it, I've been ostracized even more than I was before.

Nothing like adding social pariah to a résumé, right before you're supposed to go off to college.

Boyd doesn't approve of the idea at first, mainly because he works and thinks I need a babysitter, but eventually Fiona gets him to relent, and soon I'm spending my weeks learning AP chemistry and forensics online and fine-tuning my web design skills.

Some days, it's easier than others to push the thoughts of Aiden from my mind.

But the guilt never ceases.

Unfortunately, my brother has set up some kind of protective firewall, so even if I wanted to contact anyone in Aiden's life who could reach him, I can't. At least, not electronically, and I have no clue where I'd even send a letter.

But that doesn't keep people from contacting me.

It's not long before an envelope shows up on my doorstep, the contents inside making me vomit into the kitchen sink.

More photographs of me and Aiden traipsing around New York—even though he's got that disguise on, and I'm in those oversized sweats, I can tell it's us. At the dry cleaners, again in the park, and finally in the tattoo shop.

They're intimate pictures; ones that had to have been taken from a close vantage point.

Still, they aren't the most unsettling thing in the envelope.

Evidence of my entire existence—my birth certificate, vaccination records, and itemized lists of every class and extracurricular I've taken, every website I've ever visited, my exact locations in New York City. They all fall out with the pictures and a note that only says "We know who you are."

Tension notches against my sternum, permanently etching itself into my skeleton. I stuff the contents in the bottom of my dresser drawer, heart beating so hard that I'm afraid it might bust through my rib cage and splatter all over the floor.

Would serve me right.

I sit on the envelope for a few days in silence, trying to figure out what to do. If I tell Boyd, he'll undoubtedly start a war with the James family, and feuds like that have a history of ending poorly.

On the other hand, I find it difficult to believe the James family would send such a cryptic piece of mail without having contacted me another way, or even trying to get me to confess.

Which means... maybe the envelope isn't from Aiden's people at all.

Maybe my mother's ghost is haunting me in a new way, and the people from her past life are starting to catch up with me.

Not wanting to alarm Boyd, I set out with a plan—unsure of what I want the outcome to be, but positive in my convictions not to involve my brother.

The less he knows, the less he can be convicted of later.

I just want to put an end to all of this, and as I spend the next weeks living in fear, constantly looking over my shoulder, I realize there's only one thing to do.

Blackmail is something of a trade in the town we live in; at one point, just about everyone in King's Trace has fallen victim to extortion of some degree, and it feels like the most natural thing in the world when I finally dip my toes into that realm.

There's exactly one man I trust—outside of my brother. I haven't seen him since he saved my life after the attack, but I know without a doubt he'll be able to help me.

However, he's not a man you can approach and just ask a favor.

You have to force his hand.

15

My KNEE BOUNCES, intermittently colliding with the underside of Boyd's oak desk.

The air in his office is suffocating, though part of me thinks that has more to do with *why* I'm here than anything else.

It could also be the fact that, for the first time, I'm in public without a shred of makeup on, the scars on my face painfully visible. It's supposed to add a layer of vulnerability, but all it really makes me want to do is hide inside myself.

On the computer monitor, I watch Boyd and Fiona exit

Ivers International; they get into his car and head to lunch downtown, leaving me alone in the building.

It's a Saturday, so the only one working is my brother, giving me the perfect opportunity to continue my plan unimpeded.

Weeks have passed, silence from the sender of the envelope making me nervous. I'm still not sure what's going on, exactly—only that I need to act before the other shoe drops.

Wiping my palms on my jeans, I let the denim material absorb my perspiration.

Minutes later, a tall, slender figure approaches the front doors; I hit the code on Boyd's computer, disabling the alarm system and unlocking the building, and the man enters quickly.

Dressed in a trench coat with the collar pulled up around his neck, and a black hat too warm for spring, he crosses the downstairs lobby to the elevators, slipping inside like a shadow.

My stomach tightens, nerves bundling together like that might keep them safe.

Tremors rack through me as I wait, somehow feeling like prey, even though the man in question has no idea what he's about to walk in on.

At least, that's the hope. Somehow, I've managed to evade his identification over the last few weeks, my anonymity paramount to dragging him from whatever depths of hell a man like him lives in.

Alarm bells ring in my ears as the door handle turns, and for a second, I consider diving beneath the desk and hiding. Throwing away all my hard work because of my anxiety.

I shouldn't be fucking with a man nicknamed Doctor Death. Definitely shouldn't be interfering with his recent marriage, especially since rumor has it that he's willing to kill for his wife.

If rumors are true, he already has.

And that's not even scratching the surface of the supposed blood on his hands.

Regardless, I force myself to stay relaxed, kicking my feet up on the desk just as the door swings open. If he doesn't smite me on the spot, I'm hopeful he'll be receptive to what I have in mind.

"I don't appreciate having to wait—"

Dark eyes pierce mine from across the room, and his entire stature freezes as soon as he's crossed the threshold.

"Riley?"

Dr. Kal Anderson looks like Hades himself, if Hades were well over six feet tall and unbelievably attractive. His is a beauty so sharp and focused, it almost hurts to look at him without the benefit of a lens barrier.

He has on an all-black suit beneath his coat, and he reaches up, tugging off his hat to smooth a hand over his inky locks. So much sleek, effortless elegance in such a dangerous man, and he knows it too. Uses it to rule the underworld from the sidelines, content to collect souls while enjoying marital bliss.

As he slowly pushes the door shut, his gaze once again finds mine—irises so dark, it feels like staring straight into an abyss.

I almost swallow my tongue as he continues standing, confusion flashing across his face for the briefest moment.

Latching on to the flicker of an advantage, I feign nonchalance, grinning as he walks closer.

"You sure know how to make a girl wait." My hand moves

toward the armchair in front of the desk, cringing internally at my bumbled attempt at being casual.

Kal glances around, as if expecting someone else to step out of the shadows, and sinks into the chair.

"What are you doing here?" he asks, his deep voice stiff and unamused. "Where's your brother?"

"Boyd's having an extended lunch with his girlfriend. I was the one who asked you to meet."

His eyebrows arch. "*What?*"

"You wanted to know who your blackmailer was," I say, struggling to keep my hand steady as I sit straighter, pushing a flash drive across the surface of the desk.

He blinks down at the piece of plastic, then looks up at me. "*You?*"

It wasn't an easy feat, that's for sure; blackmail rarely is. Blackmailing a hit man who doubles as a Mafia doctor? Almost impossible.

For the last few weeks, I've thrown myself into scouring every piece of security footage that backs up to the Ivers International encrypted servers, searching for something to trap him with.

What better way to grab a man by the balls than to exploit the act of him emptying them?

I never watched the clips, of course. At least, not in full. Just enough that I knew what they led to—sex, go figure—so I could crop, download, and send them to his house.

A house on some tiny island off the coast of Massachusetts that I'd never even heard of until this all started.

I force a smile.

"Kind of crazy how much I've picked up in such a short time, but I guess that's the perk of being around hackers and IT people all the time now. Amazing what you can find out about a person, just by doing a little digging. Even one as private as you, Doctor."

My voice sounds a hell of a lot more confident than I feel, my resolve shaking beneath the weight of his stare.

He narrows his eyes and something in my chest cramps. "Is that so?"

Nodding, I reach into my purse and pull out another flash drive—this one, the inspiration behind my idea.

See, in order to secure his marriage months ago, Kal blackmailed a Mafia don into a deal of sorts. I'm not sure of the exact details, only that he feigned trouble for his employer in Boston and painted himself as some sort of savior in order to secure his wife's hand in marriage.

All of this learned within minutes of hacking the don's home security network, which is much less advanced than Kal's.

So, I'd taken a page out of his book and did the same thing, forging danger and leading him on a wild-goose chase to track down his blackmailer.

Excessive? Maybe, but there was no way Kal would help me out of the kindness of his heart.

Kindness doesn't exist in cold, darkened spaces.

I can see him mulling over this revelation; he squints, like he's trying to process, and delight swims through my veins at the thought that I've pulled it off.

That I duped a man known for his cunning, methodical nature, even if the only reason is that he was too distracted by his new wife to pay me much attention.

I'll take any wins I can get.

Finally, Kal looks up, pocketing the flash drive, and he leans back in his chair, crossing an ankle over the opposite knee. Propping his elbow on that knee, he strokes his stubbly jaw, watching me with an unreadable expression.

"Why?"

It's all he says, a single syllable uttered so simply, that it takes me by surprise.

I wasn't really expecting to have to explain myself, although I suppose it makes sense. Leave it to the doctor to want to learn the symptoms of the disease that's been plaguing him.

Swallowing, I push my shoulders back, slip my feet from the desk, and sit up. "I could ask my brother, but you specialize in secrecy, right? Well, I did something... bad, and I need to disappear."

"Disappear," he repeats, that same monotone voice sending chills down my spine. "You've tormented me, violated my privacy, and yet you're asking for my assistance? Either you're very brave, or very stupid."

"I like to think I'm a fun mixture of both."

Flipping the lapel of his suit jacket back, Kal removes a pistol and slides it against his knee. His eyes don't leave mine, and his fingers don't leave the trigger, training the mouth of the gun right on me.

Fear percolates in my stomach, almost propelling me from my chair, but I dig my fingernails into my palms, forcing myself not to react.

It's what he wants—a reaction. Proof of my inferiority, as though I haven't managed to trick him.

Kal isn't the kind of man who gets tricked often, so it's not surprising that he isn't taking it well.

Still, I don't bite the bait.

"Boyd will fire you as a client if you get blood on his carpet," I say, glancing at the ticking clock hanging on the gray wall, wondering how long I have before my brother returns.

Kal smirks. "I've already seen your blood, Ms. Kelly. I have no intention of drawing it today."

A shiver coasts over my skin, a memory flashing across my vision; the feeling of being carried, my body freezing as it's jostled in someone's sturdy arms. The smell of clean whiskey, nothing stale or repulsive like my mother's boyfriend's.

Dark eyes, soothing me as I drift in and out of consciousness. Hands showing mercy, healing when I know what they're capable of.

There's a certain level of trust you put in the person who saved your life. Maybe *that's* why I called Kal.

I trust my brother, but Dr. Anderson yields results.

He pulls a handkerchief from the breast pocket of his coat and wipes the barrel of the gun, tilting his head as he inspects it. I can't help wondering if maybe he's just come from a "job," and he's cleaning the remnants off.

"The help I can offer..." His lips twist, and he pauses, eyes lost in thought. Those pupils dilate, then return to their normal size as he looks at me. "It's a permanent kind, you know. The secrecy, the privacy. What you're asking is possible, but it requires a certain amount of dedication."

My heart pinches, but I nod anyway. "I know. That's... that's why I came to you."

"I'm sure your brother is fully capable of giving you the same thing."

"I don't want him involved," I say, my throat tightening around the words. "Not in this."

Partly because it feels safer, but also because I don't want to see the look in his eyes when I admit what my plan is.

Don't want him to try and talk me out of things, or convince me not to go through with it.

And if I stay, beyond the simple fact of my safety being at risk, I'll never stop lamenting my night in New York. The girl I left behind there, on a park bench with the world's hottest rock star.

After weeks of mourning her, I'm done.

I want to move on.

He's quiet for a long time, seeming to consider my acquiescence. "Why not just ask? Why go through all the trouble of harassing me?"

"Insurance." One word all men in the Mafia understand.

Something my mother understood, too.

You never, ever, do something unless you have a way to back it up.

Clasping his hands together, Kal nods once, then pushes to his feet.

"Okay, then. Let's kill Riley Kelly."

16

PINCHING my pick between my fingers, I drag the triangular tip over the strings on my bass, letting the sound reverberate against my bones.

Once upon a time, that somber tune would've been enough to get me out of a funk, but now, all it does is amplify the hollow feeling resonating in my chest.

I pluck absently, leaning my head back against my mattress. I'm sitting on the floor of my bedroom, shrouded by darkness. Only a sliver of light shines through a crack in the closet door, which I leave partially open now that no one bothers coming around anymore.

Callie comes, but I know it's only to make sure I haven't jumped off the balcony. She never says anything, just peeks in, lets her disgust fill the room, and then leaves.

I'd be lying if I said I hadn't considered jumping.

My fingers lift to the scars on my wrist, the only evidence of former attempts hidden beneath a myriad of colors.

Liam visits every couple of days, as well, staying the longest. He lounges on the sofa at the foot of the bed, playing video games on the television mounted on the far wall and keeping me up to date on the happenings within our inner circle.

My father hasn't been back, having gone home to my ex in LA. He says he's doing damage control, working out a plan, but frankly, I'm just glad he's staying away.

I can feel his irritation from across the country.

Even though he knows I haven't done anything, I've still brought shame to the James name, and that's practically grounds for excommunication in his eyes.

In any case, I'm trying to find a shred of peace in the solitude.

Trying to ignore the fact that I can slowly feel my sanity slipping away, breaking off into my bloodstream and disintegrating into dust.

I want to blame it all on the fact that my life was flipped completely on its axis months ago, and that I haven't been able to create a single fucking thing since, but my heart knows the truth.

My tormentor, my sweet little lying angel, keeps me awake at night. The memory of her soft voice and silken flesh, the taste of her innocence and that goddamn peppermint lotion.

Fuck, the lotion.

Digging into the pocket of my plaid pajama pants, I pull out a handful of individually wrapped peppermint candies, tearing one open with my teeth and dropping it in my palm.

Goddamn, I shouldn't crave the reminder of the beautiful viper, but even through all of the despair, her disappearance bothers me far more than it should.

It feels like she got off scot-free, and I'm here to suffer in the aftermath, even though I didn't do anything wrong.

My only sin was taking a fucking chance for once in my life.

Callie's had several lawsuits opened up against various news outlets, but they find clever ways around the situation, evading exact details and refusing to name specifics.

As if "Rock star plummets to Loserville after allegations ruin his career" could be about anyone but me.

Bringing the candy to my nose, I inhale deeply, and for a moment in time I'm back at Gio's tattoo shop in New York City, kneeling between her spread thighs and marring her creamy skin.

It should probably be more alarming that I can't seem to cancel the weekly delivery of peppermints from a candy store in Brooklyn, but I'm choosing not to think too much about it.

If I do, then I have to take note of the emerald dress, the shoes, and every other item of clothing sitting in my closet, staring me down each time I sit and try to write something.

With a sigh, I glance at the instrument in my lap, sending a silent plea to the Muses to strike me with inspiration.

I can feel myself slowly going mad, the inability to create pushing me further into a downward spiral of self-loathing and apathy.

Both the pick and instrument are hand-me-downs; the

pick, a shiny piece of purple plastic with a two-headed serpent on the face, and the guitar, a vintage Fender Precision bass that my father got from his father, who swore it was once played by Pino Palladino.

I've always considered them good luck charms. My first album, *Follow You To Hell*, was produced from a single bass line off this very instrument, and after it went platinum, I resigned to start every new project the same way.

There's a room down the hall where the walls are lined with different guitars, and a baby grand sits in the foyer off from the private elevator, but they don't spark my inspiration.

Right now, nothing seems to, and I'm starting to wonder if I should just give up entirely.

Sighing, I push the bass off my lap and get to my feet, that hollow feeling expanding inside me, its inky tendrils wrapping around my sternum. They tighten until it feels like the bone might crack under the pressure, and I make my way to the bed, crawling beneath the covers.

The heaviness that's lived in my body for years now threatens to crush me, and for a moment, I wish it would.

Wish I could erase that night after the charity gala from my mind for good.

But when sleep overtakes me, it's thoughts of her I drift off to.

LIAM MANAGES to drag me out of my bed for the first time in weeks.

He shields me under a Reds baseball cap, oversized

sunglasses, and a shapeless puffer jacket that feels a little too obvious for the beginning of summer.

I haven't seen a ray of sunshine in days, though, so I let him take me out. We hop into a blacked-out GMC Suburban and head to some dive bar on Staten Island.

Part of me expects animosity from the crowd, especially once we settle in at the bar and I shirk off the glasses and coat, but instead we're flocked by a crowd of sympathizers.

They drone on and on about my plight, how they'll always believe a man until proven guilty, and for some reason, it rankles me. Unease chinks along my spine, digging into the vertebrae until I'm practically vibrating with annoyance.

After I've signed a dozen autographs, Liam slides a beer over and raises an eyebrow at me.

"You good? Because three seconds ago, it looked like you wanted to tear into your own fans."

"I'm fine. That was just a lot to soak in." I take the bottle, bringing it to my lips for a quick sip, far past caring that I shouldn't be drinking. "Guess I've got to ease myself back into the socialization part of this gig."

"See, this is why sitting alone in your apartment day in and day out is a bad thing. Think of all the connections you're missing out on when you sit up there sulking, forgetting how to interact with people. You could be networking with people who could help you, clear your name once and for all, but you're too busy hiding."

"I'm *trying* to work," I snap, narrowing my eyes at him. Ever the publicist, always worried about my image and not the fact that I'm drowning in misery. "I don't know if you noticed, but I don't exactly have very much else going on right now. Making music is the only thing keeping me fucking occupied, asshole."

Liam sighs, taking a swig of his own beer. "I get that, man. But you can't just give up."

"I haven't."

"Really?" He quirks a brow. "Then why the hell haven't you found that girl yet? The Aiden James I know would never roll over for some cheap pussy."

My throat burns, hearing him call her that. Then, the fire inside rages even higher, my internal defense of the girl who ruined my life irritating me.

God, I'm pathetic.

I don't even know her fucking name, and yet I'm stuck on her as though she's a goddess on earth, and I've found religion in her.

"Nothing to find," a voice says from over my shoulder. We turn to see a man with a bad comb-over leaning against the counter, pudgy fingers wrapped around a half-empty pint. "Didn't you hear? That girl's dead."

I snort, and Liam rolls his eyes, leaning in to ask, "How could you know that? No one even knows her name."

"Oh, *someone* knows her name, all right. And someone took care of pretty boy's little problem," he sneers. Tilting his head, he takes me in from head to toe and chuckles to himself. "Then again, maybe she's created a whole new set."

With a hiccup, he stumbles off to the back, his gait and slurred speech confirming that his ramblings are just that.

There's no way the girl is dead.

Surely, someone would've figured that out. Even though the Internet's been practically scrubbed of her existence, outside of the claims themselves, it's not possible something like this would happen and I wouldn't know about it.

Right?

Liam and I sit in silence, my thoughts growing persistent in volume with each drink I take. I do my best to tamp it down, not wanting to spoil the night for Liam, but eventually I can't ignore the pulse in my veins.

Sliding off the stool, I clamp a hand on his shoulder. "Gonna step out for a smoke."

He hesitates, casting a glance over his shoulder to where my bodyguard, Jason, sits in the corner of the room watching us.

I sigh. "Please, I'll just be a second. I swear I'm not going anywhere. Need some air."

"Okay." Liam shrugs, scratching at his blond hair. "I'll try to stall him."

Clapping him on the back, I duck out a side exit into a damp alley and collapse against the brick wall. Shuffling out a cigarette from my jeans, I light up and take a slow drag, trying to calm the painful buzzing ricocheting off my temple.

Dead. I scoff, wondering who the fuck that girl was, and how she ended up being so goddamn elusive. Is it possible her enchantment was nothing more than a ruse, and that she was sent to ruin me?

Then again, if that were the case, I don't know why she seemed so reluctant to be my date that night. Why she ran from me, when I'd only just gotten a taste.

Tapping my foot on the concrete, I do my best to make sense of the situation, ruminating on everything that's led up to this point for the millionth time since the allegations began.

No one knows who she is, because she forged the papers to get into the charity gala that night.

But at the tattoo shop, they'd run her license, and no one said anything about it being a fake.

With the cigarette dangling between my lips, I replay that thought in my mind again, heart stalling as it gets stuck on a loop.

She used her real license to get a tattoo.

Blinking at the bare wall in front of me for several beats, I take one last puff and toss the cigarette to the ground, taking off on foot down the alley and street to where the Suburban is parked. Throwing open the back door, I quickly relay directions to the driver, sending a text to Liam that I'm heading back to the apartment and sending the car back for him.

A string of explicit texts follow, but I ignore them, adrenaline coursing through my blood as the driver whizzes through the city streets.

When he finally gets close enough, I shove open the door and sprint down the sidewalk, barreling into Gio's shop with absolutely no finesse. My hair sticks to my forehead, damp with sweat, and I'm out of breath as I ask about their records.

"Got a warrant?" Jenna barks, glaring at me as I double over with my hands on my knees, trying to regulate my breathing.

"Just show him the fucking thing," Gio snaps from the back of the shop.

Growling under her breath, Jenna reaches into a desk drawer, pulling out a binder and flipping directly to the page in question.

I blink at it, then up at her, and she shrugs. "Look, we didn't mention it because someone showed up right after you left and threatened our lives if we did."

"Threatened your lives?"

"We don't know who," Gio says. "Didn't see them. Just got the message."

The phrase repeats in my head as I grip the binder with trembling fingers, squeezing the edges until my knuckles blanch. I stare down at the picture—ocean eyes that are branded on my soul look back, as devoid of emotion as ever.

I remember the way it felt when she looked at me, as if I was the first person to make her *feel* something.

I remember what it felt like to spear my tongue inside her, lap at her juices, revel in her ecstasy. How I wished I could've recorded her sounds, so I could keep them as just mine forever.

Slipping the photocopy from the binder, I absorb everything—her date of birth, the state of Maine branding, the address.

My gaze zeros in on the address, a sinister feeling unlike anything I've ever known taking root inside me like a hundred-year-old tree.

I glance up at Jenna, cocking a brow. "No one finds out about this, or I'll report you for evidence tampering. Got it?"

She nods, and I make my way from the building, unable to stop looking at her ID.

If she's dead, fine. The obsession stops here.

If she's alive, though...

If Riley Kelly is alive, I'm going to track her down and make her wish she wasn't.

Part Two

17

THREE YEARS LATER

As a kid, I despised Christmas.

The memories associated with it—my parents' split, my mother's first overdose—soured my attitude toward the holiday pretty early on, and it didn't help that no one could ever seem to get me a decent gift.

Year after year, I'd hold my breath, hoping someone had paid enough attention to me to be able to pick something I liked.

All I ever opened was crushing disappointment.

This year, I'm buying my own gifts.

Partly because I'm spending the season alone, but also

because I'm trying to practice self-love at my brother's girl-friend's insistence.

We have over a month until Christmas, but Fiona's been dragging me all over Lunar Cove trying to find the perfect gift since she flew in yesterday.

Which wouldn't necessarily be a big deal, except that Lunar Cove is a lake town in the foothills outside of Denver, and with their population maxing at about five hundred residents, there aren't very many places to buy things that aren't souvenirs.

"What about this?" she asks, showing me a purple tie-dyed snow suit, raising her brows from across the clothing rack.

I make a face, continuing to sift through the hangers on my side. "Do I look like someone who wears tie-dye?"

Pursing her lips, Fiona glances down at my black sweater, thick black leggings, and black leather knee-high boots.

Sighing wistfully, she snaps the hanger back on the rack. "I was really hoping that hair color of yours would lead to a change in your wardrobe style."

Reaching up, I pull my fingers through the rose gold strands that graze the tops of my breasts. I've been letting it grow ever since I started dyeing it, eager to put as much distance between me and my past self as possible.

That's what the move here was about, after all.

When Kal Anderson said he was going to kill me, he hadn't been exaggerating. For the last three years, Riley Kelly has ceased to exist, and her rumored death got about the response I always anticipated it would.

No one fucking cared.

Aside from my absentee father, who left Maine not long

after my obituary ran in the newspaper, my death didn't cause so much as a ripple in our community.

On the one hand, Kal assured me it was a good thing—if no one cared, no one was going to question it, either.

On the other hand... *no one cared.* My life had left as much of an impact on the world as my own mother's, and that realization stung.

But once the plan was set in motion, there was no turning back. On the outside, I haven't been Riley since that day in my brother's office and having a clean slate has been nice.

During the day, when I'm doing freelance web design for clients that Boyd sends my way or exercising at the athletic club down the road from my house, it's easy to pretend the slate isn't stained on one side.

That I'm not just trying to keep myself distracted, because my demons lurk when I'm not actively keeping them away.

Nightmares in the shape of tattooed limbs and the scent of spicy cardamom plague my sleep every night, where I'm unable to outrun my subconscious.

Fiona's exhale draws me out of my thoughts, and she holds up a wooden pocketknife, the word *boss* engraved on the side. She raises an eyebrow expectantly, and I return her stare with a bland expression.

"Shopping is supposed to be fun," she whines, noisily putting the knife back on the display. "If I knew you were going to be grumpy, I would've just gone with your brother."

I turn to inspect a spinning rack of designer sunglasses, ignoring the pang that shoots through my chest. "He still refusing to come visit?"

She looks down at the French tips of her nails. "He just

needs a little time, Ril—" Cutting herself off, she presses her red lips together and sighs again. "It's hard for him, not having you near where he can keep an eye on you."

"Well, it's not exactly been a picnic for me," I hiss, lowering my voice.

One look at the front of the souvenir shop tells me the cashier—my elderly neighbor, Mrs. Lindholm—has her eyes glued to us, watching intently for a piece of drama to gossip about at the marina.

"Look, all I'm saying is give him some time. He *is* trying."

"It's been three *years*, Fi. I've talked to Kal Anderson more in that time than my own brother."

Her eyes soften. "Maybe that's part of the problem."

Frustrated, I ball my hands into fists and bite down on the inside of my cheek. I'm not sure how many times I have to explain the reasoning behind why I reached out to Kal instead of Boyd, but nonetheless, it's obvious I haven't yet reached the limit.

Maybe it doesn't help that I never told anyone about the mysterious envelope, hoping that if I ignored its existence, the problem would go away on its own.

And that has been the most successful part of this entire plan—whoever sent the envelope has yet to come to collect or expand on their supposed knowledge.

Regardless, the topic of my brother exhausts me, and I leave Lunar Cove Trading Co. empty-handed. Per our weekend tradition, when Fiona flies into town, providing me with the only *real* human contact I get outside our residents, we stop by Dahlia's Diner for chocolate milkshakes and walk along the makeshift boardwalk.

It's a strip of businesses that run along the lake, packed in the summer with tourists but a complete ghost town in the winter. I sip my shake, the ice cream frigid on my tongue, while the cold breeze glides over my skin, caressing the scars on my face.

"Do you ever think about it?" Fiona asks as we pass a pizzeria, then an art gallery. "About who started that awful rumor about you and—"

"No," I lie, interrupting her sentence before she can mention his name. A sinking feeling erupts in my stomach, like I'm being swallowed whole by fear. "No point in dwelling on things I know I won't ever get the answer to, right?"

Fiona grins, looping her arm through mine and resting her head on my shoulder as we walk to where her rental car is parked. "You know what that is? Growth."

But it's not.

When I stop work tasks for the day, I immediately pull up a secret folder with endless files of research. Security camera footage from every street corner we touched that fateful night in New York City, IP addresses of people who interacted with private forum posts detailing my supposed claims against the rock star.

Anything that has to do with the rumor sits in that folder, and I spend all of my free time sifting through, trying to find answers.

Every day, I come up with nothing, except the express feeling that my sanity is slipping further and further from my grasp.

I can't tell her that, though. Not when everyone thinks I've let it go.

Not until I know for sure.

18

"WE'RE OUT OF PEPPERMINT TEA."

The feminine voice startles me, and I sit up straight, leaning back against the red vinyl booth seat. A waitress stands beside my table with her arm cocked in the air, balancing a black tray on her upturned palm.

I swallow over a lump that lodges in my throat, shoulders tensing, and search her big green eyes for signs of recognition.

She just blinks, using her free hand to push a strand of onyx hair from her face.

Blowing out a long breath, I shake my head. "Sorry?"

One brow arches. "You ordered a peppermint tea, right? Our new hire, Billie, took your order, and she didn't realize we're out."

"Oh." Toying with the silver rings on my fingers, I nod. "That's fine. What about plain tea?"

"We have that in spades. Our elderly customers are the ones who drink it, and it takes them a full month to go through one box."

When I don't say anything, my gaze flickering back out the window to my left, she taps the side of her tray and smacks her lips together. "Okay, I'll grab that and be right back."

Again, I don't acknowledge her, my attention long gone before she's even stepped away from the booth. Locking on to movement across the street, I lean closer to the glass pane, surveying the strip of businesses until I find her.

She's bundled up in a black peacoat and a thick scarf, her hair catching in the breeze and obscuring her face from view.

Smirking to myself, I touch my fingertips to my lips; even three years later, I can still feel the imprint of her mouth on mine.

Still jack myself to sleep every night to the image of her breaking apart on my tongue, crying out with no sound, as if unsure of how to welcome the pleasure.

I would've taught her how to accept it. Over and over, until she was a blubbering, snotty mess of frayed nerve endings and fluttering muscles.

But she hadn't given me the chance, and now that ship has sailed.

The only thing I'm here to do is expose her as the snake

she is, drag her back to the land of the living where the truth can eat her alive.

Tracking her down was no easy feat, especially given the media's assumption that *I* had anything to do with her supposed death.

Even though I was cleared of suspicion when her death was ruled a suicide, people still look at me like I killed her myself, which is part of the reason I've been searching for her all this time.

Riley Kelly has connections, and they've gone to great lengths to ensure she remains in hiding indefinitely.

Unfortunately for her, my obsession hasn't lessened.

And when an artist has a muse, even if that muse is toxic and life-ruining, they don't stop seeking them out.

Can't stop, even when they desperately want to.

So, for three years, I've been looking. I've spent an ungodly amount of money and time, and neglected the contract with my label, in favor of scouring the earth for her.

Part of me still can't believe I finally did.

The other part is salivating, ready to feast on her fear and make her repent for her wrongdoings.

My cock jerks behind my zipper at the thought of her pleading for mercy, even knowing she won't get any.

Hand sliding across my mouth to my jaw, I chuckle softly, watching her tuck her hair into the collar of her coat. It's longer now than it was that night in New York, and I can't help wondering if it's still as soft.

Or if she thought dyeing it that blush color would mask her identity from me.

She moves to the edge of the sidewalk, turning to scan this side of the street. My breath catches somewhere between my lungs and throat, turning to smoke that threatens to suffocate me as those shiny blue eyes sweep past the window.

Tension threads through every muscle, wrenching so tight it makes my teeth ache, the thrill of being caught mixing with the disappointment that she doesn't seem to notice me.

That cocktail morphs into a vicious storm, though, when her gaze finally lands, a small smile breaking out along her pretty face.

A man exits the art gallery beside Dahlia's Diner, pausing to lock up before spinning around and heading over to her. He swings his keys around an index finger, whistling as he strides in her direction, and suddenly I'm unsure if the rosy tinge to her cheeks is from the cold temperature outside, or the dark-haired fucker invading her personal space.

Her mouth moves, mumbling something I'm too angry to register, and then he's stepping in and pulling her into his embrace. His bronzed skin is such a deep contrast to hers, and I hate seeing the two pressed together.

Curling my hands over the edge of the wooden table, I tighten my grip, allowing the pressure to build until the surface creaks.

Thoughts of murder pulse along my spine, scratching at the bone, and I bite down against the urge to bolt out there and beat him bloody for touching what belongs to me.

But I can't ruin everything I've worked so hard for, and that would certainly not go over well when I report back to Liam. He thinks this trip is my attempt at finding inspiration and completing my album for Symposium, and I don't really want to have to explain a body count this early on.

My father, the only other person who knows I'm here—

and the only one who knows *why*—wouldn't mind if I got my hands dirty. In fact, he'd probably encourage it.

God knows he's no saint.

Still, there's only one corpse I want to deal with, and she has no fucking clue I'm here.

The waitress returns, a white ceramic mug sitting in the middle of her tray, and she sets it down in front of me. Reaching into the pocket of her little black apron, she tosses two extra Lipton tea bags on the table, then steps back, hugging the tray to her chest.

She's a pretty girl—those gemlike green eyes set in a delicate, lightly freckled face, and the way she stares a bit too long makes me think she's eager to please.

Glancing at the betrayal across the street, I consider taking the waitress up on her unspoken offer. Let my mind run with the idea of taking her to the bathroom in the back and unloading all my stress on her.

In the vision, though, it's not her face I see.

It's Riley.

And though it might feel good in the moment, it wouldn't after.

Besides, that's not why I'm here. If my dick gets wet, it'll be at my sweet little angel's discretion, and not a moment sooner.

"Sorry about the wait," the waitress says, wiping her hands on her apron. "Would you like a complimentary oatmeal raisin cookie, for your trouble?"

Wincing internally, I shake my head. "No trouble at all," I say, leaning in to read her name tag, "*Jade*. Keep the cookie."

Fishing into my coat pocket, I slide out from the booth and drop three hundred-dollar bills on the table, scooping the mug into my hands.

"Keep the change, too."

I leave her standing there, stunned into silence, and head out the glass front door. An overhead bell signals my departure, and the man across the street glances my way.

His beard irritates me. It's too long—if he buried his face between Riley's glorious thighs, she'd be left with an uncomfortable itch.

Nothing like the sweet burn my stubble created at the tattoo shop.

Dick throbbing, I stuff a hand in my pocket to adjust, not dropping the man's eyes once they reach mine. He makes a face, and I pull a peppermint candy out, popping it from the wrapper into my tea.

It immediately begins dissolving, and I bring it to my mouth slowly, smiling around the rim of the mug as the first scalding drops touch my lips.

The man leans down, saying something in Riley's ear, and then he finally looks away.

My heartbeat races as he slips his hand in hers, tugging her the opposite direction, leading her farther from me.

I sip my drink, soaking in that peppermint flavor as it singes my tongue, promising silently that I'll see her soon.

19

As I RINSE a head of lettuce beneath the faucet in my kitchen sink, I try not to let my irritation bleed through my actions.

Caleb Pruitt lies on the floor in front of my dishwasher, a screwdriver in his mouth, humming Christmas tunes while replacing a hose. Despite my reassurance that I'd call a plumber in the morning, Lunar Cove's golden boy refused to pass up the opportunity to help out.

I shouldn't bitch—he's about the only friend I've made in town, aside from Jade at the local diner.

Not to mention, him fixing the appliance keeps unnecessary strangers from coming to my home.

We met at the art gallery on the boardwalk; one night, after spending nearly a year here without leaving the house, my loneliness got the best of me and I decided to go out.

He'd been standing beside a clay sculpture of Atlas, carrying the globe on his shoulders, and I'd been so mesmerized by the sleek design and the impossibly smooth edges that I'd nearly knocked it over trying to get closer.

Turns out, Caleb owns the art gallery. The Pruitts are Lunar Cove royalty, with each of the three sons in charge of various businesses around town.

From that night on, Caleb planted himself in my life, always willing to lend a hand, even when I say I don't need it.

That should probably worry me, but then I remember how boring it is here without a friend, and I ignore it. Hoping he gets the hint that my feelings are strictly platonic.

"You're spending an awful lot of time on that lettuce," he calls out from across the kitchen, tilting his head back to cock an eyebrow at me. "It's gonna start disintegrating if you don't let up."

Snapping out of my reverie, I shut off the sink and set the lettuce on the granite countertop to dry. Wiping my hands on my leggings, I check the farfalle pasta cooking on the stove, then grab my phone and shoot a text to my brother.

Me: Do you remember that time Mom made bow tie noodles for my eleventh birthday?

A few seconds later, his response pops up.

Boyd: Do I remember the day she nearly burned down your trailer, and made you eat black pasta?

Me: It wasn't all burned.

Boyd: No wonder you cleaned your plate.

I'm not sure where to take the conversation next, so I wait

for more; it never comes, and sadness works its way into my heart all over again.

Sighing, I lean against the kitchen island and lock my phone back, cursing myself silently for undoing any semblance of progress my brother and I had made in our relationship in the years before I left Maine.

"Are you okay?" Caleb asks, pushing away from the dishwasher as he gets to his feet.

I nod, forcing a smile. "Just my brother being his annoying self." Turning around, I move to stir the homemade tomato sauce—a recipe I got from Kal's Italian wife—and lift a shoulder. "You have two brothers, though. I don't have to tell you what that's like."

Caleb rests his hip on the island. "I didn't know *you* had a brother."

The cogs in my brain skid to a halt, and panic swells in my chest. My hand continues stirring, kinetic energy propelling the movement.

"We have a complicated relationship," I say, settling on a half-truth. "I don't really talk about him much."

He grunts. "Not even once in the two years we've been friends?"

Pressing my lips together, I shrug. "Guess it's never really come up."

I feel his dark eyes boring into the side of my head, but I keep mine trained on the sauce. Finally I see him nod in my peripheral vision, and he seems to relax.

"Well, I know better than to push you for information. Don't want you to lock me out on the deck again."

The tension in my shoulders lessens slightly, and a laugh pushes from my throat. "I'm not that bad."

"It was the middle of a snowstorm," he says, pointing a finger at me. "And all I asked was if you needed extra firewood."

"And then you learned I have a gas fireplace." Glancing over at the gray stone mantel, I try not to think of the one at my brother's house, and how this one seems empty in comparison.

Overall, the entire cabin is pretty empty; sure, it came fully stocked with handcrafted pine furniture that matches the paneling on the walls and vaulted ceilings, but since I can't acknowledge my old life without risking my safety, no personal effects decorate the place.

The lakefront and mountainside views through the ceiling-to-floor windows, though, are almost enough to make up for it.

Almost.

After a prolonged silence, Caleb jumps back into fixing the dishwasher, and I strain the pasta, emptying both pots into respective serving dishes and setting them in the oven for a minute to cool down.

When he's finished, I offer him a plate, and we eat standing at the island, staring out the back windows.

There's another cabin just beyond the lake, uninhabited for years, according to the locals. Movement catches my eye, though, a dark figure lurking in the shadowy corner of a window upstairs, and an uneasy feeling settles in my gut, putting me on edge.

Then I blink, and the figure's gone, the house as still as always. Leaving me to wonder if I made it all up.

Spearing a piece of pasta with his fork, Caleb nudges me with his shoulder. "So, you gonna attend the art show coming up? The focus is on indigenous folklore."

I poke at my food, pushing it around my plate. "That sounds interesting, but I don't know…"

"If you feel weird about the crowd, I can always escort you."

A cramp flares in my stomach, and I shift my eyes down, discomfort tangling in my nerves.

"It could be fun," he continues, shoving another forkful of pasta into his mouth. "That's all I'm saying. Champagne and appetizers, and you get to judge people all night. What more could you possibly want for a winter evening?"

"I'll think about it," I say, even though I've already made up my mind.

Satisfied with that, he finishes his food and washes his plate in the sink, drying it and putting it away quickly. I walk with him to the front door, my body going stiff when he stops to pull me into another hug.

Pressing a soft kiss to my cheek, Caleb pulls back, and I try not to seize up completely at his forwardness. My brain repeats that he's just an affectionate guy, and that he doesn't mean any harm, but my body rejects the sentiment.

My pulse thuds loudly at the base of my throat as he releases me, and he grins. "I'll call you tomorrow, okay, Angel?"

I nod, disgust immobilizing my vocal cords, and watch him descend the porch and head to where his Jeep is parked.

Going back inside, I shut the door and secure the three deadbolts, peering through the little glass window at the top of the door. Caleb sits in there for several beats, staring up at the house, and for a second I'm racked with nervous energy.

Afraid that he'll come back, and decide my friendship is no longer good enough.

My shaky hand grips the doorknob, tightening around

the black metal until my fingers ache, but then he's turning the engine on and driving away.

Sagging against the door, I allow myself a chance to revel in the relief. Living on my own has come with its own set of obstacles and learning to curb my fears of being attacked again is high on that list.

A pang shoots through my chest, terror trying to solidify in my soul, but I tamp it down and take the stairs two at a time. Pushing open the door to the master bedroom, I go straight for the en suite and let the porcelain Jacuzzi fill up.

While I wait, I strip out of my clothes, pausing in the full-length mirror beside my dresser. With a makeup remover wipe, I slowly clean my face, touching the jagged lines of pale flesh.

The slivers, a sharp stroke against my cheekbone and a slash at the corner of my mouth, are still rough and tender to the touch, but they're finally beginning to fade.

My gaze drops, along with my hands, and I slide my fingers over my hip, wincing at the way that gash looks; it's messy, the tissue raised and sensitive and darker than the marks on my face.

It's ugly, and I can only imagine the memory attached is even worse, so for a moment, I'm grateful that those images are just out of reach.

Grabbing my purple silk robe from where it hangs on the mirror, I wrap it around myself, dousing my shame before it can finish crawling up my neck.

Holding the tie against my waist, I walk to the nightstand beside my bed and pull open the drawer, biting my bottom lip as I stare down at the contents.

The birthday gift from Fiona stares back at me, still in its box and wrapped in cellophane. Swallowing over the sudden dryness in my throat, I reach in and pull it out, opening it quickly.

My cheeks heat, embarrassment pressing down on my chest, as if there's a chance someone might see me use it. My thumb finds the button on the wand, and it roars to life, vibrating violently where it rests against my thigh.

At the same time, my gaze lifts, catching movement through the window; immediately, I'm drawn to the second story in the cabin across the lake, my entire body hollowing out.

Lungs on fire, I can't stop my breathing from growing sporadic or the anxiety from flooding my chest. Scanning every window in the house, though, I come up short again with nothing but the light rustling of the aspen trees surrounding us to focus on.

You're being ridiculous, Riley. There's no one out there. No one is coming for you.

No one knows you're here.

For some reason, I can't shake the eerie feeling, or stop it from mixing with something else—disappointment.

Still, if it were someone coming to kill me, they'd likely have already done it.

If it were someone representing Aiden James, I don't know why they'd be across the lake and not hauling me in for questioning.

My heart thumps sadly at the thought of how badly I fucked up there. How I wish I'd never gone on that class trip or met him in the first place.

How I wish I'd let him do more to me that night in the tattoo shop.

Switching off the toy, I grip it in my palm and stand up, closing the curtains before going back to the bathroom.

And when I sink to the bottom of the tub, fitting the pulsating tip of the wand between my thighs, I fantasize about the man with the gray eyes, wishing I hadn't ruined his life.

20

I'M HEARING THINGS.

I *have* to be.

There's no other explanation as to why my name would be coming from beyond the closed bathroom door.

Waiting with my ear pressed to the wood, I hold my breath, straining for more.

Another breathy moan slips beneath the crack where light shines through; paired with the sound of water lapping at naked flesh, and my dick is already hardening behind my zipper.

But still, I wait.

A buzzing sound fills the air and my hand inches toward the doorknob. My rings clink against the fixture, my fingers clutching but not turning.

Not yet, anyway.

That same sensation I got when I saw Riley for the first time, across the room at the charity event, washes over me. The elation of, for once in my life, being on the giving end of speculation.

Of watching, rather than being watched.

It's fucking freeing.

Heady and intoxicating in a way that almost makes me sympathetic to the paparazzi vultures.

Or maybe it's just her making me feel this way.

"Oh..." Comes her deceptively sweet voice, and I reach my free hand into my pocket, popping a peppermint into my mouth. "Oh, *god.*"

Rolling the candy around with my tongue, I ignore the urge to burst inside and demand she not call out for someone who isn't me.

The invisible man in the sky has nothing on the things I could make her scream, but if she'd like a proper introduction, I'd be happy to help out.

Biting down on the peppermint until it shatters, I shake my head and release the knob, taking three giant steps back. My boots are soft on the carpet, leaving just enough of a trace on the beige shag to freak her out.

My sweet little angel is nothing if not paranoid, always peering over her shoulder, as if she expects trouble to find her at any moment.

I can't imagine my finding her was ever on her radar, which is going to make the look on her face so much more delicious.

The buzzing continues in the bathroom, so I acquaint myself with her bedroom while I wait.

There's a tall dresser against one wall, and I sift through the drawers slowly, pausing when I get to her underwear.

I tell myself not to. That I don't collect anymore.

And yet, when my palm closes around silk and lace, I can't resist; I quickly stuff every pair of panties she has into my coat pocket and push the drawer back into place.

Euphoria tears through me, a comet blazing its path to destruction, and when it implodes I know I'll be left with the usual disgust.

Right now, though, I can't bring myself to care.

Turning, I survey the rest of the room; a multicolored floor lamp sits in one corner of the room beside a pink bucket chair. Like the rest of the furniture in the cabin, the bed is some kind of ugly pine material, and there are purple satin sheets stretched over the mattress.

A leopard print throw lays at the foot, and on top of that is a laptop with a snakeskin sleeve on the lid. Scoffing at the irony, I perch on the edge of the bed and pull it onto my lap, opening the top slowly, while listening for footsteps.

With my heart in my throat, I push the power button in the corner. The computer flickers to life, and my pulse increases its frequency, excitement drumming through me.

The lock screen pops up, and I frown. Racking my brain for every bit of information I've collected on Riley over the last three years, I try to think of what she might use as a password, but none of the words work.

Tapping my finger on the keyboard, I start to type something else, but then I hear it again.

"*Aiden...*"

My spine stiffens, my gaze shooting up to the door. The bathroom light is still on, no footsteps discernible, but I *know* I heard it that time.

Shoving the laptop away, I stalk back to the door. I can't stop myself from turning the knob and pushing it slightly ajar.

I know her exact routine and have cataloged her every action. I know that when she takes her baths, she puts on a giant pair of noise-canceling headphones and slathers on some kind of green face mask.

I know she spends exactly twenty-three minutes in the tub.

And I know that when she gets out, she lathers up in that peppermint lotion that haunts my fucking dreams to this day.

I can taste it on her skin, still. Remember exactly how breathless she was, how flushed her face got when she told me about it.

Still, part of me expects her to notice when I walk in.

For her self-preservation to win out, and self-awareness to kick in, alerting her to the fact that she's being preyed upon.

I almost want her to. Want her to see the monster she's created before he inevitably destroys her.

But she doesn't notice, headphones securely in place, and suddenly I'm staring at the most beautiful liar I've ever seen.

Her pale skin, slick with water and an undeniable sheen of sweat, glistens in the vanity lighting, and she lays with her head hooked over the lip of the bathtub, pink hair shimmering over the side.

Perky breasts with sweet, peachy nipples rise and fall

with each ragged breath she draws, dispersing the water's surface. I watch as it ebbs back and forth, the moon pulling and pushing at the tide, enamored by the way it seems to move for her.

Disappointment sizzles in my chest when I realize her blue eyes are pinched shut, but then my gaze slides between parted, propped up knees, and the air escapes my lungs.

My legs quake as her hands move, guiding the bulbous head of a vibrator back and forth over her clit.

Blood rushes south, and my palm comes down, pressing against the fly of my jeans. My tongue feels heavy and dry, her tiny moans making me dizzy.

As my own breathing starts to struggle, hers picks up. Her chest heaves, caving in and then pushing back out, and my lips tingle with the desire coursing through me.

It'd be so fucking easy to march over and draw the taut peaks of her tits between my lips. To draw out her pleasure, test her tolerance for pain by sinking my teeth into the puckered flesh.

Gripping the counter with as much force as possible, I keep myself in place, unwilling to reveal my presence before I know what I want to do with her.

My father wants me to expose her. Bring her back to the land of the living and prove myself to those who doubted me.

Technically, I want that too.

But I also think I deserve a little fun along the way, all things considered.

So, I remain still, cock leaking on my thigh as I watch Riley bring herself to orgasm; I can't see all of her face from this vantage point, but I see her forehead wrinkle as she gurgles in delight, arching her back against the tub tile.

Goddamn. I'm feverish, bearing witness to divinity.

My jaw clenches so tight that stars dance around the edges of my vision.

The toy must be new, because I've never heard the sounds coming from her throat before. Not behind a closed door, anyway.

A fleeting thought flashes through my mind, and I wonder if the guy with her on the boardwalk gifted it to her.

If he's used it on her.

Fury scorches a path across my chest, crimson splashing behind my eyes every time I blink. As she comes off her high, Riley disables the vibrator and goes limp in the tub, running a hand through her hair.

I'm stuck in place when she finally stands, reaching for a towel hanging on the wall, back facing me.

My throat constricts as she rises, droplets of water dripping over the curve of her perfect ass.

Memory and screens do not do her justice.

Annoyance heats the base of my spine, clearing the fog of lust as it coasts through my brain. I dip out the door before she can turn around, knowing the next part of her routine gives me a couple of minutes to disappear into the shadows again, my malicious presence unbeknownst to her.

The bedside lamp doesn't illuminate the entire room, so I slink into a darkened corner by the dresser, willing my dick to go down.

Pressing myself into the wall, I try to think of anything else. My parents, the lake outside, my fifth grade social studies project on the Declaration of Independence.

All I see is her fucking face.

A subdued noise of frustration puffs from my nostrils, and I move my hands to my jeans. It's a shit idea, possibly the worst I've ever had, but right now my only thought is relief.

Relief of the guilt her beauty fills me with when *she* should be the one repenting.

Of not being able to create, because she's still got her claws latched into my brain, my lungs, and my *soul.*

Three years I've spent living and breathing her. Imagining the moment I'd be able to reclaim my focus.

Denying myself because of the way she dominates my thoughts.

But no more.

With shaky fingers, I drag my zipper down and wrench my cock from my boxers. It's hot to the touch, and I swipe my thumb along the tip, spreading the bead of precum bubbling there.

Releasing a harsh breath, I close my eyes and inhale, stroking up my shaft once.

Twice.

My movements are stilted, uneven as I lean to listen for her departure from the bathroom. The sink turns on, and a strangled moan escapes me as I begin pumping harder.

Palming the top of her dresser, I blow out a breath, sweat forming at my hairline. As a drop glides down the bridge of my nose, I'm reminded of her in the bathtub, body shimmering with the evidence of her exertion, and my balls draw up tight.

I envision her face, mouth parted in shock and eyes wide, if she were to come out before I'm finished.

The idea of her catching me like this, draining myself dry to the image of her doing the same, spurs me on. I'm panting, hips bucking against the air, my climax so close I can taste it in my throat, when I realize I don't have anywhere for it to go.

Swallowing hard, I slow my strokes without ceasing completely, glancing at the wooden surface in front of me. I could use a pair of panties stuffed in my pocket, but then I'd have to leave it for her to find in order to send a message, and I don't want to do that.

But I'm not leaving without letting her know that I'm here.

A bottle sitting in my line of sight captures my attention, and I lean in, squinting hard to see the label.

Something sinister weasels through my gut, weaving its way between my ribs until it's practically one with my being. Satisfaction, sick and deranged, courses through my bloodstream, and I reach forward to unscrew the lid.

Gripping the bottle in my free hand, I position it beneath the slit in my crown, resuming the languid strokes from before.

My toes curl inside my boots, my spine liquefying, as thick ropes of cum spurt from me like a hot spring. It dribbles into the lotion, musk mixing with the smell of Christmas, and I come close to blacking out from the pleasure it gives me.

Inside the bathroom, the sink shuts off, and I fumble to put myself back together. Screwing the lid on tight, I give it a little shake, my pulse skyrocketing.

Perverse contentment rains over me, and I set the bottle back where it belongs, slipping from her bedroom before she can come out.

When I'm back at my temporary residence, I set up my usual watching post at the window, propping my feet on the sill with my bass in my lap.

And as her silhouette gets dressed and ready for bed, smoothing what I imagine is *my* vile concoction on her body, I write an opening verse for the first time in three years.

21

"I'm just saying, I don't know where they could've *possibly* gone."

Crouching on my hands and knees, I sweep underneath my dresser, searching for what I already know isn't there.

Kal's voice is strained, and I don't have to turn around to know there's a harsh look of resentment on his face. I don't think the man *has* another expression. "How the hell does an entire underwear drawer go missing?"

Groaning, I yank my arm out and sit back on my knees, casting another futile glance around the room. Nothing's out of place, save for the shoe boxes I've dug out of the closet in my haste to find my panties.

When I woke up this morning and went to put on a new pair, I'd opened the drawer and discovered the whole thing was empty.

My first reaction was a deep sense of confusion, followed closely by a tinge of fear. Either that someone had broken in and robbed me of my underwear, or that Caleb had somehow slipped upstairs unnoticed and raided the contents.

Sitting here, blushing hard in front of a man who definitely has more important things to deal with in life, I still don't know which is worse.

"There's no evidence of a break-in," Kal continues. "Is it possible you've just misplaced them?"

I twist around, watching his thumb smooth over the black wedding band on his left hand. With his other, he scrolls through his phone, sharp brows drawn in, a determined frown pulling all of his features down.

How his wife deals with a man who always looks so perturbed is beyond me. She must have a spine of steel to not spend all of her time thinking he's mad at her.

I've only spoken to her a few times; she's warm where Kal isn't, a balm for his sharp edges. But there's a ferocity that blazes in her eyes. One that doesn't allow for much direct contact.

A match made in hell.

My first year here, I ended every evening with a phone call checking in with Kal, demanding to see pictures of his newborn daughter.

The guise was that we were ensuring I was safe, but really, I was just lonely, and I think he knew. Eventually, the calls became attempts at therapy sessions, and I'd ceased making them entirely, except for when he insisted.

In a way, it felt like I was cheating on Boyd, and I think that's why I withdrew. Then again, my brother's pointed absence all this time makes me feel a little less guilty.

If he can't show up when I need him most, why shouldn't I replace him?

"We're talking twenty, thirty pairs of panties here," I say after the silence goes on for so long, he actually looks up. "They aren't pens; they don't *get* misplaced."

"Perhaps your dryer ate them? I've heard of that happening."

Shifting so I'm sitting on my ass instead of my knees, I narrow my eyes at him. "Do you even do your own laundry?"

"Only the loads with blood stains."

A shiver coasts over my skin, like the featherlight sweep of fingertips. It's a barrier, one he purposely puts up any time things get too chummy, like he's as uncomfortable with our dynamic as I am.

Shaking my head, I smooth my palms over the carpet; my hand freezes mid-sweep, touching the edge of a distinct groove.

In the shape of a footprint.

I'm not sure why, but for some reason, I don't immediately point it out to Kal. My insides twist painfully, the way you wring out a wet rag, but I ignore the sensation. Instead, I force my hand the rest of the way, erasing the evidence.

Lifting my head, I try to pretend I didn't see it in the first place, sure that my mind is playing tricks on me. "You think I'm crazy, don't you?"

"I don't think that." He sighs. "However, I do think you should consider the correlation."

"Between...?"

"Solitude and preposterous scenarios. Especially for a stressed, traumatized individual."

His doctor voice is in full effect, and I shrink into myself, feeling small.

"I'm not saying you're crazy, *or* that you're making things up. But the mind is a wonderfully delirious place when we allow it to be. It can create false narratives and block out truths entirely. Sometimes, it's to shield us from bad memories; others, it's fear manifesting, conjuring things that simply don't exist, as if trying to prepare us for certain possibilities."

My fingers clutch at the carpet threads, as if the imprint might return.

"Sounds like a fancy way of calling me a liar."

Tugging at the lapels of his black trench coat, Kal shrugs. "I believe *you* believe what you're telling me. Unfortunately, the evidence doesn't support the claim, and... well, there's not really anything I can do about it, Riley. I can arrange to have more cameras installed, but maybe you should also look into—"

"Don't say it."

"—therapy." He slips his phone into his pocket, dark eyes glinting in the bedroom light. "You've experienced a lot of traumas in your short life, and now you're living on your own, pretending to be a person who hasn't felt death slip between her fingers. That's quite the charade, don't you think?"

I look at the floor, emotion circling my throat. "I've tried therapy before. It was all Boyd made me do after the attack."

Kal hums. "Try again. Even meditating or journaling would be better than ruminating. In the meantime, I'll have someone out with more cameras this week. Think you can manage until then?"

Nodding, I sit there on the floor as he sees himself out of the cabin. It's not until I hear the front door click shut, the sound echoing off the ceiling, that I get to my feet and go down to lock everything behind him.

When he's gone, I press my back into the door and glance around the main level of the cabin.

It's always so fucking empty when they leave.

Twisting the knob on the fireplace, I watch the flames roar to life, then move to the kitchen to make myself a cup of hot cocoa. While I wait for the water to boil, I stare at my phone, considering calling my brother.

If anyone understands why I don't want therapy, it's him. Not that it ever kept him from making me go. At one point, we even tried group sessions, but then work and school kept our schedules apart, and I got to a place where I was functioning through the day, so I think he assumed I was okay.

That I wasn't hollow anymore, just because I'd resumed eating and sleeping and watching television.

Or maybe that's just what he wanted to believe.

But the truth is, it's not possible to heal from things you can't see.

Even invisible wounds hurt, and mine have scarred so deeply by now that I'm not sure I'll ever be able to move on. Not sure if I'll ever stop looking over my shoulder and expecting rancid yellow eyes, or the taste of copper.

Add in the fear of being found out, of being discovered as the girl who destroyed America's once favorite rock star, and I'm pretty sure seeing a therapist would only result in me being committed.

The teakettle on the stove begins to squeal, and I remove

it quickly, pouring the water into an oversized mug. Tearing open a packet of hot chocolate, I sprinkle in the powder and stir, then top it off with marshmallows.

When I take a sip, the hot liquid burns my tongue, but I revel in the sensation. Let it scald me, a silent punishment for the sins I'm trying to outrun.

I sit at the kitchen island, drinking slowly, and stare out the back windows at the cabin across the lake. A strange, jittery feeling envelops me the longer I look, waiting for something to appear.

After a few seconds, a light flickers on in the corner of the upstairs level, and I suck in a startled breath.

But when I blink, it's gone.

Almost like it never turned on in the first place.

Leaving me to wonder if Kal was right, after all.

22

RILEY SLEEPS with every light on downstairs, as if the lack of darkness could ever keep the monsters from coming out to play.

She went to bed an hour ago, the lamp in her bedroom flickering off and beckoning me over. I'd shoved my feet in my boots and closed the distance between our cabins, satisfaction weaving through my muscles as I evaded the security cameras she has in place.

It really isn't difficult to tap into these systems and tamper with them. With the click of a button on my phone, I alter the camera parameters so my pathway is *just* beyond detection, then slip inside.

Clearly, the system is more for her peace of mind; if this were my penthouse, 911 would be dialed the second they stepped off the private elevator.

And yet, here I am, moving freely about my little liar's home while she dreams upstairs.

Dragging my fingertips along the granite countertop in her kitchen, I narrow my gaze as I walk past the sink. There are two ceramic plates sitting in the stainless steel basin.

Two forks.

Two wineglasses, both with red stains left behind.

I lift the glasses, noting the pale pink lip gloss around one rim; the other is smudged with fingerprints, but no identifying feminine features.

Before I can stop myself, I'm imagining the man on the boardwalk with her the other day. The one who can't seem to keep his hands to himself when he's here, helping her with things around the cabin.

The one she drew the curtains closed for this evening, barring me from peeping in on their little rendezvous.

My fingers tighten around the mouth of the glass, and I feel it splinter beneath them before it implodes.

Glass shards burst into the air like fireworks, sharp edges embedding themselves into my skin. Somehow, that hurts less than the betrayal of her moving on, having dinner with, and entertaining another while I've been miserable for the last three years.

Flipping my hand over, I let the pieces clatter into the sink, then turn the faucet and rinse the smaller bits off of me. The water stings as it washes over each cut, and I allow myself to lean into it for a moment.

To remember why it is I'm here.

Wiping my hand dry on the white towel hanging on her oven handle, I leave the broken glass where it sits and continue my exploration.

Let her figure out what happened when she wakes up.

Maybe it'll teach her not to give away things that belong to me, like her precious fucking time.

I don't even let myself think about what else she might be offering.

There's a small side table to the left of her staircase, and an old landline hangs on the wall above it. A red light blinks at the bottom, and I walk over, needing to sate my curiosity.

It's not like many people know she's here, and I can't imagine why she'd communicate with this phone instead of the burner she keeps on her person at all times.

With my thumb, I press down on the button, adjusting the volume as the prerecorded introduction begins.

Some crackling comes over the line, and then a man's voice. My shoulders tense, my entire body poised as it waits.

"Angel! It's me, Caleb. I'm stuck at the gallery, and my cell died an hour ago. This is the only number listed in that old as shit phone book, and it's not even under your name."

My eyebrows push together, creases as deep as canyons rippling across my forehead.

Pushing the rewind button, I let the message replay, leaning in.

"Angel! It's me, Caleb. I'm stuck—"

Rewind. Pause.

A lead weight settles in my stomach, sending sparks of hot irritation through me as it expands.

Play.

"Angel! It's me—"

"Angel!"

Angel, Angel, Angel.

Rage boils in my chest, percolating so quickly I can hardly catch my breath as it spills over. I repeat the process —rewind, pause, play, and again—until my finger feels like it might fall off, and then I switch fingers, certain in my conviction that I'm mistaken.

That someone else isn't calling her the name I gave her.

The one that fucking ruined me.

Scrubbing my hand over my jaw, the stubble coarse against my palm, I stare at the answering machine, my brain scrambling to process whatever the fuck is going on.

I don't give it much time, though, too annoyed to sit and try to reason with myself.

Without listening to any more of the messages, I slide my finger from the red button and hold down the delete one above it, waiting until the dial tone tells me there are no more messages left.

My gaze drifts to the top of the stairs, and I stuff my hands in my jean pockets, rocking back on my heels. Weighing the consequences of going up while I can still feel anger pulsing through my blood.

Gritting my teeth, my feet carry me two steps at a time, and before I have a chance to think better of it, I'm pushing open the door to her bedroom and moving to the foot of her mattress.

The floor lamp in the corner casts the room in a dull hue, and I can just barely make out the tint of her hair as it fans across her pillow.

So beautiful. So fucking delicate, and innocent—if you don't know better.

Sinking onto the edge of the bed beside her, I snake my

palm over the curve of her hip, on top of the covers; she's on her side, facing me with her tiny palms tucked under the pillow, her breathing soft and soothing.

A clock ticks somewhere in the house, echoing through the halls; combined with the heat of her body and the gentle caress of air as it escapes her nose, I can almost grasp a shred of serenity. It teases my fingertips, the edge of oblivion taunting my fury.

But I plunged off the deep end long ago, and I'm no longer interested in swimming back to shore.

Curling my fingers over the hem of her blanket, I tug the plush material away, my cock springing to life at the sight of her bare skin.

Christ.

It's the first time I've seen her naked form since the other night in the tub, and my breathing grows erratic as I recall how she came with my name on her lips.

How I would have given up music entirely, in favor of hearing that one song on her lips forever.

Still, I've never seen her this close up and naked, at least not completely. Not long enough to appreciate it.

The night at the tattoo shop, the shape of her sopping cunt and the feel of her thighs against my ears are seared into my memory, but the top half of her body is uncharted territory.

I swallow, a hard knot lodging at the base of my throat as my eyes rake over her. Those peach-colored nipples pebble as they're exposed to the cool air, and I grip the blanket tighter, resisting the urge to strum my thumb over one.

It's bad enough that I'm looking.

Perfectly swollen tits give way to a flat, slightly concave stomach, which tapers to round hips and porcelain thighs.

Folding the cover back so it rests just above her knees, I sit back and admire the shadowed view.

God, the things I want to do to her.

Depraved things—things a man like me, stuck indefinitely in the public eye, shouldn't crave. But every cell in my body screams out for her, like sheep helpless against the slaughter.

A whimper startles me, and my eyes shoot to her face, afraid she's woken and caught me staring. Her eyes are still closed, though. Relaxed as she traipses through dreamland, completely unaware of the danger sitting at her bedside.

My hand twitches, my gaze sliding over the slender slope of her neck, tracing the ridges of her collarbone, the dip of her navel. She shifts, scissoring her thighs as if trying to get comfortable, and the movement draws my attention to her partially-covered hip.

Lifting a hand, I gently reach out, trying to suppress the trembling. Eyes snapping to hers, I watch, rapt, as my fingers sweep over the ink there, tracing the slightly raised lines as if they weren't seared into my being the moment I put them there.

Angel.

Something pinches in my chest, prodding at my heart like a hot poker as I crest the point of the letter A. She shifts again, inching closer, and my finger moves higher; it brushes against something rough, and I frown, following the trail of distinctly smooth skin disappearing under the blanket.

It zips up toward her belly button, stopping at the edge, and when she rolls to her back, I see a flash of shiny white.

Planting my palm on the other side of her, I lean in to try and get a better look; the closer my nose gets to her body, the stronger that peppermint scent gets, and I'm thrust back in time to the night we met.

When I buried my head between her legs—but not before she kept me from raising her shirt.

My heart weighs heavy as I determine it's a large scar, but I have no idea where she could have gotten it.

From what I've been able to learn about Riley Kelly, her mother was a known drug addict, and they were far from well off, but there are no extensive medical records of hers detailing the kind of assault something this large would entail.

I *know* scars. This is not the kind you come by honestly.

Sitting back on the bed, I absently slip a finger beneath the band of my watch, satisfying the ever-present itch lurking beneath my tattoos.

I start to cover her back up, hating the sympathy pulsing around the edges of my soul, desperately seeking entrance. If I allow myself to feel bad for her, then I lose my advantage, and my entire reason for coming to this literal hell is moot.

Riley's head jerks on the pillow, twisting as she lets out another whimper. Her fingers tangle in the sheets, clutching them to her chest, and as she thrashes, I see the same slivers of perturbed flesh on her face; one at the corner of her mouth, the other slashed across her cheek.

What the fuck?

Those, I definitely would've noticed in New York. Most of what I did that night was stare at her perfectly symmetrical nose and imagine how soft her lips would be.

Frowning, I glance down at them, recalling they'd been softer than I ever could've imagined. That kissing her felt like coming home after a lifetime of not even realizing you'd been missing.

Deciding to return back to my cabin to investigate her history further, I lean down, inhaling and trying to see if I can sense a slight change in the scent of her lotion.

My hand comes up, fingers coasting over her jaw, and I let out the smallest sigh.

Then, her eyes pop open.

23

My vision is blurry as I peel back my eyelids, the presence of someone in the room yanking me from an Ambien-induced sleep.

At first, I'm irritated that not even pills can keep my fight-or-flight response subdued.

When my gaze focuses on the hauntingly beautiful face hovering over mine, though, I can't help wondering if this actually *is* a dream.

Tension ripples through my stomach, tying my organs into knots.

Jesus Christ, this has to be a dream.

There's no possible way Aiden fucking James is sitting on my bed right now, staring at me like he's seen a ghost.

Somehow, he doesn't look spooked; he looks like someone who lives in an abandoned house *because* of the spirits. Like he's been expecting me.

But that can't be right—I never even told him my real name all those years ago, and if he were here right now, *calm resignation* is the last thing I feel he'd be experiencing.

The longer he stares, a still silence coursing between us while our breaths mingle, the more convinced I become that I'm still sleeping.

It's the only plausible explanation.

"Pretty girl."

Oxygen catches in my throat, and I feel my eyes widen, but for some reason, I'm detached from the actual movement itself. Just like when he lifts a palm, dragging a ringed finger along my jaw; his calloused print is rough on my skin, but it's almost as if there's a thin barrier separating us.

Something protecting me.

When he pauses at the corner of my mouth, the air stuck in my esophagus escapes in a panicked *whoosh*, and my chest compresses with horror.

I glance at the lamp across the room, then back, pushing my head into the pillow in an effort to evade his touch. Hoping that he can't see well in the dim lighting.

Gray eyes narrow just slightly; his stormy gaze penetrates deep, pricking at my soul like a needle drawing blood.

"So many secrets," he says, voice as low and gravelly as ever. His hand shifts, his thumb coming to my mouth and sliding over the scar there up to the one on my cheek.

Applying the slightest pressure, he traces the jagged sliver, a blank expression on his face.

My mouth dries up, my tongue sticking to the roof of my mouth like sandpaper.

"Nothing to say, even after all this time?" he continues, cocking his head to one side. "No questions, concerns... *admissions?*"

I try to make my lips move, try to make some sort of noise to appease him, but my body refuses to cooperate.

He tsks, letting his hand fall to my collarbone. My lungs expand, expressing a gust of air when I remember I'm naked.

That my entire body is bare beneath my blankets.

Just centimeters away from the handsome phantom before me.

As if sensing my renewed panic, Aiden hooks a finger in the comforter, tugging without displacing it. I tighten every muscle in my body, folding in on myself to keep out the intrusion.

"I have a lot of questions for you." His eyes dip to my throat, and I feel his thumb sweep back and forth over my skin, just above the hem of the cover. "Should I quiz you now, or is this not a good time, with you being naked and all?"

Forcing a swallow, I finally find my voice. "How are you—"

"Ah, ah."

His free hand flies toward me so fast I don't even have time to register its direction until it lands. He claps it over my mouth, mushing my lips into my teeth, and I wince at the sharp sting of bone cutting into sensitive flesh.

"You had your chance to speak, and you didn't take it. Now it's my turn. Besides, it shouldn't matter *how* I'm here; did you honestly think you'd be able to hide from me forever?"

Yes. That was the goal, anyway. My escape from Riley Kelly was meant to provide me safety, but also keep me from ever having to face the secret my brother made me keep.

Pulling the blanket down, he exposes the tops of my breasts, keeping my nipples covered. I hiss, back bowing as the cool air lashes against me, and he tightens his hold on my mouth, pushing my head farther into the pillow.

"For every question you get wrong, or you don't answer, or that just generally pisses me off, I'll slide this blanket down until your dignity ceases to exist. Got it?"

God, please let this be a dream.

I glance at the table to my right where my phone sits, and he follows my line of sight. With a heavy sigh, Aiden rips one corner of the throw off my right breast, and I squeal as the apex pebbles because of the sudden change in temperature.

His nostrils flare. "Don't even think about calling anyone. You *owe* me this, at the very least, and you fucking know it, my little liar. So, either take this like a good girl, or I'll put some truth behind those goddamn rumors you spread about me."

His words slice me wide open, the accusation flying directly from his mouth somehow worse than knowing someone made it up in the first place.

Because not only was the rumor concocted, but now my worst fears regarding it are confirmed; Aiden believes I started them.

I can see it reflected in his eyes. The kind of anguish you gain from a personal betrayal, it hardens you and sharpens your focus at the same time it snuffs out any misguided positive notions about the world.

It's like looking in a mirror.

Heart pounding, I manage a stiff nod, and he lightens the pressure on my mouth.

Barely, but still.

"Okay. First, I want to know why you did it."

Sliding his hand to my chin, he raises an eyebrow.

I exhale harshly. "I *didn't* do it—"

The end of my sentence is muffled by his palm slapping back over me; this time, his rings scrape my teeth, and he exposes my left breast with a snarl.

"Of course, the first thing out of your mouth would be more lies. Christ, you probably don't even know how to help yourself, do you?"

A gurgling sound rips through the back of my throat as he leans in, his mouth hovering dangerously close to my areola. It tightens as hot, damp breath whispers over the peak, and my pulse races, thudding like a stampede between my ears.

Terror seizes my brain with its chilly claws, that age-old sense of paranoia flaring in my stomach and making me tremble.

But something else happens, too. Aiden's mouth parts, minty air washing over my nipple, and through the disgust, a fog of clarity appears. Something inside me that recognizes him, and my body's response to the things he's done to it.

As he stares up at me, lips a ghost of a touch away from my skin, the image of him kneeling between my thighs in a similar fashion blindsides me.

Not because I haven't thought about it since that night, but because it feels an inappropriate memory to have while he's torturing me.

Heat thrums between my thighs, arousal coiling tight in

my pelvis, and I shake with an entirely new fear; that he'll be able to tell how he affects me.

And for some reason, part of me wants him to.

When he shifts, pulling his head back, a huff of relief decompresses my lungs. The smile that graces his face as he sits up is sinister, replacing the desire with dread, and I blink to try and stave off the whiplash.

"So, *that's* how you want to play this." His thumb flicks across my now-sticky skin—so soft, I'm sure I imagined it.

That makes me ache worse.

"What kind of girl makes up such lies about the man she's so desperate and needy for?" he asks, but this time his hand stays over my mouth, informing me that it's a rhetorical question.

The blanket slides lower, passing over my stomach until air hits my belly button. I don't even have time to react, or freak out about him seeing the scar there, because the blanket doesn't stop moving. He rips it off once he passes my hips, baring most of my body and soul on the bed, just barely hiding the imperfection by my tattoo.

Gray eyes feast on my naked form; if sight were palpable, I'd be a sobbing explosion of pleasure right now, trembling from the lack of warmth as it mixes with the fire in his gaze.

Nostrils flare. His inked hand grips my knee, bending it slightly.

Opening me.

I make a noise in my throat, something that's supposed to be a protest, but it cuts off when he leans in.

Eyes on mine, he doesn't touch me any more than he already is.

He just hovers, watching for my reaction.

And then he *inhales.*

I gasp so hard my lungs nearly burst. No other thoughts process—not about him seeing my scar, or what he's doing here, or if he's going to hurt me.

Just the elation from that singular action.

There's something so pure and erotic about him *smelling* me, as if he's trying to brand my scent into his being, that a tiny wave of euphoria tears through me, threatening to break my spine with its reverb.

Aiden's smile shifts again, and he licks his lips, glancing down like a man prepping for his next meal.

As my pleasure dissipates, that familiar, comfortable feeling takes hold again, and reality crashes down, shattering the illusion that I've crafted around me.

My body stiffens, awareness trickling into the recesses of my brain that were still subdued from the sleeping pill.

This man has broken into my house.

Tracked me here.

Which means he not only knows where I'm at, but my real identity.

And I'm lying here, letting him accost me. Not taking danger seriously, which is what got me in this fucking mess in the first place.

Bucking against his hold as nausea curdles in my gut, I thrash and whimper until he finally loses his grip on my mouth. He shuffles backward, poised as if ready to grab me again, but I lean over the side of the bed just in time for vomit to spew from my mouth.

It puddles on the carpet, right on top of the slightest hint of a boot print, and my chest caves in, buckling as I realize just how fucked I am.

I wipe my lips with the back of my hand, and Aiden's wraps around my hair, pulling it into a tight ponytail; he grips hard, his fist against my scalp, and yanks my head back so I'm forced to blink up at the ceiling.

"I hope you've enjoyed your scot-free life for the last three years." His breath washes over my face, minty and fresh, and I swallow around it. "Because all of that is over now, *angel*. You're going to atone for what you did, even if I have to *coax* it from your sweet little cunt. Especially now that I know how badly she still wants me."

Twisting my head in his direction, he crashes his lips to mine, pushing them open with his tongue. I grunt, trying to shove him out—absolutely horrified by the idea of him tasting puke—but then he pulls back and drops me before I can even blink.

"Remember what I said about telling anyone about this," he says, pushing to his feet. His clothes are black, his boots clunky, and there's a degree of savagery behind his eyes that I don't remember seeing that night in New York City.

Without another word, he stalks from the room, and I collapse against the bed as apprehension breathes through my pores. My tongue shifts, curling around something foreign that wasn't there seconds ago.

A peppermint.

24

"You're sure they can't come any sooner?"

I wipe condensation from the bathroom mirror, glaring at myself when a hole appears. Phone pressed to my ear, I'm dripping on the tile in my post-shower haze, trying to figure out if last night was real or not.

When I woke up, the only evidence was the stain of vomit on the floor, which looked as if it'd been scrubbed—but I can't remember doing it.

In fact, the last thing I remember is tasting peppermint, but this morning, there was no sticky candy residue left in my mouth.

Not to mention, I had on an oversized Metallica T-shirt, which I definitely wasn't wearing around Aiden.

I've gone most of the day walking on eggshells, afraid to leave the cabin on the off chance my memory is simply failing me again. Every closed door has been cautiously opened, every light left on, and every door locked tight.

If he is here in Lunar Cove, I'm not going to make his access to me easy.

On that same note, if last night *wasn't* a dream... wouldn't he have already been back?

Grasping on to that hope, I reach for the bottle of lotion on my sink, squirting some into my hands as Kal's voice comes over the line again.

"Apparently, a wildfire in the area is messing with cell towers and power grids, so the security company is prioritizing house visits based on urgency. You're pretty low on the list." A pause, and then he clears his throat. "Right? You *are* still low on the list?"

My mouth opens to say no, no, I'm not. That the person I wasn't really hiding from has somehow found me, and something tells me this turn of events is worse than if the people related to my attacker had shown up instead.

The attackers would probably make their revenge quick; I'd either be dead or so drugged up that I'd feel dead before I even had time to process their arrival.

Aiden, on the other hand, seems like the kind to take his time.

His threat rings out like a gong, echoing in my mind as I nod to myself, sticking to my convictions—stupid and risky as they may be—not to tell Kal.

"Yeah, I'm still low urgency," I say, the lie bitter on my tongue. It tastes like betrayal, though I'm not sure whose back the knife is stuck in. "Did they give you an ETA, at least?"

"Shouldn't be any later than the weekend. If not, I'm liable to fly out to Maine and force your brother to come install the shit himself."

A small, sad smile creases my lips. "Please. Camera installation is beneath him."

"Neglecting his sister because of some long-winded pity party is beneath him," Kal says, and I can practically hear his eyes roll.

His observation stings, and I smooth the lotion in my hands down over my thighs, keeping the phone pressed between my ear and shoulder. "Yeah, well. You can blame our mom for that."

"I could, but eventually everyone comes to a point in their lives where they have to own up to their shortcomings. Our experiences are meant to mold, not define us."

"You should put that on a T-shirt."

"Maybe I'll have one made and sent out to you as a Christmas gift."

Warmth fills my chest like rays of sunshine, but it's the kind that doesn't quite reach your limbs because parts of you are stuck in the shadows.

I stand up straight, smoothing my hand over the scar on my hip. It still tingles from where Aiden crept dangerously close to it, and I blow out a breath, trying to erase the memory.

"You're *sure* everything is okay? You don't usually call right after I've been to visit."

Chewing on my bottom lip, I nod again, even though he can't see me. My heart throbs inside my chest, painfully aware that my brother should be the one asking this, but once again, a day has gone by without us speaking.

"Yes, *dad*. Maybe I just missed that sparkling personality of yours."

Kal gives a short half chuckle—as close to a genuine laugh as I'll probably ever get from him. "I'll let you know when the security guys update me. Text if you need me before then."

When we hang up, I stare at myself in the mirror for a long moment, reveling in the irony of me having asked one of the most notorious men on the East Coast for help years ago, and how he's turned into more of a brother to me than my biological sibling.

I'm not sure what it means—probably nothing.

But if a man like that can be reformed, it gives me hope for Boyd.

Sighing, I grab my robe from where it hangs on the back of the bathroom door, my abs tensing as I reenter the bedroom. Pausing at the threshold, my eyes dart from wall to wall, taking stock and ensuring everything is in its proper place.

Mainly, I'm checking to make sure there are no crazy rock stars hiding out where I can't see.

Satisfied with the lack of psychos, my shoulders slump slightly, and I walk over to the nightstand, crouching down to undo the drawer at the bottom. A simple combination lock keeps it secure, and I scroll through each set of numbers until it pops free.

The pistol Boyd gave me before my move sits inside, collecting dust from never having been used; it's been locked in the nightstand for three years, the need for protection beyond the basics never having risen before.

Dream or not, I don't want to take that chance anymore.

The weapon is heavy in my hand as I pull it out, and unease snakes along my spine, burrowing in each divot there.

Cold metal cools my skin as I turn it over, trying to remember the safety tips my brother gave when he shoved it in my suitcase.

"Keep the safety locked at all times. The presence of a gun alone is often enough to subdue an attacker; don't kill yourself in return."

"Aim to kill if you ever need to turn off the safety. You're not a cop. Do what you have to."

"Once it's out, don't ever take your eyes off of it."

That last comment sticks with me most, though not for the reason Boyd probably hoped. I walk to the full-length mirror across the room, so focused on the weapon that I don't even notice when someone steps up behind me.

It's stupid, really.

I should know better.

Just because you think you're alone doesn't make it so.

A sigh washes over my hair, and I grit my teeth.

Lifting my gaze in the mirror, I try to ignore the sudden racing of my heart at his proximity.

Looming over me, his front doesn't quite touch my back, but his presence scalds my skin all the same. A finger comes up, tracing the curve of my hip as gray eyes flash, zeroing in on the gun.

"Do you even know how to use one of these?" he asks, and I hate the flurry of butterflies his rasp sends through me.

My jaw clenches, and I clasp the neckline of my robe together with my free hand. "It's not rocket science."

"No, but it is a little predictable. Woman gets a stalker,

thinks she can intimidate him with a firearm. You know how those movies go."

"Oh, you're my stalker now? What an interesting turn of events."

I don't know why I say it, don't know why I'm antagonizing instead of demanding he leave, or calling the cops, but for some reason, logic flies out the window when I'm within spitting distance of this man.

It's got to be lingering groupie brain. The power of stardom that lets celebrities think they can treat normal people however they want, sans any consequences.

Or maybe I like the way my sarcasm makes those silvery eyes rage.

Maybe I agree—*I do owe him.*

"Was I not clear last night, *Riley*?"

My stomach cramps, hearing my real name on his lips.

Leaning in, he fits his palm around the gun's grip over my hand, his finger brushing outside the trigger. The barrel turns, resting at the hollow point of my throat, and I can't stop the gulp that ensues.

"I'm your reckoning."

In a flash, he's shifting, hitting the release with his thumb so the magazine pops out, and then he lets the unloaded gun clatter to the floor.

I swallow, steadying myself by planting my hands on either side of the mirror. My fingers curl around the frame, and he steps in, fitting himself against me.

"Three years," he says, tilting his head down so his nose is buried in my hair, words reverberating against my skull. "I've thought about you all that time. Imagined the look in your eyes when I finally found you; how wide they'd be, swollen with nervousness."

He squeezes my hip, then moves to the middle of the robe, hooking his thumb in the tie.

"Are you ready to tell me why you did it?" His other hand comes up to the other side of the tie, and he begins to pull the loops apart. My posture stiffens, fear immobilizing me, but as goose bumps trickle over my skin and tighten my nipples, it's clear fear and arousal are very close friends in my body.

A wave of nausea rolls through me at the thought, and I clench my jaw so hard that it feels like it might break, warding off the onslaught of feeling.

Willing myself to turn it off.

Block it out.

As the robe falls open, baring me once again to his hungry gaze, a numbing sensation spreads through my limbs like liquid Novocain.

His hands fall to my hips once again, pulling the satin material so I'm more exposed, and I draw in a shaky breath as he stares at me in the daytime.

"It really is a shame you turned out to be such a little snake," he whispers, shifting me back so I'm pressed fully into him.

Where I can feel *everything*.

While anger rolls off of him in heated waves, the erection digging into my ass makes it clear that's not his singular motivation.

Throat thick with an emotion I can't quite place, I glare at him in the mirror. "Why are you here, Aiden? What do you want me to do?"

"Suffer."

He grunts the word into my hair, his palm skating over my stomach, thumb swiping the underside of my breast.

Fingers ghost up, whispering over my nipple, before continuing their ascent and wrapping lightly around my throat.

"I want you to suffer, Riley. However I have to make that happen. I'm not leaving this hellhole until you have."

"I'm sorry," I choke out, unable to stop the tears from welling up in my eyes. I pinch them shut, but the complete sheen of terror remains, wringing my bones dry. "I didn't mean to—"

"Intentions mean shit when lives get destroyed. Keep your apologies, angel. It's too late for them to be of any use to me."

Downstairs, the doorbell rings—my single saving grace, if the predatory look in his stony gaze is any indication.

For a second, his fingers flex around my neck, applying just enough pressure to rob me of my breath.

"Jesus Christ. Fear looks fucking *delectable* on you."

The doorbell rings again, and his nostrils flare. He releases me with a harsh shove, stepping back and folding his arms over his chest. I take a second to study him in the mirror—noting the coarse stubble lining his chiseled jaw, the way his dark-brown hair curls slightly farther over the tips of his ears—before I turn around, quickly resituating my robe.

"Expecting company?" he asks, leaning against the pine bedpost.

Wrapping my arms around my stomach, I consider how much I should tell him about my relationships here. Clearly, the man standing in front of me is off his rocker, and far detached from the one I used to fall asleep listening to as he crooned sad songs in my ears.

Or maybe sanity is just the price of living.

Then again, if he knows enough to be able to sneak into

my cabin completely undetected, odds are he knows more about my life than I'm aware of.

"Three years. I've thought about you all that time."

Chills run along my spine, like an ice pick being scraped along the vertebrae.

A wicked smile plays at his lips, and he reaches up, dragging his thumb over the bottom one. My eyes catch on the Medusa tattooed on that hand; she stares back, angry like he is.

I wonder if he wishes he could turn me to stone.

"Go and let him in, pretty girl."

I wince, and his smile widens, clearly excited by the fact that he continues to catch me off guard.

"How do you know it's a him?"

"When it comes to you, I know everything. I've done my research." His head cocks to one side, perverse amusement flashing in his gaze. "Now, do you want to tell your friend you're unable to go to his art show, or should I?"

25

RILEY'S NERVES make my dick hard.

There, I said it.

Acknowledged the beast, so I might be able to get control of it.

There's no point in exacting revenge, in making Riley's life hell, if she stands a chance at getting off on it. And my cock really, really wants her to get off.

Over and over, with her tongue down my throat and my name on her lips.

Scrubbing a hand down the side of my face, I watch as she leaves the bedroom, the silky material of her purple robe swishing against the backs of her thighs. Gripping my knees, I take a second to collect myself and wait to hear the front door open downstairs before I follow quietly.

I see the second she registers that I've come downstairs; standing in the open doorway, her knuckles bleach in their hold against the frame and her spine straightens, but she doesn't make a move to greet me.

Or introduce me to her *friend*.

"...was hoping you'd come to the earlier viewing, so you could help me decide which pieces to put out."

The sound of a man's voice—the one I recognize from the answering machine—has irritation sparking hot just below my skin, and it takes every ounce of willpower I have not to shove the door all the way back and stake my claim as soon as I reach them.

Instead, I slink behind the door and lean my shoulder against it, letting my weight fall into her. She clenches her jaw, working it from side to side as if my being here annoys her.

"I'm really sorry, Caleb, I just don't feel like going out."

Gratification swells like a balloon inside my chest.

"You never feel like going out," *Caleb* says, and I despise the way he talks, like he knows her. Intimately. Clearly, I've been too occupied with watching her to notice those around her. "But every time you do, you end up having a great time."

Grinding my teeth together, I inch closer to her, bound by an intrinsic need to possess her. My hand lifts, grazing the lacy hem of her robe as my index finger slips under, brushing gently over her smooth skin.

She sucks in a breath and jerks her hip, trying to get away, but I go with her. There's only so far she can move before she inadvertently exposes me, and she knows it.

"That's true," she answers her guest, our intruder, and that she's giving him attention while I'm standing right fucking here has me seeing red.

My palm drags backward, gliding over the soft curve of her ass. I pause, pinching lightly just to hear her gasp again —the sound makes my chest feel light, like a thousand butterflies taking flight inside the cavity.

"I'll bet you don't have as great of a time as you did in that tattoo shop with me," I say, my voice just barely audible.

Riley coughs the second my mouth opens, covering my words while she keeps her attention on the man standing on the porch.

Pressing my lips together, I try again. "Has he made you come yet, angel? Or does he spend all his time talking?"

"Maybe you could ask Jade to go with you," she suggests, her voice an octave too loud. Even though she's speaking over me, her insistence that he go alone floods me with pride, loving that she's taking direction so well already.

Her willingness will eventually make the destruction so much sweeter.

I hear Caleb exhale. "Jade hates art in all forms. She isn't going to be any help."

"Yeah, but—"

"Come *on*, Angel. If I open without the most beautiful girl in town at my side, no one's going to bother showing up."

Her chin moves, eyes darting toward me in her peripheral vision. My hand freezes at the dimples in her lower back, my thumb stroking softly over the indentations.

Anger billows inside my throat, making it impossible to breathe as violence surges through me. Limbs twitching, I stave off the urge to throw the door open and let my rings rearrange the skin on his face, and instead focus on the anxious girl beside me.

As if sensing a shift in our atmosphere, she clears her throat and leans harder against the door.

Protecting him.

Nostrils flaring, I let my hand slip over her ass, fingers slowly sweeping between her cheeks. Riley squeaks, rising up on her toes, and grips the door even tighter.

"Jesus, are you okay?" Caleb asks, fueling my rage.

"*Angel*, hm?" I hiss, curling my fingers so I'm cupping her from behind. She's dripping, arousal slick against her silken skin, and I bite down on the inside of my cheek until I taste blood, just to keep from moaning out loud.

"Naughty girl, letting someone else call you the nick-name *I* gave you. Very disrespectful."

She shifts, trying to escape as I probe deeper, delving between her folds until I find her pulse. Swirling the tip of my index finger around her clit once, twice, I revel in the shudder that racks her body, throwing her off balance.

Leaning in, I fit myself against her side and yank the door open wider, ensuring the length of my arm is hidden from where Caleb stands.

He blinks, dark eyes going round as saucers as he takes me in, then reaches up to run a hand over his spirally black hair. He's wearing khakis and a green button-down, holding two to-go cups in his hands, and I take note of the Jeep parked in the drive, stashing that information for later.

"Oh," Caleb says, and the disappointment in his tone is *potent*. "I'm... sorry, Angel, I didn't realize you had company."

I continue the sensual assault on Riley's clit, my move-ments so slow, there's no way he can tell what I'm doing.

At least, as long as he doesn't pay much attention to *her*.

Beads of sweat sprout along her pink hairline, and she's sawing a hole in her bottom lip with her teeth. Her breathing spikes as I abandon my current task and move back, brushing her entrance.

I circle it, teasing, reveling in the blush that creeps up her neck, dyeing her skin a similar shade as her hair.

"I don't," Riley exhales. "Have company, I mean. Aiden was just leaving."

Grinning, I push the tip of my finger into her, wishing I could swallow the sound that rips out of her throat. Caleb frowns, squinting at us, but I just laugh and yank her closer.

"Aw, *Angel's* being modest. I just got here."

I'm knuckle deep in her cunt now, the wet, constricting heat of her inner muscles making it hard for me to concentrate as I move in painstakingly slow thrusts.

"Hey." Caleb takes a single step forward, and for some reason, it spurs me on; I start fucking her faster, adding a second finger even as she clamps down around me, so tight I think I could come just from imagining putting my dick in her.

Her hands ball into fists at her sides as I speed up, stroking against the spot that has her pressing her weight down into me.

She's soaked, drenching my entire fucking hand, and I hope he can smell her.

Hope the scent of her desire, as wrong and perverse as it may be, follows him to his little art show tonight, and then all the way back home. The same way it's followed me for years, haunting my fucking nightmares even when I knew better.

Anger resurfaces as another tiny noise comes from her,

and she's biting her lip again, her face straining as she seems to try to resist rocking back.

I plunge deeper, rougher, wondering how he isn't hearing the slurping sounds. I'm on the brink, my cock so hard that I think I might pass out from the blood loss to the rest of my body.

Caleb tips his head to one side, eyes darting between us.

"You're that singer Angel's always raving about," he says finally, a smile spreading across his face.

My thrusts stutter, the breath escaping my lungs in a single, harsh gust. I glance down at Riley, but she doesn't look at anyone, her face taking on a tomato hue.

Arching an eyebrow, I feel her pussy contract around me, clamping down as she tries to suck me all the way in. The sensation makes me dizzy, fucking delirious as her scent fills the air, but I continue on my mission, stroking quickly.

Trying to push her over the edge before he leaves.

"Is that so?" I ask Caleb, grinning as Riley's mouth parts. "I do more than sing, you know. I'm also very good with my hands."

Riley grunts.

"Well, whatever you do, she talks about you all the time." He glances at her, eyes widening. "Jesus, are you okay?"

"She's fine," I say, punctuating the words each time I bottom out. "I think she was starting to feel a little under the weather though, which is why she'll have to miss your show."

He doesn't look convinced, and she shifts away from him, forcing me as deep inside of her as I can go. She's fluttering around me, slowly unraveling, and I chew on my tongue in an attempt to keep from pushing her robe up and just fucking her right here.

Her movements are primal, needy, and my cock leaks against my thigh, desperate to finish what we started.

At the moment, I don't even care how wrong it is, or how stupid.

I just want her.

"I-I'm fine, Caleb," she breathes, eyelids drooping. "But I can't go with you tonight."

"Yeah, of course. You look sick. Should I call a doctor?"

"No!" she croaks, and I smother a grin.

"She just needs a little stress relief," I say, pulling her backward and starting to ease the door shut without removing myself from her body. "It was nice meeting you, Cole."

"Caleb."

"Doesn't matter. It won't come up again."

With the heel of my boot, I kick the door shut just as Riley begins to come apart around me.

She sags forward, bracing her hands on the wall as she writhes in ecstasy, pinching her eyes shut.

And then I withdraw my fingers.

The sound that comes out of her mouth is otherworldly, like the cry of an animal in heat. Whirling around, she glares at me, and I smirk, pressing both fingers inside my mouth and licking them clean.

Those pretty blue eyes flare, explosive seas crashing against the sandy shore. But then she blinks, and they're just resentful.

"What the hell?" she snaps, hands balling at her sides. Her face is flushed and glistening with sweat.

"Did you think I was gonna let you come? You haven't been a very good girl, Riley, nor did you say the magic word."

Her eyebrows knit together. "Magic word? What—"

Cutting her off, I wrap her hair around my fist, tilt her head back, and press a filthy kiss to her mouth. It's all teeth and tongue, pent-up rage and unresolved sexual tension, and I almost lose myself in it.

"Do you like the way you taste on my tongue?" I mutter against her, exploring and warring as our lips mold into each other.

She moans, fingers scratching a path up my chest, but then I shove back, breaking the connection.

"I can't believe I just let you finger me in front of my friend. What's wrong with you?"

"Nothing's been right with me for a very long time. You're just now catching up."

Wiping her mouth with the back of her palm, she huffs. "That was mean."

I brush a hand over my shirt and shrug. "That was just the beginning."

Without another word, I get the fuck out of her cabin, letting the promise linger in the air before I can make things worse.

Taking my cock out the second I'm back in my rental, I beat myself dry to the image of her spasming around me and the little sounds she makes.

My name coming from her lips.

And when I climax, hot ropes of cum staining the pair of silk panties I've wrapped around the crown of my dick, I try not to let it bother me that her friend said she told him about me.

26

GUILT IS SUCH A FUNNY, foreign little thing.

It's this entity inside us that reflects our greatest insecurities, placing the weight of shame and blame between our shoulder blades, even when we've done nothing wrong.

But there's a certain level of comfort within it, too. If we can ascertain the issue, locate it within ourselves, well... then we can fix it.

If we fix it, then there's no longer anything to feel bad about.

Problem solved.

Except, when you spend so long adopting everyone else's

resentment, that bitter, insecure feeling becomes part of you. Weaves into your soul and codes itself into your skin.

Pretty soon, *everything* is your fault. All the time.

You tiptoe around people just to avoid upsetting them, because it's easier than admitting to yet *another* of your shortcomings.

As I sit in the back booth at Dahlia's Diner, folding a straw wrapper into tiny white squares, it feels like I'm drowning in them, unable to pinpoint an exact place in my past where the blame began.

Snowflakes drift from the gray sky outside the window, and I wrap my fingers around my mug, inhaling the sweet smell of hot chocolate.

The diner's empty except for Jade at the counter and a cook in the kitchen—par for the course in the middle of the week. I don't know if it's the knowledge that Aiden's in town, or just the general sense of dread that seems to follow me, but it somehow seems less cozy than normal.

In truth, I should probably be more freaked out by the fact that Aiden James is here at all. That he spent the last three years obsessed with the idea of exacting revenge against a girl he knew for one night.

I definitely shouldn't be letting him shove his fingers inside me, especially when he's made it clear that he's only here to punish me.

The nagging thought that I hardly *let* him do it flares up in my brain for the millionth time since he left the cabin yesterday. It's followed by familiar unease, settling in the pit of my stomach where my mother's ghost holds it hostage.

You didn't exactly stop him, though, did you? Worthless little slut.

Blotting out the sound of her voice, I try to focus on what's important.

How Aiden found me still remains a mystery, as does the question if he knows where I am, who else does?

And how long do I have before they show up?

The bell hanging above the front door chimes as someone enters the diner, but I'm too busy staring into my mug to pay much attention. My body, however, sits on high alert, primed to run at the first hint of danger.

It's my heart that's having a hard time keeping up.

A shadow falls over the table, and I close my eyes, taking a deep breath. Every cell in my body expects to be shoved down the booth seat, or for the table to be jostled as Aiden slides in across from me, but neither of those things happens.

One of my eyes pops back open, snapping to the right of me; brown suede boots stand with their toes pointed in my direction, and as I drag my gaze up over faded Levi's and an Aspen University hoodie, I exhale with relief.

"Mind if I join you?" Caleb asks, pulling the black knit hat off his head.

I nod, sliding my closed laptop out of the way, and he drops into the seat across from me.

"Shouldn't you be working?" I ask, glancing out the window at his gallery, where I can see an elderly couple staring into the storefront.

"Shouldn't *you* be?" he counters, leaning his head back against the seat. "I thought that's why you come to Dahlia's during the day, so you can work undisturbed and not have to make yourself lunch."

"Hot cocoa break." I raise the mug, taking a sip. "Besides,

I don't have any clients lined up for a bit because of Thanksgiving. *You,* on the other hand, seem pretty busy."

Jade comes over and sets a red mug down in front of Caleb; they've been friends for so long, she knows what he wants without him even having to ask, and I can't help the bubble of jealousy that pops in my chest at the familiarity.

"So," Jade says, cocking one hip out as she rests a hand in her black apron pocket. "I hear I have you to thank for why I was pulled from a comfy evening at home last night and forced to put on a cocktail dress and *mingle.*"

My eyes flicker to Caleb, who just takes a drink of his cocoa. Glancing at Jade, I give what I hope is a sheepish smile.

"I only suggested he ask. To be honest, I didn't think you'd agree."

She scoffs, rolling her green eyes as she hooks a thumb at Caleb. "Yeah, try saying no to this guy. He wouldn't fucking shut up about it, and his whining was distracting me from my shows."

I smother a giggle. Though my age, Jade sometimes sounds like the oldest woman alive, and she's got the grumpy personality to match.

Boyd would probably love her.

Sadness breaks through the levee I've erected around my heart, and soon even that's bursting, unable to withhold it forever.

Caleb clears his throat, pulling me from where it feels like I'm drowning. "I don't whine."

"More than a horse, dude. But it's okay, because you make a mean apple crumble, which you promised to make for Thanksgiving dinner."

His eyes flicker to mine. "You're still coming to *that*, right?"

Pulling my bottom lip between my teeth, I hesitate. My mother and I never really did Thanksgiving when she was alive, on account of her usually being too high, so it's another holiday I don't necessarily care about celebrating.

Fiona does though, and for the last three years she's had feasts delivered to my doorstep, before showing up for the weekend and helping me eat it all.

This year, though, Caleb wore me down, and I'd agreed to go to his mother's house.

Of course, that was before Aiden James reentered my life just to sabotage it, and I'm not sure he's the most appropriate dinner guest in his current state.

"Don't you dare cancel," Caleb says, pointing his finger at me. He leans in, eyebrows drawing together. "Live a little, Angel. You don't want to end up like Mrs. Lindholm, with no friends and no one to stop by to entertain you when business is a little slow."

"Mrs. Lindholm has friends," I say, glancing out the window to her souvenir shop.

A shadowy figure sits on the bench just outside of it, long arms stretched over the back. He's got on black jeans and a gray puffer jacket, the hood pulled up so it obscures his face, but I'd know him anywhere.

My stomach knots, roving over bejeweled fingers as they grip the wood, remembering how they felt inside of me twenty-four hours ago.

Then, I remember the denial and the threat that came after.

"Mrs. Lindholm has a bridge club who she likes to gossip with, but that's about it." Caleb sighs, taking another drink of his hot chocolate. When he pulls away, foam paints his upper lip, and he licks it off.

"What's wrong with the bridge club?" Jade asks, folding her arms over her chest. "My mom's in it."

Caleb snorts. "I rest my case."

I don't know much about Jade's mom, except that she's a travel nurse and recent divorcée, but the way Jade's eyes harden leaves me with the feeling that there's more going on there than we know. And since I know all about complicated mother-daughter relationships, I feel responsible for changing the subject.

Swallowing over the lump in my throat, I reach forward for my laptop, sliding it into its leather case. "I'll think about Thanksgiving," I tell Caleb, looking out the window again.

When I do, Aiden's gone, and it feels like a pit opens up in the center of my chest, demanding to be filled—with what, I'm not sure.

"If it's a matter of politeness, you can bring your... houseguest."

Jade turns to me, her black ponytail swishing against her shoulders. "*You* have a houseguest?"

"Uh... sort of?"

"Sort of, as in it looked like he wants to be more than just your guest," Caleb says, his face scrunching up. I see a flicker of hurt there, hidden in his dark eyes, and it makes my stomach somersault.

"Well, I don't know about that."

Jade frowns. "Do we know him? Kind of rude of you to be dating and not tell us."

"No, you—"

"It's that singer she's obsessed with," Caleb cuts in, shooting me an amused look. "James something. You know, the one who was on the Sexiest Man Alive cover a couple of years ago?"

She just stares at him.

Sighing, Caleb rolls his eyes. "Jesus, Jade, you've got to join us in the twenty-first century."

Reaching into her apron pocket, she pulls out a quarter, and chucks it at him; it smacks his chin, dropping into his lap, and she sashays away to the front counter.

Rubbing the spot on his forehead, Caleb looks at me and sighs. "Seriously though, Angel. You're practically family at this point. I want to spend Thanksgiving with you."

My chest tightens. "I'll think about it."

He watches as I slide from the booth, slinging my laptop case over my shoulder, apprehension lining my insides like sticky venom.

"You'd better," is all he says, and I leave him there with both hot chocolate mugs, half expecting to be accosted the second I step foot from the diner.

The snow is falling a little heavier now, a light dusting covering the ground, but I don't see anyone outside.

Don't hear the crunching of footsteps or feel the heat from my stalker's body.

There are no gray eyes piercing through the winter air, locking in on me like they can't stand to look anywhere else.

For the first time in days, I'm completely and utterly alone.

27

"OKAY, and if we bring in the harmony here, the transition to the bridge is a lot smoother... son, are you even listening to me?"

Blinking, I sit up straight, my hands falling to the electric guitar in my lap. One single pawnshop in this backwater tourist town, and the only instrument they had was a black Viper. The irony has stuck with me since I bought the damn thing, returning to my rental before this virtual meeting with my father.

Thoughts of snakes have me looking up, casting my gaze across the lake to where Riley's cabin is still dark. She's been out all day, and I get the distinct feeling that she's avoiding me.

Like she thinks she can escape.

"...seriously, earth to Aiden? Good God, you're worse than your mother."

The mention of Callie has my eyes snapping to the computer screen in front of me, sitting forward. "You talked to Mom?"

"Not recently, no. Every conversation with her turns into a screaming match, and since I've got about a thousand conferences next week to go over your reintroduction to the world, I've been trying to save my voice."

"Well, I bet if you tried not cheating on her, she'd be more receptive."

"Christ, that was years ago, and we—" Cutting himself off, he reaches up, rubbing a hand over his bearded jaw. "You know what? Not worth arguing with you over again. Why are you asking about her, anyway? Has she not contacted you?"

I snort, leaning over my guitar. "She was barely speaking to me *before* I left."

In truth, a canyon-sized rift opened up between us when the accusations of my sexual misconduct were leaked. And even though I've maintained my innocence and provided countless hours of testimony and evidence disproving the claims, she still looks at me like I'm evil.

My thoughts drift back to Riley, the way I finger fucked her in front of her friend yesterday, just because I could.

Maybe Callie sees the truth, and that's why she stays away.

Maybe I am a monster.

"You sound disappointed, but trust me. The only thing

you're missing out on is the number of times she calls me *hijueputa* in a day."

"Yeah, well. Looks like I should've appointed you manager after all."

"Tried to tell you. There's a reason Calliope Santiago doesn't perform anymore, and it's got nothing to do with me."

Rubbing at the pair of wings inked on my left wrist, I sigh, readjusting the guitar in my lap. "Did the label listen to the demos I sent?"

"They did. Two of the three tracks were approved, but they think the last one is a little dark." My father cocks an eyebrow. "Even for you."

"We branded my entire act around grit. Now they don't like it?"

"It's not that, it's just... very niche. Harder to market. I think they want to make some tweaks, is all."

My fingers tighten on a tuner, and I frown. "I'm not interested in reworking the song."

"Aiden, be reasonable—"

"Complete creative control is *written* into my contract."

"Yes." Sitting back, he smooths a hand over his red tie and pushes his reading glasses higher up his nose. "And so is the clause about Symposium having final say on what gets put out."

Violence swims through my veins, but I bite my tongue, not in the mood to negotiate. Besides, when my father's made up his mind about something, there's very little that can be done to change it.

One of the only reasons he's still on my side through all of this.

While that should be a comfort, I can't help wondering if

the tepid support is worth everything I've given up in exchange.

We end the meeting, and I evade his attempts at getting me to promise to review the lyrics. I haven't been able to write anything in years, and the first time I do, the product is met with criticism.

Too dark, my ass.

As if damn near everything I've ever written isn't a thinly veiled call for help, backed by catchy hooks and upbeat pop music.

But people will believe anything they're told, as long as it fits the narrative they have of you in their mind.

For the people who just want to enjoy my music, or my celebrity, I guess the lyrics don't really matter.

They see exactly what my PR team wants them to.

Walking into the kitchen, I place one palm on the countertop and run the other down the side of my face.

Massaging the ache flaring up behind my brow bone, I look around the thirteen-hundred square foot cabin; it really isn't anything fancy, with its worn hardwood floors and the floral wallpaper in every room, but it was the only one available in town.

Its proximity to Riley was just a bonus.

Now that I've inhabited it for longer than twenty-four hours, it's beginning to show signs of Aiden James wear and tear; the floors and drawers are littered with peppermints, discarded clothing, and every scrap of paper with a lyric or musical notation I've written down over the last few days.

Candy wrappers, Post-it notes, a worn copy of *Metamorphoses* that I found in the upstairs bedroom and ripped the pages from. Whatever I can get my hands on when the muse speaks.

The faster I get it written, the easier it is to pretend my muse doesn't have any relation to *her*.

Grabbing the bottle of Jameson from one of the glass cabinets, I pour a finger into a glass and walk to the window, studying the cabin across the lake.

Snow blankets the ground and clings to tree branches, effectively smothering the outside world in its brightness. It sparkles as I cast my gaze over it, tracking up the pine log siding to the massive windows that face mine.

The sun is setting, the sky getting darker by the minute, but her lights are still off, and I can't help wondering where the fuck she is. If not for the meeting with my father, I'd have been tailing her all day, but part of the deal in what I'm here to do is that I have regular check-ins.

Because careers don't wait for revenge, and neither does my father.

Finally, a yellow glow emanates from the front porch, and I sip my drink, my cock hardening just at the thought of her. I'm expecting a cab to pull into her elevated drive, but instead I see a Jeep.

My grip on the glass stiffens, my rings digging into the skin on the inside of each finger.

I watch silently.

Seething.

She gets out the passenger side, and then starts up the front walk, but not before *Caleb* darts around the front of the vehicle, catching her elbow. He escorts her to the door, his hand dropping to her waist, and pulls her in for a hug when they reach their destination.

Rationally, I know he probably only helped her because the driveway is slick. I know I haven't seen her put any salt out.

Irrationality, though, is what embeds itself in my chest. It's what incinerates all logic, razing it to the ground the second he puts his hands on her.

And she doesn't flinch away.

As she disappears inside, her pink hair the last thing I see, I stand there for several beats, my heart beating so fast that I'm afraid it might pop free from my chest.

Caleb lingers in front of the door for a moment, and then he's turning, glancing out at the trees that surround the cabins, and landing on me.

I don't make a move to hide. Don't really care if he sees me watching.

Maybe if he does, he'll know better next time.

As volatile as Riley may be, as much as I may despise the little liar for what she's done, I'll be fucking damned if someone else ruins her before I can.

Or worse.

If they heal her, before my darkness can sink its talons in.

Caleb's hand lifts, though I'm not sure he knows who he's waving at. Probably just trying to be nice, like the little all-American boy he is.

My pulse thumps heavy between my ears, and I try not to envision his broken body lying bleeding on the snow-covered ground. Try not to think about how good it would feel to split my knuckles open on his bone, to maim him to the point that he could never touch her again.

I've never *really* been a violent man. Growing up, there was always a bodyguard or a security team around, and I never wanted to damage my hands and risk not being able to play anymore.

But right now, as bitterness coats my heart, hardening

around it like a wax mold, I would love nothing more than to hurt him.

Knowing I can't, though, as he returns to his Jeep and drives off, I slip into my shoes, pull on my coat, and head over to the person I know will put up with it.

28

I'M NOT sure how I can tell, but I know the second I'm no longer alone in my house.

There's just the slightest shift in temperature, like when a window's left open. The hairs on the back of my neck stand up first, prompting goose bumps to rise on my arms, and then my gut folds in on itself, warning me to flee.

Other than that, though, there's no change.

No floorboards creak, no thudding ensues as they come upstairs, and no one lurks in the shadows. It's just a feeling I have.

One second, I'm sitting at the vanity across from my bed,

removing my makeup, and the next, Aiden's standing behind me, glaring at our reflection.

He doesn't say anything. Just stares, storms raging in his gray eyes.

The kind of storms you lose yourself in. That destroy without discretion, obliterating everything in their paths, leaving behind worthless terrain.

My hand shakes where I hold the makeup wipe to my chin, but I don't move it, too afraid to see his reaction to my scarred skin in the daylight, with no barrier to hide behind.

He reaches up, brushing some of the pink hair from my shoulder.

"So, that's why I didn't notice your face before." His fingers are rough, new calluses sprouting overtop old ones, and he drags the pads across the back of my neck. "You were hiding."

I don't answer, unsure of what he wants me to even say.

Why wouldn't I hide from him?

From everyone?

It's the only thing I know how to do.

"Show me."

My eyebrows furrow at his command, and I shake my head.

His hand pauses, and I feel his fingers curl around my neck, their grip harsh. "It wasn't a fucking request."

I press the wipe harder against my face. "And my scars are none of your business."

"Wrong." He squeezes, gray eyes blazing. "Everything about you is my business, Riley. You no longer have an advantage in the information department."

All traces of the confident, charismatic rock star I met years ago are gone, and in his place stands this... monster.

An unrecognizable villain driven by the need to make me pay for something I didn't even do.

You didn't exactly make things better, though.

A lie of omission is still a lie, it's just dressed better.

"If you know so much, how come you seem so shocked by the scars?"

"Nothing in your medical history points to wounds that would leave such permanent evidence." Bending down, he moves so our faces are side by side in the mirror, and I can smell the slightest hint of whiskey on his breath.

My stomach rolls, fear seizing me like a volcano preparing to erupt.

"You looked at my medical history?"

The envelope that prompted my move flashes to mind, and I can't help wondering if he had something to do with it, after all.

"Don't sound so offended. It's not like you didn't violate *my* trust."

"What you did was *illegal*."

His brows rise. "As is lying about a crime. But don't worry, my little snake. I didn't find anything interesting."

I clench my jaw as he leans in and try to pretend I don't hear him inhale at my temple.

"Well, there was one thing," he murmurs, his lips grazing my hair as he speaks. "Something about vaginal scarring? Tell me, Riley, did someone hurt you, and you thought it'd be easier to blame me?"

Violent nausea curdles in my gut, a fiery ball of disgust spinning inside me until it's about to burst. Shame slithers down my limbs, terror mixing with hot humiliation, and I press the makeup wipe into my cheek until my teeth threaten to pierce the skin.

"You don't know what you're talking about," I grit out.

"Well, here I am, asking you to clarify." Pausing, he stands up straight again, releasing me with a shove; I brace my free hand against the white plastic of the vanity, catching myself before my chest can collide with it.

"I'm confused about what makes you think you're entitled to that part of me," I snap, growing agitated. "If you're going to torment me, then fucking do it. But don't try to get to know me better. I'm not telling you my secrets."

Walking backward, he stops once the backs of his knees hit the bed, cocking his head to one side. He studies me, silent as a mouse, for so long that I force myself to look away, glancing down at the tabletop for my foundation.

If he's going to stick around, I need to put it back on.

I don't know why it matters, but it does.

A muscle spasm works through my hand as I search, frenzied panic swelling in my chest as my eyes rove over the makeup, unable to find the bottle I want.

"I can't tell you all my secrets. Where's the fun in that?"

Freezing, I tilt my head up, glancing at him in the mirror. He's sitting on the bed now, having discarded his puffer jacket, and is working the sleeves of his black button-down, folding them back over his forearms.

Heat pools between my legs as he uncovers his inked skin, and my eyes struggle to memorize the images in person. Skulls, flowers, and music notes are among the designs, each one having a profound—and totally unwelcome—effect on the pace of my heartbeat.

It's almost enough to distract me from his words, but then I blink, realizing what he's just said.

Words I spoke the night we met, before we'd even left the charity gala.

He smirks, seeming to notice how flustered he's making me.

"What?" he prompts, switching to his other arm, working the sleeve up. "You didn't think I'd forget, did you?"

Placing his arms behind him on the mattress, Aiden leans back; his thighs are spread wide, the black boots on his feet somehow adding a layer of intimidation that makes it difficult to draw air.

It's power.

Raw, magnetic, and all-consuming as he holds it over me.

It leaves me feeling somehow sick and elated at the same time.

"Does Caleb know your secrets?"

Reflexively, my face pinches. "Caleb doesn't really know anything about me."

"Nothing? What does he think you're doing here, all by your lonesome?"

I shrug. "He thinks I'm a freelance web designer from Florida, and that I moved here because my parents used to vacation in Denver."

"And that your name is Angel," he says. A dark brow arches, an accusation lacing his tone. "Don't forget that."

"It was the first one that came to mind when I was making the new identity," I admit, spinning around in my chair. I keep the wipe pressed against my skin, reaching up to adjust my robe when his gaze drifts to where it gapes slightly.

"Sure you didn't do it to ease your guilt?"

I scoff, my agitation growing, slipping like dust between my fingers as I try to control it. "Why on earth would that have helped? It's a constant reminder of how I fucked up every time anyone speaks to me."

Aiden snorts. "Yeah, you seem real bent out of shape over it. He call you that when he comes for you? Does he bend you over, whisper the name *I* gave you, and pump you full?"

"You're disgusting." Tears sting my eyes as I push to my feet, scrambling toward the bathroom.

My hands scrape the door, nails raking over the surface just as heat floods my back; he crashes into me at the same time he pulls the door shut, flattening me against it.

"Where do you think you're going? I'm not done talking to you."

I squirm, jerking my shoulders around as I try to keep the wipe in place. His hand comes up, inked fingers encircling my wrist, trying to tug it away.

"I'm not discussing my sex life with you."

"Why not?" He shifts, grinding his hips into my lower back, and goddamnit if he isn't hard.

Does he like seeing me struggle?

The thought leaves my mind as soon as it arrives, forced out because it has no place there. It doesn't matter what this psycho likes; I'm not supposed to be interested.

"I think I deserve to know who you've been fucking since I saw you last," he says, reaching up to pull my hair to the side. "Especially since you didn't let me that night in the city."

"Good thing, too, since you've clearly turned out to be a crazy person."

"Surprised you didn't already know about that. There's a whole section of my Wikipedia page dedicated to it. I thought you used to be a fan, *angel.*"

His words give me pause, because I'm not sure if he's being facetious or not. It's been a long time since I actively stalked his informational pages, though, having opted for occasional check-ins through social media only over the years.

Do people really think he's crazy?

And if they do... am I in actual danger?

"I'm not a fan of *this*," I say, pushing back to try and dislodge him from me.

It just makes him press harder, and his low chuckle rumbles in my ear, echoing in my chest. "Sure about that? If I reached under your robe right now, you wouldn't be soaked for me?"

His free hand skims my thigh, just below my lace hem, and I squeeze my legs together out of habit. He chuckles again, the sound throaty, and its malice rains down my spine like icy drops of water.

Slamming my head into the door, the tendons in my neck scream in agony as I stretch, trying to crush his knuckles with the blow. I repeat the action, and he moves at the last second, my cheek colliding with the wood.

Pain smarts along the bone, searing a path up my nose. My vision blurs, splotches of color flashing across line of sight, and then he's turning me.

Fat tears well in my eyes as the wipe falls to the floor, abandoned as I reach up to cradle my cheek. It's hot to the touch, not that I can put much pressure on it without the sting splitting my face in half.

"Stop trying to hurt me," Aiden says, one of his hands coming up to cup the side of my face that isn't pulsing. "I might not be in the fucking Mafia like your brother, but you're not going to be able to overpower me."

My nostrils flare, anger bubbling inside me. "Don't talk about my brother."

"Another touchy subject? Jesus, Riley, you really are full

of secrets, aren't you? I wonder which ones you're willing to sell your soul to keep."

Leaning my head back against the door, I close my eyes, letting the tears spill over as the pain in my cheek crests. It throbs outward, sending jolts of misery through my body.

"Leave me alone," I say, hating that this isn't the first time I've had a breakdown in front of him.

What is it about this man that cracks me wide open?

"You hate me. Messaged received."

He doesn't say anything for a long time, but doesn't move away, either. I peek out from mostly hooded lids, looking up at him as he studies my face.

My cheek feels swollen, so I'm sure the scar beneath my eye looks worse than usual. The one at the corner of my mouth probably does too, just in comparison, and never in my entire life have I wanted to die more than I do in this moment.

Strangely, he doesn't look disgusted. I'm not even sure he's looking at the wounds, until I feel his thumb graze the one at my mouth, and my entire soul feels like it's combusting in the worst way.

Thick, scorching hot embarrassment collects in my throat, making it impossible for me to say anything else.

I have no other plea. Nothing more to offer.

The tears continue streaming down my face, a lifetime's worth pouring out in front of him, taking the shape of the physical pain.

Aiden releases me and steps back. My eyes pop open wide as he puts distance between us.

"Don't hide them again," he says, walking over to the bed to retrieve his coat. He shrugs into it, the material stretching tight over his broad shoulders, and then he turns to leave the room.

Pausing at the door, he glances back at me. "If you do, I will make this experience worse for you."

And then he leaves.

29

I'VE UNLOADED my cock probably a hundred times since the other night, frantically trying to erase the mental image of tears streaking down Riley's porcelain cheeks.

I'm doing it again now, palm squeezing my dick like I'm trying to punish it, the memory of her breaking down playing on a loop in my mind.

Sick fascination had seized my brain as they spilled over. Arousal, hot and poisonous, spread from my chest down my spine, collecting in my balls.

My tongue ached to lap at the salty droplets. To consume

the essence of her ugliest emotions and store them on my tastebuds for eternity.

I'd gone back later, after she'd fallen asleep, and studied her in the dim lamplight. One side of her face was swollen and already bruised from where she smacked it into the door, the other mutilated by scars I can't make myself comprehend.

They're clean, precise cuts, even if the skin that healed over makes them look messy.

The one on her cheek even has that crisscrossed look, proof that it was stitched up at some point, and yet I can't fathom why there's nothing about them in her medical records.

After I've finished painting the shower floor with my cum, I step out, wrap a towel around my waist, and sit down at the kitchen table to pore over everything I have on her.

My wrist itches, and I scratch my nails over the skin, then press the pads of each finger to the shattered compass on the inside of my forearm; it stretches from the bottom of my hand to my elbow, the glass shards breaking off and turning into a flight of birds.

Some of the birds take irregular shapes, sadness hidden beneath the ink.

I stare at the puckered slivers of skin, barely visible and only if you know what to look for.

It's *my* one secret.

Glancing down at the files in front of me, I'm drawn back to wondering what Riley's are. How does a seemingly normal girl like her have so many?

My phone rings, and I groan as I get up to answer. "What?"

Liam's laugh fills the line. "Mountain air isn't as relaxing as they say, I take it?"

"Mountain air is the same as the air everywhere else."

"I'm pretty sure that's scientifically incorrect, but I digress. Why do you sound so grumpy?"

"Have you ever considered that this is just my personality?"

"Many times," he says. "I've just been holding out hope that one day you'd change."

Ignoring the spark of annoyance his words cause, I move back to sit at the table, propping my feet up on the surface. "You have a reason for calling, or are you just trying to piss me off?"

"Doesn't exactly take much." He laughs, and I remain silent.

After a beat, Liam clears his throat, and I can imagine him standing in front of the mirror in his apartment in Queens, sifting through an assortment of ties as he decides what to wear for the day.

When I had more things for him to do as my publicist, the morning phone calls were part of our off-tour routine. He'd check in while he got dressed, then stop by on his way to the little office space he rents downtown, usually with scones and coffee.

Sitting in this cabin with my empty refrigerator, I've never missed that more.

"Anyway," he continues. "I just thought I'd let you know that I booked you for a New Year's Eve party."

"I told you, I'm not ready to perform—"

"You have to do it at some point, man. Consider this your reintroduction to the world as the new and improved Aiden James."

A sharp pang flares up behind my ear, and I exhale, forcing my voice to remain even. "Fine. As long as I'm done here, I'll do it."

"You can't really negotiate once the date's been set—"

"I'm not asking for permission." Carding a hand through my hair, I lean back in my chair, an abyss sprouting inside my chest, taking any ounce of joy or contentment with it. They disappear, leaving me hollow, as if they never existed in the first place.

"All right." After a beat of tense silence, Liam asks, "So, are you enjoying Lunar Cove?"

"Not particularly."

He sighs. "Are you even doing tourist shit, or are you sitting in your cabin wasting away?"

"I didn't come here to do anything," I reply. "I came to write, and that's what I'm doing. You're interrupting, actually."

"Oh, I bet." I can almost hear his eyes roll. "Well, don't shoot the messenger if you come back home with a million regrets, all because you didn't want to leave your bed while you were away. Life moves on, whether you enjoy your vacation or not."

I *don't* want to leave my bed at any point of the day. Dragging myself from it is the purest form of torture; my body sags into the mattress each morning, desperate to return to my unconscious state, where the only things that hurt me are figments of my imagination.

It's a wonder I've been productive during my stay so far, at all, when apathy hangs over me like an angry storm cloud, constantly coating my skin in its acidic rain.

We hang up a second later, and I stare down at the documents in front of me. Toying with the rings on my fingers, I skim each page again, reminding myself that *this* is the overall goal of being here.

Not to have fun, but to ruin.

And I can't very well do that from inside my cabin.

SHE LOOKS surprised to see me, which I find amusing.

It's like she still isn't grasping the severity of this situation.

If she's my pretty pink pop star, I'm her rabid fan.

And rabid fans don't give up until they've gotten something from the object of their obsession.

Situated in the back corner booth at Dahlia's, Riley pauses scrolling on her laptop when I step through the front door.

Her eyes harden, a glare marring her brows, and I smother a delirious grin.

Under the fluorescent lighting, her scars are plainly visible. Harsh pinks lighter than the blush tinge of her hair, and my dick jerks to life behind my jeans at the realization that she's following orders.

"Oh, my god, oh my god," a shrill voice calls, echoing through the empty sitting area. "Oh, my *god!*"

Tearing my gaze from Riley, I watch as the silver door to the kitchen swings open, and a girl with chestnut hair bounces out.

She's wearing the same uniform that the other waitresses wear—a long-sleeved black T-shirt and dark jeans—and has a name tag strapped to her chest that says Dahlia, but this is my first time seeing her since I arrived.

Coming to a skidding halt in front of me, the girl huffs a breath, rustling the bangs that cover her forehead. She slaps a palm on the counter, practically wheezing, and looks up at me with dark-blue eyes.

"Oh my god," she repeats, clasping her hands against her chest. "Caleb said you were in town, but I swear I thought he was lying. But he wasn't! You're *here*! *Aiden freaking James* is standing in my diner!"

I wince, wishing she'd keep her voice down. Even though the diner is mostly empty, the need for discretion was bred into me, and this girl seems like the kind of person to spread a rumor before you've even formally introduced yourself.

"The one and only," I force out, giving her what I hope is still a charming smile.

To be honest, I haven't smiled at anyone in a long time, so it's possible that the gesture looks as painful as it feels.

She squeals, lifting up on her tiptoes, and starts to reach out to touch me. At the last second, though, she seems to think better of it, and instead gets stuck with her hands extended, mouth slightly ajar.

I raise my eyebrows, then chance a glance over her shoulder, warmth flooding my chest at the expression I find on Riley's face.

Jaw set and ocean eyes blazing, she's the embodiment of jealousy. It radiates off her in waves, recognizable because I know the feeling.

The fact that she's this affected bodes very well for me.

"This is your diner?" I ask the girl, taking a slight step forward so the tips of her fingers brush my chest.

Her eyes widen, and her chin jerks up and down. "Well, I mean, technically it's my mom's, but it's *named* after me, and

I'm working on buying it from her. And you're just *standing* in it! Oh, my god."

Spinning around, she waves at Riley. "*Dude*, do you know who this is?"

Riley snorts. "Unfortunately."

I smirk, and Dahlia's shoulders slump. "What do you mean, unfor—" Cutting off, she whirls back around to me, a wounded expression on her soft face. "Jesus, ignore her. Clearly, she's going through something, otherwise I know she'd never disrespect a *god*."

I've been called that a lot over the course of my career, even though I vehemently refute it at every turn.

Would a god go years without producing a single piece of music, all because he'd become consumed by thoughts of the girl who ruined his life and then left it, like none of what happened when they met mattered?

I suppose it depends on which god's mythology you're looking at, but I've never felt like anything but a mortal.

"Seriously, *Herculean Effort* got me through my mom's chemo a couple years back," Dahlia says, shaking her head. "I had tickets to go to one of your shows in Boulder, but it..."

She trails off, as if just remembering what happened to that show, and all the others scheduled after. Her face morphs into a mask of reservation, and she pinches her lips together.

"Got canceled?" I provide, and she nods, suddenly looking extremely uncomfortable in my presence.

I try not to let it bother me, and force my smile to remain in place anyway, but the sudden shift in demeanor is a serrated knife to my heart. It slices me wide open, leaving the eviscerated bits behind as blood pours from the open wound.

"Uh, yeah." She rocks back on her heels, sliding a hand into her apron. "I was really sorry to hear about all of that."

"All of that," I repeat, blinking down at her as she now avoids eye contact. Irritation courses through me, and I glance back at Riley, who's watching with a blank expression. "You know, they never proved those rumors true. The girl never spoke up, and no evidence was ever found. The police wrote it off as the incoherent ramblings of a scorned fan."

I watch Riley as I say it, tracking the slightest movements in her face. Her left eye twitches, and her tongue darts out, swiping over the scar at the corner of her mouth.

The scar she left visible, all because I asked her to.

Instead of waiting for a reply from Dahlia, I push past her and head to the back. My cock swells painfully, pride washing through my veins as I stalk toward my prey.

She doesn't cower, doesn't move as I stop at her table, gripping her chin in my hand. Up close, the evidence of some sort of assault in her life prods at something buried deep inside of me, but all I can focus on right now is the even sound of her breathing.

The cerulean hues of her irises, crystalline as they stare up at me.

"You're not wearing makeup," I mutter, tracing the scar near her mouth with my thumb.

"Well, you said not to, and I don't really want to be murdered in my sleep, so I—"

Pinching her lips between my fingers, I stifle her sentence. My heart kicks at my ribs, and I release a strangled sound.

"Doesn't it feel so much better when you do what I ask, pretty girl?"

Before she has a chance to answer, I shove her head back

and crash my mouth to hers, needing to taste her as much as I need to formulate my next breath.

And if kissing her in public causes her problems, well.

So be it.

30

TURNING my phone in my hands, I try to suppress the anxiety coursing through me. My brother's name lights up the screen, an incoming video chat, and I'm sitting in the bath with my clothes on, hoping that Aiden's done stalking me for the day so I can talk in peace.

The odds aren't particularly in my favor, especially given his knack for showing up out of nowhere, but hope still springs eternal in my chest.

I've never been much of an optimist, but I'm trying to convince myself so my brother doesn't worry. Because I fear I may not have been taking this situation as seriously as I should have, and I already know what he'd say about it.

Sucking in a deep breath, I accept the call, and Boyd's stoic face fills the screen.

"Surprise, still alive," I joke, the words tumbling out before I can catch them.

Somehow, his expression flattens even more. "Did you turn in the hotel project I sent you before the holiday break? They're saying they didn't receive it."

The smile drops from my face, fake as it is, and sadness swirls in my stomach. Nodding, I pinch the inside of my thigh, grounding myself in that pain so I don't have to acknowledge the internal.

"I uploaded it Sunday night. It should be in their box folder, but I can double-check."

"No point in double-checking right now," he says, tone sharp, like a blade sawing against my throat. "They're gone for the week. Make sure it's there by Monday for when they come back, and hopefully they'll still pay you in full."

Leaning my head back against the lip of the tub, I don't say anything else. Frankly, I'm not sure where to even go from here. Not sure why he called.

After a prolonged silence, where we just stare at each other through the screen, I try something else. "How are things in King's Trace?"

"Why do you care?"

My eyebrows shoot up into my hairline, and my vision goes lax as my nose burns with the urge to burst into tears. Running my tongue over my teeth, I try to think of a response, but nothing comes out.

The thoughts in my head play like a broken record,

sentences forming halfway and then getting skipped over before they can be vocalized.

Boyd groans, scratching at his jaw. "Fuck, I didn't mean it like that."

"How'd you mean it, then?"

"I don't know." He looks over the camera, hazel eyes unfocusing for a beat, before returning to me. "I guess I've been hoping your new life would erase your ties to this place. Help you forget the people here and get you to a place where you don't care anymore."

My throat feels like it's on fire, but I swallow the flames down anyway. "You want me to stop caring about the people I spent my whole life with?"

"I want you to move on." His jaw clenches, a muscle jumping beneath his eye. "That was the whole point of the move, right? To start fresh. You can't do that if you've still got ghosts across the country."

Picking at a worn piece of grout in the tub tile, I consider his words, trying to decipher the place they're being spoken from.

But I just keep coming up empty.

"What did I ever do to you, Boyd?" My voice is so soft that I barely even hear it, and when he just continues staring, I'm not sure if I actually said them or not. I open my mouth to try again, and he just shakes his head.

"What?"

Chewing on my bottom lip, I shrug. "I just mean, what did I do to make you hate me? I thought things were okay for a while, before..." Pausing to take a breath, I force it shakily from my lungs. "Before New York. But now it's like we're right back where we were before Mom died."

"I don't want to talk about this."

I swallow, the fire in my throat hardening into a thick, ashen knot. "Of course not. God forbid you experience real, human emotions for once in your life."

His eyes flare, fury sparking. He's quiet for a long time, just watching me through the lens, and then he sighs, running a hand over his face.

"Emotions are overrated, Riley." Pulling away, he works his jaw from side to side, eyes shifting off camera again. "They should be reserved for things that matter."

Pain slices through my chest, and it feels like I'm being flayed wide open—all over again. Like he's reached right inside the cavity, taken my heart in his hands, and stabbed right through the organ.

Shifting, I tilt my phone toward the ceiling, unable to keep the tears at bay. Mouth open, my tongue swipes at my scar, my body's natural attempt at a defense.

It's not supposed to sting this much. Not after the physical pain I've endured, and the years of emotional abuse at the hands of our mother, and eventually, myself.

And yet, it's his words that sear a path straight to my soul. Embed themselves in my bones, rooting in the marrow and creating a hurt so deep that I'm not sure I'll ever be able to extract it.

Somehow, the invisible wounds scar the worst.

"Riley?" he's saying, trying to draw me back. Maybe to apologize, or say that he didn't mean it. Or maybe just to move on, changing the subject.

Whatever the case, I don't want to stick around for more.

My thumb hovers over the call end button, and as my name grows frenzied from his mouth, I hang up.

The phone falls from my hand into the tub, and I push to

my feet on wobbly legs. My face in the mirror is red and splotchy, and I swipe my fingers under my eyes, trying to erase the evidence before I head to Caleb's house for Thanksgiving dinner.

I change quickly, pulling a pleated lavender skirt over black knee-high socks, and slipping into a black cashmere sweater that Fiona gave me two Christmases ago.

Smoothing my hand down over the outfit, I contemplate disobeying Aiden's orders to go without makeup. No one's said anything in the days since I stopped wearing it, probably out of discomfort more than anything, but I still feel the weight of their curious glances.

Still, I'd rather them look at the scars than talk about why a rock star randomly showed up in town, and then kissed me in front of a fan at the diner.

My lips are still tingling from it, the appreciation in his eyes just before almost enough to make me forget why he's here in the first place.

Which probably makes me the village idiot, but whatever.

At least I'll die satisfied.

Smearing some cocoa butter balm onto my lips, I forego anything else on my face and exit the bathroom, hoping the puffiness around my eyes goes away before I get to Caleb's.

If I get to Caleb's.

My stomach flips as I enter the bedroom to find Aiden lounging on my bed, wearing a Sid Vicious T-shirt and jeans. His legs hang over the side, and his back is stretched out on the mattress, dwarfing the furniture.

He rolls his head when I walk in, turning to look at me. Silver eyes rake slowly over my body, and the way he strokes his bottom lip with his thumb has me clenching my thighs together.

"Have you been crying?"

Holding up a hand, I shake my head. "Please don't. I'm not in the mood right now."

His chuckle is deep, and I feel its rasp in my core. "Where are we headed this evening?"

"*We* aren't going anywhere. *I'm* going to Caleb's, and *you're* not invited."

"I'm not sure you understand how this works, angel."

"No, I can't say I'm very familiar with stalkers," I say, moving past him to head for the door, swiping my purse off the vanity as I pass by.

Closing my fingers around the knob, I start to pull it open, but then he's there, slamming it shut. I glare at his palm where it's flattened against the wood, his rings dull against his inked skin.

He slides his hand down, stopping when he's just centimeters from my face, and then I feel him press into my back, wedging his cock between my ass cheeks.

"I was hoping we'd be able to spend Thanksgiving together."

"Why would you think that?" I manage, trying to ignore how good he feels, how warm and fulfilling his touch is. "We *barely* know each other, and you've made your intentions here pretty clear. Do you think I'm going to just roll over and let you hurt me, no questions asked?"

"I think," he says, reaching down to grip my hips in both hands, squeezing them as he shoves me farther into the door. My pelvis grinds against the wood, trapped between two impossibilities. "If I told you to flip your skirt up and let me fuck you right here, right now, you'd arch your back and give me what I want."

My breathing grows shallow.

Erratic.

"No." It's all I can muster, a half-hearted whisper that barely makes it past my lips.

"No? I don't remember asking a question." His hands glide down, brushing the bare skin of my thighs as they slip beneath the hem of my skirt. In a second, the soft material is pushed over my ass, the chilly air cool against my skin.

Aiden clicks his tongue in clear disapproval. "Where did you get new panties?"

"New panties?" I frown, starting to turn my head, but he reaches up and grips my hair, keeping me in place. "Oh, my god! Did *you* steal my fucking underwear? You really are insane, I—"

My words cut off on a strained moan as his fingers slip between my legs and glide upward. Frissons of heat coil tight in my stomach, and he rubs my clit in soft, circular motions, forcing my thighs farther apart by shoving his knee between them.

"We might not know each other that well yet, but your body craves mine," he says, voice low, fingers hooking in the crotch of my satin thong and tugging it aside, giving him better access.

He alternates between swirling and pinching, fast and slow, and it's mere seconds before I'm panting and rocking into the movements.

"And if you want to talk about how insane I am, let's discuss who made me this way."

"I didn't—"

Pitching himself forward, he moves his hand down,

teasing my pussy with his index finger. I'm practically bent in half as he pushes inside, and the sound that escapes my throat hurts on its way out.

A single burst of clarity breaks through the lusty haze in my mind, and I blink, forcing myself to reject the way his fingers turn me to putty. If I don't end this, I'm going to be late for dinner.

"Stop," I whisper, but I think even when I say it, I know he's too far gone.

I think that's the only reason I *do* say it; because I know I should.

Not necessarily because I want him to—which feels odd, all things considered.

His strokes come fast, his finger curling against that spot inside me that makes my vision slacken. "*No.*"

I feel the loss as soon as he withdraws, and all I can do is brace my palms against the door. My thong slides back into place, and he shifts; the clinking of a belt buckle has my muscles drawing tight, unease skating down my spine as the hand in my hair pushes me harder into the wood.

"Wait," I say, twisting, moving my hips, trying to escape.

My throat constricts, confusion clawing its way to my chest, and he just chuckles.

"Not a very nice word, is it?" He pulls my thong aside again, and the band stings where it cuts into my waist.

"Oh, god, Aiden—"

"*God?*" he snaps, and Jesus *fucking* Christ, I can feel him pressing against me. The head of his dick prods my entrance, hot where it touches me, trying to split me open. "No, angel. There's nothing holy about what I'm gonna do to you."

He rubs up and down my seam, and I feel wet, but I don't know if it's him, or me, or both.

"Why don't you want me to go to dinner?" he asks, dragging his dick up and positioning it. I suck in a sharp breath when he starts to push inward, feeling my pussy stretch beyond belief.

It burns slightly, the pressure sending sparks of weirdly pleasurable discomfort through my limbs. They sizzle, electricity and nerves mixing to put me on edge, and I tense up, waiting for more that never comes.

"*Fuck*, my cock looks good inside you," he says, blowing out a breath. But still, he doesn't move any farther. My fingers scrape at the door, and he finally releases my hair, reaching around to continue circling my clit with his thumb.

"Answer me," he demands, and I twist my head to see what he's doing, watching as his free hand wraps around his veiny shaft, pumping slowly.

My eyes widen, the sight of him stroking himself—while simultaneously rubbing me—so painfully erotic that I lose my grip on the door and droop forward, pressing my chest into it to keep upright.

"I don't want people to get the wrong idea," I gasp, struggling to maintain a coherent thought as he switches directions.

"You mean you don't want Caleb to get the wrong idea."

"Yes! I don't want to hurt the only real friend I've ever had."

He grunts, and I feel myself starting to unravel. Arousal unspools like an old thread inside me, and even though he's not pushing deeper, my pussy clamps down around nothing, my clit pulsing to the point of pain.

"What's he gonna think when you show up tonight, smelling like a mixture of our cum?"

"I'm not—"

"Sure about that? I'll bet you're three seconds away from drenching my fingers and cock. I bet if I wedged myself inside this tight cunt any farther, I'd blow my goddamn load so fast because of how she's strangling me, desperate for release. Good thing you're on birth control, right?"

Shaking my head, I try to ignore the words. Try not to think about what they say about me, that I'm not only laughing at the absolute danger I'm in, but also once again proving my mother right.

Maybe I really am a worthless whore.

My brother certainly doesn't seem to have much faith in me.

And if family, the ones who are supposed to support and love you no matter what, can't see anything worth respecting in a person, then how could anyone else either?

Maybe this treatment is exactly what I deserve.

"Come on, pretty girl. Show me I'm right."

When I come, the euphoric sensation that rolls through me like a thundercloud almost knocks me off my feet. It steals my breath and kicks me in the gut as wave after wave of sweet relief crashes down over me.

Aiden hisses behind me, sucking in air through his teeth. I hear his hand pick up speed, that distinct sound of flesh against flesh filling my ears, and he bends down, pressing a tender kiss to my forehead.

"That's it, pretty girl. I knew you could do it. Knew you'd look so good coming on my cock."

Something between a whimper and a cry lodges in my throat, and I squeeze my eyes shut, trying to stave off the tears threatening there.

It doesn't work; they spill over with no regard for the situation—or maybe *because* of the situation. For some reason, even though I've just had the best orgasm of my life, as the pleasure subsides and I'm left with just my thoughts, disgust fills me, kicking me in the face and leaving its boot print as a reminder.

"Fuck, you're beautiful," Aiden whispers, his tongue darting out to collect my tears at the same time he pulls his dick from me.

He shifts, pressing his lips to my cheek as he continues jerking himself between my legs. His breath is hot as it fans across my face, and then he's letting out a low, guttural groan and snapping the band of my thong against my skin as he climaxes.

Thick ropes of cum splatter against my thighs, but the majority of it, he's managed to catch in the crotch of my thong. I breathe out a sigh, shaking from the entire ordeal, grateful he at least thought to be careful for cleanup.

But then he's bending, dragging the thong up instead of down, and resituating it on my hips. I gasp as his seed touches my bare pussy, and he reaches down, rubbing on the outside, smearing himself all over me.

The scent of sex fills the air as he steps back, fixing my skirt, and tucks himself back into his pants.

I'm still flattened against the door, unsure of what the fuck just happened.

"I'm going with you to that dinner, one way or another." Aiden turns me around, tilts my chin up. "Don't convince yourself there's any leeway on this. At least not until I get what I want."

Without expanding on that thought, he slides me to the side and opens the door, disappearing through it as I slump against the wall.

My heart races, my fight-or-flight response on autopilot,

and I realize for the first time since he pinned me to the door that during the entire thing, I wasn't really scared at all.

For once, I lived in that single moment and allowed myself to experience it, rather than trying to catalog everything that could go wrong.

And I'm not sure how I feel about it.

31

I STAND outside Riley's cabin far longer than necessary, waiting to see how much time it takes her to collect herself after I lose my fucking mind.

I'm still reeling when Caleb comes to pick her up, floating in a state of disbelief over what transpired upstairs.

That my dick was inside her minutes ago. Just the crown, but that was enough for me to feel her tight, slick heat convulsing around me, and to learn that I would die buried between her legs, if given the chance.

I don't know what possessed me to do it, except that the idea of her sitting beside Caleb all night, the two of them laughing at their little jokes while I sit in my cabin alone, enraged me.

Only when she's safely in his car, not having had enough time to change out of the messy thong I left her with, do I leave her house. I hop into the black Volvo I rented when I got to town and head to the boardwalk strip.

Aside from a tiny convenience store closer to the lake, Dahlia's Diner is the only place open, its big red neon sign bright against the night sky. Stuffing my hands into my pockets, I head inside with a notebook, sitting at the counter as I try to put Riley out of my head.

I don't know exactly how much time passes, but I sit there looking at the book for so long, my vision grows hazy.

Jade, who seems to be a regular here, comes out from the kitchen to take my order.

"Here on Thanksgiving?" I ask, folding my hands together. "That sucks."

"I'm just closing tonight. Better than having to listen to my mother complain about all the dirty dishes at home."

"Moms are good for that," I say, although I can't really relate. My mother stopped being one a long time ago, and we always had a housekeeper.

Her complaints usually erred on my father's tendency to stray.

"Okay, don't tell me. Peppermint tea, and..." Jade purses her lips, tapping her pen to her chin as she studies me. "And a cinnamon bagel."

My eyebrows raise. "Do you remember all your customers' orders?"

"Only the ones who tip well." She shrugs, then spins around and trots to the back.

The door swings shut behind her, and I stare down at the

blank page in my notebook, rubbing my temples to try to erase the memory of Riley coming undone in my arms.

I scribble some one-liners in the notebook, working through the melodies in my head, and by the time Jade returns, I've got a coherent bridge for a new song.

She places my order on the counter with my receipt, then moves to the cash register and starts counting the drawer.

"So, you're the rock star, huh?" she asks after a few moments, barely even glancing in my direction. "Do you make a habit of going around and kissing girls in random restaurants, or is Dahlia's special?"

Dahlia's isn't. Riley is.

"How do you know about that?"

She snorts. "You only tongue bathed each other in front of Lunar Cove's biggest gossip. Seriously, I love Dahlia with all my heart, but she can't keep a secret to save her life. I'd be willing to bet the whole town knows about it by now."

Well, shit. I'd expected it to cause Riley problems within her inner circle, but I hadn't anticipated it being the talk of the fucking town.

The last thing I need is people realizing where I'm at, before I've even gotten to dispose of Riley myself.

Pulling my phone from my jacket pocket, I notice a string of notifications from my dad and Liam, and when I open the first one, sure enough, it's a screenshot of someone saying I've been spotted with a pink-haired girl out west.

For now, it seems, my exact location is still unknown, with my father saying he intercepted rumors and redirected people to California and Vancouver, but still. I'll need to be a bit more careful if I want to go through with my revenge.

"I've gotta be honest, I never really saw Angel going for that type."

For some reason, the comment irks me.

Who did she see Riley with, *Caleb*? Please.

That man can try all he wants, but he's not ever going to *get* her.

Not the way I do.

Taking a bite of my bagel, I lift a shoulder. "You know her pretty well?"

The expression on her face fills me with satisfaction. "God, no. She's more closed off than Fort Knox."

"Maybe *Angel* isn't who she says she is."

"That sounds incredibly shady." Jade frowns, pausing with bills in her hand. "Do you know something we don't?"

My gut sours, and I wish I hadn't said anything.

"No, I'm just saying. Maybe your town is judgmental, so she keeps to herself."

"Well, that's rude."

"That's life."

Pushing some of the black hair from her face, Jade shoves her money into its till, slams the drawer shut, and puts her hands on her hips.

"I don't think I like you very much."

Smirking, I bring my mug to my lips, downing the piping hot drink in four big gulps. The liquid singes my tongue, the mint cooling my teeth, and I set it back on the counter with a loud clank.

"Join the club." Sliding from the stool, I stuff the rest of the bagel in my mouth and pull out my wallet, throwing a couple hundreds on the counter before swiping the notebook and heading out.

"People who tip this much are overcompensating for something," Jade calls, and I just laugh, waving at her over my shoulder.

The bell chimes as I walk through the front door, chewing slowly. Leaning against the building, I survey the empty streets, tucking the book beneath my armpit.

Headlights flash, blinding me as they cross over to the parking lot. I slip behind a stone pillar a few feet away, slinking to the shadows just in case. There's never any telling who is going to recognize you in public; even the biggest names can sometimes walk around undetected, depending on where they're at.

My encounter the other day, though, with Dahlia, makes me nervous about who else in town knew me as more than "Angel's" boy toy.

Fire scorches down my sternum at the thought of her having any others in the time between when she was still dead to the world, and when I found her.

Guess that's the kind of thing you'd ask someone before sticking your dick in them.

Snow begins drifting from the night sky; it's been flurrying on and off for days now, making the sidewalks slushy. The ones on the boardwalk are freshly salted, possibly because this is the most visited part of town in the winter, so when I shuffle back, I don't have to pay very much attention to where I'm stepping.

I still do, though; caution is a habit at this point.

Two figures exit the vehicle, their silhouettes starting up the road toward the diner. Their voices float to me, but it's not until they're bathed in the neon glow that I notice it's Caleb and Riley; they walk with their arms intertwined and heads huddled together, looking more like lovers than anything else.

If you didn't know any better.

My teeth grind together, and I step back slowly, ensuring

that I'm totally enshrouded in darkness as they stop in front of the building.

"You're sure you're okay?" Caleb asks, reaching with his free hand to brush a strand of hair from her face.

I don't miss the way she flinches, ever so slightly, a crooked smile forming on her lips.

"I *promise*, I'm fine. I'm really sorry I couldn't stay, but unfortunately, being a girl waits for no one."

Caleb sighs, shaking his head as he steps back. "You could've stayed at the house. My mother would've been glad to get you some shit to make you feel better."

"I appreciate that, but I think I'll feel better in my own bed."

"God, I just fucking hate the idea of you going home in a cab. It's supposed to start snowing harder really soon, and the roads are already terrible as it is."

Tipping her head back, Riley laughs. The sound rankles me, reminding me of the night in New York City and how badly I wanted to believe it was something she didn't do often.

That she'd given me a piece of herself no one else got.

Crushing my notebook to my side, I ignore the anger, letting it simmer in my soul.

"Your cabbies probably drive better in the snow than I do," she tells him.

"Fair point." Still, he rocks back on his heels, lingering. "And you're sure you're okay to wait here by yourself?"

"Positive. Jade's inside, anyway, if I need something." Reaching out, she pushes her palms against his chest. "Go, dude. I'll see you tomorrow."

Hesitating another moment, Caleb finally takes a step back, shaking his head. He pulls a hat from his coat pocket, tugging it over his hair, and then turns and jogs in the direction he just came.

Neither one of us moves, watching as he climbs into his Jeep, honks twice, and then peels away.

I'm just about to step out and reveal myself when she swivels in my direction, placing her hands on her hips.

"You can come out."

For a second, I stay hidden, not sure that I like how accustomed to my presence she's becoming. If we eliminate the element of fear, then what the fuck is the purpose of all of this?

Still, I can't resist putting myself in her personal space, so I move out from the pillar and prop my shoulder against it.

"You're terrible at this," she says, taking a single step closer.

"Oh? Are you well-versed in the art of stalking, Ms. Kelly?"

"I shouldn't dignify that with a response," she says, crossing her arms over her chest. "But, for the record, I was the president of your biggest online fan club for two full years before..."

She trails off, casting her eyes to the ground. Her boot kicks at the snow, and she clears her throat.

"Well, regardless, I was the one running it for two years. I tracked down your specific GPS coordinates when you were on tour, down to the hotel room you were staying in. I cataloged what your favorite drinks were in each individual city, so I could arrange to have gift baskets sent to your room before each show."

Riley exhales, her breath clouding visibly in the chilly air.

"One time, I even thwarted an attempted crazed fan from

breaking into your tour bus, just because I happened to know where it was sitting during your Super Bowl halftime show, and some of the girls in the fan club let me know what was being planned."

Jesus. The girl is a former superfan, and I didn't even know.

My stomach churns. "I feel violated."

A grin spreads over her face, a look of rare pride over-taking her features. "Did all of that from the comfort of my home, too. Pays to have a big brother with a wealth of technology at his fingertips."

"Oh, are we gonna talk about him now?"

Something dark passes over her. It wipes the grin clean off.

"No." She flips her hair off her shoulder. "I'm just saying, your stalking skills are very amateurish. I always know when you're around."

"And yet..." Trailing off, I move in, not stopping until I'm standing right in front of her. Close enough to see the dark blues in her eyes, like frozen tundras waiting to be scoped out. Full of depth and secrets. "You always seem nervous. Like you're not expecting me."

She swallows audibly. "I don't know what you want with me. One second, you're telling me how much you want me to suffer, and the next, you're..."

"Making you come?"

Her cheeks darken. "Yeah, that."

"*That.*" Another step, so our shoes are touching. "Does sex make you uncomfortable, Riley?"

"*You* make me uncomfortable."

"Now that can't be true. You wouldn't have come on my fingers... or my tongue... if I made you uncomfortable."

"Maybe I'm one of those people who likes pain."

I hum, my free hand coming up to wrap around her throat. Squeezing slightly, just enough to rob her of easy access to air, I arch a brow. "Would you like to find out?"

Her throat ripples beneath my hold, and I imagine it doing the same when she's swallowing my cum, gagging on me.

"I'm a virgin." She says the words so softly, so suddenly, that I'm convinced she hadn't planned on the admission.

It pulses in the air between us, collecting like snowflakes on the ground. Confusion knits my insides, and I let my hand fall to my side, searching her face for signs of a lie.

"But your medical records—"

"I've never slept with anyone," she insists, dropping her chin slightly.

My gaze flickers to the scars on her face, and I think about the one on her hip. I've never felt more confused in my entire life.

Pulling away, she runs a hand through her hair, then hugs her biceps. "I should go in and wait for a ride."

"I'll take you."

Glancing at my extended hand, she cringes. "That feels like a terrible idea."

I shrug, wiggling my fingers. "Won't know until you try."

It takes several more minutes, and my toes start to go numb by the time she finally nods. She doesn't take my hand, but she follows beside me, and for right now, I'm okay with settling for that.

32

WHAT IS A SOCIALLY acceptable amount of time to let someone bully you?

Rubbing the sleep from my eyes, I delete the text in the search bar. I don't put it past Aiden to have installed a nanny cam on my laptop when I wasn't looking, so I don't want to incriminate myself more than necessary.

In truth, he's been fairly quiet in the couple of weeks since Thanksgiving; when Fiona came to visit over the weekend, I hadn't seen him at all, though I know he's always lurking.

Being on this end of an obsession is... weird, to say the

least. I spent most of my life living vicariously through celebrities, studying their lives in the hope that maybe some of that glitz and glamour would rub off on me.

Now, my days are occupied by graphic design, bubble baths, and the animosity of the man my teenage self was infatuated with.

She didn't know better, though, so I'm trying to cut her some slack.

Aiden James hides his crazy very, very well.

I can't help feeling a little bad that I seem to have sent him over the edge, though you would think that three years is more than enough time to move on from something like that.

Just like you have, right, Riley?

Slipping from the bed, I pull on a white terrycloth robe and head downstairs. The cabin is freezing, and when I pass by the thermostat on the wall, I notice the indoor temperature has taken a dip along with the drop outside.

I can almost see my breath as I reach out, cranking it back up.

Glancing at myself in the mirror hanging by the stairs, I scrub my nails over my jaw; red, scaly patches of skin have sprouted there, and no matter how much lotion I apply, they're not going away.

Part of me wonders if I should call Kal and have him write me a prescription, but the other part of me wants to see an actual doctor. One I can talk to about my *history*.

Aiden's comment about *internal scarring* has stuck with me, and I can't stop wondering what that means.

If my mother's boyfriend took more than just my life the night he attacked me.

Maybe getting answers will unlock some of the memories, although at this point, I feel stupid for wanting to know.

I should be content in my ignorance, but something about it all still bothers me. Somehow, the not knowing is worse.

Walking into the kitchen, the scent of coffee and butter invades my senses, and I freeze in place as my eyes sweep the scene.

Caleb stands over a skillet at my stove, poking at something inside with a spatula. The island is littered with ingredients I've never bought—whole milk instead of the oat I drink, a package of uncooked bacon, corn meal, and a block of gooey white cheese.

As if sensing my presence, Caleb turns his head and gives me a lopsided grin. "Well, good morning, sunshine. Glad to see you're not sleeping the day away."

Frowning, I adjust my robe, pulling it closer to my neck. "What are you doing here?"

"Uh..." He doesn't look up from his task. "Cooking breakfast?"

"Well, I can see that. What I mean is, why?"

"I had a bunch of bacon leftover from a tourism conference this morning, so I figured, why let it go to waste?"

My nose scrunches up. "I don't like bacon."

Caleb's hands stop moving. "*What*?"

"It leaves a weird taste in my mouth." Shrugging, I walk over to the cabinet, pull out a mug that has a foxtail as its handle, and pour a cup of coffee. "Probably because my mom used to burn it any time she'd bother making breakfast when I was a kid. My brain rejects it all the same."

"Wow. You know, sometimes I feel like I don't know you at all."

He shakes his head with a little laugh. I watch as he flips a little flattened circle of dough, pressing down on the top, and try to ignore the wound his words leave on my heart.

"Doesn't like bacon. Sheesh. Well, at any rate, the bacon's just one aspect of this meal. I'm also making—"

He cuts off abruptly as he turns, eyes widening as he takes me in. "Holy shit, Angel, what the hell happened to your face?"

I groan, reaching up to cover my jaw with my fingers. "Oh god, nothing. I'm having some kind of allergic reaction to my lotion, I think."

Abandoning the stove, Caleb wipes his hands on a dish towel, then immediately walks over. Pushing me aside, he reaches up to cradle my face, tilting it in various directions as he inspects the rash.

"Do you have any allergies?"

"I—"

"Latex."

My head whips around to find the source of the answer, even though I know without looking who it came from. Aiden slips in through the glass patio door, and my heart stutters inside my chest as I rake my gaze over him.

Droplets of water cling to his tanned skin—skin that, until now, I've only ever seen the bare minimum of. In every paparazzi photo of him that exists, Aiden's wearing a shirt. Doesn't matter if he's on the beach, in a pool, or on stage.

It's never been something he's commented on in interviews, either.

As he walks inside, his dark and damp hair dripping onto the defined, inked planes of his torso, I can't figure out why he'd ever hide himself.

I can't stop staring as he comes closer, not the slightest

bit concerned that he's getting the floor wet. My eyes trail over the intricate designs etched into his chest—instruments, abstract drawings, and flowers decorate his skin, each one bleeding into the next to make a homologous collection.

A phoenix sits at the center, its fiery wings spanning across his pecs and the tail wrapping around his belly button.

But that's not the only thing that catches my eye; as I make my third pass around the colorful linework, my gaze snags on a splash of silver.

My stomach tightens. *His left nipple is pierced.*

A plain dime-sized hoop hangs off the puckered flesh, and for some reason, my first instinct is to reach out and hook my pinkie through it.

Folding my mouth together, I slip my hands behind my back, resisting.

Aiden seems to zero in on where Caleb's holding me, and his jaw tics, his tongue pushing against his cheek as he leans against the counter.

"How do you know she has a latex allergy?" Caleb asks, and I want to pinch my eyes closed, because even *I* anticipate what's about to come out of Aiden's mouth.

The rock star grins. "How do you think I know?"

He stares at Caleb's hands until they drop, then reaches for my robe and tugs me into him so I'm nestled between his legs.

To anyone else, the gesture might seem warm and romantic. But when his palm lands on my back, searing me through the thick fabric I have on, I feel his fingers dig into me.

Clawing.

Claiming.

It's not romantic, so much as it is Aiden asserting his dominance over the situation.

Over me.

Stupidly, because I still feel like I owe him—and because I don't hate the way it feels—I let him. Even though doing so causes a flash of hurt to spark in Caleb's eyes as he backs away, returning to his skillet.

"Hot tub works, by the way," Aiden tells me, reaching up to tuck some hair behind my ear.

I didn't even know I had a hot tub.

His eyebrows draw in, creasing in the middle. "What the hell happened to your chin?"

"It's *nothing*." Heat crawls up my neck, embarrassment burning into me. "Just some kind of reaction to my lotion. I'm calling the doctor as soon as everyone leaves my house."

"Lotion?"

"Yes, it's what *humans* use to moisturize their skin?"

"Are you suggesting I'm some sort of extraterrestrial?"

"More like demon spawn."

Caleb clears his throat. "My mom probably has some aloe vera mixture that might help with that, in the meantime. I know doctor appointments around here are pretty sparse this time of year."

"She'll get in to see one," Aiden says. "I'll pull strings if I have to."

"I'm not sure if you have the same kind of reach in Lunar Cove as you might in other places." Caleb flips his dough onto a nearby plate, returning to the pan for another and repeating the process. "The people around here don't really give a shit about your fame."

"Do they give a shit about money? Because I could probably be the owner of this tourist trap by sundown, if I wanted to be."

Setting the spatula on the counter, Caleb turns, crossing his arms over his chest. He looks at me, then at Aiden, and back. A lump forms in my throat, unease spilling like flames down my esophagus.

"You might be able to," he says, pinning me with a dark look, "but I don't think you'd be able to buy Angel. So, maybe consider your priorities before you go around trying to prove how big your dick is."

"I don't have to prove anything." Aiden's hand wraps around my skull, pulling me against his wet chest. "*Angel* already knows the truth. Isn't that right, pretty girl?"

My teeth saw into my bottom lip, irritation buzzing through my veins at the same time my insides preen, basking in the glow of his admiration.

Caleb's face softens, his disappointment unmistakable.

"I'm gonna head out," he says, walking over to a chair at the island where his dark-gray coat hangs.

"You don't have to—" Aiden pinches my hip, ending my sentence prematurely. I shove out of his grasp, my fist rearing back as a reflex.

It pauses mid-swing, and Aiden's silver eyes glow with amusement.

Letting my hand fall, I sidestep him and walk around the island, gesturing to the food sitting out. "Caleb, come on. You didn't make all of this for me. Stay and help us finish it."

I don't know why I say *us*, like Aiden and I are a unit, but once it's out there, I can't fish it back. The word tastes bitter on my tongue and gets worse when Caleb gives me a small smile.

"It's not a big deal, Ang. Eat up, and I'll see you later for

Christmas shopping." He reaches out, patting my cheek even though I'm sure Aiden's glare is aimed at us, and then he steps in, lowering his voice. "But, for the record, I do think you should put *something* on your face. That rash looks painful."

I nod, smiling slightly. "I will."

"Good." He steps back, sliding on his coat, then disappears from the room. My heart aches as he goes, knowing he deserves a better friend, yet selfishly not being willing to let him go yet.

It's that age-old caveat of wanting what's best for others, but also needing to keep a piece of their goodness for yourself. If not for Caleb, I don't know how I'd have survived in Lunar Cove this long, and I'm not in a place yet where I'm willing to find out.

Spinning on my heels, I scowl at Aiden. "You're an asshole."

He's standing at the stove, using his finger to taste the yellow batter in a glass mixing bowl.

"Tell me something I don't know." His face twists, and he wipes his finger on the dish towel. "Your boyfriend can't cook."

"God, he's not my fucking boyfriend."

"Good thing, because he can't cook. You'd probably die of food poisoning in that relationship."

I'm indignant on Caleb's behalf. "He can cook. I've had his apple crumble, and he makes scones and empanadas all the time."

"Okay, so he can bake." Aiden pushes the bowl back on the counter, turning to face me. "That's not the same as cooking, though, and people who can't cook shouldn't try to make *arepa boyacense* unsupervised."

I blink. "What the hell is that?"

"A Colombian breakfast dish. My mom used to make it every weekend when I was a kid, and let me tell you, it was heaven." He points at the fried dough sitting on the plate. "Those taste like ass."

"Familiar with that, are we?" I try not to let my surprise show over the fact that he's talking about his past, so candid as he stands here in my kitchen.

Like we're old friends and not, at best, star-crossed wannabe lovers.

A slow burning smile spreads over his lips, and he lets his eyes fall down over me. "Don't worry. I'll be familiar with yours in no time."

He reaches into the bowl for a measuring cup, funneling the batter from there into the pan

I frown. "What are you doing?"

"My mother would disown me if I didn't correct the golden boy's mistake, so apparently I'm making you breakfast." Glancing at me over his shoulder, he lifts an eyebrow. "Be a good girl and help out, hm?"

33

My thumb flicks against the lid of my Zippo lighter, my legs outstretched as I lounge on the bench in front of the Pruitt Art Gallery.

Caleb's been back from break for half an hour, and while every light inside has been turned on, and the open sign flipped back, he hasn't actually unlocked the door.

My dick is getting frostbite just sitting here.

There's about three feet of snow on the ground, and the entire boardwalk is decked out in Santas and beautiful, twinkling lights, each store overhang having their own specific color of bulbs; red at the diner, yellow at the souvenir shop, blue at the art gallery, and so on.

Christmas back home stopped being much of an event when I was young; even before my career took off, and my parents decided cultivating the Aiden James brand was more important than cultivating *me*, things in our household were strained.

Not unloving, necessarily. Just awkward. A severe disconnect existed between the three of us that kept happiness on the outskirts of our lives.

My mother buried her sadness in pills, becoming the caricature of a once-great singer.

My father tried to alleviate his with material things. Business ventures, vacations, jewelry, models, and cars. Anything money could buy, Sonny James wanted it delivered to our home.

Me, well. I didn't know what the fuck to do with my sadness. No one wanted to acknowledge it, because doing so was like admitting something inside of us was broken.

So I kept it close.

Bottled it up, then tucked it behind my rib cage like hidden treasure.

Leave something buried long enough, and eventually it'll wash back up, waterlogged and sandy and worse off than if you'd just dealt with it in the first place.

I toss a peppermint candy at the glass door again, and this time Caleb's face appears from behind a covered canvas. He frowns, pursing his lips when he sees me, like he isn't sure if he wants to answer or not.

After a minute, he finally trudges over like the good little boy he is. Flipping the lock on the door, he yanks it open, crossing his arms over his chest.

"What do you want?"

Pushing to my feet, I close the lighter and stuff it in my pocket. "Can't a guy come visit his favorite artist?"

"I'm not an artist. And I'm not your favorite anything." He moves back as I walk inside, taking in the rows of displays in the little room.

Six individual glass cases line the middle of the floor, with the covered canvas standing at the back. Others hang on the wall, a macabre representation of still life here in the Rockies, and a spinning display showcases different native artifacts.

"That's not entirely true," I say, walking over to inspect a landscape of the lake just outside. "You're my favorite nuisance."

Rolling his eyes, Caleb walks to the back corner, slipping behind a tall receptionist desk. He's folding pamphlets, fingers moving with ease, and I'm once again overtaken by jealousy at the thought of those being anywhere near Riley.

"If you're not an artist, why do you own an art gallery?"

"Do you have to create art in order to appreciate it?" He pauses, glancing up at me. "Wouldn't that defeat the entire purpose of your career, if the only people who could own music were also the ones who play it?"

"Well, enjoying music and owning a recording studio are vastly different things."

I shake a peppermint from my jeans pocket, popping it out of the wrapper and into my mouth. He watches the movement with cold, calculating eyes—so different from when he's around *her*, that I have no doubt about his feelings.

"It belonged to my grandfather years ago. He left it to me in his will."

"Seems an odd thing to leave a man who doesn't care about art."

"Again, I care about it. I'm just not an artist."

The covered canvas in the back catches my attention for a second, and I cock my head to one side, letting my gaze slide to his.

He clears his throat, adjusting the collar of the light-blue button-down he has on.

"In any case, I'm also not officially open right now. This is supposed to be by appointment only, and I have a showing in twenty minutes. You should probably leave."

Instead of listening, though, I make my way to his desk, settling my forearms on top of the dark wood surface. Caleb doesn't spare me a glance as I loom over him, and the lack of attention irritates me.

The lack of respect from him, in general, is infuriating, although part of me feels like I'm more bothered by the fact that he gets the soft, genuine side of Riley, and all I get are the bits I scrape from her.

"What's the nature of your relationship with Angel?" I bite out the last word, hating that I have to use it.

His brows lift. "None of your business, apparently. If she didn't tell you about it, then I don't feel I should betray her judgment."

"Maybe I want to hear it from you."

"Why? Don't you trust her?" A smirk pulls at the side of his mouth. "What do you want me to say? That I've fallen asleep to the sound of her screaming my name practically every night she's been here? That some days, it hurts to shower, because the sting from where her nails raked down my back the night before is almost too much to bear?"

My fingers curl around the edge of the desk, heat boiling inside my chest.

"I could tell you those things. Fuck, what I wouldn't give to be able to. But they'd be lies." He shrugs, folding pamphlet after pamphlet, creasing the pages perfectly and stacking them to his right. "Truth is, I barely know her. She keeps herself locked up tight, and the chains around her heart are damn near impenetrable."

Blowing out a breath, I sag against the desk. "Tell me about it."

Caleb doesn't say anything for several beats. The only sound is that of the papers shuffling and the soft tones of instrumental jazz trickling in from somewhere.

Grabbing the back of his neck with one hand, Caleb stops what he's doing and meets my gaze. "I've spent a *lot* of time wishing those beautiful blue eyes of hers would acknowledge my feelings. That she'd, I don't know... wake up one day and realize I could help her. Keep her safe from whatever it is she's running from."

Fire rages in my stomach, its flames rolling up my sternum and singeing my throat. The rings on my fingers feel heavy, leaden as they curl into my palms, trying to listen without wanting to rip his jugular out.

"But, ah... that's not gonna happen. She doesn't look at me like I'm the answer to her problems." He clears his throat once, twice, then returns to his task. "She doesn't look at me the way she looks at you."

His words fill me with a mixture of disbelief and misery, and a notable absence of happiness. They twist inside me like poisonous vines, racing to see which can reach my heart first.

Because I'm not the solution to Riley's problems.

I'm the root cause.

Pushing away from the desk, I cast one last glance at the canvas hidden beneath a plastic tarp. Suspicion pulses inside me, and I reach out before Caleb can stop me, ripping the cover away with a single swipe of my hand.

My jaw clenches so hard I can almost feel my teeth cracking. I stare at the white expanse, taking in the soft, feminine lines, the oceanic blue eyes, the pink hair that takes up the sides and top corners.

But there's no scarring. No imperfections that make it *her*.

Still, its essence is haunting. Alluringly simplistic, yet somehow bold and intoxicating with its depth.

Pressing my lips together, I turn to look at Caleb. "Not an artist, huh?"

His nostrils flare, but he doesn't answer. I wonder when the last time he looked at the painting was—last night? Months ago?

The look in his eyes holds the evidence of a recent wound, so it must not have been long.

Sliding my wallet from my pocket, I take the blank checkbook from the back and slide it onto the counter. "I'll buy it."

34

HUDDLING down lower under my covers, I roll to my side, keeping my phone against my ear.

"What do you mean the security people never showed up?"

Kal's voice is stern, too loud in the dark quiet of my bedroom.

I flex my toes under the mass of blankets on top of me. "No one ever came to install more cameras. I don't know how to explain that better."

He sighs, and I hear the fussing of his toddler somewhere in the background. *God, it's weird to imagine that soulless man with a child.*

Then again, maybe he's not totally soulless, if his willingness to help me has been any indication.

Maybe the darkness is a cloak he wears to keep himself safe.

"Why didn't you tell me this weeks ago?" he asks. "I never got an update from them, so I assumed everything had been set up."

"I kind of forgot they were supposed to come out." *I've been a little occupied.*

"Once again, I'm concerned that you're not taking this seriously."

"Yes, I am! If anything, you didn't take it seriously when I first asked for the cameras."

"And yet, you *forgot* that they were supposed to be installed? Had the matter been truly as urgent as you made me believe last month, I don't think I would've gone a single day without hearing from you."

His tone bites. "What's your point? Do you think I'm being dramatic or something?"

"I think you have a propensity for blowing things out of proportion," he says slowly, carefully enunciating each word.

"Well, then you're not gonna like what I say next."

He waits.

Pushing some of the hair from my face, I exhale, my breath visible. "Uh, I don't think my heater is working."

"Your thermostat?"

"Yeah. It was extremely cold inside the other day, so I turned it up, but for some reason, it can't keep the right temperature. The needle's been dropping steadily since."

Kal swears under his breath. "For fuck's sake. Well, at

least we know you won't die being murdered. Just by freezing to death."

I wince, a chill that has nothing to do with the air sweeping over me.

The scar on my hip throbs, and I struggle to stay present and not let the memory resurface.

"Goddamn. I'll take care of it," Kal says, and I can't help the way his tone makes me shrink into the mattress, shame clawing its way up my windpipe. I want to apologize, but the words don't come out.

Stupid, Riley. Stupid, stupid, stupid.

Mom was right.

God, was she right.

"Your brother is not going to like this."

I snort, the notion shoving me further into my spiral. "Boyd doesn't give a shit what happens to me."

"If that's the case, I'd love for you to explain why I have to report my every fucking conversation and visit back to him." Clearing his throat, I hear him say something to someone, but can't quite make out the whisper. "Some people don't know how to reach others when it's never been done for them. Just because he doesn't show up for you in the ways you think he ought to, doesn't mean he's not showing up."

A sharp pang shoots through my chest, and I turn my face into the pillow, letting the cotton soak up the tears as they bleed over. "Does it even matter if I can't see a difference?"

"It matters. Some journeys take longer to bear fruit, is all."

It's at odds with what he told me the last time he was here, and I can't help wondering if maybe Boyd told him to say it. Like he thinks he might be able to lessen my hurt if he builds a case for himself through the people I trust.

I hang up without saying goodbye and spend a couple of minutes staring up at the ceiling. Part of me expects Aiden to jump out of the shadows, and so I wait a few beats, clutching the sheets to my chest as my eyes dart around the room.

The air is still, though. Lacking the charge that accompanies him.

I wait some more.

Curl and uncurl my toes.

Finally, I get out of bed, tightening the tie on my robe and sliding my feet into a pair of fuzzy purple slippers. My teeth chatter as I walk down the hall, gripping the banister on the stairs.

"Hello?" I call, hoping he'll materialize and I can dive back under the covers. "Aiden?"

It feels idiotic, searching for some sort of comfort in the arms of a man who's made it clear he despises me, and yet I can't seem to stop.

When I'm met with more silence, I tiptoe down the stairs and scour the entire first level. Tremors roll over me as I move through the house, coming up empty.

Ending my search at the back door, I push it open and lean out, scanning the deck. The hot tub is covered up, and the darkness outside is as uninhabited as the inside.

Sighing, I pull back, moving to shut the door when light across the lake gives me pause.

This time, the shadowy figure remains in the window, his silhouette ensconced in yellow light.

My heart hammers in my chest, and I stumble back a step, my fingers shaking as I squeeze the fabric of my robe in them. Anxiety twists through my muscles like a pretzel, everything locking up as it spreads to my limbs.

Neither of us moves, and I can feel the snow seeping into my slippers, freezing where it bleeds into my toes.

A fever builds in my core, too. It radiates up my thighs and covers the chill in my bones.

Standing there, soaking in his invisible scrutiny, I realize I like the flames.

Something in me craves that heat. Feels desperate for *him*.

I turn away, determination propelling me back inside the house so I can put on a pair of boots. I shouldn't go there, shouldn't throw myself at the feet of this dangerous man. But for some reason, I think I'd rather be there than have to sit with the ice that's made a home in my veins.

I'll choose his warmth, even if it means getting burned.

At least when you're on fire, you know you're alive.

SOMEHOW, I make it around the lake in one piece; using the flashlight on my phone, I step in the soft footprints he's left behind, following the path he apparently takes every time he comes to me.

My knuckles are red and raw by the time I get to the front door, and pain splices up my forearm when I bring them against the wood.

I blow into my palms, rocking on my heels while I wait for him to answer. It takes an impossibly long time, and I step off the porch for a second, glancing up at the second-story window to see that the light's gone out since I left my deck.

Rejection ricochets around my skull, bouncing excitedly from one side to the next, causing a headache to sprout behind my brow bone.

One last knock, and I'm once again met by an uncomfortable silence. Tears well up in my eyes, but I bat them away quickly, not sure how cold it has to be in order for them to freeze on my face.

Plus, I'm *so sick of crying.*

Sniffling, I wipe my nose with my sleeve and turn to go, my legs screaming against the cold, where my calves are exposed by my robe.

My foot lands on the bottom step as soon as the door swings open, and I jerk my head around so fast that I lose my balance; my feet slide out from under me, and my back bows where it smacks against the edge of the step.

The breath whooshes from my lungs completely, leaving me immobile. For a second, as I blink up at the night sky, panic surges through me as I consider the possibility that I might actually be paralyzed.

"Jesus fucking Christ," Aiden hisses, and his sudden steps shake the porch, the thud of his quick approach reverberating in my spine.

"Ow," I whisper, unable to do anything else. I want to close my eyes when he appears above me, his too-handsome face adding insult to injury, but my eyelids won't budge.

Nothing moves, hard as I try to make my body obey.

And then an entirely new panic settles in, like floodgates being thrown open. In an instant, I'm lying on my back in my mother's trailer, bleeding and aching and wishing more than anything that I could just get up.

If I could make my legs work, I could leave.

I could fight back.

For once, I wouldn't be totally fucking powerless.

But it doesn't *work*.

Because in truth, all I am, all I've ever been, is weak.

I hear the sob pierce the air more than I feel it, but when Aiden's palm presses gently against my mouth, that's *all* I feel. Channeling the sureness of his touch, I focus on regulating my breathing, looking up at him with teary eyes.

Even though he's been awful to me, I let him pull me from the memory. Maybe that doesn't help my case, but right now I don't care.

"Are you hurt?" I try to shake my head, but I'm not sure it works. He glances down, frowning at my robe. "Fuck, Riley, what are you even doing out here? You're not dressed for the snow."

Prying my tongue from the roof of my mouth, I manage to shake his hand away. "You didn't come o-over tonight."

He blinks. "What?"

"You d-didn't come over." It's hard to speak as the feeling slowly returns to my nerve endings, the frigid air sticking to my skin. "So, I c-came to y-you."

For a long time, he doesn't say anything, and I force a cough just for something else to focus on. My heart's been shattered and left in bloody heaps on the floor, mortification winding around my windpipe and constricting until I can't breathe all over again.

"Angel," he finally says, swiping a thumb beneath my eye. "You've been waiting for me?"

"It's stupid," I croak.

Aiden shakes his head, his mouth hardening into a thin

line, but he doesn't say anything else. His eyes, though, glitter like pyrite, and I wish I knew what that meant.

I feel like a limp noodle as he bends, gathering me into his arms carefully. When he lifts, I wince, a sharp twinge splitting through my lower half.

He freezes, and I realize I must have made a sound or facial expression that alarmed him.

"Goddamnit," he grits, and I see his Adam's apple bob as he swallows. "Where does it hurt?"

I don't answer, too overwhelmed by the whiplash he's giving me. There's still an undercurrent of anger, even when he's handling me like I might break, and it's confusing.

A strangled sound tears from his throat, and he walks back up the steps, clutching me so tight that I don't jostle even a little. Once we're in the foyer, he kicks the door shut, and the heat from his cabin immediately washes over me, returning feeling to my fingers.

I glance around the room, taking in the floral wallpaper and the bear-shaped rug lying in front of the fireplace. Like my cabin, the furniture inside is all handcrafted and pine, and there's a brown suede sofa in the living room, which he spreads me out on.

"Don't move," he commands, and frankly, I'm not sure I could even if I wanted to.

The heat from the fire laps at my skin, and I roll slightly, presenting my aching back to the flames. A moan escapes my lips as the warmth soothes my pain, and I try to stifle it in one of the tacky deer print throw pillows.

"*Riley.*"

Aiden's voice cuts through the air like a reprimand, and I shift my eyes up to find him standing over me, a bottle of water in one hand, the other turned upward like he's holding something.

"Yes, Doctor?"

"Take these." He shoves his hand out, revealing two little pink pills, and I frown at them. "It's an antihistamine."

"Like for allergies?"

"And inflammatory pain. It's all I've got here." Dumping the pills into my hand, he shifts me onto my side. "Although, I notice your rash hasn't fully gone away."

"I'm still using the lotion."

His mouth twists up. "What? Why?"

Popping the pills into my mouth, I shake my head when he offers the water and swallow them dry. "The winter air dries out my skin, and I haven't been in to see the doctor yet to know what ingredient it is I need to avoid."

"So you'd rather have a rash than dry skin?"

"Don't judge me."

"I'm not. I'm just... trying to understand the logic."

A weird laugh bubbles up out of my chest, and I roll over again, this time so I'm facing him. The silver of a chain necklace peeks out from his white T-shirt, and his hands are stuffed in the pockets of his black sweatpants.

"Here's something you need to understand about me," I say. "Not all of my actions are driven by logic. Sometimes I just do things, regardless of the consequences."

"Like, walk to a man's house even though he's made it clear he wants to hurt you."

Running my tongue over the fronts of my teeth, I shrug. "You don't really want to hurt me."

"I don't?"

"Nope." My lips smack against the end of the word. "If you did, you would've left me outside to freeze."

He hums, crouching down on his knees beside the sofa. When he smooths his hand over my forehead, his rings are cool against my warm skin.

"Maybe I want to hurt you on my own terms," he murmurs, minty breath brushing my temple.

There's certainly no denying he *wants* to. I'm just starting to question how strong that desire beats compared to the others.

I turn my head, and the flames behind him somehow reflect in the harsh grays of his irises. They burn where they lash against me, pulling me in, scarring me indefinitely.

My hand lifts, moving of its own accord, and I capture his strong chin between my fingers. My thumb presses into the gentle cleft hidden by his stubble, just below his bottom lip—the one I spent *years* drooling over as a teenager, imagining getting to do this very thing.

Biting down on the inside of my cheek, I blot out every other single thought, focusing instead on how surreal this is. How I can't believe I'm sitting here, touching a god, wishing I could keep him.

"Maybe I'll let you," I whisper, and my hand slides down his chin to the back of his neck, tugging him into a brutal kiss that I just know I'll feel on my teeth for years to come.

35

Lights me aflame in places I didn't know existed.

It's fucking dangerous, but I let her pull me in anyway.

Her lips move slowly against mine, coaxing and caressing like she's trying to memorize the feel of our mouths together. My hand comes up and tangles in her hair, guiding her movements, desperate to feel *more*.

Clarity shoves through the haze of lust clouding my judgment, and I pause, my eyes popping open. Up close, I can count the light freckles dusting her nose, and see the exact shape of her scars; my hand slides around, cupping her jaw, and I trail my thumb over the one beneath her cheek.

Lips still sealed to mine, she opens her eyes; the pale, watery blues knock the rebellion out of me like wind being let out of sails, and I tilt her head, climbing up so I'm hovering over her as she sinks deeper into the couch.

Thighs trapped between mine, her robe rides up, taunting me. Disconnecting from her takes every ounce of willpower I possess, but I do it, licking the seam of her mouth as I pull back.

She scowls. "Please don't tell me you're regressing into being an asshole again."

I smirk, shifting so the rigid outline of my dick presses into her hips. "Who said I stopped?"

"We were having a *moment*," she whines.

Bringing my hand to rest on the arm of the couch, I hold myself up, using the opposite one to toy with the collar of her robe. She watches the movement, her gaze glued to my fingers, and I can tell she's anxious.

"Breathe," I murmur, trailing the pad of my index finger lightly down the valley between her breasts. "I just want to talk for a minute."

Fear pulses in those beautiful blue eyes, and they fall closed. "I can't tell you what you want to know."

"Sure you can."

"I *can't*," she snaps, and when she looks at me, tears fill her lids and spill over, staining her porcelain cheeks. "Please don't make me."

Bending, I press my forehead to hers, inhaling and letting her incinerate my lungs.

"I *have* to." There's a strain in my voice, something

untethered and miserable, because goddamn if there isn't a sick vindication in seeing her cry for me, over and over.

It's satisfying in a way I've never known, sending bolts of arousal through me like lightning striking the sky.

My cock jerks against her hip, encouraged by her tears, and I reach up to collect them on my thumb; without giving it much forethought, I slide that same hand beneath the waist of my pants, pinching the bead of precum bubbling at the tip of my shaft, and bring it back up, mixing the two liquids together.

Pressing the wet pad to her mouth, I silently ask for entry. She hesitates, discomfort etched into her face, but after a second, she parts her lips enough for me to push in.

Her tongue swirls around, licking like she's trying to embed my fingerprint into her memory. My throat constricts, my hips pinning her harder against the sofa, and something new flashes in her gaze.

Something carnal and needy that sends a shot of desire straight to my cock.

She sucks my thumb in to the knuckle, laving around like she's addicted to the taste.

I pull out, and she releases me with a loud pop.

"More?" she asks, and I swear to fucking God I almost combust on the spot.

"Are you begging, pretty girl?" Lifting my knee, I use it to pry her legs apart, fitting myself between them.

Rolling my hips against her hot center, I press my open mouth to her temple to try and stave off the visceral reaction I'm having to her.

"Do you... do you like when I do?" She clears her throat, and I feel her fingers tug on the hem of my T-shirt. "Beg, I mean."

"I believe I'd like anything you did," I say, pulling back just enough to maintain eye contact. "But yes, begging is up there."

"Why?"

A frown pulls at my lips. "You want me to explain why I like it?"

Crimson crawls up her neck, embarrassment flushing her face. She turns her head toward the fire, gulping. "Forget it, that was stupid."

"Stop doing that." I grip her chin, tugging her back so she's forced to look at me. "Stop immediately shutting down and beating yourself up when someone asks for more information. This is how humans communicate. You're not *stupid*, Riley. Stupid girls don't get away with the shit you have."

She doesn't say anything, but a shred of surrender splashes in her irises; it's not complete, but it's enough, and I rotate my hips again, notching my erection against her needy cunt. I can practically smell her already.

"It's about control, Riley." I lower my head, catching the gasp that escapes as I grind into her clit. "It's acknowledging an imbalance of power and reinforcing it for the person who holds more." *Slow thrust. Grind. Repeat.* "It's you trusting me to use that power to please you. To corrupt you."

The tie of her robe loosens with each gyration of my hips, and I push the cotton material aside, needing to see more of her.

"Are you going to corrupt me?" she asks, her voice saccharine—but not in an innocent, genuine way.

I look up at her as my fingers find her cunt, sliding deftly between already slick folds, and her lashes fan across her cheeks as she stares back.

Uncertain, but still somehow unwavering.

Circling her entrance with my middle finger, one of my eyebrows lifts. "I think I already have."

Abandoning her tight little hole, I move back up and find her swollen clit, pinching it between two fingers. She jerks into it, and I fit our upper halves together again, swallowing her ensuing moan.

"We're coming back to my questions," I tell her between sloppy kisses, unable to tear myself away as she slowly undulates below me. "But first..."

Breaking away with a pained groan, I slink to my knees on the floor and pull her to the edge of the sofa, settling my shoulders between her legs. I reach up to push her robe farther apart, but her hands slap over mine, stopping me.

"Riley." My voice is a growl, primal and irritated that she keeps denying me. "We're doing it right this time, or not at all."

Her teeth sink into her bottom lip, and she shifts, clearly trying to get away. I slip my arms under her, clamping my palms down on the insides of her thighs, pinning her in place.

"*Please*," she whines, pinching her eyes shut, her hands coming to tug at the robe. I yank harder, and she chokes on a wail. "It's fucking *embarrassing*."

The air expels from my lungs like I've just been run over by a military tank and left flattened.

"What's embarrassing? Your scars?"

She lets go of the robe, covering her face. "*Yes*. They're disgusting, and I don't want you to see."

A beat of silence passes between us.

"Riley, I don't give a shit about your scars."

"How can you not?" Her voice breaks, emotion making it so thick that *I* find it difficult to keep breathing. "*I* hate them.

Every time I look in the mirror, they're all I see. These big, ugly flaws that I didn't always have, and then one day, boom. I'm a freak. Everyone pretends, you know? They act like I don't have these nasty reminders marking me. Like they don't see them, and they don't make a difference in how they look at me, but they do."

Her hands come to her mouth, touching the scar there, and she continues shattering.

"I can't even complain about them because *so many people* have it worse, and I should just be happy to be fully functioning. Alive. I should be *happy* to be alive."

"Jesus," I mutter, crawling out from between her legs to drag her down to the floor with me. She comes willingly, burying her tears in my chest.

"I'm not," she sobs, and all I can do is stroke her hair, guilt and shame settling like a slab of broken concrete on top of my heart. "I'm not happy I'm alive. I'm not proud of my trauma, or the person it made me. It *hurts*, and I *hate* it."

The concrete gets heavier with each admission, until the organ is crushed completely, its beats slowly dwindling to a halt.

Pulling back, Riley fists my shirt, anger and pain dancing in her baby blues.

They glisten, hopelessly anguished, and she just shakes her head back and forth. She sniffles, wiping her nose with her sleeve, and then she shifts, pushing me so my back rests against the sofa.

Widening her legs, she moves to straddle me, and I palm her hips, holding her still.

"Riley," I breathe, surprised at the way she resists, bearing down in spite of my iron grip. "I don't want to do this."

"I like it better when you call me pretty girl," she says, encircling my wrists, trying to move them. "And yes, you do want this. I can feel how badly."

Gritting my teeth as her bare cunt makes contact with my erection, I dig my fingernails into her. "I don't want you like this."

"Not even if I say *please*?"

She bats her lashes, rubbing herself over me, and fuck, when she slides back, I see where she's soaking my sweats. My head lolls, my eyes rolling as she grinds hard, sending fragments of exhilaration down my spine.

The grip on her hips falters, and she seizes the opportunity, bringing my hands up to cup her breasts beneath her robe. On instinct, my head snaps back up and my fingers curl around them, squeezing the perfect handfuls.

"*Please*, Aiden. Make me forget."

Without missing a beat, she continues dry humping me, face wet from her tears and flushed with desire.

She looks so painfully perfect, so agonizingly tempting, that I can't hold back.

Fuck it, maybe this is how I'll ruin her.

I'm not even a hundred-percent sure what she's asking me to help eliminate from her mind, but fuck if I don't want to destroy everything she's afraid of until it's just *me*.

Leaning forward, I ignore the nagging thought about the fact that I'm losing control; dipping my head to one tit, I flick my tongue against the pebbled peak, pressing my fingers into the base of her spine.

Her movements stutter, a low moan peeling out of her, and I open my mouth wide, pulling her between my lips.

"Oh, god," she exhales, ecstasy coating her words.

I suck harder, laving around the distended nipple. She

reaches forward, fumbling for my dick; yanking at my sweats, she manages to tug the waistband down enough to free me, and tucks the pants under my balls.

My cock stands at attention, deep red and angry, and she licks her lips as she stares at it.

Her hand comes out, tentatively wrapping around the shaft, fingers barely touching.

She starts moving, short bursts up and down, and I bite the inside of my cheek until the taste of copper floods my mouth.

"Can you, um, show me what you want me to do?"

I curl my fingers around hers, increasing her pressure, but then bat her hand away. "Some other time. Right now, I want to fuck you."

"Oh."

"Yeah, *oh.*"

Taking her hips in my hands again, I yank her up my lap, lining her up with my cock as it lies against my abs. She sucks in a sharp breath as her lips spread around me, and I guide her over it in long, smooth strokes.

"Does that feel good, pretty girl?"

Her stomach flexes, in and out, as she moves. "*So* good."

"I want you to look at it," I say, sliding a hand up to fist the back of her hair, tilting her chin down. "Look at what's gonna be inside you soon. Get it nice and wet, so it pushes right in that sweet cunt of yours."

She watches, mouth parted. "What if it doesn't fit?"

Christ. "It'll fit, angel. Even if we have to make it."

Precum oozes from my tip, and I swipe my thumb through it, spreading it over her lips before dipping inside.

I pull from her mouth again, my nerves slowly unraveling as pleasure ebbs through me. Her pulse throbs against me, making my balls ache, and the tiny noises and gasps coming from her make me think she's close.

"Don't stop until you come," I tell her, my hands falling to her hips again, driving her motions. "Be a good girl and get ready for me."

Blue flames light her eyes, burning so hot that it's impossible not to feel their heat.

She works her clit furiously over me, her juices dripping everywhere.

"Aiden, please... I'm, I don't—"

The closer she gets, the more panic-filled her voice becomes, stretching so thin and tight that it sounds like she's on the brink of catastrophe, rather than rapture. I wrap my fingers around her throat, pressing lightly, until she looks at me.

"Are you begging me to let you come?" I ask, lifting up to speak against her mouth.

She nods, but a layer of confusion still laces her gaze, like she's intrigued but still not totally sure.

"Do you trust me?"

Her lips purse. "I shouldn't."

I grin. "That wasn't the question."

When she nods, I start grinding my hips up to meet hers and the increased friction has her cresting the edge of her orgasm in seconds.

"That's it," I croon, coaxing her through as she cries out in elation. "That's my girl. Fucking me and I'm not even inside you yet."

She rides me right off the cliff, panting and swiveling and moaning, and then I push her up, grab the base of my dick, and yank her down on top of it.

36

Pain settles between my thighs, extending from my pussy to every single receptor in my body. It's a sharp sting and a dull ache all at once, burning me from the inside out at the same time it douses the fire.

My fingers twist in the neckline of Aiden's shirt, and my knees clench around his hips, but other than that, I don't move. His hands sizzle where they roam, constantly moving since he started pushing in; knuckles dragging up my spine, palms splaying down my thighs, thumbs trailing over my collarbone.

It's such a shift from the way he's touched me before.

There's something almost reverent about it, like I'm a glass figurine he has to hold and knows he can't drop.

I should be embarrassed about my complete breakdown, but it's really difficult to feel anything else right now except his cock lodged inside me.

"Riley. Open your eyes."

Immediately, my lids peel back; I hadn't even realized they'd closed.

His silver gaze meets mine, so close I can see the different layers of gray—some slate, some cloudy, like the glittering edge of a crystal. For a moment, I lose myself in the storm that is Aiden, my apprehension melting away like lava over an ancient city.

"Very good, pretty girl." His praise makes my core clench, warmth spreading through me as he brushes his fingers over my back again, digging into the meat of my ass.

I can't help the buzz of disappointment at the lack of skin-to-skin contact where my robe still covers me.

"Take a deep breath," he says, pinching.

I gasp, the location of pain zapping to my backside. As my lungs clamor for more air, the movement somehow opens me, and I slide down his cock another inch.

The agony has almost started to subside, delicious tension ebbing in its place. I repeat the gesture, sucking in oxygen and letting him fill me.

"*Slow*, Riley, fuck." He fists my robe, the tendons in his neck straining against his tattoos. "We have to go slow."

A ragged moan tears out of me as I bottom out, my ass resting atop his thighs. He jerks forward, dipping his mouth to the hollow of my throat, his breaths stilted and hot.

"Oh, my *god*." I think my fingers are starting to go numb

from the choke hold I have on his T-shirt, but I don't even care.

Once I've had a second to adjust, the stinging sensation morphs into a warm wave, slowly unfurling in my core. My hips shift, seeking more, craving the friction.

I yank one hand from his shirt and press the palm into my stomach. "God, I can feel you here."

Aiden coughs, pulling back to look. "Fuck, angel, don't say shit like that."

Frowning, my anxiety flares back up, and I pause. "I'm so—"

"Don't you dare apologize while my cock is inside you," he says, shunting deeper, capturing my surprise with his lips. "You're just so goddamn tight, I don't know how I'm gonna hang on."

"Oh." Separating our mouths, I glance down at where we're connected, forcing my breaths to even out. Rolling forward again, I hook my teeth in my bottom lip and chase that euphoria, grinding my clit against him. "It feels good?"

His head lolls back. "Phenomenal, pretty girl. You feel fucking *phenomenal*, and you're doing such a good job. Working my dick with your sweet cunt, like it belongs to you."

Pride blooms in my chest at his words, and wetness trickles between my thighs, soaking the both of us.

Emotion clogs my throat as I continue swiveling my hips, desperately trying to cull the need building in my center. My motions falter, nerves taking the forefront as my concentration becomes distracting, but then Aiden's gripping the back of my neck and forcing my gaze to his.

"Whatever feels good for you, feels good for me." He

flicks his tongue over my lips and the quick lashing has me bowing, wanting to feel that sensation in other places.

But I'm stuck in limbo, trying to wade through the black sludge of self-loathing.

As if sensing that my mind is still struggling, Aiden grabs me and lifts, setting me on the bear rug. He scrambles to his feet, reaching behind his head to tug off his shirt, and then kicks out of his pants and boxers.

I swallow, feeling small in front of him, but in the best way. Maybe it's that power dynamic he mentioned before, but being here on the floor while he towers over me has my pussy clenching wantonly, aching to be filled back up.

Climbing on top of me, he pushes so I'm flat on the ground, kicking my legs apart and settling between them.

This time when he pushes in, there's far less resistance; he grips my thighs, pulling them back so my knees are almost pinned against the floor, and *oh fuck,* when he moves I can taste him in my throat.

"Insanity," he whispers, pulling out to the tip just to thrust all the way in again. "I'm afflicted, and I think you're somehow both the cause and the cure."

"I'm so—"

Clamping his hand down over my mouth, he shakes his head, pistoning into me with a pinch of brutality. It knocks the air from my chest, and my pussy convulses in delight.

His rings feel like a balm to my soul, cool and soothing where they dig into my skin.

"Since you can't seem to stop apologizing, I'm going to keep my hand here. Which means you won't be able to beg me to come with words. Get creative, pretty girl."

I don't even want to listen to what he's saying, because his dick is stroking and massaging places I hadn't known existed. My vision blurs as he drives in, my inner muscles fluttering around him as pleasure zings through my veins.

"Take it," he mutters, and I can't tell who exactly he's chanting to. "Take my cock, pretty girl. Fits you perfectly."

Blades of hair curl over his forehead, dampened from the sheen of sweat slicking across his skin. I reach up, pushing the dark strands back, and I swear he purrs for a moment before going back to whispering dirty things under his breath.

His words, tiny gasps, and moans of praise feel like sunshine soaking into my skin, but it's his eyes that I pay attention to. The way they vacillate over every inch of me, blazing a path from where we're connected up to where his hand keeps me mute.

They're intense storms raining down on me, elation sparking like a match that doesn't stop raging.

It's exhilarating, being trapped beneath his hungry gaze and letting it wash over me. Knowing he's breaking apart for *me*, even though not long ago he wanted to ruin me.

My fingers tingle as I reach up, tracing the lines of his tattoos, trying my best to memorize them in case this is the last time I get to see them. He bucks, canting his hips so hard that his balls slap against the crack of my ass, and I can feel us inching up the rug.

It feels so good that I'm starting to see stars, black creeping in at the edges of my vision. My pulse kicks rapidly, blood rushing between my ears, and with each thrust, an animalistic sound wrenches itself from the back of my throat.

Eyes wide, I keep them trained on him, refusing to look away as release unspools in my stomach, tendrils of euphoria reaching through and wrapping around me.

I need it, I need it, I need it.

As it crawls up the base of my spine, I'm so distracted by the heat that I don't notice my robe falling open, baring every part of me but my arms to Aiden. He drinks me in, fucking faster, the muscles in his jaw clenched so tight I can practically see the indent of his teeth.

Tears prickle behind my eyes as my orgasm crests, and he lets out a sound that echoes in my chest. "You ready for me to fill you up?"

I try to nod, something caught between a sob and a squeal scratching out of my throat, vibrating against my skin. The tears fall over as my climax reaches its crescendo, exhilaration thundering through me and making me shake.

My legs come around him, heels digging into his ass, spurring his movements as he fucks me through the bliss.

His hips jerk, his pace stuttering in time with the beat of my heart, and then he shoves in so he's flush with my skin. A torrent of hot, thick cum pulses inside of me, and the low groan he gives is desperate and gravelly, sending a shiver down my legs.

"*Fuck.*" Aiden sits back on his knees, chest heaving as he catches his breath. Sliding his hand slowly from my mouth, he runs his thumb in a soothing gesture over my lips, as if he's trying to bring the feeling back. "You okay?"

Nodding is all I can manage, my mind too gooey and sated to form coherent thoughts, much less vocalize them.

With a grin, he bends and presses a searing kiss to my mouth, letting his tongue lick lazily at the interior, like he's memorizing it.

Pulling back, he sighs, his hands never leaving my body. Like he can't possibly stand not to touch me, even for a second.

"We should get you cleaned up," he says, and I feel his fingers swipe through where our cum drips from my core.

Shaking my head, I moan in protest, exhaustion suddenly bearing down on me. "Not yet. Want to sleep."

"Fine, just for a second." He glides down my body, and I feel him pause for a second at my hip. I know he's looking at the scar, but he drags his finger over the tiny tattoo there, as if trying to pretend otherwise.

Or maybe he's reiterating how little he cares about the imperfections.

Whatever the case, my body tenses, but I'm too limp to do anything else. And then he keeps moving, shouldering his way between my legs, cradling my ass in his palms and lifting it off the floor.

I glance at him, my eyes bulging; his breath skates across my clit, making it throb painfully as he lines his mouth up. "What are you *doing*?"

One lick along my seam has my head dropping to the floor, aftershocks rolling through me.

"Cleaning up," he says, before sealing his mouth to me like it's the most natural thing in the world.

37

RILEY PASSES out almost immediately after my tongue brings her to the brink for the third time. Her thighs quake, tightening around my ears as she comes, drenching my chin in our combined juices.

By the time I've disentangled myself and wiped my mouth with the back of my hand, she's out cold, a light snore drifting from her parted lips.

Her face is red, mouth swollen, resembling the crescent shape of her cunt. After taking a quick piss, I grab a warm washcloth from the powder room and bring it back to the living area, settling it gently between her legs to try and soothe her abused flesh.

I won't lie and say I don't love the color on her. Red looks fucking good when it's painting her skin because of me.

Pulling my knees to my chest and draping my forearms over them, I sit at her side for a long time. The heat from the fireplace envelops us, calming the chill in the air that flares when I'm not touching her.

I'm not sure what that's about, but for now, I ignore it, positive that I don't want to know.

I don't feel like sullying this night with the bite of reality. *Speaking of...*

My gaze falls to where her robe gapes, pooling on the floor under her. The flames cast her in shadows, barely giving visibility to her hip, but I look anyway, *needing* to see for myself.

A pinkish-white, angry abrasion stretches from the outside of her left hip and fades on the way to her belly button. It's risen slightly compared to the unmarred skin, smooth to the touch but rough at the same time and two fingers thick at its widest point.

Nausea roils in my gut. Potential images of how she got the scar flip through my mind, dozens of scenarios playing out like the ending credits of a movie, all of them filling me with frustration and violence.

Trailing my fingers slowly over the mangled flesh, I continue down to where the word "angel" is etched into her hip. The reminder of putting it there eases my pulse a bit, and I dip my head, pressing the lightest kiss to the ink.

"Told you it was ugly."

My eyes snap to hers, surprise flooding me like a sudden wave. Her head is propped up by her arm, and she's watching me with an unreadable expression on her face.

I sit up, my hand brushing over her stomach. "It's not—" I start, the sentence stalling partway through. No matter what, I doubt I'll ever be able to convince her that the scars aren't ugly, so truthfully, there's no point in trying.

"You're right, Riley. They're ugly."

A beat passes silently, and then she huffs out a harsh laugh. It's broken, strangled, and I feel it pierce my chest the second it escapes.

"*Okay*, well. This was fun." Reaching for the lapels of her robe, she pushes to her knees, snatching it closed. "Thanks for the orgasms, but I'd better get going. Feel free to stop by when nice Aiden comes back."

Before she can get into a standing position, I reach out and grab her wrist, tugging her into my lap as I settle back against the couch.

"Seriously?" She wiggles around as I bracket her with my legs, pulling her backside flush with my front. "Let go of me."

"No."

Her jaw clenches, and she lets out a ragged screech. "I want to go home."

"I don't care. You're going to stay here until I say you can leave."

"Oh, are we adding kidnapping to your list of offenses now?"

"Depends," I say, skimming my nose along her hairline, inhaling soft floral hues and that fucking peppermint. God, she needs to stop using that lotion, or I need to get her a new bottle. "Do we think Stockholm Syndrome would affect your opinion of me?"

"Not in the way you might want it to."

"Then stop talking, so I can let you go," I murmur. She grunts, crossing her arms over her chest, and I slip my hands over her waist, toying with the tie of her robe. "I want you to feel something."

"If you say your dick, I swear to God—"

One of my hands snakes up her front, cascading through the valley between her breasts to fit tight over her mouth.

Holding my left arm up, I turn it so my palm faces the ceiling, then take one of her hands and wrap it around my wrist. Slowly, I push the pads of her fingers into the inked skin, letting her feel the grooves and too-smooth lines buried under the compass and flock of birds.

Nerves cinch my throat, pulling so tight that breathing gets painful, but I let her soak in the unspoken implication anyway.

"Three suicide attempts by the time I turned fifteen." I force the words from where they stick in my esophagus and try not to choke on them. "Each cut deeper than the last, but none of them quite enough to abate my misery."

The smell of bleach and rubbing alcohol floods my senses along with the memory of waking up in my own bed, with just my mother sitting by my side, clutching my bandaged arm like it was her life raft and not the bane of my existence.

Riley's fingers curl around my arm, a silent plea.

"I won't go into the sordid details of why I was never taken to an ER, or why my family chose to handle each ordeal as a cry for attention rather than help, but if you're wondering why you never heard about it online or in the media, it's because they scrubbed the evidence away."

Her eyes glisten, and I clear my throat, discomfort ricocheting through my veins.

"I started covering mine when I started performing. Mainly because my parents wanted me to, but also because I couldn't stand the reminders of those low points in my life. The scars were ugly, and I got tired of seeing them. It helps that tattoos add to the whole bad boy brand I was aiming for. Somehow, men's mental health does not."

I work my jaw, considering what to add next. How to convey my truths.

"Anyway, all of that is to say I'm not operating under the illusion that scars somehow enhance our natural beauty, or amplify our plights. They don't. They suck." I drop my hand, tugging on her robe, and pull it open so her hip is bared.

Knuckles bleaching white, she balls her hands into fists, as if resisting the urge to cover herself.

Spreading my fingers over the diamond-shaped reminder on her skin, I turn my head, pressing my lips to her temple.

"You *have* scars, but they don't have *you*." I'm not sure if either of us is breathing anymore. "And you, Riley fucking Kelly, are beautiful in a way that'd make the constellations weep."

The first of her tears falls, dripping slowly over my fingers, and I fit her head beneath my chin, grounding myself in her the way I've wanted to since I first laid eyes on her at that charity gala.

Three years of torment, of not knowing what the fuck happened that night, and none of it feels like it matters now that I've got her in my arms. The revenge plot, the need to make her hurt—all of that slides to the back burner in favor of the warmth she provides, the relief I find in her presence.

When my throat draws tighter, I know it's not because

I'm reliving sadness, trying to explain something I still don't fully understand myself.

It's because, for the first time I can remember, I feel a little less alone. And while I'm sitting with her, I know it isn't going to last.

"I DON'T WANT to do this anymore."

My father's sigh rumbles through the phone, and I can just imagine him pinching the bridge of his nose, leaning back in his oversized office chair in annoyance. The distinctive clink of ice against a glass tumbler accompanies his breathing, and a forlorn pang of nostalgia creeps up my chest, making me long for the days I'll never get back.

Days spent watching him rule over New York City's music industry as a kid, admiring him the way the ancients must have looked at their sun gods.

As if the horizon rose and set by his fingertips alone.

Days before he cheated on my mother, broke her spirit, and consequently left me to be the scapegoat. The reason he strayed.

Only to find out later that it was just because he was bored, and girls were easy.

At least, my ex was.

Days before I hated myself and tried to drown that hatred at the bottom of a bottle, or with razors, or eventually with music.

Music was the worst escape, I think. Use something as a distraction long enough, and it'll dissolve into the stream of resentment along with everything else.

"You suddenly don't want to clear your name?" my father asks, his tone pinched. "After you spent the last three years of your life obsessing over getting to do so?"

His words burn my throat, and I move out of my bedroom doorway where Riley's sleeping—where she's been sleeping all week, while we wait on the snowstorm to dissipate, so an HVAC guy can come fix her heat.

Like I'm suddenly the good guy in her story.

Probably not a great time to bring up that I cracked the heat exchange in her unit last week.

"I still want to clear my name. I just don't want to drag her into it."

Heading down the stairs, I situate myself on the sofa, dragging my guitar off the floor and into my lap. I pluck at the strings absently, waiting while he contemplates what I'm saying.

"Tell me you're not fucking her."

My hand freezes, C sharp echoing around me. "So what if I am?"

"So what if—" Exasperation colors his tone. "Do you understand how bad it looks for you to have been accused of sexual assault, not perform or do *anything* Aiden James related for years, and then when we reintroduce you to the world, you're fucking the whore who tanked your career?"

"She's not a whore." I rub my hand over my mouth, violence pumping through me. "Call her that again, and I'll fly back to the city just to knock your fucking teeth out."

He scoffs. "If she's convinced you to throw your entire life away, again, then I suppose she must be a fucking nuclear physicist. Christ Almighty, son, do you care about your life at all? Do you care about *anything* other than getting your dick wet?"

Part of me wants to refute his claims and tear into him for suggesting I don't care about my own career. But it's *rich* coming from him, so instead, I push to my feet and head to the small room off the kitchen, slowly opening the door.

I lean against the frame, letting his words rake over my skin and soak up the scene in front of me.

The items of clothing from my closet back home, all the scrap sheets of music and peppermints—empty and not—everything I've been hoarding for years, because of this obsessive fucking thought that they'd one day become important.

That I'd need them for something other than to scratch the weird itch in my brain.

Things I carry with me, like phantoms I can't possibly get rid of, no matter how hard I try.

At the very back of the room, an emerald-green dress hangs over a painting, and I study those baby-blue eyes for so long, I almost forget I'm on the phone at all.

And I'm reminded of that night—the hope I felt, and how it was crushed the next morning. The time I spent in bed afterward, trying to garner up the courage to try, just *one more time*, to end my suffering.

The purpose I latched on to, my entire reason for coming to Lunar Cove, and how at odds it seems in the weeks since. How Riley's managed to weasel her way into my blackened heart, confusing the shit out of me as she tries to mend the pieces she helped shatter.

"No, Dad," I say finally, my eyes glued to her still ones across the room. "I don't care about anything."

38

"Here's a hypothetical for you: on a scale from one to ten, how, um... deranged might one have to be in order to sleep with their stalker?"

The silence on Fiona's end of the line is extremely loud —to the point that I have to pull the phone from where it rests on the edge of the bathtub and make sure I didn't lose connection.

She's got her camera propped up on my brother's bed while she paints her toenails bloodred, a pink towel wrapped around her head.

"One *million*," she says, dipping her brush back in its

little bottle, before applying the second coat. "That's some serious fucked in the head, back-alley kink shit."

"Jeez, Fi, I didn't take you as a kink-shamer." Heat sears my cheeks, and I lower myself back into my bubble bath, letting the foam cover my chest and thighs.

"I'm not kink-shaming." She pauses, glancing at the phone, cocking her head. "Am I? Is this hypothetical stalker, like, a role-play kind of thing?"

"Role-play?"

"Yeah, like the criminal and the victim? That kind of thing. I don't personally know anything about it, but that seems like something my brother would be into."

Probably because her brother *is* a criminal, but I don't say that. I barely know the guy, anyway—odd, given that he's Boyd's best friend, but it's not like he shares that part of his life with me.

Or any part, really.

My toes flatten against the tub tile, and I push thoughts of Boyd away. "If it's not anything like that?"

"If it's not..." Switching to her other foot, she sighs, seeming to roll her answer around in her head before speaking. "If it isn't, then I stand by my previous judgment. Hypothetically, it sounds like you need therapy."

Popping a pink bubble against her lips, she re-caps her nail polish and sticks her legs out, picking the phone up to recline on the bed.

"What brought that up, anyway? You're not sleeping with anyone, are you?" Her brows raise, wrinkling her freckled forehead. "God, do you have a stalker? Please say no, or Boyd's gonna freak—"

"I don't have a stalker," I say quickly, cutting her off just in case my brother's lurking somewhere close by. Technically, it's not a lie—Aiden's been less of a stalker lately, and more like a vampire I let in once, who now refuses to leave.

In the days since we fucked in his living room, I've spent about every night with him. Partly because the heat in my cabin just got fixed today, but also because I'm learning I really like falling asleep wrapped up in him.

Waking up on his luxury silk sheets and smelling that spicy cologne of his gives me an immediate serotonin boost each morning, and selfishly, I'm ignoring everything that led up to this point in favor of those things.

We haven't had sex again, though not for lack of trying on my part. Each time, he shuts me down and uses his talented fingers to make me come instead.

I'd be a lot more embarrassed about it if the orgasms weren't so fucking good.

"Are you *sure*?" Fiona asks, a skeptical look on her face. "No one's contacted you from King's Trace? Because if they have, we can fly you back here—"

"No, Fi, it's fine. I'm *fine*. I've just been watching too many K-dramas, I think."

"Oh, well that checks out." She laughs, and some kind of buzzer goes off in the distance. "Shit, I've got to switch the laundry over. Call me tomorrow, okay? We'll talk Christmas logistics."

I cringe. "Do we have to?"

"Yep. I've let this little rift between you and your brother go on long enough. It's time to fix it."

Rolling my eyes, I hang up, groaning as I plunge myself into the warm water. Counting to three beneath the surface, I let it calm the uneven pace of my heart and snap back up, gulping for air.

Movement in the corner of my bathroom startles me,

and I grapple for the side of the tub as I turn, a scream catching in my throat.

When heated gray eyes meet mine, I let out a strangled breath and sag into the tile.

"Jesus, Aiden. A little warning would be nice."

He smirks, making his way to the tub. Bubbles cling to my skin in all the right places, barring me from his unabashed gaze as he settles on the edge.

"A warning would defeat the entire purpose of this dynamic."

"Yeah, but shouldn't the dynamic shift, as the relationship... um... develops?"

I can feel shame coloring my face, likely as pink as my hair, so I scoop some of the bubbles into my hands and press them into my cheeks.

Aiden grins, wiping some of the soap away. "Do you want to go back to being my stalker? I have to say, being on this end of things for once is far more refreshing than I'd ever thought it'd be."

"Stalking someone is refreshing?"

"Not being under the microscope is."

Standing up, Aiden unzips his black hoodie and discards his T-shirt. Without moving his eyes from mine, his hands reach for the fly of his distressed jeans, undoing it with a slow fervor that has something hot stirring in my core.

My breath hitches when he shoves his pants off his hips, grabbing his dick as he kicks his legs free.

God, I don't know if it's possible to get used to someone who looks as good as he does naked; the deeply defined planes of his chest that turn into finely cut abs, and that V thing that you always hear about but never actually see on real people.

Not to mention his cock with its thick, veiny shaft and the reddish-pink mushroom top. I don't know if genitals are supposed to be attractive, but seeing his lengthen in front of me causes my core to throb, aching to be filled.

As he steps into the tub, moving my legs so he can prop his back against the edge opposite me, I'm practically salivating.

"Hungry?" he asks, bracketing me in with his calves, pulling my feet over his hips.

"Huh?"

His teeth scrape across his bottom lip, and he gives me a knowing look. "You're drooling, angel."

"Oh." Alarm has me straightening, dragging my knuckles across my chin, and he tips his head back and lets out a rich laugh.

The vibrant cadence of it catches me off guard, and I realize it's the first time I've heard him laugh since that night in New York City.

It's the kind of laugh you feel in your toes, that has the power to send butterflies on their migratory pattern to the South.

I'm in so much trouble.

The Jacuzzi jets kick on, blowing out against us and displacing the bubbles. Most of them pop with the motion, and then it's just two naked people in a tub, watching one another with guarded expressions.

Like they want to act on the obvious attraction pulsing between them, but are still afraid of the other's potential nefarious intentions.

Part of me feels like Aiden gave up on his quest for revenge too quickly, and it keeps me from diving in headfirst to all of this.

The fact that he seems just as unsure pretty much proves me right.

His fingers slide up my right foot, pulling it into his lap and digging his thumbs into the bottom of my arch. My eyes fall closed as he starts massaging in tight circles, breaking apart knots that have been there for years.

A moan teases at the back of my throat as he moves up, increasing the pressure on the ball of my foot.

"I got my first guitar when I was three," he says after a moment of silence, and my brows furrow, but I don't look up, not sure if he'd want me to. "It was this cheap little thing my mom bought, even though she didn't know anything about instruments. Had a mahogany back, and nylon strings, and I loved it so much that I slept with it every night until I was seven."

Snorting, I shift, resituating my ass as it starts to go numb. "When *I* was three, my mom got really high, broke out the windows in our trailer because she thought people were after her, and ended up leaving me alone for two full days while she hid out at some drug dealer's house."

I don't know what exactly prompts me to tell that story, especially since there are at least a couple of decent ones I could've gone with, but the words pour out of me before I have a chance to think about their consequences.

Aiden's fingers stall, and I can feel his eyes boring into me. Releasing a deep breath, I resist the urge to see the look on his face, afraid of the pity I might find.

A second later, he puts my foot back in the water and grabs the other, continuing the massage there. "Where was your dad?"

"I don't know. When they were together, he worked a lot. Back then, he was trying really hard to get his contracting business off the ground, or so he said." Sorrow pinches in my chest, burrowing deep as I realize how long it's been since I've even thought about him. "I think he just couldn't stand to be around Mom, though."

"And your brother?"

I hesitate, that particular wound still not close to being scabbed over. I'm afraid that if I keep picking at it, it'll never heal, and I'll never be able to have a real relationship with him.

But, Aiden's asking, and frankly, it feels kind of nice.

"He was a preteen when I was born, and he..." I swallow, my words thickening. "She always made it sound like he abandoned us to go live with our aunt. I guess she was trying to save face with me, but deep down, I knew his animosity existed for a reason."

"She gave him up?"

"Yeah." Tears sting behind my eyes and I blow out a breath. My heart aches, grief filling the cracks like glue.

No wonder Boyd always resented my existence.

I can't imagine mourning a life that'd been stolen from me, and seemingly handed to someone else.

Aiden hums, caressing my heel with his thumb. "My mom went to rehab on my eleventh birthday. Everyone tried to tell me she was taking an extended vacation in Cabo, but I knew better."

It feels surreal hearing him talk about his life after spending so much of my time learning everything about him through a screen.

"I'm not sure you want to play this game there, rock star," I say, adjusting my neck on the tub. "You heard my villain origin story, right?"

He chuckles, the sound seeming to have a direct line to

my clit. "Okay, I see your trauma and raise you: my ex-girlfriend fucked my dad while I was on the Argonautica tour. Well, while *we* were on that tour. She was sleeping in my hotel room at night and fucking him in his suite every morning."

My eyes pop open, images of his ex, with her shimmering copper hair and model figure, swimming through my mind. "*Sylvie Michaels*? With your *dad*? And you still talk to him?"

Shrugging, he drops my foot and stretches his arms out over the sides of the bathtub. "That relationship was more of a PR stunt than anything else."

He watches as I chew my bottom lip, then leans forward to grab my hips and pull me toward him.

Water splashes around us as I land on my knees, straddling his hips; his cock brushes against my pussy, and arousal spins tight in my stomach, excited by the position.

"There was no overlap, if you're wondering." He speaks against my mouth, our breaths mingling and getting lost in the steam.

"I wasn't, but good to know."

It hits me that I definitely *should've* been wondering, but for some reason, all logical thought seems to cease when I'm around him.

That feels like a red flag, but with rose-tinted glasses, I find it difficult to care.

Regrets are for the future self.

Brushing the hair off my shoulder, he dips his head, pressing a kiss to my collarbone. "You didn't try to cover yourself when I came in, you know?"

I blink, pulling back to ask what the hell he's talking about, and then it hits me.

My scars.

They hadn't crossed my mind even once since he appeared in the bathroom.

For what feels like the first time since I got them, they weren't the dominant thought ruling my brain.

The realization is as terrifying as it is freeing, so I don't give it too much time to expand into worry.

In answer, I cup his jaw in my hands and tilt his head back, fusing our mouths together in a gesture of thanks.

39

BALANCING my guitar pick between my teeth, I quickly jot a note down on the napkin beside me, closing my eyes and letting the melody breathe through me before I forget it.

When I open them back up, I see a flash of pink hair across the street, and my heart does this weird flip inside my chest at the sight.

Rubbing at my pec, I disregard the implication, watching as Riley ignores my presence and heads straight inside the art gallery.

Irritation crackles in my bones, and I slide my guitar strap over my head and push to my feet, crossing over to where she's just gone inside. Peering in through the slightly tinted windows, I scan the main lobby, releasing a breath of relief when I spot her standing in the back corner.

Alone.

The breath gets sucked back inside, though, when Caleb steps out in the next second, arms crossed over his chest. He looks pissed, and moves in close to speak to her, their noses almost touching.

My nostrils flare, but I stay glued in place, continuing to watch so I can see what she does, and punish—or reward —accordingly.

She sighs, putting her hands on her hips as she replies, but then he's stepping forward again, reaching out to cradle her face in his meaty palms.

Anger bounces around my chest like a bundle of helium balloons, pumping furiously from my heart to the rest of my body.

It's a rage I don't fully comprehend, because somewhere in the recesses of my brain, I know Riley's as obsessed with me as I am her.

If she's proved anything in the days since I fucked her in my living room, it's that.

And yet, the singular thought remains that I trusted her once before.

I walk inside, forcing myself to remain casual as the door swings shut behind me. Both faces turn in my direction, with Caleb's immediately souring.

"Can't you read?" he snaps. "I'm fucking closed."

My stare fixates on where he continues touching her, possessiveness spearing through me like a poisoned knife. I don't address him, just meet her dark-blue eyes and lift my chin.

"Could I speak to you for a second?" My voice is calm. Stiff. Her brows shoot into her hairline and then crease into a terse frown.

"We're in the middle of a conversation."

Ignoring Caleb again, I reach up, pulling my guitar off, and prop it on the floor against the wall. Lifting my arms, I clasp my palms at the back of my skull and wait.

No one moves.

Pushing my tongue into my cheek, I sigh. "*Riley.*"

Caleb's face contorts. "Who the fuck is Riley—"

Tearing away from him, she marches over and grabs my wrist, dragging me to a bathroom behind the register. She slams the door shut, sliding the barrel bolt lock so we can't be disturbed, and then whirls on me.

"What the hell?" She's fuming, shoving at my chest.

Good, now we're both mad.

I lean my shoulder against the door, crossing one ankle over the other. "What's the matter?"

"Fake ignorance does not look good on you."

"Ah, well. Like calls to like, doesn't it?" Spinning the bloodstone ring on my thumb, I watch the orange jewel orbit slowly, then raise my gaze back to hers. "He had his hands on you, Riley."

Her mouth parts, confusion knitting her brows. "So?"

"So?" Securing the ring back in place, I curl my fingers into a fist, imagining plowing it right into Caleb's smug face. "Do you make a habit of letting men who have feelings for you put their hands on your body?"

"I don't see how that's any of your business," she says, her chin tilting up defiantly.

My nostrils flare, a bull with its red flag in sight, ready to charge.

Sliding my feet toward her, I take note of the outfit she's wearing as I invade her personal space—a maroon sweater dress that clings to her curves, and a pair of sheer black tights that disappear into thigh-high boots, laced up at the knee.

It's almost like she dressed to get fucked.

"The second you let me shove my cock inside your wet little cunt, you became my business."

Backing her into the wall beside the porcelain sink, I slam my palms down on either side of her head, trapping her in front of me.

"Actually, no. When you let me tattoo my name for you on your skin, and then spread those pretty thighs so I could have a taste of what I'd been craving all night... *three years ago*, you became my business, Riley."

"That night was a mistake," she mutters, eyes volleying back and forth from mine to my lips.

"And the one at my cabin? When I came so fucking deep inside you that you smelled like me for *days*? What was that?"

"Lapse in judgment, you psycho."

"I'm only a psycho where you're concerned. You bring it out in me." My nose dips, brushing her hair, and my grip on the wall slackens slightly. "If you only knew the things I want to do to Caleb, just for daring to speak to you."

She swallows; I hear the gulp work down her throat, feel the echo as it zings to my dick, straining obscenely against my zipper.

"What kind of things?"

Satisfaction weaves around my insides like a glittering tapestry. "You wanna know how I'd hurt your friend?"

"I don't *want* you to hurt him," she insists, though her

gaze travels down to my lips again, and then back as she says it. "But—"

Stepping in, I let my hands drift to her hips, and then I'm spinning her, pushing her body into the wall with my hips. She sucks in a sharp breath, her spine going rigid.

I'd believe she's afraid, if not for the way her ass seeks purchase against my groin, jutting back like she can't even help herself.

Dipping my head, I let my mouth scrape the shell of her ear, reveling in the way her breathing stutters in return.

"But *what*, pretty girl?" She shivers, and my hands snake around to her ass, bunching in the fabric of her dress, tugging it up. "Do you like hearing about how miserable seeing you with him makes me? How I've gotten off some nights to the thought of him bleeding out in front of me?"

"Jesus," she whispers, folding her mouth together as my fingers drift between her legs. I swipe over her center once, feeling how hot and needy she is even through her tights, and then claw at the material. "I think something's wrong with you."

A single pull has the cotton ripping at the seam, exposing her, and she makes a little noise in the back of her throat that has me palming my dick, trying to keep it from exploding already.

"The only thing wrong with me is that I'm not currently suffocating with your thighs wrapped around my head."

Kicking at her feet so she spreads farther, I drop to my knees, running my fingers over the swell of her ass before delving between her folds.

"Put your hands on the wall and bend over, pretty girl."

She hesitates. "Caleb's right outside—"

"Good. He can listen to me tongue fuck you in this dirty bathroom."

After a breath, she obeys, presenting her sopping cunt like the filthy, sex-starved girl she is. I exhale and grip both cheeks, leaning in to run my tongue from one hole to the next.

"*Aiden*," she hisses.

"When I said I wanted to see all of you, I meant *all* of you. Now, be quiet and let me enjoy my meal, or I'll find something to gag you with."

The puckered aperture in the valley of her ass contracts, and I grin, glancing up as her forehead slumps against the wall.

"Do you like the sound of that, pretty girl? Want me to stuff your mouth full, so you can't lie about how bad you want this?"

Diving back in before she can answer, I lap at her sodden cunt, savoring the tang of her desire as it dissolves on my tongue. My nose bumps her asshole as I spear my tongue and thumb inside of her, curling up to massage her inner walls.

She bucks, tiny whimpers punctuating the backward grind of her hips, seeking more.

More, more, more.

It's the singular thought repeating in my mind as I take, tasting and licking and thrusting with my fingers, my face, my entire being.

This isn't a feast—it's a *devouring*.

That's the only way to describe the surge of hunger sweeping through me, collecting at the base of my spine as my cock pulses, desperate to sink inside her.

My mouth and fingers seem to be everywhere at once,

and somehow that still isn't quite enough. She appears to teeter on the precipice, caught somewhere between warm hysteria and the edge of oblivion, clamping down around me the second I stroke her clit.

"Don't come," I command, but the words are moaned into her skin, spoken like a prayer to paradise as I unravel.

"Stop doing that then," she chokes out, and immediately I move my mouth to the inside of her thigh, sucking so hard that she mewls like a beast in heat.

Yanking my mouth away with a loud, wet pop, I lave my tongue over the lip-shaped welt forming on her skin, then withdraw my fingers and stand up.

"I didn't really mean stop," she says, completely breathless, trying to twist her head around.

The finger that was just inside of her comes up, hooking in the corner of her mouth, while I use my free hand to work my dick free.

"You're not gonna come today unless I'm inside you," I grunt, shoving my pants down to my thighs and pulling myself free. "Okay? Think you can be a good girl and cream all over my cock?"

She moans her answer, and I line up with her entrance, notching the head against her dripping center.

"Wait!" The word is garbled, and I slide my finger out slightly. "How many people have you been with?"

"What?"

"I didn't ask the last time we..." she trails off, exhaling heavily. "But you know my number, so I think it's only fair I know yours."

My dick jerks in my palm, and I consider lying. I *want* to lie, so she doesn't get the wrong idea.

But when I open my mouth to speak, the truth is what comes out.

"Two total." My fingers flex around my shaft, and I grit out, "Only one that mattered."

And none in our time apart.

The confession hangs between us, heavy with the weight of its implication.

I don't wait for her to process, or say anything else; with a quick shunt of my hips, I sheath myself as deep inside her as I can go, turning her head so I can drink up the ensuing scream that tears from her chest.

Already, I can feel my orgasm teasing my spine, within reach if I'm not careful. Breaking our kiss, I piston into her, glancing down to watch as my cock splits her apart.

"Oh, *god*," she pants, fingers scraping against the wall with each of my thrusts. "Please, Aiden, *please.*"

My vision slackens as she begs, scratching that impossible itch inside of me. I fuck her harder, the lewd sounds of her arousal coupling with the soft slapping of flesh, filling the air with an erotic quality I feel in my bones.

Tugging at the neckline of her dress with one hand, I dip my head and suction my lips where her neck meets her shoulder. Her inner walls flutter, and she moans that she's close, she's so fucking close, only stopping when I shove three fingers into her mouth.

The control I'm barely holding on to slips away as she gurgles around them, her throat convulsing in time with the gagging sounds she's making.

When I pull back, another bruise is already starting to mark her skin. "God*damn*, you're such a good girl, taking me at both ends. You look fucking perfect getting stuffed full like this."

A delighted sob wrenches from her as she retches, eyes watering from how deeply seated my knuckles are, and I watch them leak the second her orgasm begins to wash over her.

"I know, pretty girl. *Fuck*, I know. Feels so goddamn good to be fucked, doesn't it? To be owned?" I'm losing it, losing the last vestiges of my sanity as they break off and evaporate into her soul. "Take it, Riley. Own *me*. Claim me right back, and make me blow inside this sweet, filthy cunt."

Rocking her hips back, Riley chases that release; mine charges like a bullet, ripping through muscle and cartilage. With one final, brutal thrust, I bottom out, hot cum spurting in short bursts, painting and tainting her insides.

A full-body shudder rolls over her, and she follows violently, beautifully, squeezing me so tight that I see stars for a moment. When she's finished, she sags into my arms; I dislodge my hand from her mouth and steady her against the wall, running my fingers down her back in languid strokes.

Her head lifts, and she looks so positively fucked, so thoroughly *mine*, with her tear-stained cheeks and those glistening sapphire eyes, that I can't help but kiss her again.

And again.

And *again.*

In that moment, out of all the others, I realize it's not insanity that drives me to be stupid and reckless with her. It's not insanity that brought me to Lunar Cove in the first place.

It's obsession.

Addiction.

I'm a fucking addict.

A fiend for this pink-haired angel.

Unfortunately, for that affliction, there is no cure. Only

abstinence, or indulgence, and I'd sooner give up my life as I know it than go a single day further without being able to taste her.

After a few moments of silence wherein we collect ourselves, we straighten on our feet and fix our clothing. My hand slides between her legs, finding the mixture of our pleasure as it seeps from her.

I dip a finger in, swirling the mess around her clit, then back over her entrance and past her asshole. "There," I say, withdrawing and bringing the finger to my mouth, licking it clean. "In case you ever get the idea again that you're somehow not my business. Let the cum drying on parts of you that only I get to see be a reminder."

Her face flushes a deep fuchsia color as she rights her dress, then creeps over to the door. "God, what if he stayed for all of that?"

"Then he's a pervert, and now he knows the score."

She shoots me a dirty look. "He already knew the score, Aiden. You're just an asshole."

I don't deny it—can't, anyway—as she unlocks the door and goes to pull it open.

"Uh," she says slowly, pulling on the brass doorknob. "It's stuck?"

"Are you asking or telling me?"

She jiggles the metal, trying to turn it with no luck. "Oh, my god! We're locked in!"

"No, we're not. It just needs a little extra elbow grease." Gently moving her out of the way, I wrap my fingers around the knob and twist as hard as I can.

Nothing happens.

Furrowing my brows, I try to turn it again, and still nothing happens. Bracing one hand against the frame, I lodge my foot into the wall and pull; it creaks on its hinges, but otherwise stays put.

"What the fuck?" I huff, my fist colliding with the wood. "Open up, you fucker."

"God, I knew this was a bad idea." Riley's fists join mine, beating furiously. "*Caleb*! Open the fucking door!"

Silence comes from the other side, and confusion laces my nerves, putting me on edge.

Riley continues pounding, screeching at her friend and kicking with all her might. I back away, glancing at the small crack between the floor and the bottom of the door; crouching down, I flatten my palms on the tile and turn my head, looking for signs of movement outside.

Everything in the gallery is still, the shadows square and unmoving. I frown, pushing back to my feet, and grab Riley from behind.

"Why would Caleb lock us in here?"

Her hand freezes mid-knock, and she shrugs. "To be a dick? I don't know, we did just turn his bathroom into an exhibitionist site."

"Yeah, and I'm pretty sure he'd rather drag me out by *my* dick than trap you in here with me." Jimmying the doorknob again, I shake my head, frustration lancing my skull.

"Get out of the way," I tell her, rolling my shoulders and trying to loosen the muscles in my neck.

She scrambles a few steps, the backs of her calves hitting the toilet. "What are you doing?"

Without answering, I call out for Caleb one last time; silence continues to trickle in from the lobby, so I focus on the doorknob and lift my foot, aiming for the lock and pushing all of my weight into it.

The door flies open, bits of metal and wood splintering

into the air as it knocks into the wall. One of the hinges pops free from the impact, and Riley screams, even though she's clearly not in any fucking danger.

Just as I suspected, Caleb is nowhere to be found.

But someone else is.

"That seems so unnecessary," Riley says as she exits the bathroom, smoothing her hands over her dress. She comes to a complete stop at my side, a small gasp falling from her lips as she takes in the petite, platinum blonde standing at the front of the shop, looking like she's just seen a ghost.

"*Mellie?*"

40

I CAN'T TELL if I'm choking on surprise, or the imprint of Aiden's fingers pressing on the back of my tongue.

Like they're still lodged there, I can feel them cutting off my air supply and debasing me in a way I didn't think I would enjoy, given my past.

For some reason, though, it just feels *right* at his hands.

It shouldn't, I know that. I know that he was awful to me when he showed up, and that the stalking was... well, illegal.

But I also know that no one's ever made me feel quite as *good* as he has, either.

As beautiful.

Whole.

Maybe that's not the answer to everything—I know the trauma can't be reversed or healed by pretty words and forehead kisses.

They help, though.

It's so much easier to navigate when you have someone standing by you.

Tearing my gaze from the disturbingly attractive man at my side, I focus my attention back on the front door, where Mellie Simmons stands.

Her skinny fingers wrap tight around the strap of the clutch hanging off her shoulder, her pale cheeks flushed pink—from the cold air outside, or what she possibly just overheard in the bathroom, I can't be sure.

Or maybe it's the fact that her former classmate is supposed to be dead, and yet here she stands, freshly fucked and being extremely obvious about it.

My mother's voice is quieter these days, but she comes raring back with a vengeance as the silence ticks by, reminding me of what a disgrace I am.

As if sensing the tension lacing my muscles, Aiden shuffles closer to me and drapes his arm over my shoulders, tilting his head as he looks between us.

"Another Lunar Cove resident, I take it?" he asks, closing the distance to hold his hand out for her. "I'm guessing there's a fifty-fifty chance you have any clue who I am."

Mellie blinks, her dark eyes peeling off my frame and swinging to him. "You're *Aiden James*. I... I cannot believe I'm standing in the same building as *Aiden James* right now. Holy shit."

He smirks, lifting his chest. "So, you're the percent that I like, then."

"She's not from here." I shrug off his hold, trying to make this thing between us look more casual than it feels.

Her excitement dwindles, and we just stare at each other for a long stretch of time. Aiden shifts on his feet, crossing his arms over his chest.

"I'll be honest," he says. "I don't understand what's happening here."

"Tell me about it." Mellie's voice is suddenly cold, so unlike the way it was in high school. "Last I saw her, Riley Kelly was walking away from our class at the airport after our NYC trip, and the next thing I know, she's dead." Her head cocks to the side, eyes hard. "Care to explain?"

"You recognize her even with the pink hair?"

My fist lashes out, catching Aiden in the abs, and he lets out a low chuckle. "I'm just saying, you didn't really do *that* much to change."

"Maybe not in person. But on paper?" Mellie frowns, adjusting her purse. "Totally legit. Then again, I guess when your family's involved with the Mafia, you can manage arrangements like that."

Unease gnaws at my intestines, and I wrap my arms around my stomach. I feel Aiden's eyes on me, hot where they try to penetrate my defenses as soon as they start shackling back in place. Taking a deep breath, I try to figure out how to explain things without *explaining* things.

"She doesn't owe you an explanation," Aiden interjects, stepping so he's positioned slightly in front of me.

Mellie's eyes go wide. "No? I was her *friend*."

"A friend would realize that people don't usually fake their deaths without good reason."

She looks past him, glaring at me. "You literally fooled an entire town into grieving for you. Friends, teachers.

Everyone thinks you're *dead*, Riley. Not hiding, not starting over somewhere new. Dead. Come to find out you've just been gallivanting in some mountain town all this time?"

Guilt tries to force its way into my heart, but I clear my throat, shoving it down where it can't be seen.

"What *friends*? The ones who ditched me on our senior class trip at some weird auction, knowing I didn't want to go out in the first place?"

Aiden's jaw clenches. The memory of that night resurfaces like a sudden slap to the face, and I wonder if it does for him too.

A warning bell sounds somewhere in the back of my mind, telling me to get out of here while I can. Before any more damage is done, or undone, and Mellie brings more of the past with her.

Clearing my throat, I straighten my spine and give her a thin smile. "Look, I understand this comes as a shock to you. If you want, I'd be willing to meet for coffee one day and catch up. Try to explain some of the absurdity away. How long are you in town?"

"*Why* are you in town?" Aiden grumbles.

"I—"

At that moment, Caleb strolls in through the front door, carrying a coffee tray with two cardboard travel mugs in it. "Gingerbread mocha for the lady, and white chocolate for—"

The smile slips from his face when he sees us all standing in the lobby, and I cringe at how disheveled I must look as he glances at my dress, then back up.

"What's going on?"

Our group seems to collectively gulp, and Mellie reaches for one of the coffees, slicing through the tension with an easy smile. So different from the expression that was *just* on her face.

"Caleb, darling, if you advertised more that a rock star uses your venue to hook up with homeless people, you could truly do wonders for business."

"Homeless people?" he repeats, looking at me again. "Angel's not homeless."

"*Angel*?" She snorts, taking a sip of her drink. "Good lord. Well, in any case, just the fact that *the* Aiden James is standing in your gallery right now is enough to send people in droves. Shall I take a pic, post it to my blog?"

"No." Aiden reaches down, intertwining his fingers with mine. "I have no interest in being photographed, nor in letting the world know where I am."

"Oh, dear." Dangling her phone from her thumb and index finger, she winces. "Guess I shouldn't have just tweeted it, then."

For a moment, I stare at her, trying to reconcile this woman with the girl who was nice to me back home—the *only* girl who was nice to me then. Is it possible my sudden disappearance really fucked with her head that badly?

We really *weren't* friends, so I can't imagine how it would. And yet, there's no denying that there's a certain edge to this woman, in her white linen pantsuit with her neatly combed bob, watching me like the cat that caught the canary.

When she looks at Aiden, something sinister seems to gleam in her dark, almond-shaped eyes. It has me shifting closer to him, pulling him into my side—an innate need to protect him from whatever hell she's about to unleash.

There's also a strange feeling unfurling in my chest the longer I look at Mellie. If she announced Aiden's presence in Lunar Cove, how long do I have before she announces mine?

And then... what? How will I face an entire town?

And what if the people I've been hiding from all this time finally come for me?

Caleb wears a perplexed expression on his face and scrubs a hand over his dark beard. "I don't know what's going on, but Angel, this is Mellie Simmons. She's the collector I was telling you about, the one that travels across the country finding indigenous artifacts to curate in different museums?"

I nod, smiling tightly. "How interesting."

She tucks her hair behind her ear, beaming up at Aiden. "The stories we could probably trade, *rock star.*"

"No thanks." Mouth pressed in a firm line, he pushes past her, yanking me along behind him. As he shoves open the front door, he tosses a "get your bathroom door fixed," over his shoulder, and then we're winding past Dahlia's Diner, and I'm having to jog to keep up.

It reminds me so much of our night in the city, except with an added layer of danger as I try to avoid patches of solid ice. Aiden doesn't stop until we're at his car, and even then, he only does so long enough to stuff me in the passenger seat.

When he climbs in, he lets out a low breath and locks the Volvo doors.

"Well, that was weird." I watch him from my peripheral vision as he reclines his head against the seat, brushing some of his dark locks off his forehead. "What are the odds that I made it three years without a single person I know coming here, and *bam*, two in two months."

He hums, draping his wrists over the wheel, looking everywhere but at me.

My eyebrows furrow, and I shift, a pinch of soreness sparking between my legs. "Aiden?"

Blinking slowly, his head turns, and he drags his heated gaze up the length of me. "Yes, pretty girl?"

A blush lashes my skin, my chest warming the way it always does when he calls me that or tells me I'm doing something that makes him feel good.

"Are you okay?" One of my hands creeps over the console as his drops onto it, and I run my thumb over the Medusa tattoo on the back of his hand, tracing her serpentine hair as it wraps around his fingers.

He watches the movement, silver eyes softening at the corners. "Are you ready to tell me what happened three years ago?"

My hand stops, and I pinch my eyes closed.

"Riley." I feel his thumb hook beneath my chin, and then he's tugging up, his breath cascading over my face. "I deserve to know."

It feels like an elephant is standing on my chest, making it difficult for my lungs to function. I swallow, hard, and the sound is loud in the confined space of the car.

"I can't move on if I don't even know what happened," he murmurs. "And *you* can't move on until you acknowledge it."

Sorrow burns behind my lids, a fire blazing down my throat and incinerating everything on contact. My mouth opens, but no words come out, and then I feel his lips against mine—soft, tentative, and passionate in a way I haven't felt.

His tongue invades my mouth, probing and twisting and exploring. Adrenaline rushes to my head, desire spiking somewhere in my thighs and roaming upward, coiling in my stomach until I'm leaning over the console, trying to get more.

He kisses me like we have all the time in the world.

Like this relationship wasn't doomed at the start.

"Whatever this is, it's not going to end well."

The words uttered by the tattoo shop girl that night ring in my head, pulling me from the moment. I sit back in my seat slightly, disconnecting our lips, framing his jaw with my face.

Running my tongue over my teeth, I squint at him, bits of mint cooling my mouth. "How come you always taste like peppermint?"

He pushes one of the spherical candies between his teeth —just like the one he'd transferred to my mouth when he first showed up weeks ago.

"Is that some sort of oral fixation?"

"No." His voice dips an octave, smoothing over me like satin, and he leans in, pressing his lips to my neck. As he drags his tongue up, alternating between suckling and licking his way to my jaw, he inhales deeply. "It's a Riley fixation."

A memory flashes, Aiden's shoulders between my legs, his nose pressed to my skin.

"You smell so good. Like peppermint."

"It's a lotion," I'd told him, allowing myself to indulge for the first time in my life.

Pulling his head up, I stare deep into his eyes, my heart beating so brutally against my chest that I'm afraid he might be able to hear it.

When he kisses me again, I forget all about his question.

When he pulls me into his lap, grinding me down on his erection, I forget about Mellie down the street, parting my thighs so he can sheath himself inside me. It's a tight fit, both the position—my back digging into the steering wheel, his legs trapped beneath me—and the act, and yet there's something strangely freeing about it, too.

We come together, crying out into each other's mouths, and this time his kiss tastes less like peppermint and more like forgiveness.

Like understanding.

I can *almost* forget that I don't deserve it.

41

Vibrations shake my pillow, pulling me from a sex-induced slumber.

Dazed, I lift my head, feeling around for the source of the disturbance. Riley's tucked tight to my side, a tiny puddle of drool connecting her lips to my ribs, and for a second, all I want to do is lie back down and never move from beneath her.

But the vibrating doesn't stop, and I don't want it to wake her yet.

Shoving my hand between the headboard and mattress, I

pull my cell up with two fingers, not looking at the screen before I roll over and answer.

I'm expecting my father, or Liam, or maybe even the hotel I booked for the New Year's show next week, calling to confirm accommodations.

I'm not expecting my mother.

"*Hola, papi.* Merry Christmas."

The sound of her voice in my ear this early, before the sun has even risen here, immediately knots my muscles together with dread.

"Callie." My voice is groggy, but my mind snaps right to attention. "Is something wrong?"

Her laugh chirps through the line. "Does something have to be wrong in order for me to call my son?"

"Well, it's the first time you've contacted me since I left New York." Silence. I pull back the phone, checking to see if she got disconnected, but her name still lights the screen. "Callie?"

"I've never gone a single Christmas without hearing your voice first thing in the morning," she says finally, and I can imagine her sitting in her condo on the Upper East Side, feet propped up on her glass coffee table as she stares down a glass of red wine.

There's probably a white tree in one corner, the only one in the house because she can't stand the needles getting everywhere. It's likely decked out with white lights and blue ornaments—her favorite holiday colors when I was a kid—though I'm sure it was a housekeeper that got them from the attic and put them on the tree.

She'll probably host some big dinner, inviting everyone in the area within our tax bracket, and she'll remain in the living room, looking into her wineglass, wondering how the red liquid keeps dwindling when she swears she hasn't touched it.

People will filter in and out for photo ops, asking where I'm at and when the next big tour is, and she won't have an answer. Her focus will stay on that fucking wineglass, even though her mind will be in the bathroom vanity upstairs, scouring the shelves for just *one* leftover pill, even though my father and I cleaned out her stash years ago.

Parties always were her biggest stressor, so I can only imagine how difficult it must be this year without anything else to focus on.

For a washed-up pop star like Calliope Santiago, becoming her celebrity son's manager is about as good of a distraction as one can get.

And I fucked it all up for her.

After an uncomfortably long gap in conversation, Callie clears her throat. "How's Colorado?"

"Cold and snowy, mostly. Not much to report."

She laughs softly. "Sounds a lot like home."

"Yeah, only like a mile above sea level, so the air here is dry as shit." Blowing out a breath, I let my arm fall above my head, tracing abstract patterns in the vaulted ceiling with my eyes. "Liam tell you I'm doing a New Year's show?"

"He did." Pause. She clears her throat again, and this time I hear her swallow. "I think that's great, *hijo*. Can't hide from the world forever."

"I'm not *hiding*," I say, biting back the urge to mention that she'd know what I'm doing here if she hadn't been ignoring me.

"You're hardly living."

My nostrils flare, and I grip the headboard in one hand,

my rings digging into the pine. "I'm not sure you're in a place to judge, *Mother*."

Her sigh crackles through the receiver, and I hear her mumble something in Spanish. "I didn't call to fight, Aiden. I just wanted to check on you."

"Why? Just making sure I'm still alive?"

"*Ay*, no. Why would you even say something like that?"

I groan, and Riley rolls away from me, pushing my legs with her feet. "You're right, I should be the one checking to make sure you're not dead in a hotel bathroom somewhere."

She stays quiet for a long, long time, and I feel my heart flatten as my words reabsorb into the air, disappearing like I didn't utter them.

"Look." Now when she returns, her voice is cold and hard. Almost detached. "Scandal ruined my career. You were young, so I don't expect you to remember, but—"

"I remember," I cut in, my throat constricting around the words. "I remember more than you think."

Everything. My memory is completely intact, each traumatic event burned into my brain, so I recall it with perfect clarity.

It's a wonder I didn't try to off myself sooner.

"Then it should be easy for you to understand why your mother had a hard time with all of this. Sexual assault allegations are very hard to bounce back from, *papi*."

"Thank you for that brand-new information."

Another sigh. "I'd better get going. The housekeeper will be here to let in the catering staff any minute now."

I bite down on the inside of my cheek, staving off the rejection. "Don't want to keep her waiting."

Before she has a chance to reply, I end the call and toss the phone to the foot of the bed.

Throwing back my side of the comforter, I slip from the bed and pad into Riley's bathroom, quickly brushing my teeth.

Spitting into the sink, I notice the peppermint lotion by her faucet, and roll my eyes, dumping it into the garbage bin by the toilet. When I head back into the bedroom, Riley's splayed out in the middle of the mattress, snoring so loud I feel it in my chest.

And even though she's a mouth-breathing, sleep-kicking bed hog, I don't think she's ever looked more like her namesake.

I peel back the blankets as I climb back in, shuffling myself so she's lying directly on top of me. My fingers find her hip, tracing lightly over the tattoo there. I just brush the corner of her scar, and her baby blues fly open, on high alert as soon as she feels the touch.

"Merry Christmas," I tell her, threading my free hand through her blush-colored locks, fisting the base to press a harsh kiss to her mouth.

"*Ungh,*" she moans, jerking away and sitting upright. Her tits are covered in faded-red bite marks and rubbed raw from the scruff on my jaw, and my dick roars to life at the sight. "No fair that you brushed your teeth."

"Your morning breath isn't that bad." Pushing up on my elbows, I rub my nose against her chin. "Tastes like *us.*"

"Not that bad is *not* a compliment, and definitely not what I want to hear in relation to our bodily fluids."

She shoves at my bare chest, pushing me so I'm lying flat again. I go without a fight, and she glides her hands up my torso, watching my abs contract beneath the pads of her fingers with a satisfied smirk.

"Like what you see?" I taunt, and she nods, continuing her exploration.

Bending at the waist, her tongue follows the trail of her fingers, leaving a stripe of saliva up the middle of my stomach, then between my pecs, and finally over my nipple ring.

"How come you don't take your shirt off in public?"

I quirk a brow. "How come you won't tell me what sent you to Lunar Cove?"

Freezing, she bites the piercing, pushing upright again with an annoyed expression. Crossing her arms over her breasts, she glares at me. "Those questions are not equal in weight."

"I agree. I've been waiting years for the answer to mine." Swallowing, I decide to give her a little in the hopes she'll return the effort. "I like my privacy, and my body is one of the few things I've been able to keep control of in the public eye. I don't think everyone deserves to see me like this."

She licks her lips, tilting her head as she seems to consider this.

"Your turn."

Throwing her head back, she groans, as if in pain. Then, shifting her hips, she reaches behind her and grabs my cock, wrapping her tiny fingers around it. It twitches, heavy in her palm, and I let out a soft curse as she pumps up and down, just the way I've shown her.

"Riley."

"Yes, sir?" She lifts onto her knees, slowly dragging the head along her slick core, teasing me with her slit before bringing it up to grind against her clit. Her mouth falls open, and mine forgets how to formulate words, euphoria ricocheting through my veins as she takes control.

"Do you think you're going to make me forget my question?"

Shaking her head, she flutters her eyelashes dramatically, sucking her bottom lip between her teeth as she drops my cock and rocks forward on it.

"*Sir*, are you accusing me of trying to distract you?" I grab the sheets, squeezing my eyes shut as I try not to lose myself to the way her silken flesh feels on mine.

But it's a lost fucking cause.

I'm a lost cause when it comes to her.

"Call me sir again." My words come out quickly, almost garbled. Breathy and desperate, I reach for her hips, lifting her enough that she can line up with my cock. "Put me inside you and call me sir when you do it."

"Kinky." She giggles, but the smile wipes off her face when she sinks down on me. Our sighs morph into one as she works it in, her fingernails digging into my chest as her ass comes to rest on the tops of my thighs. "God, I think you get bigger every time, *sir*."

"*Fuck*." My back arches, pleasure tingling down my spine, lighting my nerve endings on fire. "You're a filthy girl, aren't you?"

"Yours," she answers, breathless, starting to move her hips. Sliding her hands up my chest, she splays her fingers at the base of my throat. Not quite holding, but not quite resting, either.

It's an act of possession, I realize, staring into her hypnotic gaze. A reinforcement of sorts, as if she's testing the water, trying to gauge my reaction to her soft claim.

She picks up the pace as our gazes remain locked, her tiny whimpers spurring me on from below. I meet each roll of her hips with an upward thrust of my own, letting her work out any soreness from last night, and then I wrap an arm around her waist and flip her onto her back.

Gripping her thighs, I spread her legs as wide as they'll go, pressing her knees into her shoulders as I plunge my cock back in.

Tight, wet heat surrounds me, and each hiccuped breath I wrench from her lungs has me spiraling more and more out of control.

"Hold your knees so I can fuck you deep," I say. She does, keeping herself open so I can cover her mouth with my hand the way both of us like. "Goddamn, pretty girl, you feel amazing. Such a perfect angel for me."

Sweat coats our skin and the bed rocks into the wall, and then it's all wet flesh slapping against flesh, primal groans and grunts filling the air.

I bend down, pressing my forehead against her as she preens, her screams vibrating against my fingers, her cunt spasming in a vise grip around my cock.

"*Mine*. My filthy girl," I grunt, pushing in one final time as I unload spurt after spurt inside her. I come so hard that I black out, feeling ten thousand pounds lighter when I return to earth.

She's still fluttering, her pussy pulsing; I can feel my cum leak out, but I don't withdraw or make a move to clean it up this time. I stay lodged inside her, half hard as my head drops to her bare shoulder.

"Merry Christmas," she murmurs after a few minutes, raking her hands through my hair. "I didn't think I'd be spending the holidays with my stalker, but I suppose stranger things have happened."

"You stalked me first, of your own admission."

My arm reaches out to the nightstand, yanking the top drawer open and pulling out a white paper bag.

"I got you something."

"Oh."

I roll off her, both of us wincing as I disconnect our bodies.

She takes the bag, then frowns at me as my fingers drift between her thighs, spreading our juices over her swollen lips. "*Hey*. Talk about a distraction."

I smirk. "Just open it."

"But I didn't get you anything. You can't give me orgasms *and* presents when I don't have anything for you in return."

"All I want is you, Riley."

Her eyes widen, and I think they must reflect mine, because I certainly hadn't planned on those words coming out of my mouth. But once they're out there, I can't take them back.

Worse, I realize as I watch her peel the bag open, my stomach buzzing with anticipation, *I don't even want to.*

Fuck me, what has this girl done?

"Uh... is this..?" Pulling the contents out, she shoves the bread against her nose, and squeals. "Oh, my god, it is! An authentic New York City bagel."

"Strawberry, even."

She tears into it, tossing the bag onto the floor, and moans around the bite. "God, it's as good as I remember. How did you—"

A door slamming downstairs cuts her sentence off, and her entire body locks up tight. The bagel falls into her lap, and she scrambles to pull the sheet up over her breasts, fear flooding her eyes.

"I'm not expecting anyone," she whispers, a tremor racking her body, gaze glued to the door.

My nostrils flare, irritated that I still don't know what makes her react so viscerally to potential danger, but I push it down.

Maybe not yet, but she will tell me.

Sliding from the bed, I tug on a pair of flannel pajama pants and tell her to stay put. When I cross the room and yank open the bedroom door, the breath whooshes from my lungs, shock jumping to my throat.

Standing on the other side of the threshold is a tall, tattooed man who looks an awful lot like the girl behind me.

Except a thousand times angrier.

42

"JESUS CHRIST, Boyd, what the hell are you doing here?"

My brother crosses his arms in the doorway, staring at Aiden like he's a convicted criminal.

As I wrap the comforter more firmly around my body, I wince at my brain's choice of words.

Not convicted, anyway.

"I was told to stop sulking and get my sorry ass to Colorado, because my baby sister would be all alone in the cabin I've been paying for the last three years." He smooths a hand down the front of his coat, toying with the frayed ends of the scarf around his neck.

Still glaring at Aiden.

"Can't you knock?" I mutter, hastily getting out of the bed and trying to locate something to put on. I spot a pair of sleep shorts and a tank top on the chair across the room and use the comforter to shield myself as I pull them on. "Or send a text, like a normal person?"

"I texted three times. Called four. You didn't answer, so I took it upon myself to come in and make sure you hadn't been strung up by your toes and left for the bears."

Horror washes over me at the image. "Do people really do that to others?"

Boyd's jaw clenches. "I'm tempted."

Clearing his throat, Aiden scratches his neck and moves backward, putting a wide berth between him and my brother.

An awkward silence settles over us as we stand in a triangle shape in the room, no one willing to make the first move or speak before the other.

"Where the hell are all your Christmas decorations?" comes a soft voice from the hall, and relief pours through me at the sound. Fiona appears, stuffing her face under my brother's arm as she peers into the room, frowning at me. "This is completely unacceptable, Riley. You don't even have a *tree*, and you knew—"

Her brown eyes flicker to the side and widen exponentially as she notices Aiden.

"Oh, hello." She grins, shoving Boyd aside so she can come into the room and make her way over to introduce herself. "I'm Fiona—"

Boyd's hand whips out, gripping the end of her ponytail; she squeaks as he tugs her back into him, securing her in place with his arm around her neck.

She rolls her eyes, hooking her fingers on his forearm. It looks restrictive, but the way she leans into it is all the proof you need to know she's *letting* him hold her there. Almost like he anchors her, in some weird way.

"I'm Fiona, and the Neanderthal behind me is Boyd. No, he doesn't have manners, so don't even ask."

Aiden shifts his weight from one foot to the other. "Nice to meet you."

"You must be Caleb?" Her smile is too bright for the situation.

Kill me.

Boyd's gaze travels over Aiden's chest, cataloging every single tattoo. His eyes narrow, jaw flexing, and his eyes cut to mine. "No," he says, answering her while staring at me. "This is Aiden, isn't it?"

"*Aiden*?" Fiona's mouth drops open, forming a perfect o-shape. "The..."

"Entire reason she had to go into hiding?"

"Well, not the *entire* reason."

Again, no one says anything for several beats. My pulse thrums heavy in my veins, loud between my ears, and I put a hand on the mattress for support.

"Look," Aiden finally says, scrubbing his hands over his face. "I know this might not look *great*, but I can promise you I don't mean any harm."

Pursing his lips, Boyd slowly releases Fiona and reaches into his coat, producing a sleek handgun. Flipping the safety, he aims the barrel at Aiden, his index finger brushing the trigger.

"*Boyd.*" I grit my teeth, my hands balling into fists. Humiliation worms its way through me, setting my face on fire.

"Go ahead." Aiden shrugs, shoving his hands into his pant pockets. "If that's what you need to do to prove yourself."

Boyd bristles. He glances at me, then back at Aiden for a long moment. I don't know what he sees, but whatever it is makes him clear his throat and lower the gun, turning to his girlfriend.

The complete adoration in his gaze for her is almost difficult to look at; he reaches out, presses a kiss to her forehead, and then abruptly leaves the room.

"Well." Fiona wiggles her fingers in the pockets of her white Prada coat and raises her eyebrows. "Now it feels like Christmas."

THE INTRUDING COUPLE takes up residence in the guest bedroom down the hall from mine, and for two whole days, I don't see my brother. Fiona tries to fill the void with endless stories about the psychology clinic she just started at, and by force-feeding me chocolate shakes, but not a second ticks by where I'm unaware that my brother is upstairs ignoring me.

I'd be lying if I said it wasn't nice to have someone other than me in the house, acknowledging the holiday so that I don't have to. For a while, I try to convince myself that it's enough, but it doesn't work.

Somehow, this is worse than him disregarding me from across the country. At least then, I could pretend life was keeping him busy, and it wasn't an active effort on his part to pretend I didn't exist.

Aiden doesn't come back over, for obvious reasons, and I

start to despise how accustomed I've gotten to sleeping with him. How easy it's been to suppress nightmares with him at my side.

In truth, *everything* seems easier when I'm around him. Navigating life in general, and while I know it shouldn't, especially given the way he treated me not long ago, I don't think I can stop wanting him.

It's a bone-deep ache. One soul threaded through the other, their fabric becoming so deeply intertwined that no amount of untangling can separate them.

I tiptoe down the stairs, shrug into my coat and boots, and head for the front door, my soul desperate to be near his.

Just as I'm turning the doorknob, the floorboards creak beneath someone's weight, and I know who it is even before he speaks.

"I don't remember you being this sneaky when you lived back home."

Slumping against the door, I turn my head to the side. Boyd stands in the living room, arms crossed tight over his chest. He's wearing a red plaid pajama set that Fiona bought him for Christmas, and his hair sticks up in odd places, like he's been yanking at it for days.

"Well, when Mom was alive, I didn't have to be. She was out of her mind so much that I could come and go as I pleased."

Not that I did, I almost add, but he doesn't need to know that my propensity for being a hermit started long before I moved here.

He walks over and slides the lock back in place, leaning against the door. For a long time, he studies me, and out of habit, my tongue darts out to touch the scar at the corner of my mouth.

I'm suddenly hyperaware of the evidence of my trauma, and as Boyd tracks the movement, I can't help wondering if he is, too.

I covered the scars extensively when I lived with him. Went to extremes to ensure that I'd never be caught off guard by my appearance in a mirror or catch looks of pity from people who otherwise didn't give a shit about me.

It was a protective mechanism, and since Aiden barreled into my new life and forced my walls down, I've thought less and less about them. Right now, they're all I can think about —all I can *feel*—and as the memories come flooding back, so does my brother's anguish in the aftermath.

Reaching up, he scratches at the back of his neck and sighs. "I used to be jealous that you called her that."

I blink. "Mom?"

"Yeah. It was stupid, but I grew up calling her LeeAnn. She'd even *asked* me to, at one point. Every time you called her mom, it was like we were referencing two completely different people."

Pushing off the door, he moves around me and into the kitchen. A light glows above the sink, and I see a tub of strawberry ice cream open on the counter, a spoon sticking out of the top. He grabs it and sits at the island, shoving a spoonful into his mouth.

I glance out the back windows to Aiden's cabin, noting that the whole house is dark. He's probably asleep, and while I'm sure I could go over and wake him up, something in my soul is telling me not to.

Not yet, anyway.

Exhaling, I kick off my boots, grab a spoon from a drawer by the fridge, and join Boyd at the island. We eat the ice cream in silence, the darkness settling around us the way it seems to have our whole lives—quickly and fully, enveloping us in its warm embrace.

Leaving just a tiny sliver of light.

"Kind of weird that we're eating ice cream when there's snow on the ground," I comment after a few minutes.

He points his spoon at me. "Neither one of us is exactly normal."

"Yeah, I guess that ship kind of bypassed our docks, huh?" Pushing my tongue into my cheek, I stab my spoon into the pint and sit back, folding my arms on the counter. "Do you think we ever could be?"

"Normal?" I nod, and he laughs.

Laughs.

My broody, angry-at-the-world, too-serious-for-his-own-good brother *laughs.*

And I hate how my heart still has the courage to hope.

"I think normal is boring. Abnormalities make life more interesting."

Groaning, I drop my forehead to my arms, burying my face. "I think I'm dating my brother."

"Well, I would not suggest telling that to Fiona."

Snorting, I shove at his bicep, rolling my head to the side. "Not literally, dick. But the tattoos, and the *philosophy*? You guys would probably get along great. You know, when you're not pointing a gun at him."

A small, sad smile tugs at Boyd's lips, and he pushes the ice cream away, turning his spoon in his hands. "I failed you, a *lot*, when you were growing up. Let all the resentment and anger I had toward... our mother cloud my judgment. Let it bleed onto you. An innocent bystander just caught in the middle of things."

My throat tightens, emotion winding around and around my sternum, a boa constrictor prepping its next victim.

"I didn't think it was hurting you. Or, rather, I didn't want to see if it was. And every time I came over, you were always so excited to see me, and it felt like the universe was just driving the metaphorical knife deeper into my gut." He swallows. "Then... you got attacked, and I walked into the trailer to find you..."

Boyd pauses, sucking in a deep breath as he presses his palms into the countertop. "He was standing over you, and you didn't even..." His fists curl, knuckles bleaching, and my sinuses burn as I watch him struggle to relive it.

There's blood everywhere.

The memory flashes across my vision, assaulting my senses with its force, and I latch on to it the way one might their comfort character, letting it permeate my skin as if it deserves a place in my life.

"You didn't look like *you*," he finally manages, his words harsh. Rushed, like they're as painful to utter as they are to hear. "I don't think I'd ever seen so much blood in my life, and I knew things couldn't be good if that much of it was outside your body. And I felt so fucking *guilty* that in the milliseconds before I processed, I wished for the universe to open up and just swallow me whole. To punish me, once and for all, for being an absolute piece of shit brother."

His voice cracks, and so does something in my chest.

"I swear, Riley, if I had ever thought something like that would happen to you, I would've done anything to have prevented that."

Tears sting my eyes, and I turn away, the agony etched into his face unbearable. "You couldn't have known, Boyd.

It's not like I told you how Mom was, or what her boyfriends were like."

"But I *did* know. I lived with her. I knew what she was capable of, but I was fucking selfish. So selfish, and you paid for my mistakes." Palming the sides of his face, he lets out a ragged breath. "I thought bringing you to live with me might be my second chance. That I'd... I don't know, fix you, or something. Reverse the damage I'd caused and absolve myself of my sins. But I still didn't know what the fuck I was doing, or how to help, and then you were growing up and begging to go to New York—"

"And then I left," I finish, mashing my lips together.

He peeks at me through his fingers. "And then you left."

Every cell in my body is screaming to apologize—for leaving, for not going to him for help, for being the one our mom kept. The words claw their way up my chest, heavy with the weight of self-flagellation I've carried my whole life.

Shame I felt for things I had no control over. Grief for the girl I could have been—*should* have been, had Boyd been able to see past his own experience.

"I want to tell you it's okay, and that I forgive you," I say in a soft voice, and the spark of hope that flares in his eyes almost breaks me.

It slices through my heart, shredding it to pieces, leaving me bleeding and helpless on the floor all over again.

Biting my lip, a tear spills over, and Boyd's shoulders slump. "But you can't tell me that."

"No." I shake my head, looking down at the counter, drawing tiny circles on the granite with my middle finger. "Not yet."

I've never seen my brother cry, or even come close to it, but as he sits in my kitchen, soaking in our shared regret and misery, his eyes grow red and puffy like he's trying to hold it in.

And as much as I want him to stop fighting, I know that path isn't linear. Or easy. So, I don't say anything, letting the quiet ebb around us like soft waves kissing the shore.

Clearing his throat, Boyd reaches into the breast pocket of his pajama shirt and pulls out a little brass key. "I know I can't make up for everything in one night. Hell, I might not ever be able to. But I would love for you to come home. Maybe one day we can even talk about the boy you're apparently seeing."

I take the key as he places it in my palm. "Home? I still have my old house key—"

"Not *our* home. *Yours*, if you want it."

My eyebrows furrow. "You... bought me a house?"

"Well, I had several birthdays and holidays to make up for."

Shock seizes my chest, and I stare down at the scrap of metal, letting his words soak in. "But what about—"

The small jerk of his chin is sharp, and his eyes meet mine for the first time since I sat down beside him. "They're all dead, Riley. Anyone who ever might have come back to hurt you. I spent the last three years hunting them down and destroying their operation. No one is ever going to come after you again."

He glances down at his hands, clenching and unclenching his jaw. "I know you thought I was just being a dick all this time. That I didn't want to see you, or didn't want you to come back. And maybe, deep down, that was a stupid part of it. But... I just wanted you to be safe, Riley. To *feel* safe. Now, maybe you can."

Curling my fingers around the key, I try to let his words

warm my soul. Try to think about how good it'll feel to go back to King's Trace, even if reintroducing myself back into the land of the living will be difficult.

But one sentence he said niggles at the back of my mind, and I note that it's not entirely true.

I can think of one person who might come for me.

43

THE PEOPLE in Lunar Cove are no different than the ones in the rest of the country, I'm learning.

They're just slower, like time travels at a wildly different rate here than anywhere else.

But now that word is out about the famous musician in their midst, the townsfolk can't seem to stay inside. I haven't even been to the boardwalk strip in days, because each time I'm swarmed by a mob of people begging for autographs and pictures.

Some are genuine fans—you can always tell by their reaction to you, whether they blush or stutter, or if they stand just a little too close, possibly hoping a droplet of your sweat will splash onto them.

Others, though, are clearly only interested in a cash grab. Something signed or touched or breathed on by me that they can put in their shitty little souvenir shops and sell for an outrageous price, as if my existence matters any more than the other seven billion people on the planet.

Newsflash: it doesn't.

It doesn't help that since Riley's old "friend" told the Internet my geographical location, people are flocking to the little mountain valley town in an attempt to run into me, or say they spotted me from afar.

Somehow, my actual accommodations have remained a secret, though I don't suspect they will for long.

Just as well, since I'm on a flight to New York in an hour, anyway. Due to perform on a rooftop stage, returning to my life as though I haven't spent the last several weeks living an entirely new one.

I don't even know the man who came here anymore.

Not because I'm any less confused, or bitter, or angry. In fact, I feel as though I'm leaving with the same amount of knowledge I showed up with.

But somewhere along the way, I've started to convince myself I feel a little less empty.

Liam's voice drones on as he goes over the preshow itinerary for the fifth time, as though I haven't done enough of these to be able to prep for them in my fucking sleep.

I've got an entire suitcase stuffed full of peppermint candies, the underwear I never gave back to Riley, and every other piece of my obsession with her, that I'm trying to zip up, and Liam's incessant chatter feels like a cheese grater being dragged down my back.

"Fucking Christ, Liam." Huffing, I give up and flip the lid back, turning to glare at him through my laptop that sits on the dresser. "I get it, I have a lot of shit to do when I land. Can't we deal with it then?"

"Your father said the label wants to ensure you're as prepared as possible, so as to avoid any more... hiccups."

"Hiccups," I repeat, voice flat. "If they think someone else is gonna accuse me of sexual assault or some bullshit again, I think we've proved that we're more than capable of handling that hiccup."

"You think that girl will ever come forward?"

My fingernails dig into my knees through my black jeans, biting against the skin. "It doesn't even matter at this point. Those who care are always going to, even if I had her stand up on stage beside me and admit she made the whole thing up because she was in love with me and wanted my atten-tion. Those who don't want to believe it have already forgot-ten. Probably did the second another scandal hit, three years ago."

His lips twist as if in thought, and then he jots something down on a notepad, sticking a pencil behind one ear. "You think that's why she did it? Because she was in love with you?"

I can't help the snort that huffs out of me, amusement bitter as it pumps through my veins. "All I know is that I don't care."

It's easier to pretend that's the case than acknowledge how insane the ignorance still leaves me. How I can know practically everything about a person—from their favorite color, the name of their kindergarten teacher, the sounds they make when they orgasm—and still be left in the dark when it comes to something as fundamental as intent.

Maybe it's better that I don't know the truth behind Riley's actions. Maybe if I did, I'd see them for what they most likely are; a lost girl enjoying the embrace of a man who lost his fucking mind the second he met her.

I haven't been the same since that night in New York.

For many reasons.

And I guess part of me is afraid to find out that she is.

Hanging up with Liam, I close the laptop and slide it into its carrier, dragging my luggage to the foyer and propping instruments against the wall. I head back into the bedroom and try my hand at closing the suitcase that would be a hoarder's wet dream, when a soft gasp startles me.

"You did steal my panties!"

Jaw clenched, I turn as Riley strides into the room, irritation lacing her delicate face. She stomps over to the bed and hooks a finger in one lacy pair, holding them up as if I can't see what she's talking about.

I force a smirk. "What did you think happened to them?"

Both her hands dive in, picking up over a dozen scraps of different feminine fabrics. "I'll have you know my friends thought I was insane when I told them my underwear drawer vanished. Fiona was threatening to schedule me a psychological evaluation if I didn't stop claiming a ghost had robbed me."

"Ah, well. I had to get your attention somehow."

Perching on the edge of the bed, she continues sifting through her things, and shoots me an exasperated look. "Dude, are you a peppermint connoisseur now? You know, I don't smell like this all the time. Just seasonally."

"Shh," I say, reaching down to clamp my hand over her mouth. "Don't ruin the illusion, angel."

When I release her, she giggles, crossing her legs as she

looks out the door. Her eyes grow sad, and I turn to follow her gaze to where my things are packed up and ready to be loaded into my Volvo.

"You're leaving," she says, and even though her words are even, there's an undercurrent of disbelief hidden in them. Almost like she'd been expecting me to stay.

"Duty calls. All the time we've spent together, and our futures were never discussed? We both knew this wasn't going to last."

She tilts her chin up, finding my eyes, and the misery that swells in her sapphire gaze is almost my undoing. Almost enough for me to say fuck it, drag her to a back room and keep her my happy little secret forever—not because I'm ashamed, but because I don't want to fucking share her with the rest of the world.

Which is exactly why I'm not asking her to go with me.

"Don't look at me like that, pretty girl." I pinch her jaw, slightly rougher than necessary, and swipe my thumb over the scar at the corner of her mouth. "This has been quite the learning experience for the both of us, but you know what they say. All's well that doesn't end well."

She frowns, jerking away. "That's not the saying, and you know it."

"Doesn't matter. If a crabby tattoo shop girl says it, it must be true, right?"

Surprise flickers across her face, and I smother the satisfaction that crests inside me. "You heard her that night?"

"I heard everything." My hands fall to my sides, and I spread them out over my thighs. "I won't lie and say I wasn't hoping that my quip about fate intervening was true, but it probably makes sense that it wasn't. We're from far different worlds, aren't we?"

"Yeah," she says, dropping her gaze and the underwear in her hands. "I guess we are."

She swallows, and my heart aches. Begs. Yearns. For all of her—body, mind, soul. Whatever pieces of herself she'd allow me to enjoy, I believe in this moment that I'd take them and run, damn the consequences.

"Were you always planning to leave?"

I nod, not wanting to add lies to my list of offenses. "I was supposed to ruin you."

She laughs, but the sound is hollow. Empty. Not the lilted caress I've come to love from her.

"Do you think you haven't?"

Glancing away, I scrub at the underside of my jaw, sucking on my teeth. "Then I guess I've accomplished what I needed to, hm?"

"Oh, good. Asshole Aiden's back."

"He never left."

Her shoulders slump, and she tucks her pink hair behind her ears, scoffing. Christ, she's never looked more beautiful than when she's upset with me.

Hurting her shouldn't arouse me so much, but it does, and before I know what I'm doing, I'm dropping to my knees at the foot of the bed and crawling between her jean-clad thighs.

Her nostrils flare as she looks down at me. "Do you honestly think sex is going to soothe my wounds?"

"I don't fucking care if it does," I say, pushing her back so she's flat on the mattress. I hook my fingers in her waistband and tug them down, ignoring the look of disgust on her face. "I'm trying to soothe mine."

"Well, I don't think we should—"

"And I'm still not taking no for an answer. Shut up and let me taste you one last fucking time."

She doesn't utter another word as I yank her pants off her feet and throw them over my shoulder, then bury my face between her thighs. Within seconds, she's pulsing against my tongue, hips grinding desperately, fingers twisting in my hair and pulling tight.

I ignore the expectant gleam in her eyes as I wipe my mouth on the inside of her leg. My mouth dries up as she continues lying there, slightly dazed and dripping.

My cock throbs behind my zipper, but I will it to soften, knowing without checking the watch on my arm that I don't have time to fuck her fully. At least, not literally.

Riley doesn't move as I continue about the room, double-checking to make sure I've grabbed and packed everything of significance. When I go back to the suitcase on the bed, she rolls to her side and watches me struggle to close it.

"You wanted to know what happened that night," she says after a few silent moments, and the blood freezes in my veins, curiosity spinning an intricate web inside my chest.

I don't want to miss my flight, but I don't want to miss this more.

"My scars," she begins, her hand automatically reaching up to sweep over the ones on her face. I glance down at the one on her hip, emotion lodging in my throat, and she looks up at the headboard. "One of my mom's boyfriends was this drug runner for a local mob outfit. She'd been involved in that kind of thing for as long as I could remember, so I never thought anything of it when she started bringing him around. In retrospect, he was her longest relationship, and now... well, I guess I know there was a reason why."

Blowing out a breath, she rolls onto her stomach,

spreading her palms over her abdomen. I note that she's not even trying to cover herself in any capacity, leaving her pussy bare for my eyes only, and I'm not sure if she's too engrossed in her memories, or if that means something.

It probably doesn't.

How could it? All I've done is take from her.

"Anyway, most of the attack is a blur. One second, I was sitting on our ratty old couch doing homework, and the next, my back had shattered our coffee table." A pause. She glances at me as if checking to see if I'm still paying attention.

I inch closer, my mind stuck on the word attack.

As if I could focus on anything but.

"I was legally dead for like, two full minutes. Maybe that's why faking my death was so easy."

It's an attempt at a joke that she punctuates with a nervous laugh, but it doesn't hit. I don't move, don't blink, and she sighs, crossing her legs.

"It, uh, took me to a pretty bad place for a long time. The stuff the doctor said he'd done to me... I can't remember it fully, just bits and pieces, but I know it was bad. New York was the first non-school function I'd gone to since the attack, and, well. We both know how that night ends."

My eyes are glued to her hip, and now I'm imagining a man standing over her and carving into her flesh. Stealing a life that didn't belong to him, taking innocence he wasn't worthy of.

I try not to think about how my coming here and torturing her must have felt, after all that.

"I've never slept with anyone," she'd told me, and I don't know what the fuck I thought she meant, but it wasn't something as gruesome as this.

"I swear to you, I had nothing to do with that rumor." Licking her lips, she sits up. "I hadn't even told anyone but Fiona about meeting you, and I didn't even know about the allegations until I'd gotten back home. You have to believe that, Aiden."

I don't say anything. *Can't*. The words don't form, my lungs struggling to work properly the longer I listen to her horror story.

One I punished her for.

Agony rips through my spine, notching like a knife between each vertebrae, and bile teases the back of my throat. I press my palms harder into my legs, trying to catch my breath.

"I didn't come forward because I couldn't. In case... the man who attacked me, he was involved in sex trafficking. I guess my mom had made some sort of deal with him, and I was the product he was supposed to deliver, and never did. Both he and my mom wound up dead, and my brother was worried that if I came forward and people recognized me, I'd be in danger."

"Look, we didn't mention it because someone showed up right after you left and threatened our lives if we did." Jenna's words at the tattoo shop, making me think it'd been Riley who'd contacted them.

Riley continues. "And then I got an envelope in the mail, and it was this extreme breakdown of my entire life. My location, my medical history, and a note that said they knew what I'd done."

Tears well in her eyes as she looks up at me. I reach out, because I can't stand not to touch her right now, and she leans her cheek against my palm.

"I didn't know what else to do," she admits, closing her

eyes. "I was scared, and... I don't know. I copped out, I guess. It was selfish, and awful, and I'm so sor—"

My hand slides from her cheek to cover her mouth, my chest pinching at her apology. God, no wonder she lives with shame on the tip of her tongue.

"Why are you telling me this?" I ask, moving my hand just enough so she can answer. "Why now?"

Her hand lifts, reaching into my suitcase; it dives to the very bottom, and she tugs out a garment, draping it over my extended arm.

Emerald green.

Satin.

I can still picture how perfect she looked in it.

"You kept it," she whispers, smoothing her fingers over the material. "And you were right. You deserved to know."

44

I'M NOT sure what I was expecting my confession to do.

Not even sure what I *wanted* it to do.

The idea of keeping Aiden sounds good in theory, but he's a rock star and I'm a social pariah from Maine. He's a bad guy, and I'm a traumatized girl who finds solace in his depravity.

Star-crossed doesn't even begin to cover our story.

He doesn't even say anything after my spiel; just kisses me and says he can't miss his flight. He stops by the bathroom one last time, and I quickly stuff my hand in my pocket, pulling out the late Christmas gift I came to give him in the first place.

I store it down in the side of his duffel bag, and then slip out the front door before he comes back out, disappearing into the brush by the cabin so I can watch him leave.

When he strolls outside and starts loading his Volvo up, I try to memorize every little thing about him; the slight, almost imperceptible limp in his step from a stage injury when he was a teenager. The tattoos that cover his body, the smirk that seems permanently etched into his lips.

The circle imprint in his cheek as he sucks on a peppermint.

He glances around the area, and for a second I wonder if he can see me. Or if maybe he's checking for paparazzi, or a stray fan.

His head turns toward my cabin, and he takes a step in that direction.

I hold my breath, waiting.

Go, my mind screams. *Go over there and make me come back with you. Or stay. Don't pretend you're done.*

But then he shakes his head and gets in the vehicle anyway.

The last thing I see as he drives down the road is the fiery glow of his brake lights, reflecting off the white snow, and then he's gone.

"I'm going to throw that television off the fucking balcony if you don't turn it off in the next three seconds."

"Good luck explaining that to the owners. What if they're

sentimental people, and you destroying their stuff sends them into a murderous rage?"

Silence.

I roll over in bed, looking at the light filtering beneath my closed bedroom door.

"Fiona. Are you not hearing what I'm saying? *I'm* about to start breaking necks, and I can promise I have the rap sheet to back that threat up, unlike the elderly owner of this fucking cabin. Turn it *off.*"

Folding back my sheets, I get out of bed and peek into the hall; Kal Anderson and Fiona stand at the top of the stairs, locked in some sort of face-off.

Her arms are crossed, her face as red as her hair, and his flat expression somehow holds enough aggression that I feel it waft toward me.

"I hate men." She spins on her heel, stomping downstairs, her ponytail swishing back and forth between her shoulder blades.

Wiping the sluggishness from my eyes, I venture farther out into the hall; Kal's head whips in my direction, surprise lighting his sharp features.

"Riley." He nods, as professional as ever.

"What are you doing here?"

"I was told you're returning to King's Trace." He holds up a detached security camera in one gloved hand, shrugging. "Supposed you wouldn't need these anymore."

"God, you guys don't waste any time, do you?"

"Procrastination is a poor man's game." He sweeps past me, the air chilling as it bends around him. The tail ends of his trench coat fly behind him as he walks to a cardboard box at the end of the hall, dumping the camera inside.

I watch him disassemble the device and then seal the box, mesmerized by his precise movements.

"If you have something to say, Ms. Kelly, by all means. Before I'm dead."

Smirking, I rock back on my heels, a tiny vein throbbing in my forehead. *Weirdly, I think I'll miss this.*

"Thank you."

He blinks. "For?"

"Everything, Kal." Emotion wells in my throat, and I bite down on my tongue, suppressing it. "*Everything.*"

For a few silent beats, he just looks at me; his black eyes unfocus slightly, as if he's seeing through me, but then he blinks again and nods. There isn't a single shift in his expression, nothing to suggest that he feels anything right now.

"You don't owe me your gratitude," he says finally. "You owe it to *yourself.*"

I nod, starting down the stairs with that sentiment knocking around my skull.

Then, "But you're welcome, anyway."

Rolling my eyes, I go in search of Fiona, finding her crouched in front of the living room television with her ear pressed against the screen. I stop behind her, crossing my arms and cocking my head to the side.

"What are you doing?"

She screams, practically jumping out of her skin. Stumbling back onto her ass, she glares at me, her hand flying to her chest. "God, Riley, you can't fucking sneak up on people. Aren't you supposed to be asleep?"

"It's hard to sleep when you and Kal are arguing outside my room—"

My eyes flicker to the television, bright flashing lights catching my attention; the camera pans around a rooftop stage where some color guard is performing for a New Year's Eve party.

A banner of text glides across the bottom, an array of upcoming acts streaming on a continuous loop.

Only one stands out, though.

Aiden James, in big block lettering. *The Man, The Myth, The Legend.*

Fiona follows my line of sight, wincing, and lifts the remote in her hand. "See, this is why you were supposed to be asleep. I'll turn it off—"

"No, it's fine." Holding my palm up, I shrug, pasting a fake smile on my face.

Her mouth twists up. "I just wanted to watch the ball drop."

"So, watch it." I shrug, flopping down on the sofa across the room. My laptop sits on the coffee table, so I pull it into my lap and open up my portfolio, pretending like I don't want to look at the show with every fiber of my being.

She keeps it on a low volume for a long time, sitting with her arms wrapped around her legs, and I manage to tune it out while Kal and Boyd pack boxes of my non-personal stuff outside.

I really hadn't expected to be leaving Lunar Cove so soon, but I suppose if there's no longer any threat, staying here doesn't exactly make sense.

A pang ripples in my chest when I think about telling Caleb that I'm leaving, but on the other hand, it's probably better that I do. Nip any lingering feelings in the bud, just in case.

I'm trying to concentrate on a web concept for some kind of paywall story app, but Fiona keeps muttering things under her breath and scooting closer to the television. Her face is almost squashed against it when I glance up again.

"Fi, for fuck's sake, just turn it up—"

The color guard is gone from the stage, and in its place are an array of purple and black instruments, a two-headed serpentine design painted on the face of the bass drum.

My stomach churns violently, my breath hitching in my throat as I see a mop of dark brown hair and long legs cross over to say something to the keyboardist off the side.

He moves effortlessly, in black jeans and a gray peacoat, with a black electric guitar slung around his back. Commands the presence of his audience, though I don't think he can even *see* them on the streets below and watching from home.

A god among mortals.

Silver eyes flash as he moves behind the mic, and I'm not really sure if the camera is broadcasting the setup part of his act, or if this is part of it.

Maybe he's so out of practice that the whole performance is off.

But then the laser lights dim, blacking out completely for exactly three seconds.

Just how long he'd keep them off at the start of every show.

Sliding my computer off my lap, I abandon the façade of work and just watch; in seconds, the stage lights up in different hues of purple and the opening chords to one of his older songs begins, a fast-paced melody I'm having a hard time paying attention to.

All I can really see and hear is him.

Tapered, inked fingers strum and pluck, and his lips seem to move in time with each stroke. The way he goes from rigid and grumpy as soon as the song begins, to lithe and free with the first verse, falling back into his music as if he never stopped playing.

I realize as I'm watching that I never asked him to play for me.

Dozens of times, he worked my body like it was his favorite instrument, but I never got to see him actually play. Never got to witness the passion bleed from his pores or see the way his art makes those silver eyes of his light up like lightning striking through storm clouds.

Wrestling the remote from Fiona, I turn the volume up, inching closer as he launches into the next song, and then the next.

My throat burns watching him. Smoke unfurls in my chest, dissolving into my bloodstream; it's like aching for home without even realizing you left, and not knowing how to get back.

He's mesmerizing. Captivating.

The longer I observe, the deeper into awe I fall.

It happens all at once, my descent into hell; a single sin that snowballs into something uncontrollable.

It's madness.

Surrender.

Like staring straight into a sunset, or a religious awakening.

Ironic that I'm quite literally *kneeling*.

As the transition into his fourth song starts, though, Aiden glances down at the pick in his hand and freezes, staring intensely at the piece of plastic. He looks at it for so long, one of the event hosts cuts in to ask if everything is okay with his equipment.

Lifting his head, those stony eyes immediately find the

camera. I suck in a breath through my teeth, feeling like he's peering straight into my soul, even though there's no way he can know I'm watching.

Removing one of his earpieces, he turns his head and says something to the drummer, who nods and makes some sort of hand gesture, cutting the rest of the music.

"What the heck?" Fiona says at my side, frowning. "He wasn't even on as long as the other acts!"

But I'm not paying attention to her, my focus glued to the man on the television.

He swallows, his Adam's apple working in his throat, and then he lets out an inaudible laugh. Adjusting his mic, he inhales deeply, and I think he's about to start into an a cappella version of a song, but he doesn't.

"This was supposed to be my reintroduction into the music world," he says slowly, gripping the handle of the microphone with his fingers, keeping the pick wedged between them. "Most of you probably know, I went on hiatus about three years ago, because of some stuff that went down that kind of ruined me."

Pausing, he tilts his head, as if considering that. "Well, ruined the *old* me. The Aiden James every one of you have come to love. I wish I could say the one standing here today is as into performing as he once was, and that it feels amazing to be back here, doing what I've dreamed about since I was a kid watching my mom do it first."

I feel Fiona's eyes on me, but I can't look. Can't breathe, hanging on his every last word.

"Don't get me wrong. It's great to be back, but ever since I landed in New York, I've felt like something was missing." Clearing his throat, he twirls the guitar pick around in one hand, and I know then.

I *know* it's the one I put in his suitcase. That he found it, after all, and brought it on stage.

Used it to perform.

"Three years ago, my life shifted completely on its axis. A single night rocked my entire world, and it took me that long to realize it wasn't the aftermath of scandal and bad press that did it." Pause. Another glance at the camera. "It was the girl."

Fiona gasps, her fingers clawing my knee.

"One day, I'll be able to go into the specifics of how I lost her, followed her to the underworld, and left without her. Like a dumbass. I'll never be able to understand why I didn't tell her today that I wanted to bring her back with me."

My heart swells, painfully pressing into my ribs, trying to burst free.

"Pretty stupid of me, in all honesty. A test of faith that I failed, and will probably spend the rest of my life trying to make up for. Among other things."

He scratches the back of his neck, lifting a shoulder in a half shrug.

"I don't deserve her. I know that much. And I'm sure if I could see her right now, her face would be the same color as her hair. I don't even know if she's listening right now, but in the event that she is... well, now she knows. I'm pretty sure you've been it for me since the second I laid eyes on you, angel. Three *years* I've been completely fucking obsessed, and I don't see that ending anytime soon."

He clears his throat, and the music starts back up, playing softly.

"*Anyway*, I've wasted your time enough here tonight. You came for a show, so that's what you're going to get. I just wanted to get that off my chest, so when I announce my official retirement from music, the world doesn't seem so shocked."

A grin tugs at his lips, and he raises a hand in the air, signaling his bandmates. "This one's for you, *pretty girl.*"

The ballad feels like a smooth caress over my skin, his baritone voice flooding the speakers and sending a shiver down my spine.

Launching into a sensual number, I barely even hear the lyrics over his declaration. It repeats on a loop in my brain, tuning itself to the music he plays, and I'm struggling to process it.

Fiona's hand falls from my knee. "Did he just tell the entire world that he's in love with you?"

I stare at the television, but everything's blurry now. Emotion ratchets up my sternum, warmth spreading from my heart outward, filling me with that same nostalgic sensation I got when he first took the stage.

Like missing home. Weird that I didn't realize until now that I've been going without.

Still, I sputter, shaking my head. My instincts say to write it off, deflect the reality he's trying to push on me. A month ago, he wanted me to suffer. This morning, he left because of his show, and instead of telling me any of this to my face, he chooses a stage with millions of people.

Sane humans don't do that.

A sane, morally upright person would tell the girl before announcing it to the world.

Right?

"He's crazy," I say, a nervous laugh pushing past my lips.

The television goes black, silence filling the air. Fiona and I blink at each other, then whirl around to see Kal standing behind the sofa, his jaw set in a harsh line.

But his eyes seem soft at the edges.

"He's not crazy." He drops a backup remote onto the sofa and points at me with a long finger. "He's in love."

My eyes narrow. "It could easily be a stupid publicity stunt."

"At the same time he announced his *retirement*? Odd strategy, but I suppose if you're trying to garner interest, perhaps that could work." Crossing his arms over his chest, Kal shrugs, impassive as ever. "If there's even a tiny part of you that feels the same way, though, you should go to him."

"Go to him? What is this, the end of a romantic comedy blockbuster?"

He smirks, seeming to get lost in his thoughts for the briefest second. "Waiting is the worst part. Don't make the same mistake I did."

My mouth parts, ready to ask what the hell he's talking about, but then he sweeps from the room, leaving just me and Fiona. She meets my eyes and lifts a shoulder, moving to lean her back against the couch.

"I don't know about all that," she says, taking the remote and switching the television back on. "But I do know what love looks like, and I'll tell you this: I've never seen it shine as bright in anyone's eyes as it did the morning we walked in on you two together. Do with that information what you will."

When I'm in bed later, I toss and turn for hours, trying to figure out what I want to do with that information.

Is it completely fucked to find comfort and trust in the arms of a man who once hurt you?

A *criminal.*

For all intents and purposes, that's what Aiden is.

He's not a good guy by any stretch of the word, and yet neither is my brother. Or his friends.

Or Kal.

Maybe it doesn't matter how society paints them, or what stains mar their pasts.

Maybe what matters is the lengths they're willing to go for the people they love.

While the rest of the cabin sleeps, I slip into my boots, not bothering to change out of my pajamas, and pad downstairs. I grab my purse off the island counter, disarm the security system, and am trying to book a flight to New York as I step out onto the porch.

My thumb hits the checkout button as soon as my feet clear the threshold. I don't feel the presence at my side, don't feel the hands reaching to silence me until it's too late.

And then, I don't feel anything.

45

"I UNDERSTAND he just signed another contract with us. *Clearly*, he'll be buying himself out of it."

My father glares at me from across the dining room table, rubbing at the dark circles under his eyes as he speaks into his Bluetooth earpiece. Leaning back in my chair, I tilt my head toward the ceiling and turn the guitar pick in my hand, smoothing my thumb over the engraving on the front.

Aiden James Fan Club.

A smile plays at my lips when I recall Riley's rushed admission one night about how she'd run the online fandom for years.

My number one stalker, existing right under my nose. No wonder it was so easy to curate an obsession with her; kindred souls call to one another, and who better to understand me than someone who's been in my shoes?

It's more than that, though; hot lust and volatile emotions that at some point gave way to real affection and an attraction magnetic fields would be envious of.

I tried to do the valiant and noble thing, aware that I don't deserve her. Aware that I hurt and violated her, without remorse. Knowing we have a million different things to work through, and our lives to figure out.

But the confession had just poured out of me as soon as I saw the custom pick, and like a torrential downpour, I flooded the earth with my feelings.

A gesture I'm hoping is enough to bring her to me.

My father hangs up his phone, slinging the Bluetooth onto the table. "The next time you decide to make a major life-changing announcement, maybe at least *discuss* it with me first."

"Well, I didn't know when I went up there that I was going to be doing that."

"That's not *better*, son." Sighing heavily, he drags a palm down his face. "If anything, that proves how fucking impulsive the decision was."

Dropping the guitar pick on the table, I steeple my fingers together. The halo tattoo I got three years ago on the underside of my thumb winks up at me, and I shrug, wishing I had something more to tell him. Something better that would benefit everyone involved.

But the fact of the matter is, finding something that benefits the James family is what I've been doing since the start of my career. The rock star brand was our saving grace when I got signed onto Symposium, giving the three of us tasks to do and things to focus on outside of our misery.

The difference between the last time I took the stage before my hiatus and when I was up there tonight was staggering. Not only in the renewed sense of passion and energy I felt, but in the actual creative material.

I got stagnant before my break. My love for music was overshadowed by fatigue, drinking, and sadness. Symptoms of an illness I was trying to cure by ignoring completely.

My muse was tired, so I set her free.

Now, she can rest for good knowing she served me well. Knowing someone else inspires me now.

"You're throwing everything away that you worked so hard for," my father says, pinching the bridge of his nose. "For a girl. A girl who quite *literally* ruined your life."

"Guess so."

"What happened to exposing her? To reclaiming your innocence and fixing your public image?"

"I told you I didn't want to do that anymore. I'm not interested in further traumatizing someone who was, inevitably, a victim of the same shit that I was. She just couldn't be vocal about it."

His face hardens. "So, what? She tells you a sob story, and you're keen on believing it without any proof? What, is her pussy made of magic or something?"

My tongue gets heavy in my mouth as an image of the brutal scarring on her body flashes through my mind. The recollection of an equally brutal attack—one that had me seeing fucking crimson on my way to the airport, and if not for the fact that she'd mentioned the perpetrator is now dead, I probably would've skipped out on the concert altogether in favor of finding the fucker and sodomizing him with the neck of my guitar.

Still, I don't tell him any of that.

He doesn't deserve to know.

"If you're asking, am I giving up a lucrative career at its height just so I can spend my free time balls deep inside of a girl completely removed from this fucked industry, then yes. Yes, I am. I'm surprised you're not more proud that I'm finally understanding the power of pussy."

Pushing to my feet, I pocket the pick and smooth my hands over my coat, placing my palms flat on the dining table as I stare him down.

"Don't worry though, *Dad*. Maybe I'll follow in your foot-steps. Start up a record label, monopolize clientele, fuck over my family, and create an empire that Great Britain would be proud of." I rap my knuckles on the wood and straighten my spine. "Maybe... maybe I'll come for yours."

Several hours later, with a full moon high in the sky, I get antsy sitting around waiting to hear from Riley. Whether she watched the show or not, I need to know.

Even more, I need to tell her this shit in person.

Need to look in her eyes when I admit that I'm fucking ridiculously gone for her, so I can know for sure that I'm not alone in it.

I pack an overnight bag and leave the penthouse without telling anyone where I'm going; naturally, the second I step outside, I'm bombarded by a slew of paps. Everyone is trying to figure out the identity of my mystery girl, where I've been all this time, what my next steps are, and if I'm giving up music for good.

A million questions hurled at me by the same vultures

willing to tear me down three years ago, just to catch a quick buck.

"No fucking comment," I snap, losing them at the gated entrance of my building's underground parking structure. Hopping into my blacked-out Range Rover, I make it to the airport in record time, for New Year's Eve especially, and board a flight back across the country.

When I land in Lunar Cove a couple of hours later, I'm jet-lagged as fuck, barely able to see straight. A cab takes me across town, and I note fireworks at the boardwalk as we drive around the lake, headed for the sleepy cabins tucked away in the corner of town.

Parking in front of the two at the end of the street, I add an extra hundred to my bill, asking the driver to sit idle for a minute while I collect myself.

Technically speaking, Riley is too good for me. Pure and innocent, candy-coated with an ooey-gooey center. She could—and should—reject me, based on the simple fact that I initially set out to hurt her when I came here.

I couldn't even tell you when the exact intentions changed. Only that they did, and at some point my being here became less about finding out what happened to *me*, and more about what happened to *us*.

I can only hope my leaving earlier didn't fuck up any chances I have of explaining that.

Finally, I get out of the cab and hike my duffel over my shoulder, starting up the front walk to her cabin. A fuzzy yellow glow shines in my peripheral, bouncing off the melting snow, and when I turn in the direction of the cabin I'd been staying in, I see it.

One of the windows on the second floor is lit up, and a

shadow moves behind the curtain. My nerves pull tight in my stomach, knotting together.

Is she in my old cabin?

My steps slow as soon as they change direction, suspicion creeping up my spine. If she is waiting, if she saw the show... wouldn't she have reached out?

Chest tight, I narrow my eyes as the figure in the window disappears, almost pulling a direct page from my book. On the one hand, I wouldn't put it past Riley to mimic the days before I made my presence fully known to her, but on the other, she has no way of knowing I'd even be here.

Making my way down around the lake, I move in slow, soft steps and stick to the shadows, doing my best to go undetected by whoever the fuck is in the cabin. Rounding the back, I go for the entrance off the laundry room, moving to shimmy it open as quietly as possible.

The air is eerily silent and still when I get inside, easing the door shut behind me. I peek down the hall, noting the distinct lack of voices and movement, apprehension licking down my back like the flames of an uncontrollable wildfire.

I have a bad feeling, and it lodges itself deep in my gut, refusing to dissipate.

Just in case, I glance around the room quickly for something to use as a potential weapon. My father, for all his faults, always taught me to never go into a blind negotiation without a trick or two up your sleeve—I'd like to believe that extends beyond the boardroom, to dangerous situations, as well.

Unfortunately, my options are incredibly limited, so I grab the object closest to me; an iron. Detaching the cord, I drop it to the floor, hook my fingers around the plastic handle, and exit the room.

Shuffling my feet, I do my best to avoid creaky floor-boards, advancing down the hall with my back against the wall, flipping on lights as I go. The main level is clear, completely empty from what I can tell, but that yellow glow still drifts from upstairs, so I move toward it.

I'm hoping that maybe I just forgot to turn the light off. Or maybe, for some insane reason, Riley decided to come back and wait. Maybe she watched the concert and hoped I'd be back, so she cut out the middle territory.

Even as those thoughts swim in my brain, I know they're not plausible. And when I crest the top of the stairs, my grip tightening on the iron as my stomach sinks to my ass, those fears are confirmed.

Riley lies prone on her back, hands zip-tied behind her, duct-tape slapped across her mouth. She's staring blankly at the wall in front of her, and I see a little puddle of blood trickling out of a wound in her side.

My eyes go wide, bulging so hard that I think they might fall from their sockets, as I take her in; in the pale lighting, I can see bruises scattered across her forehead, and there are claw marks on the wooden floor around her.

Like she tried to fight off whoever did this.

I slip to the end of the hall where the bedroom is, leaning in to scan it quickly. Other than Riley, I don't see anyone else, and since I'm not sure what the fuck is going on, or how much time we have before they come back, I spring into action.

Her blue eyes snap to mine as I hurry over to her, immediately using my keys to try and saw the zip tie apart. It doesn't work; she's squirming, freaking the fuck out as I try to work her free, and the keys are too dull for the material keeping her bound.

Fear swirls in her ocean eyes as I turn her head up, ripping the tape from her mouth.

"What the fuck is going on?" I ask, brushing my fingers against her temple. "What happened to you?"

"Oh god, oh god, oh god," she sobs, spitting blood onto the floor, and I can't tell at first if she's having some kind of breakdown or what. Gripping her shoulders, I roll her so she's on her good side, trying to get her to focus.

"You can't be here," she says, tears welling up in her eyes.

Under any other circumstance, my dick would be positively fucking throbbing at the sight, but right now, with her fear and hysteria aimed at someone other than me, all it does is enrage me.

"Why the fuck are *you* here?"

"I was coming to you," she whispers, pausing mid-sob to say it. "I saw your concert, and I wanted... I wanted—"

"She wanted to let you know that she's a dirty little trailer whore who doesn't deserve you."

The addition of a new voice takes me completely off guard, and I whirl around to see a somewhat familiar face lurking in the doorway.

Platinum-blonde hair. Dark, almond-shaped eyes.

A sneer I'd love to smack off her smug little face.

The girl I met at the art gallery walks into the room, grinning maniacally at the two of us. *Fuck, what was her name? Moira, Molly, Michelle?*

Keeping her hands behind her back, she enters the room slowly, her gaze volleying between Riley and me.

I shift so I'm positioned more in front of Riley's face and chest and turn to glare at the intruder. "Didn't you two used to be friends? Why have you tied her up and beaten her?"

"Not my fault you couldn't finish your job." She moves to

lean against the full bed on one side of the room, and when she does, she folds her arms across her chest, brandishing a giant kitchen knife.

My eyes widen, my posture stiffening at it casually rests against her hip.

"Sometimes, people get distracted on their journeys," she says, lifting a shoulder. "You're lucky you have me to help finish things, Aiden."

The way my name rolls off her tongue, smooth and heavy like whipped cream, makes the hairs stand up on the back of my neck. People I've never met knowing my name and using it in conversation is something I had to get used to over the years, but the attempt at adding a layer of seduction is something most people don't really do.

Usually, they're too starstruck to really flirt, or my general disposition puts them off. But this girl is clearly trying, and it almost keeps her words from registering as I try to dissect her tone.

"What the hell are you talking about?"

She laughs, her face tipping toward the ceiling. "You were *supposed* to ruin her! It's what all the correspondence between you and your father stated up until you came here. Expose her for the lying snake she is, tell the world she faked her death because she felt guilty about accusing you of raping her, and turn the entire public against her. That was the *plan*."

When I glance at Riley from the corner of my eye, I notice hers are closed. Unease cramps my gut, and I scoot so there's less space between us, hoping the warmth of my presence is enough to counteract our ugly reality.

Taking a deep breath, I nod at the girl across the room. "How do you know that?"

"I'm your *soul mate*, Aiden James Santiago. I know everything about you." A strangled noise comes from Riley's throat, and the girl cocks her head, pushing off the bed to make her way over to us. "Is there a problem, little girl? I don't think I was fucking talking to you."

"You're not his soul mate," Riley mutters, her cheek pressing into the floor and garbling her words. "You're just insane."

The girl's dark eyes flare, unkempt fires blazing as she angles the tip of the knife in Riley's direction. "Shut the fuck up, or I'll carve the other side of your mouth so your scars match."

Swallowing, I keep my gaze on the blade, watching for the slightest movement. My fingers find the iron handle beside me, and I inch my way around them, trying to determine how quick I'd have to be with the brunt force before she lashed out and nicked me.

"Look, M—" I trail off, cringing hard when her name still doesn't come to me.

Her face twists up, horror flashing across her features. "*Mellie*."

"Yes, right. Mellie. I have to admit I'm out of the loop here, could you help me understand? Did... did my father put you up to this?"

When she laughs, it's so high-pitched and squirrelly that I almost have to cover my ears; it echoes in my skull, the way nightmares begin.

"Your *dad*? No. As if that man would ever dare speak to a *fan*. Like we're somehow beneath him, and not the entire reason for your career and success."

"Well, then I don't—"

"It was *supposed* to be me that night!" Her voice raises,

sharp and grating. "In New York. The whole trip to the charity auction was *my* idea, *I* placed a fake name on the ballot, *I* was supposed to be the ticket you bid on. But the incompetent gala aide got the buzzers mixed up, and when I saw you walking toward the bar... toward *her*, I knew there'd been a mistake."

I frown, confusion creasing my forehead. "I bid on Riley, though."

"Oh, I know." She scoffs, hatred pouring off her in waves. "I was behind the ticket counter when your friend placed your bid, and I switched up the buzzers. Or, at least, I *thought* I did. But somehow, you still found your way over to her."

Her nose turns up as she bends, poking the back of Riley's calf with the knife. "*Riley*. I couldn't understand what you *possibly* wanted in her, so I followed you to see. Figured maybe if I learned what you saw in this *freak*, I'd be able to mimic it ten thousand times better. Who would choose scars and shyness over perfection?"

Perfection seems like a bit of a stretch, but sure.

"Imagine my fucking surprise when little miss agoraphobia lets you go down on her in a tattoo shop." Pressing harder as her words get angrier, the blade pierces the material of Riley's pajama bottoms, making her squeak in protest.

"You would've done the same," Riley mutters. Her voice is weak, faded, and I glance at the blood pooling beneath her side again, fear creeping into my bones.

"I would've done *more*. Anything to get Aiden to see we belonged together. You left him! Opportunity of a lifetime, and you *bolted*." Mellie's eyes flash to mine, something wild and unhinged reflecting back at me. "She didn't deserve you, darling. Trash like her doesn't deserve anything but to be taken out."

Nostrils flaring, I clench and unclench my jaw, her words slowly processing in my mind. "So, you started the rumor."

She grins. "Started the rumor, made sure it spread through every online platform, leaked names and pictures. You guys did a good job trying to scrub the evidence away, but the Internet is forever, baby. I knew once people heard, they'd never stop talking about it."

Nerves somersault in my stomach, flipping over and over as the realization sets in. I can barely process what this stranger is saying, much less the fucking gravity of what she's done—what she's ruined.

Three years of our lives, completely wasted.

All because some bitch thought she deserved my time.

Tilting her head, a wicked smile spreads over her mouth as she looks at Riley. "I sent the envelope, too. Knew it'd freak you out. Didn't think you'd kill yourself, but hey, that was a nice little bonus." Her face stiffens, mouth mashing into a firm line. "Although, I was surprised to find out it was just another lie."

My hand whips out as she begins sliding the knife down Riley's leg, causing her to cry out in pain. I move to knock the weapon from Mellie's hand, bringing the iron up, but she spins just out of reach, cackling as she points at me.

"Don't try to be a hero, Aiden. It's beneath you at this point. We all know you're not a good guy." She leans forward, tapping my chin with the blade, and grins. "Like I said, I'm trying to help you. Clearly, you've fallen for Riley's little innocent victim act, and have lost sight of what's important."

"I haven't lost sight of anything," I say, resting the iron on my knee. The cool metal of her knife against my chin is grounding, keeping me focused despite Riley's whimpers. "Though I'm feeling pretty enlightened right now."

She groans, pulling back to glare at Riley again. "I heard your confession at your show tonight. I'd planned on flying to New York to be with you, but I knew as soon as I heard that you'd failed in your mission and needed me to help. That's why I grabbed her, and brought her back here. Thought it would be poetic to end her life where you woke up this morning. I read between the lines, baby. Don't worry. I know what you need."

"What I *need*," I say, speaking slowly in the hopes of distracting her, "*is* Riley."

Mellie inhales, but Riley doesn't stir. Her face is so pale, coated in sweat, that I wonder if she's even conscious.

"You don't know what you're saying," Mellie insists, shaking her head.

"I do. Whatever you think there is between us, I'm in love with Riley. I have been since I first saw her, I think." Pausing to roll the words around in my mouth, my chest warms as they settle, permeating my skin like they belong. "Whether or not you'd switched your tickets at the auction that night, I would've found my way to her eventually."

The scream that splits the air makes me flinch, dropping the iron as a body hurls in my direction; I'm not expecting to be tackled, so I go down easy, my head smacking hard against the floor. Mellie looms over me, thrashing as she straddles my hips and grips her knife in one hand, using the other to drive her fist into my face.

"You're supposed to be with me," she screeches, punctuating each word with a punch. "I'm your biggest fan, I'm willing to do anything for you, but you're going to choose her?"

My hands grapple for hers, but she's fast, propelled by adrenaline. I finally get a hold on one wrist and shake the knife from her hand. She hits me in the balls; I deflect the brunt of it with my knee, but it still catches me off guard, and the breath shoots from my lungs as pain zips up my spine.

Her fingers find my neck, and she digs her claws in, cutting off my airway as she reaches into the back of her waistband and pulls out a pistol.

"Jesus, you are fucking crazy," I wheeze, and she replaces her fingers with the gun, jutting it right under my chin.

"I didn't work the last three years chasing you, only to lose you to some dumpy little slut. If you won't be with me, she sure as hell doesn't deserve you."

She presses the barrel against my jugular until I can feel its imprint inside my throat; I force a swallow, glancing at Riley as much as possible without turning my head.

My insides tangle together, dread and resignation filling me.

"Angel," I say, dropping my hand to the floor, reaching for her. Her eyes are open, watching me, and she scoots closer, her nose brushing my fingers. "I mean it, okay? You're it for me. Promise you'll remember that, even when you recall all the shit I put you through."

"That's stupid," she whispers. "I don't need to *remember*, because you're not going anywhere."

Mellie flips the safety, and I laugh.

"I love your optimism, pretty girl. Don't let anyone change that, okay? And I know it doesn't much matter right now, but fuck, I'm so sorry for everything. If I could spend my entire life trying to make up for the way I've treated you, I would."

"Don't apologize." I hear her tears and let their presence soak into me.

Mellie presses harder, and I choke out a strange sound.

"You deserve so much more than words, Riley. The entire fucking universe should bow at your feet in awe of your strength and goodness. I must be the luckiest fucker in the world to have gotten to experience you, even for a little while."

"I love *you*," she says, and the sound of those three words from her pretty lips is my undoing.

I break inside, hating myself for the way I've treated her. Hating that she's caught up in this mess and that I brought it to her.

Mellie rolls her eyes. "Cute," she says, and I watch her finger hook against the trigger, prepared to pull. "But you—"

Blood spurts from her neck, cutting her off as it splatters everywhere; her hand falls from the gun, and I reach up as a reflex, taking it and switching the safety back before I've even fully registered what's just happened.

Mellie reaches up, eyes wide in shock and her breaths coming in sharp, hollow gasps; the knife she had when she walked in now juts out from the side of her throat, lodged all the way to the handle and coming out the other side.

As she collapses, my eyes find Riley crouched on her knees, the zip tie hanging from just one of her wrists now. Her pink hair is tinged with red, her face slightly swollen, and even though there's a girl bleeding to death on top of me, she *smiles*.

"Rookie mistake, leaving a weapon unattended. Guess you should've spent less time being a bitchy psychopath, and more learning your surroundings." Riley spits in Mellie's direction, anger etched into her face. "Or your *people*."

I slide out from beneath Mellie's body as it goes limp, kicking the gun away and drawing Riley into my arms. My heart races, battering against my ribs, and I thread my dirty fingers through her hair, tilting my head to look down at her.

"Holy shit. What the actual fuck just happened?"

"I told you I had nothing to do with the rumors," she says hoarsely, and I chuckle, stroking her cheek with my thumb. "And you were going to ruin my life because of them. A shame, really. Imagine what you'd have lost out on."

Grinning, my mind not quite caught up with the severity or finality of the situation, I press my forehead into hers.

"I'd never have been able to go through with it," I say. "Leaving you earlier was the hardest thing I've ever done. Stupidest, too."

"You came back, though."

Huffing a laugh, I nod, cradling her head in my hands. "And I'm not leaving without you again."

EPILOGUE

"You're absolutely *sure* you want to do this?"

Turning my head, I glare at my brother as he sits on the plastic chair beside me, hands on his bouncing knees. His eyes dart around the room, coasting over every piece of artwork hanging on the walls, tension threading through his jaw.

"Boyd." He glances at me, and I pinch his thigh. "Your nervous energy is contagious, and I'm gonna need you to stop."

He groans, reaching up to pull at his dirty-blond hair.

"God, you're right. It's just... tattoos are *permanent*, you know?"

I give him a flat look, cocking an eyebrow. "No shit? I thought you were just bad at showering."

Rolling his eyes, he pushes to his feet and paces in front of me. I know the nerves have more to do with his evening plans than anything else, so I sit back and continue scrolling through my phone, refusing to let his anxiety bother me.

Not adopting other peoples' thoughts and feelings is something I've been focusing a lot on at therapy lately, and while rewiring that part of my brain is still a massive work in progress, starting with Boyd has been monumental in helping us repair our relationship.

It's by no means perfect, and after the attack in Lunar Cove last year, it almost fractured again when Boyd's fears gave him another excuse to try and control me.

Mellie didn't die that night, unfortunately, but she was charged with about a dozen different felonies while recovering in the hospital. She pleaded insanity, her lawyer citing parasocial relationships and their effect on the brain and wound up in a psychiatric hospital somewhere across the country.

Regardless, she won't be hurting anyone else anytime soon, but it was hard for my brother to accept that I'd been accosted *again*, while he slept in the house right next door.

When I moved back to King's Trace, taking up residence in the lakefront house Boyd bought me, I also started dragging him along to therapy. Both of us have a lifetime of issues to work through, and I refused to allow any sort of regression after having come so far.

I don't want my intervention to be the sole credit for the reason he's *finally* proposing to Fiona, but I'd be lying if I said I didn't secretly pat myself on the back for giving him the push to do it.

"She's gonna say yes," I tell him, crossing one leg over the other. "You're spiraling for no reason."

He stops pacing and sighs. "They wouldn't call it *spiraling* if it made sense."

The tattoo artist finally calls me to the back, and I tell Boyd he can go and that I'll see him after his date to help celebrate. He pins me with a look that says I'd better be right, and then heads outside, disappearing down the street.

As I lie on the table in the back, letting the artist put the stencil on, I smile through my own nerves, memories of my first tattoo flashing across my mind the way they often do.

Aiden's hands on my hip, his head between my legs, his scent on my skin. Things I'd never have imagined I'd experience in a million years, that now I can't seem to live without.

Even now, I'm wearing a flannel of his that I stole from our closet while he's been in New York, finalizing a project he's been working on with his mom for the last few months.

When he "retired" at only twenty-five, he didn't want to leave the music industry altogether; just wanted to recapture his passion for it and create on his own time. Maybe even navigate through his mental health issues through music in a way that didn't drain him, he'd said.

In an attempt to slowly fix his relationship with his mother, he'd proposed starting a small joint label, and said that their primary goal would be finding and signing new, undiscovered talent.

So, his best friend and former publicist, Liam, was brought on to scout talent. Aiden produces, and Callie takes care of the business aspect of things. They're small but growing steadily; enough that last month, Symposium called with an offer to buy them out of business.

Aiden refused, of course, and now Orphic Productions is handling the relaunching of Calliope Santiago's pop career.

My thighs tingle as the tattoo gun flickers on, and tendrils of anticipation stretch through my limbs. The design takes approximately six hours, and by the time it's done, pain radiates up my side. The artist slathers me in antibacterial ointment and wraps it, and I resituate my clothing before heading out.

It's dark now, which is my preferred time of day to venture into public. My return to King's Trace was met with about as much fanfare as my fake death—so, none, essentially. I sometimes wonder if anyone even really registered that I'd "died" in the first place.

We'd released a small press statement after Mellie was taken away, explaining what had happened three years ago, and that seemed to sate most curiosity on the subject.

Still, on occasion, people will turn and stare, maybe a little longer than necessary. And while before that may have made me cower, now I just let it happen, aware that the only thing I can control in life is my own personal thoughts and feelings.

And my scars, while not pleasant to look at, are *mine*. I won't let anyone else's reproach dictate how I feel about them any longer.

The only one whose opinion on the subject that matters would never make me feel bad about them, anyway.

Besides, acceptance comes from within. Having someone around to remind me of that is nice, but my worth is supposed to start with *me*.

At least, that's what I tell myself. Sometimes I still want to hide, to protect my brain and heart from more pain.

It's not always easy, but I'm trying, and that's what matters to me.

Parking outside the house, I notice the lights are on in the bedroom; not wanting to block our view of the lake, Aiden refuses to ever close the curtains, which means the wildlife is often an unfortunate witness to our frequent trysts against the window, or on the floor in front of the bed, or whatever surface he can pin me to.

Aiden James is insatiable, and he doesn't take well to separation from me.

Then again, neither do I. It's been three days, and my core is already clenching wantonly as I head inside and up the stairs.

He's just getting out of the shower when I walk into the bedroom, my toes sinking into the plush white carpet. His back is to me, and I take a second to admire the colorful smattering of images etched into his skin, soaking in the fact that I get to stare at them for the rest of my life.

Chin tilted up, he's studying the painting hanging above the bed, eyes narrowed, but his back muscles tense when I enter, so in tune with me that he knows before I've even said anything.

"I don't know if I like this here," he says, turning to face me as I approach. I push up on my toes, and he threads his fingers through my pink hair, angling my face so he can press a hungry kiss to my lips.

"You bought it," I say against his mouth. His tongue flicks out, and my clit pulses at the promise of what's to come.

"Yeah, but I'm not sure I want the reminder of Caleb in our bedroom."

I snort, rolling my eyes as he deepens the kiss. He'll never admit it, but he and Caleb became pretty good friends in the recent months; we take turns flying out once a month to visit, and the two have bonded over art in its various forms.

He even commissioned Caleb for album artwork.

It was awkward at first, coming clean to Lunar Cove about my real identity, but they moved on pretty easily, accepting Riley Kelly without too much fuss. Well, all except Mrs. Lindholm, who still looks at me like I'm a demon when I visit.

Aiden grunts, snaking his free hand around my waist, tugging me into him. When I wince, he retreats, scowling down at me. "What were you doing at a tattoo shop today?"

I quirk a brow. "Are you stalking me again, boyfriend?"

His nostrils flare, possessiveness rearing its head in those stormy eyes. "Always, pretty girl. You know I'll never stop."

My body hums, electricity zinging through me with his words. Maybe his obsession shouldn't please me as much as it does, but part of why we work so well is that we're both fucked in the head. Equally tangled up in one another.

Pushing away from him, I lean back on the bed and spread my legs, teeth digging into my bottom lip. "Undress me and find out why I was there."

Dropping to his knees quickly, Aiden's ringed fingers glide up my thighs, flipping my skirt back to my waist. He dips his head to my pussy, licking my seam once, before the plastic wrap on my hip catches his attention.

Reaching up, he slowly peels the cover away, revealing the two-headed serpentine design that starts at the corner of my thigh and stretches over the scar there, incorporating it so that you almost can't even tell the skin beneath is mangled at all.

It winds around the angel tattoo he gave me, bright purples and greens and blacks that I fall in love with all over again when he unveils it.

"My logo?" he says, tracing the inflamed edges almost reverently.

I smile, letting my head fall back on the mattress. "Seemed fitting, considering you gave me the idea."

A strained sound tears from Aiden's chest, and he crawls up my body, peppering kisses along the way.

"How bad does it hurt?" he asks, discarding his towel and pressing the head of his cock against me.

Shifting, I spread my legs wider, answering silently. We groan into each other's mouths as he pushes in, and it throws me momentarily—as it always does—how *right* it feels for our bodies to connect like this.

When he fucks me, it's a religious experience. Something ethereal and eye-opening that leaves me gasping for breath and begging for more, all in tandem.

Every time, it feels like coming home.

And maybe you're not supposed to find that in other people, but I can't imagine what a lonely existence it must be to leave your heart with empty buildings only.

I happen to like that my home has a heartbeat.

ACKNOWLEDGMENTS

This was a hard one to write.

Normally, I'll restart a book a handful of times as I'm fleshing out and learning my characters, and once I hit a groove, things click into place. It took me a long time to get to that point with V&V—I must have over twenty different drafts sitting in my Google Drive graveyard.

Part of the reason it was so difficult was how deeply I connected with Riley, on so many levels. Her internal and external struggles are some that I have personal experience with (though maybe not to the same degree), and so writing her was both cathartic and emotionally draining.

But her story needed to be told, and I'm so happy with how it turned out. Riley and Aiden were so much fun to write, and I am already sad to be leaving them.

As always, none of this is possible without a whole host of people behind me. I'll make these quick, and try not to use the word "y'all" so much—you know, since I'm a legitimate published author, and all.

To my family: I'd never have gotten this far without your support over the years. Thank you for believing in me, even when you're not sure you should.

To Emily: my best friend, my soul sister, the person who calls me out on my BS but is also always on my side. Without a doubt, I would not be where I am today without you.

Thank you for being the best human I've ever known, and for making me a better person. Love you the most. Can't wait for champagne in the Smokies.

To Jackie: thank you for being more organized than me, all your hype, and for keeping my life in check. Sorry for all the times I leave your messages on read.

To Cat: thank you for being a creative wizard and for bringing my cover concepts to life. No one could have made this series as beautiful as you.

To Ellie and Rosa: thank you for making my words pretty and for not firing me. I promise to one day get a manuscript to you on time.

To Sav's Sirens and my ARC team: thank you for your constant excitement and support, and for being the official hype squads for each release and new project. You guys are the best.

And lastly, to every reader: literally none of this is possible without you. I'm forever grateful for every single one of you. Thank you for allowing me to continue on doing my favorite thing in the world by writing these stories.

ALSO BY SAV R. MILLER

King's Trace Antiheroes Series

Sweet Surrender

Sweet Solitude

Sweet Sacrifice

Monsters & Muses Series

Promises and Pomegranates

Oaths and Omissions (coming March 2022)

Standalones

Be Still My Heart

ABOUT THE AUTHOR

Sav R. Miller is an international bestselling author of dark and contemporary romance. She prefers the villains in most stories and thinks everyone deserves happily-ever-after.

Currently, Sav lives in central Kentucky with two pups named Lord Byron and Poe. She loves sitcoms, silence, and sardonic humor.